TRACEY MARTIN

MISERY LOVES COMPANY

MISS MISERY

BOOK THREE

MISERY LOVES COMPANY

TRACEY MARTIN

CITY OWL
PRESS

MISERY LOVES COMPANY
Miss Misery, Book 3

CITY OWL PRESS
www.cityowlpress.com

Cover Design by MiblArt. All stock photos licensed appropriately.

Edited by Danielle DeVor.

For information on subsidiary rights, please contact the publisher at info@cityowlpress.com.

Print Edition ISBN: 978-1-64898-215-6

Digital Edition ISBN: 978-1-64898-214-9

Printed in the United States of America

PRAISE FOR TRACEY MARTIN

"The action in *Wicked Misery* was great, as was the suspense. Each character felt authentic, and the dialogue had me laughing. I definitely want to continue this series."
– *Bad Bird Reads*

"Readers of *Wicked Misery*...will surely be turned into fans, and will find themselves eager for the next installment."
– *RT Book Reviews*

"*Darkest Misery* is recommended for paranormal romance readers who enjoy a high-stakes story."
– *Library Journal*

"This world is rich, it has a lot of non-human, mystical elements in a human setting... I also loved the plot. A nice murder mystery with twist after twist."
– *Fangs for the Fantasy*

"Jess is finding out it's not so easy to let go of her past as she discovers the terrifying truth behind the Gryphons' treachery in this riveting urban fantasy romance, *Misery Loves Company*."
– *Evampire*

"The action was intense and the danger and mystery behind Jess's case brought along lots of drama and suspense in *Dirty Little Misery*."
– *Urban Fantasy Investigations*

To the readers—I hope this book provides you with some good company.

THE MISS MISERY SERIES

BY TRACEY MARTIN

ONE

IN RETROSPECT, CHOOSING TO LIVE NEAR A SYLPH WHO COULD wield a straight razor might not have been one of my best decisions.

True, the sylphs hadn't done more than shoot me dirty glances during the past few weeks, and also true, razors were essential tools in a barbershop. But neither of these things made me feel better. Sylphs plus razors plus an apartment building reeked of a bad idea.

Or maybe I was just nervous about living on my own. For the first twenty-eight years of my life, I'd always had to share space with people, be they family or roommates. What if I discovered the hair in the shower drain had been mine all along? What if the peanut butter got moldy because no one was sneaking spoonfuls of it behind my back? What if the glorious peace and quiet drove me insane?

"Jess, I'm not holding this door forever."

What if my satyr-with-benefits was getting impatient while I rambled about stupid shit?

I snapped my gaze away from the sylph-owned barbershop on the bottom floor of my new apartment building, and let it fall on Lucen. Six feet of mischief-eyed, blond-haired, and sweetly muscled satyr adjusted the box he was holding and motioned impatiently.

Who was I kidding? I would never have peace and quiet as long as I had him in my life, and for that I was grateful.

I picked up my suitcase and hurried over to where Lucen had the building door propped open with his back. "Coming. I'm coming."

He let the door swing shut behind him as he followed me into the dimly lit lobby. There were four mailboxes on the right, an ancient art deco-style chandelier dangling from the ceiling, and a wide set of stairs in front of us. Cozy.

"Second floor," I told Lucen, and led the way.

The wood steps had been polished to a dull sheen by years of shoes, and they were slippery as a result. But the beige walls, unpainted wainscoting, and warm light gave the building a homey feel. Not bad for a place that, by Boston standards, was dirt cheap.

Thank dragons for Shadowtown rents. The only humans who lived in this neighborhood were crazy or desperate, and the preds owned more buildings than they could fill with their own kind.

Technically, their own kind included me since I'd recently discovered that I was a strange subspecies of satyr. It was a fact I was slowly learning to accept, although most people—human and pred alike—had no idea about my true biological makeup. They both believed I was just a reckless human freak.

One of these days I would have to enlighten some of them. Sooner rather than later if Lucen had his way.

The old brick building contained only two tenants per floor, with the second and third floors given over to apartments. I stopped on the second-floor landing, setting my suitcase down once more to fish my key from my jeans pocket.

The lock gave way and I grabbed the suitcase before pushing open the heavy door with a flourish. "Welcome to my new apartment. Much nicer than my old one. And roommate-free, to boot."

"I'm glad you're so proud of yourself." Lucen smirked. "Welcome to adulthood."

I stuck my tongue out at him and dropped my suitcase in what would become a combined living room and dining room space.

Lucen followed suit with the box and circled around. "Do I get a tour?"

"It'll be the briefest tour in history." I walked him over to the picture window that overlooked the street and pointed straight to the back of the apartment. "You can see everything from here except the bathroom."

Frowning, Lucen crossed his arms. "So you can. It's...quaint."

Fine. So the apartment wasn't much, but even so, it was more than I could currently afford. I'd signed the lease the same day I unexpectedly quit my consulting job with the Gryphons. Which meant I was temporarily unemployed. Again.

Like the last time I had found myself jobless, Lucen had offered me a waitressing position at his bar, The Lair. He'd even offered to pay me more this time, but that was no surprise. I could actually work, seeing as I didn't have a sprained wrist. Plus, Lucen was probably so thrilled that I no longer associated with the Gryphons that he'd do anything to prevent me from missing the generous hourly wage they'd paid me.

Then again, it could have been Devon's fault that he was willing to pay me more. Devon was Lucen's best friend, lieutenant to the satyrs' Dom, and now—thanks in part to me—the sole owner of the strangest nightclub in Boston. He'd also offered me a job as a cocktail waitress.

Kind as it might be for both of them to keep me gainfully employed, I didn't really want to return to my pre-Gryphon life as a server. Ever since I'd been forced into finding the guy who'd framed me for murder, schlepping drinks and food didn't have as much appeal. My short stint working for the Gryphons had driven that point home.

Alas, there was no way I was going back to the Gryphons, but there had to be another job out there that let me use my brain to help people and that paid me better than the satyrs were offering. No offense to Lucen or Devon.

I had time to figure it out. My first three months' rent had been paid upon signing.

"It might be small, but it's all I need," I told Lucen.

It was the truth. Behind the living room was a narrow galley-style kitchen, and behind that was the bedroom. Another door in the bedroom led into the narrow bathroom that ran parallel to the kitchen. There wasn't much space to fill, but I didn't own much stuff.

While Lucen went to check out the kitchen, my phone rang. Pulling it out of my pocket, I scowled. The number on the caller ID had become very familiar to me over the last week.

It was Olivia Lee, director of the Boston Regional Office of the Angelic Order of the Gryphon. The woman who, a few weeks ago, had blackmailed me into working for her as a consultant, and as a result had almost gotten me killed on my first case.

Okay, I suppose *I* had almost gotten me killed, or Lucrezia—the satyr I'd busted had almost killed me—but it was Olivia's fault I'd been sucked into the mess.

She wasn't pleased that I'd quit afterward, though it had nothing to do with her or the case and everything to do with a Gryphon named Tom Kassin and his damned Gryphon fraternity, *Le Confrérie de l'Aile*, aka the Brotherhood of the Wing.

The Brotherhood were the ones who'd made me the satyr-ish freak that I was, and they had done so when I was a teenager, without my consent or even my knowledge. When I'd discovered the truth, I'd had a good rant at Tom, and had then told Olivia she could shove her consulting gig she-knew-where.

I hadn't heard from Tom since. Olivia, on the other hand, was more persistent. So far, she hadn't followed through on her original threat to have me arrested if I refused to work for her, but I didn't know why. Especially seeing as she wouldn't leave me alone. I could only assume Tom or the Brotherhood had something to do with her hands-off approach, but that didn't exactly reassure me. The Brotherhood had to count some damn powerful Gryphons as its members, both in the magical and political senses.

I was still frowning at the phone when Lucen emerged from his self-guided tour. "Nice, new stove in there. Too bad it will be wasted on your cooking skills. Was that the evil winged-one calling again?"

Distracted by Olivia's call, I let the slight on my culinary achievements slide. "Yeah, only this time she left a message."

That was unusual. Olivia had left a voicemail the first time she'd called me, but none since.

Lucen yawned. He'd gotten up early to help me move. "Well, you going to play that message for my amusement?"

"Sure, if this is what you really find entertaining."

"Oh, you know what I find really entertaining." He grinned. "But we've got to finish unloading my car first. So give me a quickie with this."

"I'd rather give you a quickie with something else, but if you insist on listening to my voicemail…" I pressed my body against his, wrapping my free arm around his back. It was hot outside, and hotter inside with the apartment's stagnant air, and a thin sheen of sweat glistened on his skin. The scent of his cinnamon-tinged pheromones was stronger because of it, and I breathed him in deeply. My muscles, achy from loading his car this morning, decided they didn't ache as badly as my need for him.

Lucen was easily the most gorgeous person I'd ever met, and he would have been hard enough to resist if he were human. With his satyr magic, he was damn near impossible.

Sensing my desire, he leaned down into me and pressed his lips against mine. I let him for a second, grazing my teeth over his bottom lip and sliding my tongue gently over his skin. With a sharp breath he yanked me closer so that my chest pressed into his hard muscles.

I pulled away. My body whined at me for it, but I loved watching the fierce heat on his face when I teased him like this. I was probably the only person who could. Pred power—be it satyr lust, goblin greed, fury rage, harpy jealousy, or sylph insecurity—barely registered with me if I noticed it at all.

But Lucen was the exception. Well, Devon too, but it made me uneasy thinking about him.

Still, I had way more resistance to Lucen's power than I should, and it drove him crazy when I did resist because he wasn't used to it.

"You said you wanted the message now?" I reminded him innocently.

Putting the phone on speaker, I played Olivia's voicemail, which turned out to be far less exciting than the foreplay. Big surprise.

"Jessica, this is Olivia Lee, but I assume you know that and that's why you're not picking up. Whatever your issue with Agent Kassin, it does not concern me, and I want to remind you of the agreement we struck. I expect you to return my call at your earliest convenience, or I will be forced to arrange a meeting using methods you won't like."

I hung up. "Damn. Sounds like Olivia's getting bored with playing nice."

"That didn't take long, and she's calling on the weekend too. Did she forget your threat?"

When I'd told Olivia our deal was off, I'd also told her that if she arrested me, all the dirt I had on *Le Confrérie*—and the Gryphon organization as a whole by association—would go public. "Maybe. Or she's calling my bluff."

Or she didn't know exactly what dirt I had and thus didn't understand the magnitude of my threat. She'd been confused by my quitting, and now that my rage had blown over, it had crossed my mind that Olivia was probably ignorant of what the Brotherhood had done to me and at least four other children.

Ignorant, and perhaps as likely to be appalled by it as I was.

But I wasn't going back, even if that were true. They were all guilty by association in my mind.

Nonetheless, Lucen must have picked up on some of my internal conflict. "If Olivia is going to get on your case and put you on the outs with the Gryphons again, you know what you should do."

I lifted my ponytail and fanned the back of my neck. "Let me guess. You mean tell Dezzi the truth."

"You don't have to make it sound like a death sentence."

"How do we know it's not?"

Lucen didn't bother to respond to my question verbally. He just gave me a quit-being-stupid look.

Fair enough. It wouldn't be a death sentence. Not literally. In fact, Dezzi, the satyr's Dom, was very pleased with me since I'd exposed the plot by Lucrezia to oust her.

Yet telling Dezzi about my quasi-satyr status was a death sentence in one very important way. In my mind, coming out of the pred closet meant the death of my ruse. My entire self-concept. Despite having lived with the truth about myself for a few weeks, I still thought of myself as mostly human. So long as only a handful of people knew otherwise, it was easier to cling to that illusion. Once Dezzi knew, all the satyrs would know, and soon enough, all of Shadowtown would too. I was certain.

I wasn't sure I was ready for that, and for what felt like the hundredth time, I explained my thoughts to Lucen.

"You can't conceal this forever, little siren." He sighed. "I have obligations to Dezzi. If you don't tell her, at some point, I should."

"Then why don't you?" I asked, suddenly irritable. I blamed it on the heat, but the truth was, my satyr status was growing to be a touchy subject between us.

"It should be you. I don't understand why you don't want to do it. As unfair as what the Gryphons did to you was, it's got to be a relief to finally know the truth."

I picked at my T-shirt. It was one Steph had gotten me for my last birthday, black with the words "Bite me" in blue glitter. "It is a relief for me to know, but other people knowing is something else."

"Dezzi will be happy. The domus owes you a thanks for catching Lucrezia. Besides." He came up behind me and put his hands on my arms. I held my breath as his mouth brushed my ear, and sweetly cinnamon lust drove away my irritation. "You're supposed to be embracing your satyrness. Part of that should mean owning up to it."

He had a point, but I didn't like it. "I'm working on it. On every part," I added before he could interject.

The other part I was supposed to be working on was coming to terms with the fact that monogamy was impossible where he was concerned. Lucen was a satyr, and like all preds, he needed to addict humans to his magic to live. For a satyr, that meant he needed to occasionally have sex with those addicts so they remained healthy. I didn't particularly like it, but as far as I knew, there was nothing I could do about it.

Because Lucen understood that I linked sex and emotional attachment, his grand plan was to break my association. And he believed the best way to uncouple them was for me to have lots of mindless sex. We weren't even talking one-night stands. More like one-hour stands. Preferably with people whose names I never bothered to catch. If I did it enough, Lucen was convinced I would separate my feelings for him from my lusty urges.

No surprise, this was easier said than done. We'd had a conversation about it a week ago, and I hadn't done a damn thing since. Merely thinking about it bugged me. Satyr or human, I'd never been the sort of person who felt interested in hopping from one person's bed to another. Lucen's insistence that it was no big deal was a potent reminder that although I wasn't truly human, I also wasn't a normal satyr.

Lucen tugged on my earlobe with his lips, his arms locked around me from behind. I closed my eyes, not for the first time wishing for a magical solution to the problem we faced. But though I didn't know much about magic, one thing I did know was that it wasn't a solution for all problems.

"We should finish unloading," I reminded him.

"I think I changed my mind. Now might be a good time for a break, after all." Hot breath fell on my neck, followed moments later by his lips nibbling their way to my collarbone.

I breathed deeply, trying to be strong. "This place is a dusty mess. There's no furniture and no drapes over the windows yet."

"Satyrs aren't modest."

I twisted around in his arms. "I'm not a normal satyr, and I don't need to give the people at the pizza place across the street a dinner show."

Lucen laughed. "Fine. If you insist." He kissed me hard, as though to remind me what I was delaying, then let me go.

It took another hour of carting boxes and bags, but we finally headed downstairs for the last load. While packing this morning, I'd been impressed that I could fit my entire life into two trips in Lucen's midsize sedan. Now, on further reflection, I felt the serious need to do some furniture shopping lest I eat all my meals off cardboard boxes.

Sweat rolled down my neck and I massaged my throbbing hand. Getting my damn futon frame up the stairs had resulted in minor scrapes and bruises for both of us. Lucen's healed almost instantly, but being the abnormal pred that I was, I healed more like a human. Slowly and painfully.

Outside, Shadowtown was coming alive. Though I'd joked about giving the pizza place a show, they were only now opening for business. As was the chain drugstore next to it, and the barbershop and magic-supply shop on the ground floor of my apartment building.

Waving politely at the satyr who owned the magical-supply shop, I turned down the alley next to the building where Lucen had illegally parked his car. In Shadowtown, no one had to worry about tickets. The

Gryphons, who policed all magical matters, had more pressing responsibilities, and so did the preds, who policed themselves for pred-on-pred offenses.

Lucen grabbed the last box, which contained my pots and pans, and I grabbed my comforter. "You owe me for this, little siren. You owe me so much."

"I'm looking forward to it."

"Oh, no." Lucen was grinning again as he shook his head. "Not that way. I'm repainting my apartment this fall. I hope you know how to use a roller."

I banged my hip against the building door to open it. "Your apartment is gorgeous. What does it need repainting for?"

"It doesn't. I just want to watch you work."

I called him a few names as I climbed the stairs, but my laughter faded when I reached the top. Lucen smacked me in the back with the box, and I jumped out of his way.

His brow furrowed as he noticed what I was staring at. "Where did that come from?"

"No idea, but someone was sneaky." And fast. Lucen and I couldn't have been outside for more than a couple minutes.

I pushed the gift basket aside with my toe so I could open the apartment door. After I dumped the comforter on the partially assembled futon, I stuck my head back outside and scanned the landing and stairwell. They were both empty. Not exactly surprising. I didn't see a reason why whoever had left the basket would hang around to watch me take it. Yet its presence left me with a bad feeling.

Lucen had been moving my kitchen boxes around on the scant counter space, and he opened the fridge and took out the two beers we'd stuck in there earlier. I put the gift basket down in the spot he'd freed. Wrapped in cellophane was a bottle of wine, some cheese, crackers, and nuts.

"That's a harpy-owned shop that sent it." He must have recognized the logo on the envelope. With a nod, Lucen handed me one of the beers. "So who's it from?"

The beer hadn't chilled enough, but it was better than nothing. I took a swig and contemplated. "Dezzi?" I couldn't think of anyone else who might send me a welcome basket.

"I wouldn't count on it. What about your family?"

"I wouldn't count on it. They wouldn't contact a pred-owned business."

"The suspense is killing me. Open the damn thing." Lucen made to grab for the envelope, but I snatched it away and tore into it for the card. Almost immediately, I wished I hadn't.

Miss Moore, welcome to the neighborhood. I request that you grant me the honor of your presence at four o'clock tomorrow for tea.

Best wishes, Gunthra

I swallowed and reached for more beer. Shit. My gut had been right to be wary.

Lucen grabbed the card from my hand. "What does the goblins' Dom want with you?"

Since I suspected the answer and knew it wouldn't please him, I opted to say nothing. During the week when I'd been framed for murder, I'd made a bargain with Gunthra. She'd known what I was, and in desperation, believing knowing the truth about myself could help save me, I'd made a deal with her. The truth about my gift in return for an unspecified future favor.

I'd been right to a degree. Gunthra's information had probably kept me alive. But now I'd bet she was ready to collect. I'd also bet that I wasn't going to like upholding my end of the deal.

Welcome to the neighborhood, indeed.

TWO

HAVING LIVED AND WORKED WITH PREDS MOST OF THE LAST month, I'd become nearly as nocturnal as they were. But I sure didn't feel it tonight.

By the time seven o'clock rolled around, I was ready to collapse onto my reassembled futon. I liked to think I was in good shape, but a full day of moving and cleaning had worn me out. And Lucen hadn't helped. Or rather he had with the actual moving and a bit of the cleaning, but then we'd gone about breaking in every room in my apartment. That probably contributed to half of my exhaustion right there.

Alas, I had to suck it up because I wasn't about to flake out on Steph, or her cousin whom I was excited to meet. Dutifully showered and changed, I hauled my strongly caffeinated butt across town, hoping that leaving Shadowtown would boost my energy.

Part of being a satyr meant I got a high off human misery. Preds called the magical hit "feeding," and they needed it to survive. I had no idea if the same were true for me, nor did I wish to find out. It was enough to know I tasted other people's negative emotions, and they kept me energized. Unfortunately, I couldn't feed from preds or their addicts. Only un-addicted humans would do, and there weren't many of them roaming Shadowtown.

Until recently, Steph had been the only human who knew about my misery-sucking ability, and she'd been okay with it. It was my other pred-like power that had become a point of contention between us, and that contention gave me a serious case of angst each time I saw her. Tonight was no exception, and my nerves buzzed with tension as I got off the subway in Cambridge.

Regular preds exuded power everywhere they went, and they could use it to control the humans around them. At its strongest, this magic was the way preds turned humans into addicts. I couldn't addict humans, but I could still use that magic in some powerful ways. Specifically, by binding people to me with lust, I could influence them.

The last time I'd done so, Steph had freaked. Although she'd gotten over it, or claimed to, I wasn't sure I had. I worried because Steph didn't know the half of it.

She didn't know that my pred-like abilities existed because I was a pred.

Like most humans, Steph feared and hated preds. They fed on suffering, turned desperate humans into addict slaves. But I was what I was, and I couldn't help but think Lucen wasn't so bad. And if he wasn't so bad, and I wasn't so bad, then likely not all of them were so damn bad.

I was fairly certain, however, that Steph would require more convincing than that. So I kept my mouth shut and lied by omission to my best friend of ten years.

Which meant that maybe, actually, I *was* so bad.

I did my best to push these unfortunate thoughts aside as I approached the bookstore where I was meeting Steph for her cousin's book signing. I was tired of feeling guilty along with feeling just plain tired. One day, I would get the guts to tell Steph the truth, and when that day came, I prayed she'd be okay with it. But that was not today.

The evening was warm and humid, and a line snaked down the block as people waited to get in. I found Steph near the front of it and joined her, pleased to see she'd ditched the blonde wig she'd been sporting the other week and returned to her dark reddish brown one. It went much better with her style. At over six feet in her heels and dressed all in black, the people near her in line gave us a wide berth.

"Are all these people actually going to fit in the shop?"

"Got me," she said, stuffing her hands into her pockets. "I'm only waiting in line for the signing because you asked me to. Otherwise, I'd have gone straight in and attacked the coffee they set out."

I shook my head. "You don't want Eric Marshall to sign a copy of his new book for you?"

Steph snorted. "You're talking about the man who used to drive toy cars over my head when we were kids."

"So? He's Eric Marshall. Internationally renowned bestseller. They've made movies off his books."

"Bad movies."

"Whatever. Lots of stuff explode in them. Anyway, I can't believe I've known you for ten years and only the other week did I learn that he's your cousin. You've seen my bookshelves, and you never thought to mention this sooner?"

The line shuffled forward, and Steph looked like she was fighting a smile. "I hadn't talked to him in about eight years. It had occurred to me to mention it when he reached out to me, but you were a bit preoccupied at the time."

I sighed simply to be dramatic because Steph was right about the timing.

When Steph had transitioned, most of her very conservative family had refused to acknowledge her for the person she was. Some had immediately cut her out of their lives. Others had eventually forced her to be the one to take that step thanks to their flagrant disrespect. Eric, who was five years older than she was, had been among them.

Then about a month ago, right around the time I'd been framed for murder, Steph had gotten an email from Eric. He'd wised up and educated himself, and he felt terrible for having gone along with the rest of the family. He wanted to reconnect and have Steph back in his life. Since then, they'd met on a couple occasions, and Steph had been willing to forgive him.

Given the vitriol with which Steph usually spoke of her family—when she could be bothered to speak of them at all—I'd been surprised by that. It was nice to know that my friend, whose mantra had always been that forgiveness was for suckers, wasn't as hard-hearted as she liked to pretend.

It gave me hope that one day she could forgive me for hiding my secret from her.

"So any more work from the Gryphons?" Steph asked as we approached the door.

I bit my lip. Yet another thing I hadn't told Steph was how I'd quit. Such was the problem with lies. They built on each other. I had no way to explain to her about why I'd quit without explaining what I was. "The director called me this afternoon. We'll see."

Could you lie with the truth?

I really was a horrible person.

For half a second, I almost capitulated under the pressure of all my guilt. I felt it pressing down on my heart, on my conscience, like a lead weight. But my breath that carried the words stuck in my throat, and the moment passed. Just as well. This was the wrong time and the wrong place. If I ever did tell her, it would have to be somewhere more private.

"You okay?"

I nodded and faked a yawn, which quickly became a real yawn. "Tired. Too much moving today."

"Did your satyr friend help?" The dubious emphasis Steph put on friend was as good a reminder as any as to why I wasn't spilling my guts.

"Yes, Lucen helped. I'm just beat."

We shifted forward again and at last entered the building. I kept Steph busy with my own questions about her job and her boyfriend so she couldn't ask me anything else about the Gryphons.

Finally, the woman ahead of us in line finished gushing over Eric's book and took her signed copy away. With no one left between me and Steph's cousin, I got a good look at the guy whose many books adorned my shelves.

And I swallowed, completely unprepared for what I found.

It wasn't as if Eric Marshall appeared all that different in real life than how he did on his dust-jacket photo. Sure, he was older, although he sported no gray hairs or obvious wrinkles to back that up. Yet his face had clearly aged, leading me to assume he'd been using the same photo since he sold his first book.

For all that though, he wasn't an unattractive guy. His brown hair was spiky, and a touch of a five o'clock shadow graced his chin. The top couple buttons on his blue shirt were open, and he wore a slightly rumpled sports jacket. It was all very authorly in a manly, I-write-thrillers way.

But what I noticed in particular was something that probably no one else in the bookstore could see. Eric Marshall was an addict.

"Steph!" Eric stood to greet his cousin, a genuine smile replacing the practiced one I'd first seen.

Steph wormed her way around the table, and they exchanged a tentative hug. The sort you give someone when you don't know them well but feel like it's the appropriate thing to do.

"This is Jess." Steph motioned to me. "She owns all your books."

Eric beamed and offered me a hand. "Thank you so much."

I grinned back as we shook, and I tried not to let my concern for his addict state influence my opinion of him. "Nice to meet you," I said, and meant it. Part of me was glad Steph had never told me he was her cousin before they'd reconciled. I would have hated knowing I'd bought books by a transphobe.

And that was that. We exchanged a few more words, Steph told him we were staying for the reading, and Eric signed his new book for me. Then we stepped out of line, and Steph made a dash for the coffee just like she'd said she would. I could have used another cup myself, but I made my way to the register to pay for the book first.

The bookshop had cleared out an area near the back for people to gather for the reading, and the space was mostly filled. With my receipt tucked into the book, I leaned against one of the rustic wood pillars and once more examined Eric Marshall.

I shouldn't have been surprised that he was an addict. Selling one's soul for success was a cliché for a reason, and Eric Marshall's success was the sort that should have led to those rumors. He'd been twenty-six when his first book sold for an enormous sum. Twenty-nine when the blockbuster film came out. And that was only the start. Five books and three movies later, Eric Marshall was big news.

To be fair, his books were good. I liked to think I had excellent taste, and I liked them. But sometimes good wasn't enough to lead to riches and fame, and if those were a person's goals, there were ways to cheat fate. Eric must have used them.

He was a greed addict, which meant he'd struck a deal with a goblin. I had no clue what the exact terms would have been, but somewhere lived a goblin who owned Eric's soul. Eric had gotten everything he'd probably wanted at first, but now it would never be enough. The goblin's power would make him crave more, and that unrequited longing would feed his goblin master.

I shivered and hoped Eric had known how to bargain. Hoped he'd known to set a time limit on the deal so that it would end without his soul being fed upon to the point of no return. Hoped he'd have some life left at the end that he could enjoy.

"Coffee?" Steph slid the steaming paper cup under my nose.

I breathed it in, relieved to stop thinking about her cousin. "Thanks."

Fifteen minutes later, the line for signed books trailed away, and everyone had gathered around the reading area. The store had to be violating some fire code to squeeze in this crowd. Grateful for the coffee, I buried my nose in the cup's dregs so that the aroma would overpower the perfume that the woman standing in front of me was wearing.

Eric chatted about his book and the research that had gone into it, which was interesting, then settled in to do a reading. Yawning, I adjusted my position against the column supporting my weight. I let my gaze un-focus, concentrating on the sound of Eric's voice to stay awake, but it didn't help. He kept speaking more and more quietly. I wondered if he was tired too.

Then he stopped reading altogether.

An unquiet pause overtook the store, an emptiness that soon filled with the sound of chairs creaking and people shuffling. Someone sneezed, a noise as loud as a 747 in the unexpected silence.

That stopped my mind from drifting, as the mildly butterscotch confusion of the crowd increased. Frowning, I stood on my toes to see what was going on.

As I did, Eric dropped his book. It hit the wide-beamed floor with an ominous thud, and Eric doubled over in his chair. My stomach knotted, and mine likely wasn't the only one. Under the confusion ran a river of fear that swept away the butterscotch-candy taste in my mouth and replaced it with something like a sour cherry cough drop.

Steph grasped my arm as someone ran forward. The crowd swayed, blocking my view again, and I wished for Steph's height.

"Eric, you okay?"

I couldn't see what was going on, but he must not have responded because the same voice then yelled for someone to call an ambulance. Wide awake, on the awful high from everyone's emotions, I cringed.

Steph's grip tightened something fierce on my arm. "Jess, look."

Calling Eric's name, she yanked me through the people surrounding her cousin. Her horror was a sour blue raspberry slushie, urging me on. People drew back like they always did for Steph, and I grabbed one of the cheap metal folding chairs at the front of the room as she knelt next to her cousin. I swore, understanding her panic at once.

Right before my eyes, Eric's skin was slowly turning a sickly gray, his eyes glassy and unseeing. Everything within him—everything that *was* him—seemed to shrink away, to fade and die.

People called a person's soul a lot of things. But whether it was the light in Eric's eyes, or the spark that made him human, all those things were gone. Drained from him in seconds. And all any of us could do was stand around helplessly and watch.

I swallowed, tormented by the disparate emotions coursing through my blood. My humanity was horrified, yet my pred-self was alive and buzzing with everyone else's fear. I was frozen in shock, but capable of bouncing in place with energy.

Unbidden, my thoughts strayed to Lucen and my secret. What I was. What he wanted me to do. I wanted to embrace my pred power for his sake, but staring at the creature that had once been Eric, my old loathing for preds reasserted itself more strongly than ever.

In the back of the room, someone yelled that an ambulance was on its way, but an ambulance was of no use. Eric was beyond paramedic help. He was beyond anyone's help.

His goblin master had just sucked his soul dry all at once and turned him into a ghoul. And I hadn't the faintest idea how that was possible.

THREE

"Everyone back off. Give him space." One of the store clerks shooed us away. "Clear a path for the EMTs."

Excess energy crawled along my skin, and I rubbed my arms. I wanted to help, but I was as useless as everyone else. Or was I? Something wasn't right here, in more ways than the usual wrongness that surrounded anything pred.

Leaving Steph and the crowded bookstore behind, I stepped outside and called the Gryphons' emergency line.

The mere act of someone turning into a ghoul wouldn't get the Gryphons to come running, but this wasn't an ordinary way of turning someone into a ghoul. "Magical attack," I told the operator, which was true enough as far as I knew. "Someone's seriously injured." Also true.

I declined to leave my name since that was only likely to complicate matters these days. Then, taking a deep breath, I weaved my way back inside. The store clerks were still trying to appeal to everyone's good sense, but though some customers were leaving, almost as many were hanging around and gawking. Already, down the narrow street, I could hear sirens approaching.

Steph pulled me closer. She must have told the clerks that she was Eric's relative, so they let us be.

"Jess, what the hell?" Hair fell in Steph's face, and she swatted it away. "He's breathing, he has a pulse. Is this some kind of spell?"

"Not a spell. He's become a ghoul."

Shaking her head, Steph sat on one of the deserted chairs. "Ghouls are what addicts become, aren't they? Eric..." She stared at him, her eyes widening with realization.

"Excuse me." A shadow lengthened by my feet, and a woman cleared her throat. "Are you a Gryphon? Did I hear you suggest Mr. Marshall was an addict?"

I glanced up. The woman hovering over me had been standing next to Eric during the signing. I hadn't paid much attention to her because I'd been pondering Eric's little addict problem—which apparently wasn't so little—but I'd assumed she was his wife or girlfriend. If that were true, then she was one of the last people I wanted to talk to. Explaining this was going to suck. It sounded like she hadn't even known he was an addict.

Unfortunately, Steph jumped in before I could respond. "Yes, Jess is a Gryphon."

"Well, not exact—"

"Oh, God." The woman collapsed on the chair next to mine. "It's true then? Gryphons can identify addicts, can't they? I'm sorry. I should have introduced myself. I'm Marissa Walker. I'm Mr. Marshall's assistant."

"Oh." I pulled myself together. Assistant wasn't good, but it also wasn't as bad as I'd feared. The smorgasbord of stressful emotions around me was hard enough to deal with. A weepy or angry significant other would have been too much of a head rush. "I, uh, consult for the Gryphons. Sometimes."

"So Eric was an addict?" Steph's voice was as strained as her face. She was sickened and in total disbelief.

Slowly, I nodded.

Before I could say anything else, I was saved by the EMTs. As they burst into the bookstore, I scurried out of their way, leaving the awkwardness of that conversation behind.

It's no good, I wanted to tell them, but they'd figure that out themselves soon enough. Eric's assistant ran over to meet them, as did the store clerks. I debated joining them and explaining, but Steph maintained her grip on my arm.

"I thought..." She made a queasy face. "I don't know much about addicts or ghouls, but doesn't it take a long time to become a ghoul?"

Over Steph's shoulders, I could see the EMTs checking Eric's vitals and discovering they were fine. I dragged my attention from them.

I rubbed my eyes, no longer with tiredness but with frustration. "Yes. Turning into a ghoul is what happens to addicts whose pred masters suck them dry. If a soul is a person's life energy, then it means the pred has taken away all the good parts of it. And yes, it takes a long time in many ways. First, it takes years of being fed on. Second, it happens slowly, over a long period. People don't become ghouls in a matter of seconds. Eric..." Shit. There was no easy way to point it out. "Eric likely sold his soul in order to gain his success. He could well have been an addict for years. But even if that's true, he shouldn't have become a ghoul this way."

Steph groaned and closed her eyes. "What the hell was he thinking?"

I forced a humorless smile. "Probably what everyone thinks—something else is more important than their own suffering."

"But you're saying this isn't normal?"

"Definitely not normal." I shrugged. "At least I've never heard of such a thing before."

"Great. You're supposed to be my encyclopedia of magical knowledge."

I couldn't stop myself from snorting. "Sorry. I'm nothing of the sort."

Across the room, someone said "Gryphon," and both Steph's head and mine snapped that way. Marissa was gesturing to me. Peachy. I might not have been an encyclopedia of knowledge, but Steph wasn't the only one who assumed I was.

Repressing a curse, I headed over, Steph on my heels.

"Jess?"

I paused, turning at the sound of a familiar voice. The real Gryphons had arrived, and my friend Bridget was in the lead. A wave of black-and-gold uniforms parted the shop's remaining gawkers.

"Hi." Checking out the new faces, I let out the tiniest of sigh of relief.

My former partner, Andre, wasn't one of the four Gryphons who'd shown up. Until this moment, I hadn't thought to worry about running into him again. Our last—and only—case together had ended in some serious, naked awkwardness thanks to Lucrezia and her powerful magical drugs. Oh, and I'd hit him with a chair.

It was too bad because I liked Andre, but the last time we'd talked it had seemed like he wanted it to be the last time we talked. It was hard to blame him.

Two of the Gryphons kept right on walking to where the paramedics were tending Eric, but Bridget frowned at me. "Did you call this in?"

"Yeah. That's Eric Marshall over there. He was doing a reading."

"And?" Bridget's raised eyebrow made it clear she had no idea who Eric Marshall was.

"He became a ghoul," Steph said. "He's my cousin. Jess says it shouldn't have happened."

Bridget glanced between us. "Why not? Was he an addict?"

I held up a hand in Steph's direction. Her nerves were getting more frayed by the moment. "Let me start from the beginning."

I filled Bridget in on what happened. The remaining Gryphons returned by the time I finished, and the paramedics were packing up. Apparently, they'd discovered they weren't needed, or the Gryphons had told them they'd take over.

"So he was fine earlier?" one of the unknown Gryphons asked. "Were there any indications that his health was declining?"

Steph had no idea, but Marissa had joined us as well, and she shook her head forcefully. "No, he was fine. He competed in a 5k run yesterday. It was his hobby. He was telling me on the way here that he'd made his best time yet."

"That shouldn't be the case, right?" I asked Bridget.

She sighed. "No. That wouldn't be right. He should have been undergoing a steady decline. There would have been signs."

"So was this some kind of curse or something?" Bending under the pressure, Steph had pulled out her cigarettes and was tapping the pack against her hand.

The Gryphons glanced at each other, baffled.

One of the guys held up a vial. "We've got a blood sample. Initial analyses look normal so far—for a ghoul, I mean—but I'll be analyzing it at the lab in more detail."

Bridget produced a notebook and a pen from her bag. "I doubt you'll find anything unusual if you haven't yet. My guess is that this is exactly what it looks like."

I placed my hand over Steph's jittery one because the tapping was getting to me as badly as the spearmint anxiety that she radiated. "How is this possible?"

"Honestly, I don't know," Bridget said. "It's rare magic, but I've heard of it being done. It's also illegal. We need to find the goblin who did this."

"Because that will be so easy," Steph muttered.

"It's what we do." Bridget sent two of the Gryphons back to headquarters to begin work on analyzing the blood sample. Then she and her partner interviewed Steph, Marissa, and the bookstore staff.

I hung around with Steph while she went outside to smoke. "Does Eric have family to take care of him? A wife or something?"

She shook her head and exhaled a cloud of smoke into the night sky. "Nope. He divorced a few years ago. I don't even know his ex-wife's name. What happens to him?"

"Without someone to take care of him?" I let the silence be my answer.

Sadly, ghouls comprised the largest percentage of the homeless population in any city. They were mostly unable or unwilling to take care of themselves. Just shells of people. If you gave them food, they would eat. If you didn't, they might not think to find it themselves. Holding down a job was impossible. Those without family to take care of them almost always found themselves on the streets.

Luckily for Eric he had family, and he was wealthy. I didn't see why some of his money couldn't be used to pay for care if his family didn't want to bother.

"They won't," Steph said, crushing her cigarette butt. "Mark my words. My family is evil."

"Come on, you used to include Eric in that. Now you're getting along. Or were."

Steph adjusted her earrings with a wry expression. "We were getting along because he admitted he was wrong. I know the rest of the family didn't approve of him making nice with me."

I winced. For all my issues, a loving family was not something I lacked. My choices confounded my mother, but that seemed normal enough. Of course, I'd never come out to my family like Steph had. I couldn't imagine what it was like for Steph to tell her family: "I'm a woman, and from this day on, I'd like you to call me Stephanie."

All I knew from Steph was that it had gone over every bit as badly as she'd anticipated. Since I dreaded finding out what would happen if I ever sat my mother down and said, "I'm a really messed up type of satyr, and just so you know, I feed on misery," I'd never done it.

Steph had way more courage than I did.

"I should take him home," Steph said.

"What about his assistant? She came here with him."

"He pays her. I'm family. And all signs suggest he's not going to be selling any more books so that he can keep on paying her."

True enough. Eric's writing career, or any career, was over.

We went back inside the dead store. All the people who'd turned up for the reading and signing had left. The clerks spoke in hushed voices, their faces long. The inviting atmosphere given off by the heavy wood and book-lined walls weighed on my shoulders. All it struck me as now was a jungle of dead trees. Dark and depressing.

Bridget was getting off the phone, and she beckoned us both over. "If what we're thinking happened is really what happened, then it's dawned on me that not all is lost. We might be able to save Eric if we move fast."

Hope lit up Steph's eyes. I felt it too, a quickness in my heartbeat, but I tried to suppress it. Me and hope didn't usually end well. "How? What do you mean?"

"Assuming Eric was healthy, there's no way the goblin who did this would be able to feed on his soul to the point of depletion so quickly. That means the goblin must be storing it somewhere, and if it's stored, theoretically, it can be returned. But we might not have a long time to do it."

"How long?" I asked.

"I'm not sure. I need to do some research."

Steph turned to me, and I didn't like the desperation on her face one bit. "Jess, you have connections in Shadowtown, don't you? You can help."

"I..." *I don't work for the Gryphons. I hate the Gryphons.*

Bridget's phone buzzed. She glanced at the caller ID and ignored it. "I'd be happy to bring Jess in on this case if the director approves it."

"I..." Dragon shit on toast. *How could I say no to Steph?*

Easy answer. I couldn't.

I swallowed down a thousand rebuttals. "Yeah, of course. I want to help."

"Thank you." Steph draped an arm around me, the closest my not-so-touchy-feely best friend came to hugs.

I forced a smile, though I felt sick. After my epic storming out of Gryphon headquarters and vengeful vow that I would never, ever work with the Gryphons again, here I went.

Wouldn't Lucen be so pleased?

And, oh, wasn't I? The Gryphons had experimented on me as a child. They'd withheld damning information about what they'd done and what I was. Yet they, and the knowledge and resources they possessed, were the best hope for helping Steph's cousin. So sick as it made me, I would do this for Steph because she was my best friend, and she and her cousin deserved my help.

Much as I hated to admit it, by doing this, I was acknowledging that the Gryphons weren't all bad. They served a useful purpose, and sometimes they were the only people who could be counted on to help humanity.

Although they'd destroyed my life, they saved other lives. How could I condemn them all for that?

As usual, nothing could ever be simple.

FOUR

GETTING ERIC HOME BECAME A COMPLICATED DANCE OF
logistics. Marissa offered to help, but Steph didn't like turning over the
key to Eric's house—and his BMW—to someone she didn't know, so it
was up to us. Eventually we worked it out, got Eric into said BMW, and hit
the road.

"You haven't explained to me how we're going to return to Boston," I
said, trying to get Google to cough up directions to Eric's house. We
wouldn't need them until we were well out of the city, but Steph's driving
was making me constantly botch typing the address, so it might have take
me that long to be successful.

Steph braked nervously yet again as she wound through heavy
Cambridge traffic, and I grimaced as my seat belt choked me. "I'll drive us
back. It's not like Eric needs the car tomorrow."

"Okay then." It was just that she was as anxious driving the car as she
was doing things like entering Shadowtown.

"Stop it."

"What?"

She tightened her grip on the steering wheel. "You're making this face
like you do when you taste spearmint."

"Yeah, well, that's your fault."

"I know, and it's making me more nervous. I'm driving a fucking BMW. The last car I drove was Jim's Honda, and that thing's almost as old as you."

"All right! Sorry."

She shushed me, and we made the rest of the drive in near silence.

"WHOA." ERIC LIVED IN A RITZY DEVELOPMENT ON THE NEW Hampshire seacoast, about forty-five minutes north of Boston. It actually took a couple seconds to scope out the entire brick mansion. It was that big. With a shaky laugh, I shut the car door. "To think, I contributed to his ability to buy this monstrosity. What does a single guy need so much house for?"

Steph opened the back passenger-side door for Eric. "Got me, but I bet my family's going to be wondering that too." She pressed her lips thin.

With a bit of coaxing, Eric stumbled out. His eyes were unfocused, and he seemed to be moving on autopilot as he lumbered up his front steps without assistance. But that was as good as he got. He stood in the shadows by the door, as if waiting for it to magically open.

Sighing, Steph unlocked it.

Eric's house was as amazing inside as the outside had led me to believe it would be. There was nothing modern here. Nothing glassy or sleek. The floors were beautiful parquet, the furniture heavy and dark, and the rugs thick and soft. Everywhere I turned—on the walls, in a cubby, or simply standing around on a pedestal waiting to be appreciated—was art. No wonder Eric needed such a house. It was as much a gallery as it was a home.

It took us a few tries before we found what appeared to be Eric's bedroom, though in our defense, I counted six rooms on the second floor, not including the bathrooms. We convinced him to lie down on the oversized bed, which was done up in very manly shades of plaid, and Steph removed his shoes.

"Will he sleep?" she asked.

"I assume so."

"You assume?"

I backed out of the room so Eric could have whatever peace ghouls could find in solitude and darkness. "I've never seen one sleeping. I told you—I'm not an expert. I see ghouls hanging around Shadowtown. Some are more lucid than others, but I don't know why."

"Fucking preds." Steph stormed down the hall. "I swear, Jess, if I could kill the one who did this to him with my bare hands, I would do it. I'd kill them all."

Since I could sense her fury, I didn't doubt it.

I took my time catching up to her at the bottom of the stairs. I knew her rage wasn't personal, yet my internal conflict writhed and burned in my gut like a salamander trapped in water. The only thing that was clear was that the drive back to Boston would be the wrong time to confess my species.

"Most preds don't let their addicts become ghouls," I said cautiously. Like Lucen. Lucen would never allow that to happen. I'd seen him take care of the ghouls that hung around Shadowtown, making sure they got fed and sheltered.

Steph threw me what I called her Medusa expression, the one that turned the hapless people who pissed her off to stone. It didn't have quite the same effect on me, but it was the first time she'd ever directed so much aggression my way. "Don't defend them. Ever."

Right. I opted to change the subject. Not only was now not the time for personal confessions, it was also not the time for a more nuanced discussion on pred personalities. Steph had a right to be angry. Respecting that was appropriate behavior for a friend.

Not cowardly avoidance.

"We should leave out some food," I said, pretending to be distracted by a glass sculpture of a seahorse.

"Will he eat it, or do you not know that either?"

I decided to assume that wasn't intentional snark. "The latter, but if we leave stuff out, there's a better chance he'll eat than if we don't leave stuff out."

Steph nodded. "Okay. Let's find the kitchen."

That was easier than finding the correct bedroom, although I did get sidetracked by a gorgeous library on the way. Apparently, Eric Marshall didn't only write books—he coveted them. His library was two stories of books, covering nearly as much floor space as my entire apartment. He even had one of those cool ladders for reaching the second story.

Steph tugged on my sleeve. "Focus, girl."

"Yeah, sorry. But did you see he has a signed first edition of *Pet Sematary* in that case over there?"

"My cousin always liked to collect things. It was Matchbox cars when we were kids."

"His taste improved."

Steph's smile was thin and highlighted the cracks in her fading lipstick. "He paid a high price for all this shit."

In that, we were in agreement.

Unsurprisingly, the kitchen was also enormous. We searched the cabinets for stuff to leave out on the center island, settling on cereal, some snack food, and protein bars. By the sink, we left a glass of water.

Forlornly, Steph added a banana to the stack of food. "This is the best we can do? Pathetic. I guess I'll make some calls later. Maybe someone else can check in on him during the day while I'm at work."

"You're a good cousin, especially considering you didn't talk to him for most of the last ten years."

She rolled her eyes. "Someone in my family needs to not be an asshole. Let's get out of here. It's depressing seeing so much money go to waste and knowing what was used to buy it all."

"Don't knock Eric too hard. He's a good writer. That alone might not have been enough to get him this." I spread my arms wide. "But it's not like he sold his soul for a winning Powerball ticket. He still had to put in a lot of work."

"True. I guess." A sweet, vanilla sadness overtook her anger as Steph locked the heavy front door. Our footsteps sounded loud as we crossed the stone-paved driveway, but the night was louder. The insects chirped a lonely chorus. "Thanks, by the way. For helping. I'm sorry I snapped at you earlier. I'm just…"

"Yeah, I know. No worries. But if you want to kiss and make up, you can drop me off at my new home."

Steph paused before shifting into gear. "In Shadowtown? That's one hell of a make-up smooch."

ON THE WAY BACK TO BOSTON I FOUND A RADIO STATION THAT was playing Barry Manilow, and Steph and I belted out our best version of "Mandy." Alas, our best was by no means good.

Still, Steph was in better spirits by the time we got home, and she didn't even whine about driving through Shadowtown. I took pity on her and let her drop me off at one of the main roads instead of at my building.

Once I turned the corner, I caught sight of the sylph's scissors flashing in the barbershop and decided I'd be happier seeking out Lucen than hanging out at my new, mostly bare home.

Since it was Sunday, The Lair was closed. After dropping off my signed Eric Marshall book—now certain to fetch a very high price once word of his condition spread, and if I were crass enough to auction it off—I gave Lucen a call. I needed to know if he was unoccupied with…things.

Addicts.

It seemed no promises or vows to be a better satyr could kill the bitterness I felt about them or my unease about our relationship.

Fortunately, Lucen picked up quickly, and I put those thoughts out of my head and strolled over. It was a short walk, and moving my legs felt good after being cooped up in a car.

Shadowtown was more subdued than usual, but I wrote that off to it being a Sunday night. Preds didn't like the weekends coming to a close any more than humans did. The few I saw out and about paid me little attention. The satyrs acknowledged me, the harpies and the goblins ignored me, the furies gave me strange glances, and the sylphs sneered. But none of them approached me or made any aggressive moves. That was a pleasant change where the sylphs were concerned, in particular.

Between my showdown with the fury who'd framed me for murder a few weeks ago, and my takedown of the satyrs' former number two last week, I was apparently building a bit of a rep. Although I was still considered defenseless human prey by most, I must not have been considered defenseless enough to be worth the risk.

Without needing to worry about pred aggression, I was able to keep a lookout for ghouls, which was more difficult than I'd have expected. It was as though my brain had wired itself not to notice them, to move past and look away rather than face the sadness of their plight. They crowded together in the shadows like wraiths. I'd catch them only as I passed, hollow eyes, sallow skin, and greasy hair. Usually they clustered in small groups, though they acted like they didn't notice each other's presence.

And this, if I were to be honest, was why I didn't normally "see" them. The awfulness of their existence threatened to overwhelm me when I did. Worse than feeling sad, I felt helpless. Even if I could afford to feed and clothe and shelter each one, I could never give them back their old selves. All the years I'd journeyed into Shadowtown I'd turned away, letting the knowledge of their existence rub a thick callus over my heart until they became almost invisible. It wasn't nice, but it was necessary.

Tonight reminded me of why. I didn't even know why I was studying them. Nothing I could see gave me any greater insight into their situation. There was nothing to help me help Eric. If Bridget was right, our only shot was finding the goblin who'd drained him and getting his soul back in time.

But I guessed I'd needed the reminder of what I was up against and the cruelty of it to harden my resolve to return to the Gryphons. Because the satyr I was about to meet? He was so going to try to talk me out of it.

Bracing myself, I knocked.

A muffled voice came from behind the door. "You have a key, little siren. Use it!"

I sighed and dug into my pocket for it.

After closing the door behind me, I crossed the tiny entryway. To my left was Lucen's kitchen. To my right, his living room. That's where he was, flopped on the sofa with his bare feet resting on a table. Something was playing on his TV, but whatever it was, it wasn't as distracting as his chest. He was shirtless and in jeans. Just the way I liked him best.

He smiled at me as I stood in the doorway. "Did you forget you had a key, were you trying to make me move, or were you testing my ability to sense your presence at the door?"

"None of the above. I was being polite and not barging in. Although I am a bit miffed that you couldn't be bothered to get up for me. No respect."

He sprang with the more-than-human speed that all preds possessed. Muscular arms wrapped around me, and he picked me up and spun me around the living room. I shrieked.

Laughing, Lucen set me down but didn't let go, and I buried my face against him. He leaned forward and kissed my forehead. "God forbid the day I don't get up for you, little siren."

I groaned. "That sounds like a bad pun."

"Are there any other kind?"

"Fair point." He loosened his grip around me enough that I could move, and I slid my arms around his waist. Mmm...freshly washed satyr. I could detect a faint scent of lemongrass soap intermingling with his cinnamon pheromones. Damn. I would never get tired of that scent. "You smell good. Bet you taste good too." I tested that theory, first by licking the closest patch of skin then kissing my way across his pecs and slowly downward.

His breaths quickened, but he let me continue for only a moment. Then he tugged me upright so he could kiss me. I melted into him, as he entwined his tongue with mine before pulling away. "So what brings you here?"

"I can't get enough of you?"

"That much we know. But something's bothering you."

Ah, preds. You couldn't hide anything around them. Well, not unless anything was something happy.

I removed my arms from his waist because it was hard to concentrate while standing so close to him. As usual, my brain wanted to shut off and my body, well, it became very *on* in its place.

I motioned toward the beer sitting on the table. "Got another?"

Lucen obliged and retrieved one from the fridge. "So?"

"So." I drew out the word, settling on the sofa. Did I give him context first, or did I rip off the metaphorical bandage and get on with it?

Lucen raised an eyebrow.

I ripped. It was more my style and totally what he would do to me. "I'm going back to work for the Gryphons."

Though he said nothing in return, the eyebrow remained raised, frozen on his face along with every other feature.

When he didn't so much as blink for a disturbingly long time, I figured context was now appropriate. "There was a magical attack on Steph's cousin. You know, the guy whose book signing I went to earlier? It was a goblin. Steph is in a bad state, understandably, and she's my best friend. She asked me to get involved, and so I am."

Slowly, the eyebrow lowered. Lucen took a long drink of beer and shut off the TV. "You couldn't help without going back to the Gryphons?"

"What happened is out of my league. This isn't some soul-swapping case where I can go all vigilante."

If I had known Eric was an addict, I could have offered my services to him before this happened. But he was a prize-worthy soul, no doubt. It would probably have taken a lot more than the usual creeps I went after to get the goblin to relinquish him in a trade. "I need the Gryphons' resources to do this, and besides, they were already involved."

I neglected to point out that I was the one who'd involved them. If it hadn't been me, the paramedics would have done it eventually.

"I see." His tone didn't leave me very confident of that.

For Lucen, there would never be a way to see. To him, the Gryphons were the enemy and always had been. I supposed they were my enemy too these days, but it wasn't the same. I hated them because of what they'd done to me. Lucen, and every other pred, hated them because they tried to keep preds in line. To make them actually obey the laws, both mundane and magical, rather than give lip service to them.

Historically, neither side had bothered with laws. Preds and humans had been at war until only the last couple centuries. Then a peace agreement known as the London Accords had been drawn up. While a couple of centuries was a long time for most of us, preds lived long lives. Their memories were likely just as long, and the peace was uneasy at best.

Sighing, Lucen ran his fingers through his hair. "After what they did to you, little siren, I can't believe you're willing to even walk into that building."

"Me neither, and I wouldn't normally. But it's Steph. She helped me commit a felony a few weeks ago to clear my name."

"Aren't you even? Didn't you once commit a felony for her?"

I shrugged. Ten years ago, the night I'd met Steph, I'd gotten revenge— or justice, depending on your perspective—for her by trading away the souls of the two bullies who'd beaten her up.

Was that a felony? There was no law specifically for soul-swapping, probably since I was the only known person to ever try it, but Olivia Lee had threatened to charge me with endangering humans for it. That was very much a felony. "Since I've never been charged with anything, there's no legal precedent that says I'd have been convicted for endangerment. So no. But that's what best friends do for each other. Commit felonies and work with the enemy."

"Then consider this is what your boyfriend does for you—try to talk you out of it."

It was my turn to raise an eyebrow. "Boyfriend?"

And it was Lucen's turn to shrug. There was almost something self-conscious in the gesture. Maybe it was my imagination, but it made my heart beat faster. "What would you call me?"

Self-conscious myself, I reached for my bottle. "I've been thinking of you as my satyr-with-benefits."

Lucen choked on his swallow of beer. "That's so cold. I don't even get labeled a friend?"

"I thought that part was obvious."

Friend. Frequent bedmate. Lover? Ugh, that sounded so cheesy. But "boyfriend" didn't sit right with me. "Boyfriend" implied total commitment, something I wasn't sure we could have since Lucen was always going to be sharing a part of himself with other people.

I cleared my throat, hoping to change both topics of conversation. "So were you hanging out here with your TV tonight? I hope I'm not interrupting any quality alone time since the point of me not crashing here any longer..." Was so I wouldn't get uncomfortable when he had addicts over.

So much for changing the topic.

"You weren't interrupting. I was working, but I can entertain you and do that at the same time."

"You sure?" I pushed my bottle away. "Because I wanted to talk about what happened, but if you're busy, I can leave."

He grabbed my arm and pulled me closer. "I'm sure. It was just some satyr business. Not anything so important I couldn't do it while watching TV."

I nestled my head against his shoulder, but my stomach twisted. Was that some sort of euphemism for having an addict over? "Satyr business means what?"

The question tumbled off my lips. Dragon shit on toast. I was supposed to be learning not to care. Instead I was acting like a jealous wife.

Across the room, Lucen's pet dragon, Sweetpea, snorted smoke. It had to be my imagination, but I could have sworn the scaly rat was laughing at my paranoia.

Lucen shifted position, running a finger up and down my spine. In spite of my tension, I closed my eyes. "Stuff for the domus, little siren. Not what you were thinking."

Because, of course, he could tell. "Sorry. I'm trying to be okay with sharing you."

"But that's the thing, Jess. You're not sharing me." He put his finger under my chin and lifted my head so I faced him. "This is what's important. It's your head on my shoulder. Feeling your heartbeat. The way your breath glides over my skin. The smell of your shampoo. It's knowing you come to me to talk about important things, and me trying to help you. Even if you refuse to take my good advice." He smiled wryly. "But it's not sex. Sex is fun. It isn't what's important."

I swallowed, returned my head to his shoulder, and tightened my hold on him. His words warmed me inside. Snuggled up against him, I felt safe and wanted and loved, although neither of us had yet to use that word. But I felt like I belonged. I was content.

He was right too. Those were the things that were important. That emotional intimacy. There was no denying we'd had a connection like that for years, but I'd been afraid of indulging it. Yet I didn't know if it was really enough. I didn't know if I could let go of this need to have all of him to myself.

And if I couldn't? Would I lose the part I had too? How did a person learn to accept this situation? Was it possible? Just wanting to accept it was clearly not enough.

Lucen had told me to sleep around with other people. Get it out of my system. Begin to see sex as no big deal. Why couldn't I be one of those people for whom it *was* no big deal?

I kissed the patch of skin beneath his lips. So warm. So tantalizing. "I know that's what's important. I do know it."

But I love you and I want you all to myself. I clamped my lips together. Thinking it was scary enough. Saying the words opened me up to too much possible pain in the future.

Lucen stroked my hair. "I know you know it. This, little siren, is what I can't have with anyone else. We're a work in progress. Think how far we've come already."

"True. Two months ago I wouldn't let you touch me."

"Exactly. And it only took ten years for you to get over that. Let's hope it doesn't take another ten for the next step."

"Yeah." Although ten was preferable to never-going-to-happen.

The hand running through my hair stopped, leaving me disappointed until he slid it under my shirt. "Don't think I'm done trying to talk you out of the Gryphons, by the way."

I laughed once. "Yeah, I know that much too."

And that was okay because I understood it meant that he cared.

FIVE

I SPARED LUCEN THE AGONY OF AN ALARM GOING OFF EARLY BY returning to my new place around one in the morning. After closing my cheap, hand-me-down drapes, I fell onto my futon and promptly stared at the ceiling for the rest of the night. Exhaustion be damned.

I was alone. In a tiny apartment. In what should be a dangerous neighborhood.

But mostly, I was alone. Funny how when I'd lived with roommates, I'd cherished those evenings when they would be gone and I had the place to myself. I could watch what I wanted, blast my music, or take up the entire kitchen.

Now I lay awake, contemplating my life choices. That was never a good thing to do, and it was an especially bad one at two...then three...then four in the morning. At that point, I might actually have fallen asleep long enough to dream because I woke up at nine with vague memories of fires, intense, skin-searing heat, and choking on smoke and blood. So much blood. Mine, I thought.

Goose bumps broke out on my arms, despite the sweaty sheets that clung to me.

Just a stress dream, I told myself. The result of it being the first night in an unfamiliar place after I watched Eric Marshall's soul be devoured by an asshole goblin. Oh, and I was going back to the Gryphons today. Back to an organization that screwed up my life so I could be some kind of super warrior for them.

Yup, stress, and no wonder. So fuck that anxiety. I needed coffee. Everything was easier to deal with when I was caffeinated.

I dragged my butt into the shower and let the hot spray wash off the remnants of the nightmare. Once cleaned, fed, and clothed, I only required a minor pep talk—*think of Steph, remember Eric*—to get over my reluctance and head over to Gryphon headquarters.

Sometime around two thirty last night I'd realized I should call Olivia Lee and let her know I'd changed my mind and would be coming in today. Alas, the good director hadn't answered, which would have been sweet revenge for the several mornings she'd woken me up with her damn calls. But instead, I'd left her a voicemail.

She hadn't called back yet. Standing in the bustling downtown lobby, I wondered what to do. When I'd quit last week, I'd thrown my ID badge at her. As a result, I'd been reduced to just another visitor.

After I cleared the visitor's security check, I hopped on the elevator to the top floor. If Olivia wanted me back so damn bad, she could have returned my call. Since she hadn't, she'd have to deal with my unscheduled arrival.

The elevator stopped on the second floor, and a petite woman about my age got on. Anna had been the lab technician who'd worked on the case with me and Andre.

I steeled myself for questions about my sudden departure, but Anna threw me a genuine smile. "Hey, Jess. I didn't know you were back. Did they find a new case to bring you in on?"

She didn't know. She had no clue about how I'd stormed out or why.

I let out a breath, discreetly I hoped. Anna was reminding me of what my conscience had been whispering for days—that I shouldn't condemn the entire Gryphon organization for the actions of a few.

Truth was, there was no reason Anna should know what happened regarding my leaving. Based on the little I knew myself, my entire existence was top-secret stuff. None of which was Anna's fault, or

Bridget's, or probably even Olivia Lee's. It was hardly right of me to hold a grudge against any of them for it.

No, my grudge—make that my very righteous fury—should be directed at the group within the Gryphons behind this. The Brotherhood of the Wing.

But making that distinction emotionally, not just logically, wasn't easy. Especially because the Gryphons were a good target. I'd already felt spurned by them when they'd denied me entry for being a magical freak, and then they'd come after me when I was framed for murder. In both cases they'd been doing their jobs, but knowing that didn't lessen the sting.

Hell, knowing that some of them had been responsible for turning me into a freak, which was why I'd been denied entry, which had led me to engage in activities that had gotten me framed for murder... Well, that made it harder.

Still, not Anna's fault.

My body remained tense, although I tried to cover up my misplaced angst. "Yeah, looks like I'm going to be working on a case that came down last night."

"Great! Maybe we'll get to work together again." She got off one floor below me.

Stepping out on the fifth floor, I squared my shoulders and checked my surroundings. A couple people nodded at me, but no one seemed all that concerned or interested in my presence. Possibly they recognized me from my recent stint here.

I took off down the hall toward Olivia's grand office, and was waylaid at last by her perky receptionist as I approached.

"She's in a meeting," the woman told me, "and I don't have you on her calendar."

"Find time." I plopped on one of the chairs by the door. "She's been asking to see me."

The receptionist started to say something else, but she cut off as two large doors on the other side of the reception area opened and out walked none other than the director herself.

"Jessica." Olivia peered down on me with disapproval. She held up a finger in my direction, and I snapped my lips shut without uttering a word. Sure, I'd wait.

Behind her, three other people emerged from what appeared to be a conference room. The two humans were unfamiliar to me, but the magi bore a face I'd seen before and had never wished to see again.

Xander, the magi in question, was a falcon shifter with bright red plumage on his head and an expensive suit on his body. He was a liaison to important political people within the state, and a plain old self-important jackass. Our first and only run-in had not gone well.

I clenched my teeth in anticipation, but he cast not so much as a disparaging glance my way before striding off. Either he didn't recognize me, or he simply hadn't thought a woman in jeans and a T-shirt was worth his attention.

Win for me.

Olivia finished exchanging pleasantries with her companions and turned my way as they left. "Let's talk."

I popped to my feet. "That's why I'm here."

I followed her into her office, tasting the strange blend of generalized unhappiness she was feeling. So much was going on in her emotions that I couldn't sort it out, but it tasted awful.

"Have a seat." Olivia took her own recommendation, and she faced me from across her large desk. Small in comparison to it, she nonetheless radiated authority and a don't-mess-with-me attitude that I admired even if I didn't personally like her. She tucked strands of graying black hair behind her ears and got down to business. "I got your message last night, or should I say this morning."

I adopted the same attitude. "But you didn't call back."

"I didn't see the point. I'd been calling you and you weren't responding."

I almost rolled my eyes but managed restraint. "So you were getting revenge?"

"I think we can both be more mature than that. If you were going to follow through and return today, I assumed that you'd do it on your own time." Disapproval weighed down her voice.

I shrugged. "The only reason I'm back is because of what happened last night."

"That's another reason I hadn't returned your call." She closed her eyes, and for a second I saw her stress etched clearly over her face. Then she pulled herself together. "Being as famous as he is, what happened to Mr. Marshall has become a rather large and popular topic in the media. As I'm sure you're aware."

"Actually, I wasn't. I haven't gone online all morning."

"Lucky you." Olivia waved a hand around idly. "There were over fifty witnesses at that bookstore yesterday. The story of what happened is all over the news stations and Internet. There's even video. Multiple people were recording his reading at the time."

"And they made the videos public?" Stay classy, Boston.

Olivia's face was a mask of distaste. "When don't people share everything these days? Anyway, as you can imagine, it's been a busy day around here. We haven't had to deal with such a high-profile case in years. The last time anything with this much gossip potential occurred it was about that actress who got caught planting curses on a baseball team."

I remembered the incident although it had happened several years ago, and it wasn't baseball, but basketball. Selena Troy had sold her soul to a harpy for her big break, and the harpy had used her to try to take down the Lakers over some complicated gambling deal. "It wasn't this office that had to handle it, was it?"

"No, thankfully. That was the Los Angeles office, but this office does have to handle Eric Marshall. So we've been busy."

I clasped my hands together. "Good thing I'm here to help."

Judging by Olivia's expression she wasn't so sure about that. "Yes, I've been informed that Agent Nelson requested your assistance."

Thank you, Bridget. I think. If nothing else, she'd kept her word. "Eric's cousin is a good friend of mine. You could say the family has requested my personal involvement."

Olivia took a deep breath and tossed a hefty manila file folder my way. "You need to sign a new consultant agreement and fill out those forms again. Given the way you left, I had to make sure your clearances were formally revoked. Also, turn in your request for a new protective charm to

Agent Nelson, and she'll make sure it gets passed down to the lab. You can have your old cube back."

I opened the folder. My former badge was clipped to the agreement. "Great. Thanks."

"You're welcome."

"So does this mean I'm officially working with Bridget on Eric's case?"

Olivia leaned forward. "Yes, but let me explain two more things." She raised her index finger. "One. Gryphon policy is to not allow agents with a personal connection to a specific case to get involved. I'm making an allowance in this situation since the family has requested your assistance, you were a witness to what happened, and this is such a high-profile case so I want to use every resource we can spare. That includes you and your dubious contacts in Shadowtown."

Dubious? Wait until someone in HR discovered my updated contact information included a Shadowtown mailing address. "And the second thing?"

"Again, this is high profile. It's entirely possible that during the course of the investigation you'll get people from the media asking questions and pressuring you for information. If you do, let Agent Nelson handle it. She knows where to direct those inquiries. All you do is tell people to talk to her. Got it?"

Where to direct those inquiries—sounded like code for the trash bin.

"Got it. The less people I have to talk to, the happier I am anyway."

A shadow of a smile appeared on Olivia's face. "That doesn't surprise me."

Taking that as my dismissal, I got up. "Should I drop the rest of these forms off in HR later?"

"Yes. And, Jessica? One more thing." Olivia stood. "Whatever your issue is with Agent Kassin? It doesn't concern me. Next time, leave me and this office out of it."

I gritted my teeth, but since I'd just been pondering the same thing on my way here, I managed to nod rather stiffly. "Understood."

Olivia's dark eyes were hard. "I hope so because I want to be clear. My responsibility is overseeing the Boston Office. And Kassin, although he's been working out of it, does not report to me. After you stormed out of here, I made some calls because he refused to speak to me about it. I was shut out fast and told this was above my clearance. Since I'm not allowed to know what's going on, I have absolutely no interest in being caught in the middle again. Now do you understand?"

Though Olivia kept her voice controlled, I tasted the heat of her anger. I couldn't blame her. Yet interestingly, her anger didn't seem directed quite as much at me as it was at whoever had told her to fuck off.

I nodded. "I apologize for taking it out on you. I didn't realize at the time..." Hadn't been thinking straight, more like. "Didn't realize who or what was responsible for the issue. I'm still angry with the Gryphon organization, but not everyone in it. I just want to stay away from Tom Kassin."

Surprisingly, Olivia seemed mollified by my response. She probably hadn't anticipated an apology.

For that matter, neither had I until one left my mouth. Who knew? I could be reasonable, after all.

"Then you'll be pleased to know Agent Kassin left for World soon after you quit. Although I suspect he'll be back. He left a lot of his belongings here."

Well, wasn't that interesting. I'd told Tom to fuck off, and he did, in fact, fuck off and run back home. No doubt straight to his creepy fraternity to get his orders for what to do next. Olivia was right about that. No question—Tom would be back, and he and his superiors weren't likely to be done with me.

But for the moment, at least, I could breathe easier. Tom was on the other side of the Atlantic, in France. That left me room to think about more important things, like why I was here.

ANOTHER THING I SHOULD BE THINKING ABOUT? WHERE I WAS going. As Olivia's door closed, I realized I didn't know where to report.

Shifting my grip on the file folder, I decided the paperwork was a good place to start. Olivia said I had my former desk back, so I went downstairs to where my cubby had been located. Much as I didn't like sitting around and filling out stupid forms, I wasn't sure anyone would let me touch the case until I did. Besides, Bridget might have a clue where to find me if I stayed put.

I clipped on my badge and found my cube much as I had left it. With some amusement, I noted that someone had retrieved the Gryphon windbreaker I'd once asked for—and then had thrown at Olivia on my way out the door. It was draped over the back of the chair.

That saved me the embarrassment of asking for it back.

There were no notes from Bridget or anyone else, and I'd been locked out of the computer as Olivia had hinted. So I got to work on form after form with a pen I found in the desk drawer. Ten minutes into this, as I was recalling that I had a phone and could have texted Bridget, she showed up.

"Knock, knock." She had her light brown hair pulled into a tidy bun today, but instead of it looking formal or elegant, with her serious face, she looked about twenty years older than her age. "Director Lee told me you were here. Ready to go into a briefing?"

"And tear myself away from all this?" I held up the folder. "Please, yes."

Bridget smiled. Barely. But that was so very Bridget.

"It's nice to finally work together," she said as we entered one of the boring conference rooms. "Maybe nice isn't the right word under the circumstances, but you know what I mean."

"That's kind of the hazard in your line of work, isn't it? I mean, Gryphons don't get involved in things when they're all rainbows and kittens."

She acknowledged the point with a shake of her shoulders. "True."

There was one other guy already in the room, with shaggy black hair and tan skin. He held out a hand to me. "Wes," he said, then followed it up with a last name that I couldn't possibly repeat without making a fool of myself for trying.

"Wes is our lab lead on the case," Bridget explained, taking a seat.

Aha. So I wouldn't be working with Anna this time.

Wes stretched out in his chair, his fingers sweeping through his hair. "Not for long."

"Why not?" Bridget asked.

"You won't need me. Magically speaking, this is a simple case."

"Well, that's a nice change." The conference room door opened, and one of the assistant directors entered. Brian, whose last name I couldn't remember, had been the supervisor on the last case I'd worked on. He dropped into a chair at the head of the table. "Let's get this wrapped up as fast as possible then. I've got goddamned journalists from as far as Germany calling."

Bridget groaned. "One way or another, I suspect this will be fast. But Wes should probably go first with the lab results in case I'm wrong."

"Nope, don't think so. I've got nothing to report." Wes switched on the blank screen on the far end of the room to show his analysis results. "Marshall's magic profile was completely normal. For an addict-turned-ghoul, that is. No anomalies. I could have pulled these results from any dozen ghouls roaming Shadowtown's streets."

Brian scratched his chin thoughtfully. "So what the hell happened? Nelson?"

Bridget passed out some papers, but I only glanced at them. "I did some research this morning and confirmed the theory I shared with Jess last night. There are several accounts of preds draining addicts quickly and completely. There haven't been any reported cases of it happening in the US for years, but unless someone knew about it and filed a report, we wouldn't know. Odds are, it's happened without our awareness."

"How does that work?" Wes asked. "Each race feeds on specific emotions. Just draining someone of all their emotions at once doesn't seem like it would cut it."

"I had the same question," I said.

Bridget glanced between the two of us. "I'm not sure of the answer. It's true each pred race draws power best from a particular emotion, but they can feed off any negativity. So my best guess is that this would be far from ideal, but still feasible."

"Kind of like eating processed food instead of fresh?" I suggested.

Wes laughed. "Canned greed. Yum."

Brian wasn't amused. "And so now what?"

Bridget tapped her papers. "According to my research, the pred who did this couldn't have used up all of Marshall's soul immediately. It would have to be stored somewhere. Depending on how far gone Marshall was in his addiction at the time, we should have anywhere from five days to two weeks to get it back. After that, it's impossible to return it. Jess identified Marshall as a greed addict. So we know who to start questioning."

"That narrows it down, but not by much." Brian pushed his glasses higher on his nose. "You know how many goblins we have in this city? We need Marshall's contract."

Bridget sighed. "I've been working on it. So far as I can discover, his next of kin is a brother. I've tried calling him several times and have gotten nowhere. I left him two messages—one last night and one this morning."

"And you need his brother, why?" I asked.

"Like Brian said, to get his contract."

"You can't get a warrant?"

"We can't even prove a crime has been committed yet. A pred letting an addict turn into a ghoul isn't illegal in most situations, and with Marshall in the state he's in, legally speaking he's as good as dead. Once his brother gets the court to acknowledge that Marshall's a ghoul, he takes over the estate, and that's just a legal formality at this point. We learned this morning that his brother has already initiated proceedings. So if he wants to, he could cause a stink if we go barging into Marshall's house without his permission. Remember, we're dealing with a high-profile case. It would be best if we could get his cooperation."

I tapped my pen against Bridget's handouts. "You said yourself—there's not a lot of time. Sitting around playing nice with his family is putting Eric at risk."

"You have a better idea?" Brian asked.

I quit fidgeting with the pen. "Maybe. From what I've heard of them, Eric's family is likely to be a pain in the ass. But I know someone who is family and who wants to help, and she has a key."

Bridget tidied up her papers, frowning. "That's not technically legal at this point. Marshall's estate is in limbo."

"So's Eric's soul."

Brian held up a hand. "Bridget is right. We need to tread very carefully right now. So here's what I propose. On our end, Bridget will start putting together all the evidence that Marshall was cursed so we can get legal authority to search the house, family cooperation or no. But Jessica also has a point. Time is short. If Jessica is friends with a family member who has a key, and she happens to see the contract while she's there and her friend is checking on Marshall, and she happens to get us the name of the goblin..." He cleared his throat. "That would not be unfortunate."

I smiled. I hadn't thought much of Brian one way or another on the last case, but he was growing on me.

SIX

THE FIRST THING I DID AFTER THE MEETING BROKE UP WAS
call Steph and see if she was up for driving back to New Hampshire this
evening.

"It wouldn't be a bad thing to check on Eric," she said. "Why?"

I faked a cough. "Unofficial official Gryphon business."

"Sounds underhanded and sneaky."

"Extremely." I yawned. "So are you in?"

"If it will help Eric, sure. Besides, we can try that brewery up his way
for dinner. He was telling me how good the beer was last time we…" Her
voice trailed off, and I could imagine her feelings even though I couldn't
sense them.

"Sounds good. I'll be ready to go when you get off work."

After hanging up, I flipped through the notes Bridget had passed out at
the meeting, but they didn't tell me anything new. Bottom line was that
this was a simple case, like Bridget had laid out. Get the goblin's name,
track him or her down, retrieve Eric's soul.

How one returned a soul, well, I was going to have to assume that
Bridget had researched that too. No point worrying about it until we knew
we'd gotten it.

My day passed quickly. IT came around and re-granted me access to my computer, then Bridget and I went to lunch, during which she caught me up on what was happening with supposed mutual friends—the people we'd attended the Gryphon Academy with years ago. People I barely knew anymore. Soon enough, it was three o'clock, and I needed to get to an appointment I'd rather skip.

Shadowtown was waking up as I got off the T and made my way toward Gunthra's for tea. Though the July sun was high, it was hard to tell. All the buildings in the neighborhood gave off a kind of aura, as though they absorbed negativity right along with their owners. By some trick of the eye, they appeared to stretch skyward, blocking out the light. Their colors were muted, the shadows between them darker. Heavy stone and brick gave even the most mundane of businesses, like Lucen's bar, a slightly menacing air.

Gunthra's house epitomized the architecture. Stately yet gaudy, with tall, narrow doors and windows, it nested deep inside Shadowtown. The stairs to the front door were steep, and the empty urns on the portico hosted ugly stone gargoyles instead of flowers. Indeed, one got the impression that flowers couldn't bear to grow in such conditions. But if they did, they'd be darkly colored and poisonous. Monkshood maybe.

I knocked once with the heavy brass knocker and waited, hands behind my back to hide my fidgeting. The door swung open, and the Dom's liveried butler beckoned me in without a word. His large eyes appraised me, and his ears flattened against his head. I assumed he disapproved of my attire but was too well trained to speak of it.

To be fair, I looked out of place. If the outside of Gunthra's house belonged on the cover of *Pred Homes and Gardens*, it had nothing on the inside. Dark brocade covered the walls, an enormous crystal chandelier hung in the foyer, and a goblin-sized suit of armor stood in an alcove under the stairs. It was deeply moody and atmospheric, but in a way that screamed old money rather than wannabe goth.

The servant opened the set of doors on the right. "Miss Moore for you."

I had to force my feet to enter the room. The last time I'd been in here was the day I'd learned what I was—not a woman whose gift was cursed, but a part satyr. "An abomination," in Gunthra's words.

Since then, my understanding of my true species had gotten better. Or worse, depending on your perspective. According to Lucen, there was no such thing as a part pred. I was more like a subspecies of satyr. Whether his or Gunthra's description was more accurate, I couldn't say, and I wasn't sure I wanted to know anyway.

The goblin Dom rose from her fainting couch as I crossed the room. "Miss Moore, thank you for accepting my invitation."

Like I had any choice?

Gunthra dressed like a regal old woman, but not one nearly as old as she must be. I wouldn't have been surprised if all the antiques in this house had been purchased new.

Yet with too many rings on her spindly fingers and a too-long strand of pearls around her neck, Gunthra blended in with her décor. The sofa I sat on was upholstered in a gorgeous silk fleur-de-lis pattern, and the many artfully placed knickknacks scattered about the room and the paintings on the walls could give Eric Marshall a run for his money. The centerpiece in Gunthra's room, however, were the butterflies preserved in glass that rested on top of her mantle.

The Dom had a thing for butterflies. She liked the idea of metamorphosis, comparing humans to caterpillars and preds to their prettier, flying brethren. Personally, the analogy had left me with a disdain for butterflies, which I now thought of as pretentious moths.

Same as she had on my first visit, Gunthra had set out a fancy china tea set, and she poured me a cup. "No milk or sugar, correct?"

"No, thanks." If she was trying to impress me with her memory, it had worked.

"Have a muffin. Lemon poppy seed. My favorite." She smiled at me in a creepy, predatory way. Either she enjoyed playing hostess, or she enjoyed testing my patience.

Reluctantly, I took a muffin. Refusing her hospitality would be impolite, and if I recalled, Gunthra had a damn good cook working for her. "So," I said, trying not to spill tea or muffin crumbs over what had to be a very expensive couch. "Thanks for the invitation, but since I know you're not just being neighborly, shall we get on with it?"

Shall we? Being surrounded by so much pomp and elegance must have brought out the pompousness in my vocabulary.

Gunthra sipped her tea, and the silence dragged out. "Young people have no appreciation for the niceties of etiquette these days. Very well, Miss Moore. Since you insist, I did ask you here for a specific reason. You owe me a favor. I'm ready to collect."

I'd been expecting that, so I managed to swallow my bite of muffin without choking on it in panic. My stomach, however, was knotting in spite of being forewarned, and I forced myself to wash the bite down with unfortunate-tasting tea before responding. "So long as what you're asking doesn't violate the rules we agreed upon, I'm ready."

Those rules were fast and loose, something I thought I'd done well with until Gunthra had agreed to them easily. Thereby making it clear to me that I must have screwed up.

One favor that did not involve me hurting, killing, or otherwise ruining an innocent person's life. Including my own. Yeah, in retrospect, I should have done a better job of that.

"I think you'll see your concern is unwarranted." Gunthra smoothed a wrinkle on her skirt. "All I want is for you to retrieve some information for me from the Gryphons."

"Oh, that's all? You realize—"

"Information you should be able to access."

I'd almost forgotten about Gunthra's talent for talking over people. "I'm not exactly in good standing with the Gryphons."

"That, Miss Moore, is not my problem. You are consulting for them, are you not?"

"You're lucky. I went back to work for them this morning."

Gunthra clasped her hands together, and the diamonds on her fingers caught the sunlight streaming in through a gap in her blue, brocade draperies. "Consider this serendipity then. What I want you to bring me is whatever information the Gryphons have on the furies' recent actions. You don't need to give me any original documents. Copies of whatever they have will be sufficient. But I want all of it."

"The 'furies' recent actions' means what exactly? If I'm going to try to steal case files, I need to be clear about what I'm supposed to be stealing."

"Is it stealing if you're not taking the only copy of the files, nor depriving the Gryphons of any monetary value they might have?"

I rolled my eyes. "Fine. It's sharing information you're not supposed to see, whatever. Either way, you need to be more specific."

"Very well, if you want me to spell it out. I want to know whatever intelligence the Gryphons have gathered on what the furies were scheming when they used one of their addicts to frame you for murder and tried to start a pred war."

I didn't choke on my muffin, but I did almost drop the delicate china plate it sat on. I'd suspected those were the "recent actions" Gunthra had been referring to, but to hear her state plainly her suspicion that the furies had been trying to start a war...that was something else.

Lucen had speculated on it at the time, but idly. In the end, the satyrs had gone with the simplest, most-likely-to-be-true assumption—the furies who'd framed me had been working alone. There had been no larger conspiracy.

Were they wrong? If so, it raised the very good question as to why the furies might have been trying to start a war.

Gunthra cocked her head to the side. "Thoughts, Miss Moore?"

"Many." And when she chose to continue with her unblinking stare, I merely smiled. Thoughts didn't come for free around here. Just because she'd shared a theory didn't mean I needed to share questions about it.

"I'll refrain from imposing a deadline on you," Gunthra said at last, breaking the silence, "unless I feel you're taking too long."

"Good. Because you do realize it will take me some time to figure out how to get hold of that information."

"Acceptable and acknowledged."

Really? She was being disturbingly agreeable, so I pressed my luck. "Do you mind if I ask why you're interested?"

Gunthra shook a finger at me. "Actually, yes. Let's say it's a topic I find fascinating. Information is a commodity, Miss Moore. Scarcity is what creates value. I believe I explained the same thing to you when you came asking me about your heritage."

"Yeah, I believe you did. Speaking of which, it's been suggested to me that calling me part satyr, as you did, wasn't entirely accurate. Would you care to comment?"

Gunthra raised an overly plucked eyebrow. "Semantics. You are what you are, and what you are is not what most people would consider to be a satyr. I called you 'part,' and you understood me."

Damn goblins and their weasel-wording technicalities. But it didn't really matter. I couldn't claim she'd lied to me and hence our deal was void. She'd told me enough of the truth, and I owed her for it. How I was going to fulfill my end of that deal, and for what nefarious reasons she wanted that information... Well, it was too late to worry about the latter, and the former would just have to be figured out. Somehow.

I let it go.

Shoving aside my plate with the mostly uneaten muffin, I plunged ahead with an idea that had occurred to me on my walk over. "While we're having this lovely etiquette-filled tea, I was hoping we could discuss a not-so-small matter that occurred last night."

"What would that be?" Gunthra's massive brow wrinkled in what could have actually been genuine confusion. Was it possible that the Dom didn't yet know what one of her subordinates had done, or was she merely a skillful liar?

I watched her carefully as I spoke. "When I told you I went back to work for the Gryphons today, it was to assist them with a new case. You've heard of Eric Marshall, the writer?"

Gunthra nodded. Of course, she had. Not only was he famous, one of her own people had snagged him as an addict. With his value as such, the Dom would know which goblin it was. Assuming it wasn't herself.

And if Gunthra was his master, and had been the one to drain him? That would be a whole bowl of salamander shit to deal with given that I was in her debt.

"Last night, Eric's master turned him into a ghoul. He was drained completely, all at once. Like that." I snapped my fingers and paused, waiting for a reaction, but Gunthra remained impassive. Damn.

We were back to having a staring contest. Silently, I counted in my head, refusing to break first.

Gunthra took a long sip of her tea and sighed at last. "I see."

"It's illegal, and one of your people did it."

"If that's true, then I will handle it."

"Let me save you the trouble. Tell me who the goblin is, and I'll handle it."

Gunthra laughed, but not in a friendly way. "I'm afraid I don't know. I'll have to look into the matter, just as you are looking into it, I'm sure."

She was lying. There was no way she didn't know who the goblin was, but I couldn't prove it. "There's still time to save Eric from being a ghoul. I'm sure you don't care about his well-being, but my understanding is that good preds"—oh, saying that without sarcasm was hard—"don't approve of letting addicts become ghouls."

Gunthra stood. "We don't. But if one of my people is behaving badly, I reserve the right to deal with them. If, after I investigate, I come to the conclusion that what you told me was true, and I believe it's possible to restore Mr. Marshall's soul, then perhaps we can work out another deal. But no more deals until you prove yourself capable of upholding your end of our first one."

She clapped, and the servant goblin opened the door. Like that, I was dismissed.

Bitch.

I WAS SCHEMING WAYS TO GET GUNTHRA THE INFORMATION she wanted and not feeling too happy about any of them when Steph picked me up half an hour later. If there was something in those files that Gunthra wanted to know, then she probably shouldn't have them. On the other hand, this was a lot less unpleasant a favor than I'd feared she would ask. Hell, for a pred, this was almost benign.

That alone told me I had to be missing something.

I knew I should tell Lucen what Gunthra had said about the pred war, but Lucen didn't know I'd struck a deal with the Dom. He wasn't going to be pleased when he found out.

"Jess, are you listening?"

I yawned as Steph drove us through the I-95 tollbooths. "Yes?"

She flipped me off, her eyes remaining on the road as the traffic merged. "You won't even lie convincingly to me anymore? What did I do to you to deserve this neglect?"

I smacked her upraised finger. "Nothing, sorry. Long day and I got crappy sleep last night. I'm spacing out. What did your boss do?"

"Nothing, never mind."

"I am sorry."

This time she did take a moment to glance my way. "I know. You look stressed. A little under-eye cream would have served you well today."

"Gee, thanks."

"And while you're at it, color on your cheeks wouldn't have hurt."

I punched her arm. "What is this, revenge? I do not need makeup tips."

"Yes, Jess, actually you do. Tip number one—it won't kill you to wear some."

And so we continued to bash each other's style until Steph found a parking spot in quaint Portsmouth, New Hampshire, and we'd gotten seated at the local brewery. The silliness helped. I needed a distraction from my conversation with Gunthra, and Steph—I was certain—wanted one from the task that awaited.

After we'd given our orders and chosen our beers, she turned serious. "I called my cousin Tim today, Eric's brother. It's the first time I've talked to him in I don't know how many years. I swear, if I could punch people over the phone, he'd have a broken nose."

"Wait, did you get hold of him?" Tim was the brother Bridget had been trying to reach. The one who wasn't returning her calls.

"Yeah, I reached him." Given her tone, it was no surprise Steph drained a good portion of her beer before continuing. "I told him what your friend told us last night. That there was a chance we could get Eric's soul back. Know what that asshole told me?"

I winced in anticipation. "What?"

"Eric doesn't deserve it."

"Nice. I can feel the brotherly love."

"He doesn't fucking deserve it," Steph went on as though she hadn't heard me. "By Tim's logic, Eric cheated fate and is only getting what was coming to him. You see why I didn't care when my family disowned me? These are the sorts of assholes I'm related to. I'm telling you—Tim couldn't wait to initiate proceedings to get Eric declared incompetent. He doesn't see anything wrong with what happened. All he sees is Eric's money. Fuck these people, Jess. I don't know how I'm related to them."

I sipped my beer, savoring the flavor that washed away the memory of Gunthra's tea. *And I can't believe I'm related, in a sense, to preds. But we don't get to choose these things. Biology isn't destiny.*

Again, I had my opening, and again, this was the wrong time.

"What about the rest of your family? Have you heard from them?"

Steph shook her head. As befitting her mood, she wore her skull-and-crossbones earrings today, and they peeked out from under her wig. "No, but I'm sure Tim's been in contact with people. To be honest, I'm surprised he took my call, but since I was there when it happened, I guess curiosity got the best of him. No one else will talk to me. I'm unclean or some bullshit. They refuse to acknowledge my existence unless I forgo my unnatural lifestyle and embrace their bigoted version of God."

She lowered her arms from making air quotes around "lifestyle" and smacked her hands on the table as our server returned. We both kept quiet while the food was served.

"Is there any way the Gryphons can do something?" Steph asked as we dug in.

"What do you mean?"

She doused her fries in ketchup and offered me the bottle. "Is there any method they can use to prevent Tim's motion to get Eric declared incompetent? As long as there's a chance Eric can get his soul returned, it's not right for Tim to do this. Besides, someone needs to take care of Eric if he can't do it himself. His money will make it possible to hire someone, and I don't believe for a second that Tim will see to it except in the most basic, shitty of ways. Eric needs that money."

It was a good point, and I was glad to see Steph was thinking through all the angles. "I don't know, but I can certainly ask Bridget. Let's also look for the name of Eric's lawyer while we're there. Maybe he can file some kind of counter-motion. If nothing else, maybe we can tie Tim's hands until we know whether we'll be successful with helping Eric."

"Good idea. He's got to have a lawyer, right?"

"Got to." So we could hope.

We finished dinner and headed to Eric's house, which appeared all the more impressive now that I had some fading sunlight in which to view it.

"You know, it's a good thing he doesn't have an alarm system."

Steph opened the door and stuck the key back in her pocket. "New Hampshire," she said, and I could hear the shrug in her words.

Once more, my eyes were drawn immediately to the artwork and the impressively high ceiling. As a result, I was unprepared for being attacked around the ankles. I swore and nearly hit said ceiling as something banged into me.

The something let out a plaintive meow.

"Oh, shit." Steph dumped her purse on a table. "I forgot all about the cat last night. He was sleeping."

Bending down, I rubbed the cat's head. He was a handsome thing. Black with white around his paws, like he was wearing shoes. He closed his eyes, enjoying the attention to all appearances, but most likely wondering how long he'd have to do this before I fed him. "Cat food?"

"I'm sure we'll find it. You want to check? Take the downstairs, and I'll look upstairs for Eric?"

"Deal."

I paused in all the rooms en route to the kitchen, checking for Eric, but I didn't see him. Finally, I heard Steph yell that she had. Letting her tend to him, I opened and closed all the kitchen cabinets, on the hunt for cat food. I found some in a pantry and set out several scoops for my hungry feline friend.

Eric's food and water, I noticed, hadn't been touched. Bad sign. If he wasn't foraging for himself, he was really far gone. Most ghouls had enough sense of self-preservation to seek out food and water. They might not seek it with a lot of effort, but they weren't comatose either.

Maybe it was the shock to his system. Maybe it would wear off? I had to hope. Otherwise, Eric was going to need more help than anticipated, and that was definitely going to cost a lot of money.

"Steph!" I yelled upstairs from the foyer. "You'd better make sure to get food in him. I'm going hunting for that contract and a lawyer."

"He didn't eat?" she called back down. "Oh, fucking-A."

Leaving her to it, I decided to attack the most logical room in the house first. That such a room also happened to be the extremely impressive library was a bonus.

I could hear Steph coaxing Eric down the stairs as I flipped on the lights. Last night, aside from all the books, I'd noticed a corner of the room had been given over into what could be an office. A large, stately desk sat in front of the window. Behind it, blending in nicely with the bookcases, was a cabinet.

Eric was neat. Good for him. Very few items cluttered the desk—a planner, an L.L. Bean catalog, and some papers on which he'd scrawled notes about Swiss bank accounts, Nazis, and World War II. Judging by a couple nonfiction books sitting on the desk, I assumed he'd been making notes for his next thriller.

Eric's laptop, no surprise, was password protected, so I moved on to the drawers next, but they contained nothing illuminating. Just copies of book contracts, more research notes, and invoices from contractors, along with the usual things like spare USB cords and pens.

Dragon shit on toast. If I'd made a contract with a goblin for my soul, I'd have kept a copy of that contract in a secure place. Assuming it was a legal contract, that was. But that's exactly what I *had* been assuming.

Contracts for black-market deals—the ones that bought you things like curses, unlicensed disguise charms, and other illegal activities—well, those were usually not written down for obvious reasons. But massive success or luck? Totally legit and probably signed in triplicate. After all, a contract like that protected not just the stupid human, but also the pred should the human decide to renege on the deal and try to break the contract once they got what they wanted.

The cabinet then? I tried the door, but it was locked. Unfortunate because I didn't see a key anywhere. Perhaps Steph had a bobby pin. I wasn't bad at picking cheap locks, but I needed something to work with, and Eric didn't have so much as a paperclip in his desk.

Next, I scanned Eric's planner for the name of anyone who might be a lawyer, but the thing was empty. Clearly, whatever Eric used to keep track of his calendar, it wasn't this fancy leather volume. No, he probably used his phone, like I did. Speaking of which, I'd bet that was where I'd find the name of his lawyer.

Brilliant.

With a sigh of longing and frustration, I left the library and joined Steph in the kitchen where she was eating a cookie from the bag I'd seen in Eric's cabinet. At the table, her cousin was feeding himself a sandwich with a sadly comical lack of coordination.

Steph held out the bag for me. "He had a bunch of cold cuts in the fridge, but I didn't find much to cook. I can't believe he hasn't eaten all day. Is that normal?"

"Wish I knew."

"Will his coordination improve? He knew what to do when I handed him the sandwich."

I watched Eric struggle to take a bite. He got it, but not on the first attempt. "Same answer. So long as he is eating, though…"

Then what? I didn't know how to finish my own sentence.

All these depressing thoughts convinced me to grab a cookie. "I can't find a contract in the library, but this house is huge. I need to do a lot more searching. In the meantime, did you find his phone? His lawyer's number is probably in there."

"Phone's in his bedroom," Steph said, clipping the bag shut. "I found his charger in there last night and plugged it in. There's also another small room upstairs that's got filing cabinets in it. You might try that. It's at the end of the hall, after his bedroom."

"Excellent. I'll go to it."

Eric's bedroom was huge, and it took a minute to find the phone. It also smelled, kind of like Eric had been sitting in it all day, in the heat. Since I hadn't noticed the odor downstairs, I assumed Steph had covered him in deodorant. Thank you, Steph. Poor Eric. If he did get his soul back, I could only imagine how he'd feel about the ordeal, assuming he remembered it.

I grabbed the phone and was halfway down the hall when I heard a door slam on the main floor. Mid-stride, I switched direction and darted down the stairs in case Steph needed help.

But it wasn't Steph making the noise. An unfamiliar man, who nevertheless bore a passing resemblance to Eric, stood in the foyer. If I'd been paying attention a moment ago, I'd have noticed his foul combination of butterscotch confusion and curry-flavored annoyance.

He glowered at me, annoyance turning to alarm. "Who are you?"

"Tim?" I shook my head. "I mean, are you Tim?"

"How do you—?"

I was saved by Steph, who charged into the room. "What are you doing here?"

Tim blinked at her. "Stephen?"

Steph's hands balled into fists at her side. Though her shot of rage wasn't directed at me, the intensity of her anger almost bowled me over because I wasn't braced for it. Hot, smoky energy flooded my mouth and veins, giving me a head rush.

"It's Steph. And what are you doing here?"

"Taking care of my brother, as is my right and responsibility. Now get out. You don't have my permission to be here."

Steph stepped forward, her hands still clenched. "Taking care of him? By planning to bleed him dry?"

Tim pulled a phone from his pocket. "Out before I call the cops."

"Jess, are you—?"

Frantically, I shook my head at her. *Not officially*, I mouthed.

Steph scowled, but she apparently remembered what I'd explained earlier. "Fine. Your brother is having dinner. See to it that he eats everything. It's been his only meal today. And while you're at it, you might want to give him a bath."

"A bath?" Tim repeated.

Steph pushed by him. "Oh, and make sure to leave out extra food and water for the cat."

"Jesus," Tim muttered. He held out a hand. "Where's the key?"

"I left it in the kitchen." With that lie, Steph threw open the door and stormed out.

I hurried after her before Tim could discover there was no key in the kitchen and that Steph was driving Eric's BMW.

SEVEN

"HE'S NOT GOING TO KILL ERIC, RIGHT?" STEPH ASKED, pulling out of the circular driveway.

I opened the contact list on Eric's phone. "You would know him better than I do."

Steph's scowl deepened. "I do. That's why I'm worried and turning to you for reassurance that Tim wouldn't be so stupid."

"You want me to lie?"

"I want you to give me comfort."

"You know I'm no better at the warm and fuzzy stuff than you are, but it seems unlikely that your cousin would be that big an asshole."

Steph exhaled. "All right then. I shouldn't feel guilty about leaving Eric in his brother's care. I don't suppose you found the contract before we got kicked out?"

"Nope, but I do think I found the name of his lawyer." With a cry of triumph, I sent the information to myself as backup in case I lost control of Eric's phone. "Maybe he knows about the contract."

Unless Steph could sneak us both back into her cousin's house, it might be the best I could do.

Steph dropped me off outside The Lair, and although she looked like she could use a drink, she laughed at my offer to go in. I hadn't expected anything else.

Monday night meant the bar was pretty dead. I saw a few familiar faces nursing beers or eating the pred equivalent of lunch, but no one I'd had much contact with. There were a couple harpies, a table of satyrs, and not a single human. A typical crowd for the day and time.

Lucen's gaze locked my eyes as I snagged an empty stool near the back. Before I could say anything, he put my favorite beer in front of me. "Long day?"

"Yeah." I reached for his hand, trailing my fingers over his skin. Delicious, tingly warmth ran up my arm.

Smiling, Lucen leaned against the bar and took my hand in his other one. "So what did Gunthra want with you?"

I held in my groan. She was the reason I'd stopped by, but that didn't mean I wanted to discuss it. The subject was unlikely to end well. "You remember how you once thought the furies were trying to start a pred war when they framed me for their murders?"

Whatever Lucen was expecting me to say, it didn't appear to have been that. He frowned as though assuming I'd changed the topic. Boy, he was in a for a bad surprise. "Yeah. Why?"

"Gunthra believes it. She asked me over because she wants me to give her all the information the Gryphons have on the furies' activities from around that time."

"That is interesting." Lucen let go of my hand and stole a swallow of the beer. "Almost as interesting as why she would think you'd give her that information."

He said it like a statement, but it was obviously a question. I became grateful for the beer and stalled, taking a drink. "I owe her."

"You owe her?"

I shrugged sheepishly, trying for my most endearing face. "I never did explain to you how I found out that I'm part, er, quasi satyr. She's the one who told me."

Lucen stared at me, then without a word, set a shot glass on the bar and poured himself some top-shelf bourbon. "When?"

"Before the Meat Match when we took down Victor Aubrey. It was

Gunthra's information that kept me alive." I cleared my throat, wincing. "I struck a deal with her. The truth about myself in return for a favor at a later date. This is the favor she's calling in."

"For sin's sake, Jess. Every time I think you couldn't possibly do something more reckless, you remind me just how impossible you are."

I crossed my arms. "Yeah, well, you were acting like an overprotective jerk at the time. I had to be able to take care of myself. Besides, I was cautious about how I worded the deal. In the grand scheme of things, what she's asking me to do isn't much."

"But it's something." Lucen raised his hands like he wanted to strangle me. Or punch someone. "It's something that's reckless and unnecessary and could have gotten you in a world of pain."

"But didn't because although I might be reckless, I'm not a sucker. I put certain conditions around the deal."

"No, you're not a sucker." He lowered his voice, although I don't think anyone could have heard us. "I didn't say you were, but why am I learning about this now? Why didn't you tell me how you found out earlier?"

I raised an eyebrow. "Really? Because you're doing exactly what I feared you'd do. You're freaking out."

"This is not a freak-out. But if it were, it would be justified. You made a deal with the goblins' Dom."

"A well-thought-out deal." Okay, that was stretching the truth a bit. "To get information that was vitally important and that no one else seemed to know."

Lucen downed his bourbon. "You didn't give us any time to check around."

"We didn't have time, if you recall. The sylphs were gunning for my soul."

"Some days, I swear, I would like to see Assym try for it. Then you could drive him up a wall instead of me."

"That's not funny." I had no reason to fear Assym going after my soul, not any longer. But at the time, it had been a very real fear, and it was Gunthra who had clued me in to the nature of my abilities. Particularly the part about how I could reverse the pred-addict bond and take a pred's power from them.

Lucen grabbed my hand again. "You're right. It's not funny, but neither is you making deals with the goblins and not telling me. I don't want to see you get hurt, little siren."

I sighed. "I know that, but this is why I didn't tell you. You're upset."

"Damn right I'm upset. I care about you."

Which, naturally, was why he was pushing me on other men. I didn't say it aloud, but the irony of it stabbed me in the heart.

Alas, I didn't need to say things aloud for Lucen to pick up on what I was feeling. "Now what?"

I rested my head on my arm. "Just thinking about how screwed up we are."

"We're not screwed up. You just have a talent for getting into trouble and some unfortunate hang-ups."

I raised my head to find him smirking. At least his bad mood had passed. "I do not have hang-ups. I simply fail to find anyone else as fascinating as you."

"There's an obvious reason for that."

I tossed my drink napkin at him.

Lucen left for a minute to go fill another round for the harpies, but I remained with my butt planted on the stool, finishing the beer. My emotions swirled—relief, confusion, worry. Whichever. It was all negative. All giving me more of a buzz than the beer could and feeding the preds in the bar. Ugh.

The Lair's door opened, allowing a cool breeze to blow through the room. Behind it, came Devon. I dropped my gaze to my bottle, more unwanted emotions rising to the surface.

I'd spoken too soon earlier. There *was* someone out there who was almost as fascinating as Lucen, for no other reason than that his satyr magic had the same effect on me as Lucen's did.

And I didn't like it.

I'd attributed Lucen's ability to stir lust in me to our personal connection. The fact that I liked him and cared about him. For a while that had made sense because he was the only satyr who had that effect on me.

Not so anymore. The more time I'd spent in Devon's company recently, the more his power had begun to creep over me in the same way. At first, I'd thought my immunity to pred power was wearing off, but it was dawning on me that wasn't the case. It was just something about Lucen and Devon.

To use someone else's words, I had a thing for powerful satyrs.

Or did I? Devon was Dezzi's lieutenant, the second-highest-ranking satyr in Boston, a fact I usually forgot until I did something that pissed him off and he very subtly reminded me of it. He was friendly and—I supposed—funny when he wanted to be. Oh, and he flirted with me at every possible opportunity. Although he was nowhere near as hot as Lucen, he wasn't bad looking either, with bright blue eyes and a mouth that was rarely serious.

If he weren't a satyr, Devon would have his charms.

But he was, and I didn't like one bit that I could sense his power. I didn't trust him and didn't want to like him. The fewer satyrs I had any interest in whatsoever, including as friends, the better off I would be. Who wanted to get attached to people who you weren't sure could get attached in return?

I kept my head down until I heard the door open again, and I caught Devon's back as he left. The quick visit suggested he'd been here on satyr business. Devon had his own job to do in the evenings.

My sigh of relief might have been silent, but no doubt Lucen had noticed my tension and the way it lifted. He returned a moment later.

"Don't mope," he said, taking away the empty bottle. "We are going to make this work."

I forced a smile. "I hope so."

"Yes, we will." Lucen practically growled the last word. "Just as long as you stay away from humans."

I narrowed my eyes at him. "I can't restrict who your addicts are. You don't get to restrict who I decide to sleep with on the side. If I do that at all."

"You have a bad track record with humans. Also, you're not human, so it's not like you have so much more in common with them than with us. Also, again, polyamory isn't a lifestyle with us. It is life, so I don't have to worry about someone else trying to steal you away from me. That's a lot less certain with humans. And four... Wait, am I up to four or five points now?"

"Four."

"Fine. Four, most importantly, satyrs excel at sex. Trust me, after having been with me, you'll never be content with a human again."

"First you think you're the most fascinating guy in the world, and now you're a sex god? No self-confidence issues with you."

"Why should I have any? I am amazing. Stick to satyrs. Plenty will be happy to help out, and none of them come with emotional baggage. We'll both be happier. In fact, throw yourself at Devon again. He's dying for it."

"What?" Damn it. I could feel the blood rush to my cheeks. "I have never thrown myself at Devon."

"Oh, no? I heard there was a time at Purgatory when you almost pulled his clothes off."

He was laughing at me, which only made my blood hotter. "I was under the influence of drugs and magic. Doesn't count. I would have thrown myself at a rocking chair if one had been nearby."

"Wouldn't have been nearly as satisfying, I bet."

"This is the second time tonight that you've made light of me almost dying, you know."

"Consider it revenge for you holding out on me about Gunthra. Besides, you turned a lovely shade of tomato. I think you have a crush on Devon."

I glowered at him, wondering what sort of emotions of mine he was feeding on. Only I would have a boyfriend who was amused that I might be attracted to his best friend. "I'm a grown woman. I do not have crushes."

"Then I stick to my original statement. You want to drag him to the floor and rip his clothes off. It's okay. He'd enjoy it."

I raised my middle finger at the idea, but for all my faking it, Lucen had to know he was skirting close to the truth by the way my blood pressure was up. "You're satyrs. You do have that effect on even the most prudish of people."

"Which is what you're acting like. Just admit it. Have some quality naked time with Devon. Shag like rabbits. It'll be good for all of us."

Glaring at him, I slid off my stool. "Tell you what. I'll consider it if you do something for me. I want to go on a date."

That surprised the smirk right off his face. "You what?"

"A date. You know, what normal human people do? I'll consider sexy, naked time with your satyr friends, embrace your licentious ways, if you'll consider embracing some human ones. Dinner out and real conversation. I want something more than just tearing each other's clothes off for a change."

I must have stumped him because Lucen gave me a Gunthra-like, creepy, unblinking stare. "Okay, fine. A date. But I pick the place. It's got to be somewhere pred-friendly, and you've got to be honest with me about future dealings with our enemies."

"Fine." I held out a hand.

He shook it. "Done. And we get to get naked afterward, right?"

"You're hopeless."

"I could invite Devon along."

"Now I'm done." Using work as an excuse, I kissed Lucen good night and went home, thankful that living alone meant I couldn't embarrass myself in front of anyone else this evening.

IF I'D KNOWN WHAT MY DAY WAS GOING TO BE LIKE, I'D HAVE actually gone to sleep last night like I'd told Lucen I was going to. Instead, I'd stayed up late, my thoughts drifting constantly to our conversation while I tried to read what might be the last ever Eric Marshall novel.

As such, I was tired again and in the perfect state to be blindsided.

"Do I want to know how you got the name of Eric Marshall's lawyer?" Bridget asked, examining the paper I gave her.

"From his cell phone. Nothing sinister. We got kicked out by Eric's brother before I could find the contract, but I thought the lawyer might be able to help."

Bridget added the information about the lawyer to her case notes. "So you were snooping through Eric's phone. That's all."

"In my capacity as a friend of his cousin's. Not in any official Gryphon capacity that could get anyone in trouble. Brian told me I could, remember?"

Bridget shook her head. "Fine. I won't ask any other questions."

"Good. I take it this means I shouldn't hand his phone over to you?"

Her brown eyes opened wide. "No, and I don't even want to know you have it. I'm going to pretend I didn't hear that."

"You know, you haven't changed at all since the Academy."

"Neither have you." She smiled and spun her chair around. "I'm going to go call Mr. Marshall's attorney and see if I can get us in to chat. That…" she pointed at me, "…will be in an official capacity."

"I'd have just broken into his office and snooped through his files. Unofficially."

She either laughed or choked on her diet soda. My guess would be choked. "I'll let you know what I find out."

Feeling useful—also unofficially—I returned to my desk with a spring in my step. Bridget had left me some tasks to do and some questions about what I knew of the goblins, and I figured I could grab a much-needed coffee from across the street and get to work on them. I could also brainstorm ways to get my hands on the information Gunthra wanted.

But someone was waiting for me at my desk. My feet faltered and my good mood evaporated like a puff of dragon smoke.

"Jessica, I see you're here." Tom Kassin's smile was smugger than ever.

In my sleepy daze, I actually took a step back, feeling as though I'd been punched in the gut. He wasn't supposed to be here. Olivia had told me he was in France.

My heart pounded against my rib cage like it was begging to break free and beat on Tom itself. At my sides, my hands curled into would-be fists. "Yes, I'm back. No thanks to you. Go away."

"I was hoping your presence here meant you'd rethought your position." Tom's accent had confused me at first—part southern twang, part British. It sounded stronger than ever with both geographical regions right now. Like he'd been honing it just to irritate me. "Apologizing for your outburst seems unlikely, but I do hope we can be colleagues."

"Not a chance in hell."

"Unfortunately, it might come to that."

I closed my eyes briefly and pushed by him. "Back to your end-of-the-world shit?"

"It's not shit. It's real and it concerns you."

"No. What concerns me is what you did to me, but I'm trying to overlook that so I can help a friend. *That's* why I'm here. Now, if you'll excuse me." Coffee. Must get that coffee. I needed to be alert so he couldn't ambush me again.

I left for the elevator, and Tom followed. "I've been in meetings at World since we last spoke."

"I don't think 'spoke' is the right word."

"You don't know how your existence and your gifts have shaken things up. There is a lot you need to know. It's why I came back yesterday."

Yesterday? He came back to Boston the same day that I came back to the Gryphons? Coincidence could bite me.

The elevator arrived, and Tom entered on my heels, a short, blond shadow.

"I know all I need to know," I told him, "which is more than I can say for Director Lee. She's extremely curious about you and your interest in me, so if you don't want me yelling it to the heavens, you should leave me alone."

"Nice try, but I don't believe you have any desire for the director—or anyone else—to discover the full extent of what you are and what you can do."

"I'd risk it." But that was a lie, and Tom didn't need to be a misery-sucking, quasi-satyr freak to detect it. "Don't think you're so clever. You don't know the full extent of what I can do either."

Brilliant, because now that I'd told him... I silently cursed my tendency to run off at the mouth when I got angry.

I stormed out of the elevator, thankful that Tom kept silent while we strode through the busy lobby. As soon as I pushed open the doors though, and the building's AC gave way to hot summer air, he started up again.

"If you won't cooperate, Jessica, I've been authorized to make you cooperate. But I'd rather it not come to that."

I paused at the bottom of the steps. "What are you going to do? Arrest me? Isn't it bad enough that your people worked serious magic on me without my knowledge? Do they think they own me too? And why are you following me? Don't you have other things to do?"

"If I don't follow you, I won't get to speak to you. And no, I don't. This is what I was sent here to do."

Peachy. World Headquarters or the Brotherhood or both had sent him to Boston to stalk me. Since that was the case, I gave up.

Tom crossed the street with me and entered the coffee shop. "To answer your other question, we don't pretend to own you. But I have been tasked with the important job of making you see the light, of making you understand what's coming and why we created you. You're not stupid, Jessica. Nor are you devoid of any curiosity. How bad can it be to hear me out? Hate me, if you like, although I had nothing to do with turning you into what you are. But listen. You returned to work for a friend? Listen for your friend's sake."

"Why? What's going to happen to my friend?"

"The same thing that's going to happen to everyone unless we can stop it."

I breathed deeply to control my frustration and inhaled the lovely coffee aroma. It alone didn't wake me up, but it was soothing. As I calmed down, an idea came to me. Toying with it in my head, I placed my order.

Tom waited by the door. I took my time sprinkling cinnamon on my foamed milk, and when I was certain I had my best move, I returned to him. "I'll make you a deal. You have some information I'm very interested in seeing. If you let me read it, I'll hear you out."

Tom regarded me suspiciously. "What sort of information do you want?"

"When we first talked, you told me you were here investigating the furies. I'm curious about that, seeing as I'm the person they framed for murder. I'd like to see those files, if you actually have them."

He pushed open the door and didn't say anything until we'd crossed the street once more. "I was investigating the furies, true, although that investigation has been put aside temporarily. I'm not sure there is anything in those files that would interest you."

"I'd like to be the one to determine that."

Although Tom must have sported some serious charms that dulled my ability to feed on his emotions, his warm chocolaty suspicion was strong enough for me to notice. Yet he nodded. "I don't see why that should be a problem. I'll share the information I have on them, and you'll devote some time to learning about the magi's prophecy."

"Deal." I sipped my coffee, wondering how many deals with the devil I could make in the span of two days.

Still, I'd known there would be a price to pay to Gunthra, and since Tom wasn't going to leave me alone, in a way, my plan was kind of genius. Or, at the very least, convenient.

"Let's go to my office," Tom said, holding open the door for me. "I'll get you the files and we can talk."

I hid my grimace behind my coffee cup. I wasn't ready to start this crap today. Fortunately, my phone buzzed with a text, saving me from an immediate need for excuses. "I can't now. Bridget got us an appointment with a busy lawyer, and we're leaving ASAP."

I held the phone up for him as proof because he looked like he needed convincing.

"I'll be here when you get back." With that, Tom walked away.

No doubt he would be.

EIGHT

Getting to Eric's lawyer's office required a drive to New Hampshire. Frankly, after three days in a row of it, I was getting tired of this stretch of I-95.

"He couldn't do this over the phone?" I grumbled as I got out of the car.

Bridget peeled off her sunglasses as we entered the office lobby. "He refused to discuss client issues over the phone with anyone who wasn't that client."

To add insult to injury, or annoyance to irritation as might be more accurate, Eric's lawyer kept us waiting for an additional twenty minutes even though we'd arrived exactly on time. When a secretary finally ushered us into the guy's cramped office, I was daydreaming of letting loose a salamander in the building.

Eric's lawyer was an older man with just the right amount of gray around his temples and wrinkles around his eyes to fulfill every lawyer stereotype I could dredge up. For Eric, he'd have made a perfect stock character, which is what critics usually accused him of writing.

He shook hands with both of us, then gestured for us to take the two chairs in front of his desk. "Your paperwork arrived right before you did. I needed to review it and make sure all the legalities were in order. Protecting client confidentiality is of utmost importance to us. You understand."

"We do, of course," Bridget said, and I decided I'd better let her do the talking because I wasn't as good at faking politeness. "But time is also important if we're going to have any chance of getting Mr. Marshall's soul back to him before it's too late."

The lawyer folded his hands. "I understand, and I've had the pleasure of working for Mr. Marshall for years. Anything I can do to help, I will."

Not making us drive up here would have been a start, I thought, but I bit my tongue.

If I had to guess based on her smoky impatience, Bridget was thinking the same. "We were hoping you might have a copy of Mr. Marshall's contract with the goblin in question. That would be the simplest and quickest way to solve the problem."

The lawyer's shoulders sagged slightly. "Unfortunately, I don't. Mr. Marshall hadn't sent it to me yet."

"Yet?" Bridget and I both leaned forward. "So it was a recent contract?"

"No, not to my knowledge. I meant Mr. Marshall and I had a meeting scheduled for this week to discuss it. I believe the contract itself is several years old."

Hope deflated in my chest. We'd assumed as much, but for a brief second, I'd thought we might be wrong. That would have meant we had a longer timetable.

"What were you planning on discussing about it?" Bridget asked.

The lawyer raised a bushy, graying eyebrow. "Is that pertinent to the case?"

"Anything could be pertinent at this point. Anything could be a clue that points us toward the goblin."

I didn't see how the discussion was likely to matter, and clearly, neither did Eric's lawyer, but he shrugged it off. To most people, the Gryphons worked in mysterious ways, and maybe this guy was one of those who put unwarranted faith in them.

"Mr. Marshall was interested in seeing whether there was a way to break the contract. Such proceedings are not my area of expertise, but I was going to take an initial look at it for him and recommend a friend for him to talk to."

Bridget's expression was impassive, but her cool surprise mirrored my own. I couldn't see how this information would help track down the goblin, but at last things became a little clearer. We had a motive.

Bridget spoke my thoughts out loud as we got back in the car a short time later. "If the goblin knew Marshall was trying to break his contract, he might have been worried Eric would be successful. It's not as though Marshall couldn't afford to hire the best lawyer to have a crack at it."

"And even if Eric wasn't going to be successful, the goblin could have done it out of revenge."

Bridget turned out of the parking lot, chewing on her lip. "It would be a stupid move to make for revenge. For the average person, the attack might not have been brought to our attention, but for a semi-public figure like Marshall, the goblin should have expected we'd be alerted."

"Possibly. But to be fair, if Marshall hadn't been in a very public place when the attack happened, we might not have known it was an attack at all. People would simply have assumed Marshall's master let him become a ghoul. And besides, we haven't found the goblin. They might yet get away with it." I yawned. Coffee was no longer doing it. I needed a nap. "Preds aren't any smarter than humans. I can definitely see a vengeful pred acting without thinking."

"No, they aren't smarter, true. And also like humans, the best way to shake information out of them is to catch them off-guard." Bridget handed me her phone. "Brian's number is in there. Call him for me and tell him I want backup to be ready to meet us when we get to Boston."

Warily, I opened her contact list. "What do we need backup for?"

"We're going to question the goblin's Dom. I wanted to avoid this, if possible, but we don't have the contract or much time left. There's a decent chance she'll know who the goblin is."

"We need...?" Backup for this? I bit my tongue. No point in letting Bridget know that I thought taking a group into Shadowtown to question one goblin was overkill.

Definitely no point in letting her know I'd met Gunthra by myself yesterday.

If she wanted backup? I'd get backup. And hope Gunthra didn't laugh out loud when she saw me.

AFTER A QUICK DETOUR THROUGH GRYPHON HEADQUARTERS, we were on the road again. Bridget had insisted I get my protective charm updated, and she and the two additional Gryphons who would be our backup armed themselves with salamander-fire-forged blades.

Since I didn't feel like explaining why I didn't need the charm, I let the lab Gryphon draw a new series of protective glyphs on my back. That was as much defense as I was permitted to bring. Only the real Gryphons got real Gryphon weapons. I thought of my own salamander-fire-forged knife, Misery, at my apartment, but I didn't need it. I mean, my apartment was in Shadowtown, for the love of dragons. I felt silly enough going to an interview with a posse.

Lucen would likely laugh himself to tears if he heard about this.

For the Gryphons though, it was serious business. They had more than the average resistance to pred power, but only I had my immunity. Their protective charms would help, but for them, this was entering enemy territory. Once, I'd have thought no differently, and I tried to focus on that, although it was hard empathizing when their anxiety made me jittery.

Soon enough, the two SUVs pulled up outside of Gunthra's gothically weird house. On the way over, I'd explained to Bridget that I was acquainted with the Dom from my stint as the furies' patsy, but I left out the details, and thankfully Bridget didn't ask many questions.

It was fairly early for Shadowtown, and the street was quiet. Relegated to the back of the group, I stood with my hands in my pockets, casting glances down the road. Any minute I feared seeing a satyr I knew. Lucen would just laugh, if I was lucky, but Devon would probably try to sabotage my standing with the Gryphons for his own amusement.

Bridget knocked a second time on the heavy door. It opened a moment later, and Gunthra's servant regarded us with comical disdain, but no surprise. Certainly he and Gunthra had realized who was outside.

"My lady has a very busy morning," the goblin said. "You will have to set up an appointment for later."

Bridget's hand brushed over her knife's sheath. "Your lady has to answer some questions. We can do it now, or she can come down to headquarters with us. I promise you, that will take far more time."

The door shut in her face.

The Gryphon standing next to me pulled out a stick of gum. "Always the same game with this one." He offered the pack around.

Spearmint. Ugh. I was already tasting enough of that because of their nerves, and I held up a hand to decline. "Wouldn't you need a warrant to bring her in?"

"Not to question her, although it's easy enough to get one if we need it. But Gunthra's just playing games. It's about power. She can't let us in until we threaten her or else she loses face."

That sounded about right. The various pred races only got along because they all hated the Gryphons. So they were always watching each other, keeping an eye open for weaknesses. Cooperating with the Gryphons counted.

Gunthra's door opened again, and the door goblin frowned at us even more deeply than before. With his grayish-brown skin, he looked like a woodcutter had gone a little too deep with his knives and chisels. "She will see you."

"I expected so," Bridget said with perfect composure.

I had to give her credit. Internally, she was as rattled as anyone there, but for a change, her subdued manner served her well. Of course, if I could sense her nerves, so could the goblins. But at least she put on a good show.

The goblin's disdain turned to disgust as he spied me bringing up the rear, and I fought to keep from laughing.

Gunthra, however, was not so discreet in her acknowledgment of me. She was seated on the same couch as she had been yesterday, but there was no tea and treats set out on the table. Nor did the goblin servant close the door behind us after we entered the room. He left it open, and I suspected he, and any security Gunthra kept around, were waiting nearby and listening to every word.

"Miss Moore, I didn't expect to see you again so soon." Her smile was genuine enough. She was enjoying the expressions of surprise she'd elicited from Bridget and the others. "Hard at work, are you?"

"As you can see."

Fortunately, that was the last thing Gunthra said to me during the conversation that followed. Bridget did her best to get the Dom to cough up information on the goblin who took Eric's soul, and Gunthra pretended ignorance.

"It's come to my attention that this thing happened, yes." Her large eyes shifted my way, and her lips upturned in a sly, not-quite-there smile. *Test me*, she was saying. *Give me a reason to let them know that you were the one who told me.*

So I played ignorant too, and let Bridget and the others waste all our time by asking Gunthra questions that she pretended she couldn't answer.

Five minutes into the most fruitless interrogation ever, Lucen sent me a text. Peachy. He'd arranged for me to meet with Dezzi later. I slipped my phone away, both wishing for the end to Bridget's questions and that they'd never end so I wouldn't have to deal with my own interrogation.

Obviously sensing my mood, Gunthra flashed her large eyes my way. "Everything all right, Miss Moore?"

I faked a smile. "Everything's fine. Thanks for asking."

Jaw clenched, I waited for her to say something else and expose what she knew about me, but Gunthra was smarter than that. She had to realize if she said anything to make the Gryphons distrust me, it would make getting the files she wanted more difficult.

I gestured for Bridget to get on with it, and soon we were back on the fast track to nowhere.

"That worked real well," the gum-chewing Gryphon muttered as we left.

Bridget unlocked the car door. Her face remained placid, but I could sense her annoyance. "I didn't have high hopes, but Gunthra's on alert and knows we're taking this seriously. She's going to want to take care of the problem so we don't come back. We just need to keep watch on the fallout and try to intervene when we get an opening."

"How do you keep watch?" I asked, getting in the car.

Bridget didn't answer until we'd left Shadowtown behind. "There are preds we can put pressure on for information. They act as our eyes and ears on occasion."

"They don't simply cooperate, do they?" I couldn't imagine that.

"No. We have leverage on a few. No different than how the police lean on informants."

I waited for more information, but Bridget wasn't forthcoming. Giving up, I changed the subject. "So now what? We wait around and see if Gunthra shakes anything loose?"

"Now, since Marshall's lawyer was a bust for the contract, I focus on getting access to Marshall's information other ways. From what you've said, it sounds like Marshall's brother was stonewalling me while he tried to get everything tied up in court. We fight that."

"How?"

"By making it very clear to the brother that this is a legal investigation and any attempt to block us gaining access to what we need will be considered obstruction. Once we have the legal authority to do so, I take a team and search Marshall's house for the contract in an official capacity. At the same time, we reach out to the rest of the family, question them and Marshall's associates. Even if Marshall never spoke a word directly about his addiction to any of them, he might have said something that we can use. He might even have mentioned the goblin by name."

"And what do I do?"

"I was hoping you could catch up on Shadowtown gossip. Someone's got to know who Marshall's master was. Preds talk."

She had a point. They must, but none had ever done so in my presence. "If the goblins know we're searching for this person, they're not going to talk in front of me."

"But the satyrs and harpies might."

Maybe. Neither of those races cared for the goblins, but whether they would have any information on which goblin had snagged the famous Eric Marshall for an addict—that was another story.

"Think you can talk to your satyr acquaintances soon?" Bridget asked.

I tapped my phone, pondering the text from Lucen and my meeting with Dezzi later. "Yeah, I can talk to them soon."

Getting any useful information was another thing entirely.

NINE

BACK AT MY DESK, I DISCOVERED A THUMB DRIVE AND A NOTE from Tom explaining that it contained all his information on the furies. I had to give credit where it was due—that was a much faster response than I'd been expecting.

He'd also left me a book. Faded black, with creases in the corners and a disintegrating cover, it looked like it might fall apart if I opened it. Tom had stuffed a lot of similar books in his office, a few of which I'd snooped through once. When I'd accused him and his fraternity of ruining my life not too long ago, he'd tried pressing one of those books on me, so it wasn't surprising he was doing it again. Perhaps the only surprising thing was that this wasn't the same book as last time. He must have found a creepier one to replace it.

Maybe I'd skim it later. I wanted to stop at my apartment to get Misery and mentally prepare myself before my meeting with Dezzi. I pocketed the thumb drive, which I figured I'd read before passing its contents on to Gunthra, and stuck the book in my backpack. Then I checked both ways down the hall and dashed for the exit. Tom's habit had been to work late, and I didn't want to be caught trying to sneak out without our meeting.

At home, I changed into a pair of jeans and a clean shirt, then strapped Misery around my hip. Although I had no need to take the knife into a meeting with Dezzi, feeling the sheath against my thigh comforted me. I'd acquired the blade around the time I'd acquired the information about what I was. We were on this journey together. It only seemed right to have it with me when I spilled my guts.

Besides, wearing a salamander-fire-forged knife made me feel a bit like a badass. Silly as that might be, I would take whatever mojo I could fake, because I was so not looking forward to this conversation.

Leaving Tom's thumb drive on my bureau, I silently and quickly rehearsed what I was going to say to Dezzi. Then I squared my shoulders and took off for The Lair and whatever it would hold for my future.

The bar was open for business, but Lucen had moved a couple tables around, effectively turning the back of the room into a semiprivate seating area. Apparently he didn't think the conversation at hand warranted opening the bar late for true privacy, which I took to mean he didn't consider my forthcoming confession that big a deal. I hoped he was right and that Dezzi wouldn't treat it as such.

As for myself, I still considered it a big fucking deal, but I'd live. Lucen was right about one thing—better Dezzi hear it from me than from him.

Lucen set an empty glass in front of me. "I thought you might want something. You're nervous."

"With good reason."

"Horrible reason."

"You don't know that." I took the bottle of Jameson's that he had set on the bar and poured myself a heavy shot. "This is my deepest, darkest, dirtiest secret. I haven't told anyone else."

Lucen poured himself a shot to go along with mine. "I like the sound of deep and dirty. Anyway, little siren, other people do know it. Gryphons know it. Gunthra knows it. Don't you think you'll be better off with people who are on your side knowing it too?"

"Since when are the satyrs as a whole on my side?"

He downed his shot and cupped my hand in his. "Since you saved Dezzi's backside."

If you'll recall, I was trying to save a bunch of humans, not the satyrs. On some level, I was certain Dezzi understood that, but supposedly she'd appreciated the way I'd handled the situation, allowing her to escape any legal issues for Lucrezia's crimes. Alas, that had mostly been luck. Not that I was admitting it.

"What if Dezzi expects me to bend my knee to her like the rest of you do?"

Lucen laughed and stuck the bottle away. "No oaths or pledges of loyalty are required."

"Uh-huh. What about stabbing me with a pin and making us satyr sisters?"

"You been drinking before you got here?"

"No, but I should have been."

Lucen came out from behind the bar and trailed his fingers down my arm. His touch soothed my nerves in spite of myself. "Relax. You're one of us, and Dezzi is the Dom for this region. She needs to know the truth, and it will most likely work in your favor. Dezzi protects her own, and she likes you."

To be fair, I liked Dezzi too, as much as was humanly—or inhumanly—possible, all things considered. Every interaction I'd had with her suggested she was fair, and, like Lucen had said, she took care of the satyrs under her. She'd even taken in one who'd been cast out by another domus.

That said, she was a damn powerful pred, and in my experience, no one ever got to be damn powerful by being kind and generous all the time.

The Lair's door opened as I drank the last of my whiskey. Dezzi had arrived. All the satyrs in the bar quietly deferred to her in their own ways as she walked past, and she stopped to talk to most of them. Her dark eyes, however, remained fixed on me. I pushed the empty shot glass aside, watching her right back. I wondered if she noticed my unease, and if so, what she made of it. Lucen hadn't told her what the meeting was about.

Tall and curvy, with perfectly unblemished dark skin, wide eyes, and an enviable set of eyelashes, Dezzi was nothing if not memorable. Today, just a few of her long braids wrapped around her horns. When she moved, she swayed like a queen, and when she spoke, she commanded authority, though her voice was soft. She was the definition of stunning, and yet her magic had no power over me.

Lucen jokingly referred to her as "mother," although I didn't think she was the one who'd made him a satyr. Devon was the only one who I knew owed their magical second life to Dezzi. And on cue, the bar's door opened a second time, and in strode Dezzi's lieutenant.

I swallowed, cursing my stupidity. Bad enough that I was about to confess my darkest secret to someone I could barely call a friend. I hadn't counted on spilling my guts to Devon as well. In hindsight though, I should have expected it. Devon wouldn't be an effective backup if he didn't know everything that Dezzi did.

Together, Lucen, Devon, and Lucrezia had once made up Dezzi's inner triad—or the three top-ranking members of her council. Since Lucrezia was now in Gryphon custody awaiting trial for murder, that left a vacancy.

"Did Dezzi choose Lucrezia's replacement yet?" I asked Lucen as Devon also stopped to talk to a satyr on his way toward us.

Lucen set a pitcher of beer, some glasses, and a bowl of pistachios on the table for us. "No. So no one else will be joining us, if that's what you're asking."

It was, so I nodded in reply. Adding another satyr to this conversation would be worse, especially since there were few others on Dezzi's council whom I knew by name.

Across the room, Devon winked at me. Raising an eyebrow in return, I hopped off the stool. Glad one of us was cheerful.

He came up behind me as I contemplated which chair to grab. I was feeling defensive, so I wanted my back to the wall, but that meant I'd be hemmed in on all sides by my company.

"So Jess has a secret," Devon said close to my ear.

I'd noticed the faint clove scent of his magic a second earlier, but had been lost in my thoughts. Now I jumped, and the realization that I was sensing his power left me flustered. Damn it, that shouldn't be happening, and it was one of the biggest reasons why I didn't want him here.

Tucking a strand of hair behind my ear, I inched away from him. "Hardly a secret," I said, thinking on what Lucen had pointed out a moment ago. "It's just not common knowledge, and the blond one behind the bar thinks you should be let in on the news."

Devon smirked. "Will it answer the question of how you got past my wards at Purgatory?"

"Still hung up on that, are you?"

He pulled out a chair and sat, affecting a lazy, disinterested manner that didn't fool me one bit. "You keep not answering the question, so yes. You know what they say, the chase is often what makes something exciting. This uncommon knowledge, everything you keep covered up and out of my reach—the more you dodge and deflect, the more intrigued I become by what you're withholding until it's all I can think about. All I dream about. So close I can almost taste it. It makes life hard."

Heat spread across my chest, driven by the intense expression in his eyes. Clearly he wasn't talking about the wards anymore.

"I might have the explanation about your wards, yes."

His smirk morphed into an evil grin. "Well, that solves one of my hang-ups. Now when are you going to do something about the other?"

Before I could escape, Dezzi appeared at Devon's side. Lucen followed with a glass of wine for her. I grabbed the closest chair and sat, trying not to fidget. Dezzi took the seat to my left. Although I could see the rest of the bar over Devon's shoulders, his height and Lucen's broadness to my right formed a warm wall around the table. I felt cut off, trapped in our own room after all.

Everyone was silent while Dezzi sipped her wine, then she gestured to me. "My number two called this meeting because he said you have important information to share."

"Wait, you're number two?" I stalled, glancing at Lucen.

"I was promoted since Lucrezia's gone. This is your meeting, Jess."

In other words, get on with it.

I took a deep breath, feeling three pairs of eyes drilling into me and three auras of magic assaulting my senses. Unlike the other two, Dezzi's was faint, but the strength of the power she emanated suggested that I had her full attention.

"Fine. So here's the thing. You all know I have unusual abilities for a human. The reason for that is because..." Living with the knowledge for a month made it no less difficult to get out the words. My tongue wanted to trip over them, but somehow I forced the correct sounds to form, though they did so slowly and ugly. "Because I'm not fully human, or maybe not human at all, depending on your perspective."

Whichever perspective, I was resigned to it being a matter of semantics. I was what I was, and the news of that seemed to have stunned Dezzi and Devon. Her face was uncharacteristically blank, and Devon's mouth was uncharacteristically silent.

Finally, Dezzi took another sip of wine, and Devon poured himself a glass of beer from the pitcher.

Unnerved, I slapped my hands on the table and stood. "Okay, so that's all. Meeting adjourned."

Lucen grabbed my wrist. His grip was light, and his face twisted into a smile, but his message was clear. "Would you relax?"

"No."

"So what are you?" Devon asked.

"A freak," I grumbled, but I sat back down.

Dezzi leaned forward, weaving her fingers together and resting her chin on them. "I've had suspicions, although the details elude me."

Devon blinked at her. "You know?"

"I said not for certain." She waved a finger at me. "Tell me everything and start at the beginning."

I poured myself some of the beer. This could be a long story if I knew where to start. Was it with what the Gryphons had done to me as a teenager, or when I bargained with Gunthra for the information?

I decided on Gunthra, and spent the next ten minutes going over everything I'd learned about myself in the past month. The beer loosened my tongue, or I blamed the beer anyway. Although I'd rehearsed this part, the truth was, I hadn't done a good job of it. As I spoke, it dawned on me that it was damn near impossible to explain my sordid life story without sharing details I'd have rather not shared about my abilities and about the Gryphons.

I talked about the deal I'd struck with Gunthra. The explanation she gave me—how humans with magical blood didn't always die when preds tried to change them, but on rare occasions became something other, not quite pred but no longer human.

I mentioned the unique abilities my quasi-satyr status gave me—how I could influence humans, my stronger resistance to pred power, and most importantly, my ability to reverse the bond that preds used to feed on human emotions. Then I explained how I'd used that ability on the fury who tried to addict me, and how the Gryphons had discovered some of what I was capable of.

Finally, I told them about the Gryphon files Steph stole, getting them decrypted, and finding out it was the Brotherhood of the Wing that had done this to me.

When I finished, Dezzi and Devon knew everything I'd told Lucen, and the shock waves I'd elicited had me squirming in my seat. Shock tended to blunt a pred's power, but shock was temporary. Once it passed, preds threw off heavy power from their heightened emotions, and I'd given Dezzi and Devon a lot to think about. Not only was I well aware of Devon's clove scent, but Dezzi's coconut pheromones settled against my skin too.

I slid my chair back from the table and pulled my knees in. It didn't help dull my senses, but it made me feel more secure.

Devon raised his glass toward me in a mock toast. "So you're one of us. Congratulations on your promotion. This changes things."

"Changes what things?"

"Before you were interesting because you were a strange human. Now that I know you're your own species? That is way beyond interesting." His blue eyes opened wide as he turned to Lucen. "You can't hoard her. It's not fair."

Lucen laughed, but I groaned. "Can you be serious for a minute?"

"What makes you think I'm not?"

Fortunately, Dezzi didn't seem to be in a joking mood, and a glance from her made the boys shut up. "I suspected something like this but not to this extent. Changing someone with magic in their blood—I knew that it did not always kill the person, but I did not know it could lead to people with Jessica's abilities."

"I didn't even know that much," Devon said, sounding petulant.

Dezzi's expression was mock pitying, and she patted him on the arm like a child.

I snickered into my beer, and Devon tossed a pistachio shell at me.

"So is that what you were thinking?" Lucen asked. He still held my wrist, but now his grip felt more protective than controlling. I appreciated the warmth of his hand.

"Not quite. Gunthra's knowledge appears more extensive than my own." Dezzi smiled apologetically, but she didn't sound happy about that. "The implications here are intriguing. If the Gryphons have found out how to ensure the survival of people like Jessica during the transformation, that would be good to know. As is whatever else this Brotherhood is doing in secret."

Devon tapped his fingers around his glass. "It could change the entire power balance between us and the Gryphons. It takes away our only real threat to them."

"Please." I crossed my arms, letting my feet fall to the floor with a thud. "All it would do is put you on equal footing with them."

"But there's a lot more of them, in case you haven't noticed."

"There's a lot more humans," I countered. "Not a lot of them with Gryphon talents."

"But they have the magi working with them."

The only race that preds hated more than other pred races was the magi. The bird shifters possessed just as much magic as preds, but they allied themselves with the Gryphons.

Lucen cleared his throat. "Speaking of Gryphons, since Jess has gone back to working with them—"

"You what?" Devon shook his head at me. "After what you said they did to you?"

I glared at Lucen. Dezzi hadn't taken it well the first time I went to consult for the Gryphons. At least in the end, it had worked out in her favor, so she'd forgiven me. "It's not permanent. I'm only doing it to help a friend. One case, then I'm done."

"Would they have you for longer?" Dezzi watched me, her near-empty wineglass at her lips.

I frowned, confused by the question. "I'm sure Director Lee would love it. Why?"

"I like this. I think it is a good thing for you to work for them."

Lucen gaped at her along with me. "How is this good?"

"As I understand it, the only ones who know what Jessica truly is are us, Gunthra, and some within the Gryphons who will not want her secret made public. Correct?"

I wet my lips. "Yes."

"Then it should be obvious. Jessica is one of us, though the Gryphons want her to be one of them. This council will benefit greatly from having an insider among them."

Devon raised his eyebrows at me, and Lucen scratched his scruffy chin. Much as he didn't want me to work for the Gryphons, Dezzi had gotten his attention.

She'd gotten mine too, but I wasn't contemplating the idea like they were. "No. Look, I appreciate what you've done for me in the past, but any debt I owe you, I consider paid by foiling Lucrezia's schemes."

Dezzi said nothing and reached for a pistachio.

It was Devon who broke the uncomfortable silence. "Jess, I know you used to have this strange notion about supporting the Gryphons, but after what they did? You're not human. You don't have to be Team Human by default anymore."

"I'm Team Me. And me is not a team player."

"So why are you siding with the Gryphons?"

I started to bang my head against the table, then thought better of it. "I'm not. I'm furious at the Gryphons for what they did, but I'm not a part of your domus, and I'm not going to be anyone's spy."

"Actually," Dezzi said, and that one word made my blood cold.

I cut her off before she could finish, glaring at Lucen. "You said no oaths."

"Jess." His voice was annoyingly condescending, but his expression was confused. His blue-green eyes left my face for Dezzi's.

"Jessica."

I sighed. "Yes?"

Dezzi pursed her lips in response to my tone. "I cannot force you to join my domus, nor would I. We live like we do for our own protection, which you do not need because you pass as human."

This time. You don't need our protection right now because the Gryphons aren't hunting you right now. Dezzi didn't say it, but the reminder was evident in her inflection.

I forced myself not to twitch.

Dezzi spun one of the silver bracelets around her wrist. "It is tradition that if a member of the domus uncovers betrayal or a similar crime by a member of the Dom's council, then that person is rewarded for their intelligence and loyalty by being offered the newly emptied seat on the council. As I did not believe you were one of us, I'd been considering who should fill the opening left by Lucrezia's departure. But things have changed, as my number one so astutely pointed out earlier." She cast a sarcastic smile his way, which Devon returned.

I watched their exchange, mind reeling as I processed what she was implying. "Wait, you're offering me a seat on your council?" I had to say it aloud to grasp it. It was insane.

It was also, admittedly, kind of brilliant. Dezzi wasn't forcing me to join her domus or be her spy. She was offering me a place of honor within it, and in such a way that the other satyrs would have to respect me. In one gesture, she told me I'd earned her confidence. In one gesture, she dangled out power. Protection. Belonging—something I hadn't had since the Gryphons had dumped me from their Academy.

And if I took it, how could I not spy on the Gryphons for her? If I took it, I'd have chosen a side. The Gryphons had used me, then cast me out. Once again, Dezzi was willing to take in the satyr who'd been tossed aside. She was the benevolent queen, and this was why people like Devon and Lucen were devoted to her.

I had to admit, the offer was tempting. That willingness to trust me and treat me with respect was very different from the welcome I'd gotten from the Gryphons. Director Lee had called me stupid and reckless before blackmailing me into being a consultant.

But more than that, it was the idea of finally belonging somewhere that called to me. I'd been an outsider for so long, prey among the preds and a freak among the humans.

Dezzi took my hand, but I barely registered the lust that should have stirred from touching her. "You are one of us, though a unique one for sure. You have proven yourself extremely capable. You have won the trust and affection of someone I hold in high regard. And you live among us. By tradition, I have no qualms offering you a seat if you will have it."

With Dezzi touching my left hand, and Lucen my right, I felt pulled in two directions, although they were undoubtedly pulling me the same way.

Yet when I looked up from the table, it was Devon, sitting across from me, who I saw. Devon with the horns in his black hair where I had none, and Devon whose magic affected me still, reminding me that I wasn't as free of pred influence as I liked to pretend.

And that was really the crux of it. Deep down, I still wasn't one of them. Council seat or not, I would be different. Dezzi's satyrs could feed off my emotions, and I identified as human, much to Lucen's dismay.

Swallowing, I withdrew my hands from both Dezzi and Lucen. I would have to choose my words carefully. "I'm flattered by the offer, but I'm not ready to commit to anything."

"Think on it," Dezzi said. "The offer stands for the time being."

TEN

DEZZI LEFT SOON AFTER, BUT DEVON LINGERED, TO MY dismay. He hung out at the bar with Lucen, and together they planned my future on the council.

"Standard council initiation for a nonstandard satyr?" Devon asked. He pushed a stray curl out of his eyes, which were focused on me and filled with mischief.

I was hoping to ignore him and have a word with Lucen before I left, but that was looking less and less likely. The two of them had been doing their best to goad me since the meeting broke up, ignoring the fact that I was in no mood for joking. Something they should have been well aware of.

Lucen leaned against the bar, scratching the scruff on his chin. "You mean the one where...?"

"That was it."

They both stared expectantly at me.

I gritted my teeth and checked my email. I was not going to ask whatever they wanted me to ask. *Go away, Devon. You make me nervous.*

"That's always good fun, although it's also been a long time since we had a proper orgy around here."

"Save that for the after-party, perhaps." Devon pointed at him. "I'm not hosting it at Purgatory. Too much cleanup."

"Fine. Forget it. I get the feeling Jess would never admit to liking it anyway."

Paulius, one of The Lair's usual bartenders, furrowed his brow in my direction and took my empty glass. "What are they going on about?"

"Nothing. They're being dorks and trying to get a rise out of me. That's all."

"Actually, I think you've got the rising thing reversed," Devon said. "But initiation should clear that up if Lucen hasn't managed it yet."

Lucen punched him in the arm. God, it was like I was surrounded by teenage boys.

Paulius grinned. "So what's initiation?"

"I was waiting for someone to ask." Devon sighed heavily. "We expect new members to make a vow with each existing member."

"In front of the whole council," Lucen added.

"In the position of the existing member's choice."

"And a good time will be had by all."

I tucked my phone away, very conscious of how close they stood. I could close my eyes, spin around until dizzy, and still sense the precise location of both Lucen and Devon thanks to the pull of their magic. My skin itched with it, longing for two pairs of hands to descend and quench the irritation. Lucen's hands slipping between my thighs... Devon's tongue burrowing in my mouth...

Damn it, my clothes were getting uncomfortable. Anyway, what the hell was wrong with me? I could barely control myself around Lucen. The two of them together might rip me in half, and I didn't even like Devon.

Liar, a traitorous voice in my head whispered. *You think he's funny and attractive.*

But I don't trust him.

Why not? When has he ever done anything to deserve that? Is it because he's a satyr? Newsflash, little siren: so are you.

Go piss on a salamander, I told the voice. I hated internal arguments, and they were a hundred times worse when the subject of said arguments was gazing at me like he could read my thoughts as well as my emotions.

My life had been so much simpler when I'd shunned relationships altogether.

I mimicked Devon's impish expression. "You're both so full of shit that it stinks in here."

Laughing, Paulius got back to work. It was time I did the same since I was obviously not going to get that private, serious conversation with Lucen accomplished.

"Jess, are you leaving?" He slid a beer down the bar to Devon.

I stuck my hands on my hips. "Yes, unless either of you can tell me what goblin addicted Eric Marshall."

"Isn't he that writer guy?" Devon asked. "Highly controversial thrillers, right? I didn't know he's an addict."

"Was. Not anymore. I take it that means you're not useful."

"I'm very useful when it's important, as you should know. And that reminds me, I'm still waiting on my thank-you present for saving your life last week."

"Sorry, I'm too busy saving someone else's life this week. It's called paying it forward, and I have work to do. For the Gryphons."

Lucen had grabbed my hand and was kissing it when I said that. He smacked the back of my fingers before releasing me.

"That there is your problem," Devon said as I walked away. "You could be so much more fun if you ditched the beasts."

"No one who knows me thinks I'm fun."

"But we can fix that," Devon called after me.

I left, exasperated. Hands in my pockets, I stomped the whole way back to my apartment, unsure why I was annoyed. Was it because of how Dezzi had sprung her offer on me, or because I didn't like that it tempted me?

Lucen and Devon had been taken by surprise too, but if they had any misgivings about Dezzi's decision, they kept quiet in front of me. Good little satyr boys. Loyal and trusting of their Dom, at least in public.

Truthfully though, I doubted Lucen had concerns. He was probably thrilled by the idea, which made being annoyed about not talking to him all the more absurd. What was there to discuss? He'd want me to go for it. Was I hoping he'd talk me into it?

I didn't think so. I just wanted someone to talk to about the meeting, and Lucen was my only option. Steph didn't know enough, and like Lucen, I knew what her opinion would be. As for Devon, he didn't count. The only times we managed to have serious conversations were when he was threatening me to get my nose out of satyr business. Sometimes I wondered if he was capable of being serious at all where I was concerned.

"Oh, lookie here. It's my favorite satyr's girlie."

I paused with my hand on my building door and swallowed. The fury I liked to call Mace-head because of the way he wore his spiky hair—and because I didn't know his real name—was leaving the magic shop on my right.

All I knew about him was that he'd hung around with the fury who'd tried to frame me for Victor Aubrey's murders, and a week or two ago he'd inexplicably chased off a couple of his brethren who'd been out for revenge. Then he'd told me the fury Dom had plans for me.

My blood turned cold. Funny how I'd forgotten about that until this moment.

Bells on the shop door jingled as it closed behind Mace-head. He tucked a package under his arm so he could pull out a cigarette. "Not just strolling about anymore, are you? Moved in?"

"I do hope that's not a problem." My tone was icy, but really—I did hope that the furies wouldn't consider it a problem. Because, shit, they hadn't bothered me in a while, which was very much a good thing.

Mace-head flicked his elaborate lighter and blew a puff of smoke into the air. "Nope, no problem. Just saying hi. Being neighborly."

Yeah, I bet. "Hi. All right then. See you later." Probably sooner than I'd like.

Mace-head grinned. "As you say. Take care, girlie. Take very good care."

I opened my mouth then shut it. Just like with Lucen and Devon's joking at The Lair, some questions were best left unasked, though in this case for a very different reason.

I hurried into the building, and by the time I turned around, he was across the street.

Weird. I'd swear he was doing all this to freak me out, but I doubted I'd be so lucky. Especially thanks to Gunthra's interest in the furies, I had a bad feeling about Mace-head's interest in me.

My phone buzzed as I climbed the steps, and I checked the text, pushing thoughts of Mace-head from my mind.

Talk about this tomorrow for real? Lucen had written.

Yes.

I'm taking you to dinner. Be ready at eight.

Ah, yes. The date I'd demanded. He got his meeting. I got my normality. *Damn right.*

Somewhat appeased, I armed myself with a mug of tea, my laptop, and the thumb drive, and spread out on futon. Time to get to work. I'd feel a lot better when I was out of Gunthra's debt.

Whether it was purposeful to spite me, or whether Tom was just hopelessly disorganized, I couldn't say, but the information on the drive was chaotic. Since my thoughts were already scattered thanks to Dezzi throwing me for a loop with her offer, sorting through the confusion was almost too much. But I had to try. If Gunthra wanted this information enough to call in her debt for it, she must have a good reason.

Tom hadn't skimped on what he'd given me, but much of what was here was information that I already knew. One month ago, violent psychopath and part-pred like me, Victor Aubrey, had gotten lucky and discovered we shared the same unusual misery-sucking ability. He'd gotten my name and contacted me, trying to get me to join in his fun. No doubt, at some point he'd hoped to entice to me to go along with his disgusting game of rape-torture-murder while feeding on his victims' suffering.

I'd declined. Victor hadn't taken it well and had framed me for a few murders. Or so the story went in the press, and with Victor dead— murdered in his high-security prison—no one was contradicting that tale.

The truth was more complicated. Victor was a rage addict, although I had no idea whether that was by choice or because no one had clued him in to the fact he could reverse the pred-addict bond and drive his fury master out of his head. I suspected it was both, and Victor had enjoyed being an addict.

But whichever, by all the Gryphons could determine, he'd been working with his fury master to choose which women to kill and had mutilated their bodies per the fury's instructions. Specifically, his victims were vanity addicts, which would enrage the sylphs. Victor had also removed their hearts after they died, throwing suspicion on the magi, who —unbeknownst to most people—enjoyed human hearts as a forbidden delicacy.

It was a situation certain to spark tensions among the preds, as well as between the preds and the magi. By framing me, Victor and his master had only fanned the flames since I was on good terms with Lucen. That had turned some of the sylphs' anger directly on the satyrs.

With regards to this information, Tom's files contained little I hadn't already learned with a couple exceptions, mainly how the Gryphons had tackled the investigation before focusing their energy on me. Apparently, at one point, they had covered the local magi black market in human hearts. Lovely. I hadn't even known such a thing existed.

Nonetheless, I couldn't see anything there to interest Gunthra. The details of what happened were boring.

The why of it all was another story. Gunthra had indicated that she believed the furies used Victor to try to start a pred war, and the facts of the case bore that out. Why else had Victor's master been intent on getting the various pred races at each other's throats? But I'd forgotten about the way Victor had implicated the magi too. If this had been about a war, it hadn't only involved the preds.

Swallowing the dregs of my tea, I read on.

Victor had been killed in prison at the behest of the furies, although the Gryphons couldn't prove it, and no one seemed to have tried too hard. Victor's fury master had disappeared after Victor was arrested. I hadn't known his name, so I couldn't have identified him, and the furies' Dom had played clueless. But all signs pointed to that fury's demise.

Boo-fucking-hoo.

Tom hadn't done much to follow up there. Most of his attention to the case had gone into me. Hardly surprising since uncovering information about my gift was a large part of why he'd been sent to Boston.

Tom had wanted to know if my selection as Victor's patsy had been more deliberate than first suspected. Alas, he left more questions behind than he did answers. Who concocted this scheme—was it an order from the fury Dom, or had Victor's master been acting alone? Had the furies known about Victor's pred-like abilities? Had they told Victor to involve me? What, if anything, did they know about what Victor and I truly were?

I read through file after file, stared at magical scans of my blood, Victor's blood, and the many victims' blood. None of it came close to answering the question that Gunthra had raised. Why? Whatever Gunthra was hoping to find, it was unlikely to be here. Tom, and the other Gryphons who'd worked on the case, had thought the furies were behaving oddly, but neither the main investigation nor Tom's follow-up investigation focused on that. The Gryphons had wanted to catch a killer. Tom had wanted to catch me.

In the end, I was left with the same possibilities that Lucen and I had once discussed. Furies instilled rage in people, but confusion and fear were the emotions they thrived on. The furies—or a lone fury—could have been hoping for nothing more than to gorge on those feelings by causing a magical shitstorm, or they could have been trying to raise the sort of power they liked most for some other nefarious purpose. Who knew?

Not the Gryphons, and if Gunthra could make anything out of this mess, then more power to her, I supposed. Satisfied there was nothing in here that I needed to "accidentally" delete before turning the information over, I shut my laptop.

Thinking it was time to relax with a good book and a light dinner, I dumped the dregs of my tea in the kitchen sink. But it wasn't Eric's novel that caught my eye when I returned to the bedroom. It was Tom's book.

I frowned at it. I didn't want to read. Didn't want to talk to Tom and hear his batshit excuses for what the Brotherhood did. Yet for some reason I grabbed the book anyway.

"Fine. You're going to make me hear you out? I'm going to read your shit so I know exactly how to call you on it when I do."

And now I was talking to myself. Peachy.

I got a yogurt from the fridge then opened the book to the first bookmark. As I didn't own a table, I leaned against the counter as I ate.

What I'd thought might be a journal turned out to be more like someone's notebook. Each bookmark—there were three of them—had been left on a page describing a vision some magi had had. After spending a couple minutes completely confused, I wised up at last and realized I needed to read more than just the bookmarked page to understand what was going on.

The three visions Tom had pointed me to appeared to be of the same event, but the visions themselves were different. Each had been experienced by a different magi in a different time and location. Whoever had written this journal back in 1911—I'd found a handwritten date on the back of the front cover—had discovered similarities between the visions and made notes describing the way they were linked together.

I wasn't sure I'd have picked up on the similarities myself. The first vision had been recorded in the fifteenth century. Along with the original Latin text was the journal-writer's translation, which was the only way I could read it. Even so, it bore faint resemblance—at the surface level—to the second recording from the seventeenth century, and less so to the third vision from the nineteenth. The second had been recorded in Latin, as well. The last in English.

The world had changed drastically during those times and since then, but eventually I figured out the "gray mountains of man" and "teeth of steel thrust into the sky" that were described in the earliest vision must have referred to modern cities and skylines filled with what would have seemed like impossibly tall buildings.

The second vision described the cities differently but was similar in other, more disturbing ways. According to this recording, the first demons —whatever they were—would be freed by fire and flood, and rise to enslave humanity. More talk of blood came after that. Rivers of blood. Tears of blood. Oceans of blood. Blood of something called the Others.

The second vision was obsessed with blood.

I remembered reading something about Others and Firsts in one of the books I'd paged through while snooping in Tom's office, but this journal contained no more information on what they were than that book had. Just lots about blood, and fires too.

Oh, the fires. All the visions described the purple smoke and blackened skies of salamander fires burning through the cities.

The hair on my neck prickled as I read the description of them given in the third and most recent vision, and I clenched my jaw. I'd heard something similar, too similar for comfort, before.

Olef, a friend of mine among Boston's magi population, had thrown me for one hell of a loop not too long ago. It was only recently that I'd learned he was a clairvoyant, and not just any clairvoyant. A clairvoyant who'd had a vision of me.

He'd described the same sort of scene—cities burning in salamander fires—and he'd claimed to have seen me in the middle of it all.

Much as I hated to admit it, the visions in this journal did sound familiar. Olef had said nothing of Others and Firsts, but his timing was eerily on cue. Each vision had come every two hundred years, right around the turn of the century. Fifteenth. Seventeenth. Nineteenth. And now the twenty-first for Olef.

And Olef, like Tom, seemed to think this somehow concerned me.

I slammed the book shut. Did. Not. Like.

My yogurt remained before me, mostly untouched, but I didn't feel hungry any longer.

"Stupid. Who's to say any of this is real? Not all visions come true, and besides, maybe whatever this is doesn't happen for another two hundred years."

Of course, Olef hadn't indicated the cities he saw were futuristic looking, and I wouldn't be there if his vision was of two hundred years in the future. Satyr subspecies or not, I seemed to age like a normal human, not a pred.

"And anyway, Olef's visions might not even be related. Why am I talking to myself? First internal arguments at The Lair, and now this. I'm losing it."

Cursing, I stuffed the yogurt back in my fridge and nearly jumped out of my skin when my phone rang in the bedroom. Pulling myself together, I realized that was Steph's ringtone, and I dashed to get it. A distraction couldn't have come at a better time.

"I got your message," Steph said as I paced the short length of my apartment. "Can we meet up for lunch tomorrow so you can fill me in on how Eric's case is going?"

Right foot, left foot, spin around in front of the window and do it again. "Yeah, yeah, sounds good."

"You okay? You sound spacey. What are you doing?"

I let my fingers graze the cover of Tom's book as I passed through the narrow kitchen. "Oh, you know. Contemplating the end of the world."

"Sounds like fun."

I paused, catching my reflection in the bedroom window. I looked like shit. Very much like someone contemplating the end of the world, indeed. "You know me. No one who knows me thinks I'm fun."

ELEVEN

I met Steph for lunch the next day at a crowded sandwich shop near the hospital where she worked. She'd already commandeered a booth for us, and I joined her without anticipating a fun conversation. I hadn't slept well thanks to my not-so-light pre-bed reading. Plus Dezzi's offer stuck in my head like a tack. One pinning a piece of paper to me with a giant scarlet *S* on it for "satyr."

Steph didn't look so hot herself. She sported circles under her eyes that were only partially obscured by her concealer, and she had on her glasses instead of the freaky bright green contact lenses she normally wore.

"Tired eyes?" I asked, spinning my buzzer around on the table.

"Tired Steph. I ripped my contact this morning because I was half asleep, and I didn't feel like getting out a new one." She took a long draw from her soda. "This stuff doesn't have as much caffeine as coffee, does it?"

"Don't think so."

Steph wrinkled her nose. "I'll get coffee to go. So what's going on with Eric?"

I shifted in my seat as I filled Steph in on everything that had happened with the lawyer, Gunthra, and the other leads and tactics the Gryphons were pursuing.

"That's it?" Steph stared at me.

I spread my hands helplessly. "Bridget's good. She knows what she's doing, and they're doing all they can."

"Then why aren't they using you to help too?" Her buzzer went off, and she scowled like she wanted to throw it at someone.

Ironic that I'd always thought Steph put way too much faith in the Gryphons, but for once, when I thought they were doing their best, she didn't seem to agree. I supposed it was always different when it was your life or your family on the line. Then nothing would seem to be enough.

My buzzer went off as she was returning to the table, so it was a few more minutes before we could resume our conversation.

"My family is sick," Steph continued, picking at her sandwich. "I thought they were awful before, for what they did to me, but in contrast to this, I could almost respect them for that. It's one thing to stand by your convictions and tell me you think I'm wrong because I don't fit with your version of religion. If that's what you need in your life, fine. But now they've swarmed in like vultures circling over Eric's money. Of course, it's all under the self-righteous guise that he did this to himself and got what he deserved. So I told Tim last night that if Eric's money was all ill gained through deals with the devil, then they should plan to give it away instead of keeping it for themselves."

I swallowed my bite of sandwich. "And what did he say?"

"You have to ask?" Steph flung her hair over her shoulders and finally started to eat, but she managed only a couple bites before she went on a new rant.

I listened quietly, understanding her need to vent and grateful that I'd thought to order food that went well with the spicy rage her emotions stirred. As she spoke, it dawned on me that Steph hadn't cared so much about an update on the case. She'd just needed to talk. Likewise, she wasn't upset with the Gryphons' lack of progress so much as she was with the world in general.

"This is why I never talked about or to my family." Steph tossed her half-uneaten sandwich on the plate. "They make me ill. I swear to God, Jess, some humans are as bad as preds. They feed on misery the same way.

I think they enjoy it. You should hear the way my family moralizes over Eric. They're lapping up his suffering like preds."

I cleared my throat. "Hey now, misery-feeder right here. Let's be kind to those of us stuck getting head rushes from other people's emotions. Okay? Not all of us actually enjoy it."

A half-smile cracked Steph's lips. "You're different. You use your ability for good, and you don't create misery just to feed on it. You're not a pred or one of my relatives."

My own smile faltered. Well, I wasn't one of her relatives anyway.

Tell her, I yelled at myself. For the love of dragons, I'd told Dezzi yesterday. All the satyrs probably knew by now. It was hardly a secret.

But nope, still couldn't. I rationalized it as usual—not the right time. Steph had more pressing concerns.

"What is it?"

I quit poking at my sandwich. "Nothing."

"Liar. Your entire body twitched when I said you weren't a pred or a relative, and since I'm pretty sure we're not related..." Steph lowered her glasses so she could stare at me better. "You're not beating yourself up over your freakishness, are you? I thought you'd made peace with your curse years ago."

I opened my mouth, shut it, opened it again, and took a bite of my pickle to delay speaking. "I'm at peace. Total peace. See me being Zen."

"Then what was it?"

"Um, you know, just stuff." I shrugged. "Not important. You and Eric and your stuff is important. Don't let me bother you with my crap."

Steph flopped back against the booth. "Bother me, please. I need to talk about something else. It's only fair. I ranted at you for ten minutes. Go on. Something's bugging you if you were thinking about the end of the world last night."

Oh, crap. What exactly did I have to talk about? The actual end-of-the-world stuff was out because it skirted too close to Tom and the Brotherhood and the truth about me. There was also no way I was bringing up my deal with Gunthra. So what did that leave? The oh-so-pressing decision I'd been contemplating about cutting my hair?

I blurted out the next thing that came to mind, which at least was a problem believably agonizing. "What are your thoughts on monogamy? Lifestyle choice or biological imperative?"

"Say what?" I had her attention if nothing else. "Last I knew you weren't in one relationship, never mind more."

I scratched my neck, suddenly wishing I'd brought up the magi visions after all. "For argument's sake, let's say I'm in a casual relationship with someone. Nothing committed." Lucen would hate that characterization of our relationship, but he wasn't here to remind me that committed didn't necessarily mean monogamous. "But let's say I'm also attracted to someone else. What does that suggest?"

"I don't know, but I'm intrigued." Steph tapped a finger over her lips, a gesture that usually suggested she was craving a smoke. "And I don't see the problem as long as everyone is okay with it."

"So you don't think it's weird?"

Steph snorted. "If it involves you, it's weird by definition. But no, I don't see the big deal. Is Person One this Gryphon you mentioned a couple weeks ago? The one you said was hot and you went out with?"

I cringed at the memory. Poor Andre. My former partner was hot, and a nice guy, and now most definitely wanted nothing to do with me thanks to Lucrezia's damn sex drugs. I wasn't sorry that Lucrezia had ruined any chance for us to have a relationship, but losing a friend sucked.

"No, that thing fell apart before it went anywhere, unfortunately."

"Damn, bummer. So who is it, and why haven't you mentioned him before?"

Because he's a satyr and you'll lose your shit?

"It's not that satyr, is it?"

Score a point for Steph. Damn it. "How did you do that?"

Steph blinked at me like I'd slapped her. "Are you kidding me? It is?"

I slumped in my seat, hoping to end up under the table. But Steph kicked me in the shins, and I bolted back up. "It's...you know, we're friends, and..."

She shoved a finger in my face. "No, bad Jess. Satyr. Evil. Pred."

I knew it wasn't an accusation, but it sure felt like one. "That's not entirely fair. He's not evil."

"I'm not even going to go there, Jess. Suffice to say he's not boyfriend material. You were asking about weird? That's beyond weird. We're in serious fucked-up territory."

I grabbed her hand and pushed it out of my face. "I'm resistant to pred power. They don't affect me. Can't feel it. Can't be mind-fucked or addicted. How's that for fucked-up territory?"

Her hand fell limp in mine, and I released it. "Say what? Since when?"

"About a month ago. Long story that I haven't wanted to plague you with, but the upshot is that I can't sense pred magic anymore unless the pred touches me. Except Lucen's magic, that is. And what that tells me is that I'm attracted to him for more than his magic."

"You..." She waved her hands around like a madwoman. "You cannot drop a bombshell like this on me when I need to go back to work in twenty minutes."

"You wanted me to tell you something interesting."

"Jesus. I didn't expect *that* interesting."

We sat in silence for a moment. She stared at me, and I did my best to meet her stare with a confidence I didn't feel.

Eventually, Steph pulled out her lighter. "Thanks to you, I need a smoke before returning to work. Is the other person a satyr too?"

I coughed. "Yes."

"And I thought *my* dating history served as a cautionary tale." Steph stood, shaking her head. "I can't offer you advice, my friend, because this is so far outside the realm of anything normal that I'm stumped."

Awesome. Because when your transgender, ex-hacker best friend who listened to obscure death metal and who paid her way through college by running a website from which she sold underwear allegedly worn by BU's sorority girls (but was in fact bought at Wal-Mart and used to wipe the sweat off gym equipment)—when she told you you're dating life was outside the realm of normal...

Well, that kind of said it all, didn't it?

I followed Steph into the sunlight and walked with her toward the hospital. "So I guess you and Jim are out for double dates, huh?"

Her expression was withering. "Do not get yourself hurt."

"I'm trying not to."

"You're not trying very hard, that's all I'm saying."

"When have I ever done things easy?" My phone rang, preventing me from hearing whatever snark was surely dancing on Steph's tongue. "Bridget?"

"Hi, Jess. Are you busy?"

I paused on the corner. "Nothing that can't be put off. What do you need?"

"Can you come in? We got a ton of information from Eric's house—hard drive, papers, bank receipts, you name it. I have a plan, but I could use all the help I can get to go through this."

"I'm on my way."

Steph crushed her cigarette. "They got something?"

"A lot of something, just don't ask me how it'll be useful. Will keep you posted."

"You do that." She clucked her tongue at me. "You're a Gryphon dating a satyr. Do your coworkers know this? Isn't that like treason? You're a double agent."

I laughed, but coming on the heels of yesterday's conversation with Dezzi, it struck me as too true to be funny.

TWELVE

Bridget had taken over a conference room and turned it into a war room. A messy war room.

I stood in the doorway, searching for her amidst the nine other Gryphons running around and the piles of paper spread over every surface like snow. As the AC turned on, some of the paper snow beneath the vent lifted off the table and blew like the real thing. As I tucked a pile of receipts beneath a box, I spotted Bridget behind a computer at the far end. She saw me at the same time and beckoned me over.

I wove across the room, dodging Gryphons and gingerly stepping over boxes containing yet more paper. "What's going on? It looks like you have everything here but Eric's contract."

Bridget slid the laptop over to another Gryphon. "We might have the contract somewhere in this mess and not have found it yet. We got permission to search Marshall's things this morning."

"I see."

She pulled her hair back as we spoke, ignoring my comment. "We just got back. In case we don't have the contract, we're expanding our search to include other ways to track down this goblin. That's why I need your help. I was able to recruit a bunch of people, but there's a lot to go through, and what we're searching for might be obscure."

"Sounds like a blast. What are we searching for besides a contract?"

"That's the problem. It's one of those situations where you'll know it when you see it."

I peered into the closest box. It was filled with green hanging file folders, each stuffed with papers. "Will I?"

"Possibly. Will any of us?"

"Your optimism is inspiring."

Bridget grabbed the box I was poking through and handed it to a passing Gryphon. "Since when do you care for optimism? We're searching for patterns in behavior. Marshall lives in New Hampshire. There are no pred communities in his area. Boston is the closest, so his goblin most likely lives in Shadowtown. See where I'm going with this?"

I really did try, but my brain was not up to the task. "Pity me. Agent Kassin's reading material kept me up last night, and I'm sleepy."

"Oh, yeah. Kassin's top-secret stuff. I heard he was looking for you earlier."

"Great. Hide me behind a stack of papers if you want me to stay here, or he'll pull me away. My understanding is that he outranks Director Lee."

Bridget smiled. "He does, and can do. So to explain—addicts need to meet their masters every now and then to keep the bond strong and healthy. As a rule, preds don't go to their addicts. They expect their addicts to come to them. Marshall would, therefore, have to travel to Boston on a somewhat regular basis. So that's what we're looking for—anything to suggest when or where. Some preds let their addicts go to their houses or places of business, but others don't. They could have met at a place in or around Shadowtown. If we get the place, we get a lead on tracking the goblin. Make sense?"

It did, but it sounded like dreadfully dull, possibly fruitless work. On the other hand, it beat going door-to-door in Shadowtown and asking people if they knew which goblin addicted Eric Marshall. With my Shadowtown contacts—aka the satyrs and Gunthra—tapped out, that was all that was left to me if Bridget insisted on it.

Bridget set me down with a box of my own, this one filled with manila file folders instead of green ones. While the other people around me pored over bank statements, credit card receipts, and who knew what else, I discovered my box was mainly filled with all the information Eric had kept regarding the building and upkeep of his massive house. Nothing remotely helpful.

We'd been at it for over an hour when an older woman at the opposite end of the table jerked me out of my searching stupor. "I might have something."

Wearily, I rubbed my eyes, hoping it was the damn contract so I could stop this tediousness.

The Gryphon cleared a spot among the papers she'd been going through and laid out what appeared to be a series of bank records. "These show Marshall's debit card uses. It's not much, but every other Thursday evening he's dropped money at some place called Vine. Looks like a Beacon Hill address."

"That's a wine bar," one of the other Gryphons said. "Pricey place too."

Bridget sucked on her lip. "Not exactly near Shadowtown."

"No, but it's near this." Wes pointed to something on the laptop. "I found a recurring appointment on Marshall's calendar—a support group for addicts. It meets every Thursday out of Mass General."

"So maybe Eric goes for a glass of overpriced wine before or after his group." I stretched my arms. "It's not likely he goes to the group and meets the goblin on the same day, is it?"

Bridget turned to me. "Maybe, maybe not. But why make more than one trek into the city if he doesn't have to? We should check it out, and the support group too, to see if Marshall talked to anyone in it."

I'D BEEN RECRUITED FOR BOTH TASKS, AT LEAST IN PART because I wanted to get out of the building and therefore out of Tom's reach.

Bridget explained more on the drive to Vine. "These support groups are usually semi-anonymous because there's such a stigma to being an addict. I could send over a plain-clothed Gryphon to talk to people, but I'd rather not."

I rubbed a smudge of dirt off my sunglasses, parsing that one out. "Are you suggesting I lie to people about why I'm there so they're willing to talk?"

Bridget's lips thinned at the suggestions. "Of course not. You're only a consultant, so you don't have to lie, and you could truthfully explain that you're a friend of the family."

I almost laughed. "That still sounds fairly devious for you. I thought you were all about being straightforward and official."

Bridget frowned at me. "That is straightforward. Nothing there is a lie or devious. It's about putting people at ease."

Right. Because sending a pred into an addict support group instead of a Gryphon would be much less stressful for the addicts.

Of course, Bridget didn't know what I was. It was the advantage of being able to pass as human, as Dezzi had mentioned.

I held up my hands in defeat. "Okay, understood." Still devious though, I thought.

Vine had just opened when we found it tucked into one of the neighborhood's quaint brick buildings. Inside, I pulled off my sunglasses and blinked while my eyes adjusted to the dim light. I spent a fair amount of time in bars, but this was the first one I'd been to that made me feel uncomfortably out of place.

When I went out with Steph, we favored her cousin's bar. Kilpatrick's was one of dozens of Irish, or faux Irish, pubs that dotted the city. It was a step down from The Lair, more boisterous and more likely to see a fight break out. But The Lair, though Lucen kept it nicer than any satyr bar had a reason to be, had nothing on *this* place.

Everything here was chic and shiny, from the glassy black tabletops to the mirrored lighting, and the artful arrangement of empty wine bottles and corks that graced the walls. If I touched something, I feared I'd leave dirt behind, but I tipped one of the menus closer with my finger anyway for a better look. Then I let go of it quickly when I saw the prices.

"We don't open for another five minutes," one of the servers said with barely a glance in our direction. She was dressed all in black, her blonde hair slicked behind her ears, and she was lighting the votives on the tables.

Bridget made a show of checking her watch. "It's three o'clock by my time, but we're not here to drink. We need to ask some questions of the employees about one of your regulars."

"Oh." She deigned to check us out, and surprise registered on her face when she saw Bridget's uniform and her badge. "Um...let me get the manager." Smoothing down her skirt, she headed into the back.

Two more people emerged from the back room almost the instant after the blonde disappeared. They were both also dressed in black. The man headed behind the bar with a curt nod, and a black-haired woman approached us. She had a pinched expression, and I could taste her displeasure. Whether that was because we weren't paying for our time here or because this was legal business, I couldn't be sure.

She dismissed me with a glance, so maybe she also disapproved of my jeans and sneakers. "Cat Williams." She held out a hand to Bridget. "How can I help you?"

"We're investigating an attack on one of your regulars," Bridget said after introducing us. "His name is Eric Marshall. I don't know if that means anything to you."

Cat's spine straightened, and I bit my lip, amused by her indignation. "Absolutely we know Mr. Marshall. It's always an honor when a celebrity shows favor to our establishment. We've only been open for six months, but Mr. Marshall was one of our first guests. It's terrible what happened to him, but I wasn't aware there was an attack too."

Bridget let the misconception slip. "There was, and we're following all leads in the case. Unfortunately, because of what happened to Mr. Marshall, we're unable to ask him questions directly. We do know he came here regularly and were wondering if he ever met anyone."

Cat's eyebrows shot into her hairline. "I hope our establishment is not involved in any way." After Bridget assured it was not, she went on. "He never met anyone here, no. But he usually came in with a friend. A girlfriend, possibly. I couldn't say."

"You wouldn't happen to have the woman's name, would you?"

"I'm afraid not. Jenny might be of more assistance if it's the woman you're interested in." Cat waved over the blonde waitress.

The door jingled open as Jenny approached. Cat told her to stay and answer our questions while she attended the customers.

I listened again as Bridget gave a brief rundown of our purpose. Unlike Cat, who seemed to be well-informed about what happened to Eric, Jenny only knew she'd heard something on the news.

"He was attacked with magic?" A spot of color bloomed on her pale cheeks. "That's awful. He usually sat in my section when he'd come in. He was very polite and tipped well."

"What about the woman he was with?" Bridget asked. "Do you know her name?"

Jenny thought for a moment. "Yes, I know I heard him say it occasionally. It began with an S. Sharon maybe? Or Sienna? I want to say it makes me think of something warm. I'm sorry I can't remember better."

My gaze roamed the floor for a waiters' station. "If she ever paid with a credit card, you'd have her name. We know when she came in, so the search would be narrow."

"Good idea," Bridget said.

"Former waitress here," I reminded her.

But my good idea was for nothing. "Mr. Marshall always paid, which I always thought was very nice of him because I didn't get the sense that they were together, if you know what I mean."

"So she wasn't his girlfriend?"

"Not the vibe I got. They talked quietly, but there was no touchy-feely-ness, if you get me."

"What kind of vibe did you get?" I asked. Jenny questioned me with her eyes, so I tried to explain without tipping her off or freaking her out. "I mean, was there anything unusual about her?"

Like you know, a cold aura or a prickly sensation in your mind? Did she awaken any greedy urges or impulses? Did you occasionally see her from the corner of your eye and something about her appearance seemed unnatural, like it was a disguise charm?

If the mystery woman was obviously a goblin, surely Jenny or Cat would have mentioned it. But preds often donned disguises when they mingled in the human world. Those came easy for satyrs, who only needed to hide their horns. Goblins would need more elaborate magic, but it could be done.

"No, nothing really," Jenny said. "She seemed pretty normal. Sorry."

"That's all right. Can you give us a description of her?"

"Thirties, I'd guess. About your coloring." Jenny pointed to me. "Tall and very thin. She kind of looked like a model, and she wore lots of rings. That's one thing that always weirded me out about her. Every one of her fingers had two or more rings on it, even her thumb. I always thought it looked so uncomfortable."

Bridget wrote down everything Jenny shared, and let her go.

"The rings make me think of Gunthra," I said. "She wears them like that too."

Bridget stuck her notes away. "Does she? I never noticed. It doesn't sound like this person is our goblin, though. I'm sure Jenny would have noticed if something was off about her. Even the most clueless people tend to be aware of disguised preds at a subconscious level. We should check with the bartender and manager to be sure."

We did, but neither of them provided any useful information. The excursion seemed to me to be a bust, but at least it got me out of scanning Eric's water bills for part of the afternoon.

Jenny ran up to us as we were leaving. "I just remembered. The woman's name is Shawna."

Bridget wrote that down too, and thanked her.

"Did you see anything about a Shawna in Eric's stuff?" I put my sunglasses on as we returned to the car.

"No." Bridget pulled out the keys, and the SUV beeped as it unlocked. "But now we can look again."

Peachy. So much for getting out of more paperwork.

THIRTEEN

I SUSPECTED BRIDGET WOULD HAVE KEPT ME AROUND ALL evening searching for Shawna or other leads in the mess of papers she obtained from Eric's house, but when I told her I had plans, she grudgingly let me go. I felt bad for cutting out early, but Lucen was taking the night off for our date, and it wasn't fair to screw up his plans either.

Speaking of my horned demon, he called me as I got off the T. "Wear a skirt tonight."

"What?"

"You heard me. A skirt. A short one."

"I don't think I own a skirt. Scratch that—I know I don't. I just finished unpacking my clothes the other night."

"You don't own a single skirt? What sort of woman are you?"

"One who likes pants, obviously. When have you ever seen me in a skirt?"

He sighed into my ear. "Never. That was the point. If we're doing this whole date deal, we should do it right. You, a skirt, an easy way for me to slide my hand up your leg during dinner."

"Not a skirt person."

"You lack imagination. Picture a quiet, candlelit corner. You're sipping your wine, waiting for the food, and that's when you feel my hand brush your knee under the tablecloth. You do nothing to give it away, and slowly, I draw my fingers up your leg, nudging your skirt higher. You're tensing with anticipation, but still not moving as I glide my fingers between your thighs. You breathe a little faster, feeling your blood rush. And still I reach higher and higher, caressing your smooth skin, watching you stifle a gasp as my finger grazes the edges of your hairline before sliding lower and spreading your folds."

I realized I'd stopped in the middle of the sidewalk and hastily started moving again. "Okay, you've got my imagination going."

"Really? Then imagine that I can tell you want me to stop, but you can't help spreading your legs just a touch, leaving me room for another finger and another, delving deeper until I find your clit, stroking and caressing it. Again. And again, feeling it grow harder while you grow wetter. And maybe you move slightly now so I can slide one of those fingers deep inside you. Your hands are tight around your wineglass, and your nipples are poking through your shirt. You're afraid people are watching you, sensing what's going on, and as your breathing—"

"All right, all right. Been giving this a bit of thought, have you?"

"All day, Jess. You need a skirt."

I swallowed. "You said eight o'clock? There's time for me to buy one then."

"Do that." Then he hung up on me.

Men.

I WASN'T SURE HOW I DID IT, BUT WITHIN NINETY MINUTES I'D shopped, showered, and changed into the first skirt I'd owned since high school. It wasn't a very nice skirt, but I'd been pressed for time, and it didn't look bad when paired with a lacy tank top and my knee-high black boots. Too bad for Lucen, though, I was not going commando beneath it. The skirt flared in the wind a bit too much for that.

He showed up exactly at eight, part of his insistence that we do this thing properly. He wore a plum-colored button-down shirt tucked into a pair of black pants. It wasn't as much to my taste as his tight T-shirts and jeans, but it showed off his narrow waist and broad chest nicely.

"Anyone ever tell you, you clean up well?"

"Not if they want their jaws to continue working. Anyone ever tell you that you have legs?"

"You're well acquainted with my legs."

He grinned. "But the rest of the world is not. That needed to be remedied. You have so many lovely body parts. You should be sharing them with people more often."

I poked him in the chest. "We do not need to go down that road tonight. This is our date. Just us. Two."

"Fair enough." In a couple steps he'd rounded on me, pushing my back against the door. His lips found mine, then his tongue, pulling and taking insistently as I let him in.

I wrapped my arms around him. The warmth of his skin beneath his shirt seeped into mine, and my blood burned hotter. His cinnamon scent flooded my senses, driving away thoughts of anything but his body and the way his hard muscles moved beneath the thin layer of cloth.

I broke away from his mouth, hungry for air. "You always smell good enough to eat."

"Is that so?" He flattened me against the door again, retaking control of my lips. One hand snaked its way beneath my skirt. Fires ignited up my leg as his skin pressed against mine, and I remembered his little tease on the phone.

With his other hand, he tugged aside the low-cut collar of my blouse, slipping the strap down my arm. I held my breath but made no move to help him. I wasn't wearing a bra because the tank had one built in, and the fit was tight. Lucen's face was a mask of intensity as he struggled to free my breast, and I enjoyed watching him almost as much as I enjoyed the feel of his hand. When his fingers brushed my nipple through the material, I clenched down to my toes.

Lucen breathed my name, then the hand beneath my skirt stopped abruptly. "What's this?"

My body wailed as his grip on me loosened. I wanted to scream at him to keep going, but he'd like that too much. "That would be my thong."

"What happened to no underwear?"

"I never promised that. I didn't feel the need to flash my lady parts to all of Boston should there be strong breeze tonight. Besides, I know you know what to do with thongs."

His hand squeezed my butt, but he moved backward slowly. Heat and hardness vanished, leaving me burning but empty. "I'll rip them off."

"You'll owe me a new pair."

"I'm going to need to buy stock in a lingerie company because of you."

My body sagged with disappointment as he let go of me altogether. "Not my fault you can't behave around underwear."

"Your fault for being silly enough to keep wearing it around me. Now look at you, you're a mess." Lucen adjusted my shirt, taking care to rub my sensitive nipples as he did, then he pulled down my skirt. "How can we go out with you looking like you've been ravished?"

I squeezed his hands. "I haven't been. That's the problem. I thought I might be a bit more of a mess before we left."

"Don't be impatient, little siren. That was just an appetizer."

"Steph was right," I said, flinging his hands away. "You are evil."

"And your sexual tension feeds me better than anything we're going to eat tonight." He burrowed his face in the crook of my neck from behind, an arm locked around my stomach. "I can smell the lust on you."

I elbowed him in the gut. "If that's all you're going to do, then back off. So where are we going?" I grabbed a purse because the stupid skirt didn't have pockets.

"You'll see." And that was all he would say about it. We spent the drive discussing Dezzi's offer. Lucen reacted to it exactly as I'd expected, encouraging me to say yes. That allowed me to fine tune my case for why I shouldn't, although whether that served to convince Lucen or myself I wasn't sure.

Either way, I dropped the topic when Lucen pulled up in front of one of the North Shore's more famous seafood restaurants. "We're going here? Seriously?"

In response, Lucen threw a cheap disguise charm around his neck, and his horns winked out of view. While I gaped at him, a parking attendant opened my door for me. In a state of disbelief, I got out of the car. We'd left Boston proper for one of the outlying coastal towns, and the evening was heavy with the smell of the ocean. Even the air tasted salty.

A shudder of lust swept through the valet as Lucen handed over his key, and half dazed, the man got into the car. I hoped he didn't crash it.

"Seriously?" I asked again. Lucen seemed to make decent money, but the prices at this place had to put those at Vine to shame.

He took my arm and escorted me inside. "You think I have no class."

I made a noncommittal noise. It wasn't that so much as I didn't know enough about him to judge. But hey, that was partly what tonight was about. Probing Lucen for his life story. "When I said date, I imagined a burger-and-beer joint."

"When do I ever do things half-assed?" Lucen fell silent as the doormen ushered us inside. "Let's just the say the owner has a lusty little problem."

I groaned. "One of yours?"

"No, not one of mine, little siren, but it helps get us a table. It also helps that it's a Wednesday. I'm not sure anything would help if this were a Saturday."

The restaurant was small and dimly lit, but Lucen's connection meant we got one of the best tables the place had to offer. Tucked into a corner, I had a brick wall at my back and to my right, a large window that overlooked the water. Since it was rapidly getting dark outside, however, my best view was sitting across from me.

I kicked him lightly under the table. "For all your evil plans, you can't even reach my leg from there."

"No, pity. I should have scoped the place out ahead of time and found somewhere more suitable for mischief." He handed me the wine menu. "There'll be time enough for that later though."

"I expect so. For now, we get to talk for a change."

Lucen raised an eyebrow. "Because we don't usually do that?"

"Different talk."

"Different? Like we're going to speak in pig Latin?"

I picked up my napkin as if to throw it at him, but I worried that sort of behavior would get us kicked out. Lucen's laughter died away as our server came over.

After he left, my date adopted his serious face. "Okay, little siren. You obviously have something on your mind. What do you want to talk about?"

"Nothing in particular, but I feel like we don't talk about real things enough."

"Real things, unlike when we discussed who could have framed you for murder, or the ethical implications of you working for the Gryphons, or—"

"Yes." I leaned forward. "Real things, unlike whatever our current crisis is. We've known each other for ten years, and yet how much do we actually know about each other?"

Lucen was silent as our wine came, and we both quickly scanned the menu and ordered. Once our server disappeared a second time, he sipped his wine thoughtfully. "I know you are the most fascinating person I've ever met. That's been enough for me."

"Even now that you know what I am? I'm hardly so exciting anymore."

He shook his head. "It's true enough that I became interested in you because of your gift. It's the reason I contacted you that first time."

That first time had been the day the Gryphons had kicked me out of their pre-training program, the day of my eighteenth birthday when they lost all hope of my gift developing normally. Lucen hadn't merely contacted me. He'd followed me and kept me from doing something stupid in despair.

"My unhappiness was probably an all-you-can-eat buffet for you." I'd never had any delusions that he'd helped me out of kindness.

"I'm not a cruel person. Misery isn't exactly my favorite emotion, but you were full of it. But that's not it either, Jess. Just having a weird satyr-like gift interested me, but it's what you did with it that got my attention for good."

"You mean with the souls?" That was the night I'd taken up soul-swapping. I'd decided if my gift had gone evil, then I would use that power for good. Since that night, I'd made a lot of trades. Only when the Gryphons had started forcing me to work for them did I stop. All of Shadowtown knew about my new job, and therefore no one was inclined to trade with me anymore.

"Yes, that's what really made you interesting," Lucen said. "Your gift?

It was curious, but it's not something you can control. What you did with it was. It was clever and it was gutsy, and I knew then that you were someone to keep an eye on. Someone I'd better not mess with too, although that's exactly what made me want to mess with you."

"Really?" I sipped my wine, feeling those words wrap around my heart.

"Really, little siren. You're smart and reckless and sexy, and I've never met anyone quite like you, your gift aside. I wouldn't have chased you down for ten years if I didn't think you were worth it."

I could feel my body flushing. These were the most words Lucen had spoken at once to describe his emotions. "Show me, don't tell me," he'd once said. And he had shown me, time and time again, what I meant to him. But I hadn't realized how much I craved to hear it too. How hot words could make me feel. What a rush it was to hear this damn sexy, powerful satyr say these things to me. Lucen wasn't hitting me with his power, but my nerves were on fire, and all I could think about was that he'd teased me about my skirt. All I could imagine was his hand slipping between my thighs. I'd never wanted to throw myself at him so badly before.

"I always thought it was just my gift that interested you. You never said anything to make me think otherwise."

"I know that's what you thought, but you are amazing, so some things I expect you to figure out on your own. What's also amazing is how someone so smart can be so clueless too." He smirked, but any urge to kick him vanished as he kissed my hand.

The sensation of his lips seemed to travel up my arm and straight down to my groin. I squirmed in my seat. His gaze was molten, heavy and sticky, as he watched my chest rise and fall. Catching on, Lucen dragged his thumb slowly over my skin, and oh God. Little ripples of desire ran through me and pooled between my legs. I held my breath a moment, then took my hand back before I did something unseemly.

This was probably one of those reasons why we never talked except about essential topics. He would just say or do something irresistible, or touch me in the right place, and I was a goner. Satyr magic was hard enough to ignore without one trying to make you melt. If we weren't in public, I would have been all over him by now. Him sitting so close and so clothed was maddening. In fact, if he told me to, I'd start doing something obscene now and damn the consequences.

I want you now. Inside me. I didn't have to say it. He could sense it and was enjoying every second of it from the look on his face.

He bent over, his voice low and his breath on my face. "One day, Jess, I'm going to make you scream without even touching you. That's my life goal. To leave you writhing, begging for my touch, but be able to make you come with just a look or a word. To know you want me that bad, that our connection is that strong."

My heart pounded. I suspected he was closer to that goal than he might realize if my reaction tonight was any indication. Sitting still, not touching him was torture.

Lucen straightened with a smile. "So what else do you want to know about me that you don't already?"

I reached for my wineglass with an unsteady hand. "I want to know how you're planning to do that. Exactly how you're planning to do that."

"I don't think you want to have that conversation here. I'm too close to being successful." Lucen touched my hand again, proving the point as my eyes closed. "We've covered the basics. I'm obviously brilliant, which is why I'm on Dezzi's council. I make a damn good martini. And I like you on top so I can see you all the better when we fuck. So next?"

I choked on the overpriced wine. "You also know how to take a sweet and sexy moment and ruin it with your arrogance. Moving on then. You're always chiding me and saying things like 'if I ever bothered to know you better,' so that's what I'm trying to do."

"Interview me." He held open his arms.

I pretended to crack my knuckles, but I was still recovering from a serious case of horniness. "We'll start with your name."

"You know my name."

"I meant the name you were born with."

Lucen stared at me a moment, his fingers tracing the stem of the wineglass. "Why does that matter? It's not my name anymore."

"A name says a lot," I replied as our server brought over our dinners. My scallop concoction smelled wonderful, but food was far from my mind.

My tongue, like the rest of me, was hungry for other things. "A name gives a clue about a place or a time—your where and when."

Lucen assured the server we were fine. "Where and when I was born originally aren't important if you want to know more about me. You'd be better off asking, say, if I chose Lucen for my new name. That would be more telling of my personality."

"Did you?"

"No."

"Then why bring it up?"

"It was an example."

I rolled my eyes. "Fine. Then share the most telling thing about your personality with me—did you choose to become a satyr?"

Lucen refilled our glasses with the remains of the wine bottle. I had the sense he felt he needed the alcohol to deal with my questions, but I didn't understand why. Why poke fun at me for not knowing everything about him, then get defensive when I asked questions? He was lucky he had other good qualities that made up for him being so frustrating.

After he finished drinking, he went back to studying me. "Does that matter? It's all in the past. Any decision old me made is old."

"It's a very telling decision."

"Is it? Without knowing the circumstances surrounding it, your conclusions might be completely false."

"Well, if you told me the circumstances instead of telling me they don't matter..."

"But they don't. That me is dead. The decision would tell you nothing about me now."

I frowned, confusion turning to irritation. "It would tell a lot, I think. It would tell me whether you chose to prey on innocent people."

"This again? Jess." He sighed. "Better to be a predator than prey, don't you think?"

"So you did choose this?"

"Is that what I said? What I'm saying is—it doesn't matter. We're all predators, every single one of us." He pointed at my plate with his fork. "Something has to die in order for you to eat. At least as a so-called pred, nobody has to die to feed me. People even enjoy doing it. You were, just a couple minutes ago, if you'll recall."

I said nothing, but suddenly my scallops didn't smell so appealing. I pushed them around on my plate before deciding on more wine.

Lucen's hand landed on mine. "You hate what was done to you because you didn't have a choice. I get it. But don't keep hating yourself for what you are."

"That's not it." I wasn't sure what was it, but I didn't think I hated myself.

"Then don't hate me for what I am, or because I can't give you what you want. Whatever I decided or didn't decide, it was a long time before I met you. And if I could turn off being a satyr to make you happy, I would. But I can't stop needing to feed any more than you can."

I wrapped my fingers around his. "I believe you."

"Good." He gave my hand a squeeze. "Then can we go back to talking about happier things? I'll tell you my favorite movies and discuss politics, and we can make fun of the other diners, and I'll whisper the twenty different ways I intend to serve you up as dessert later."

"Do any involve whipped cream?"

"They do if you want them to, although I love the taste of your skin just the way it is."

I smiled, concentrating on his touch, letting it burn through the last of my annoyance. "Then tell me about that. Tell me more about this goal of yours."

"Happily." He released my hand, but before he could get out another word, my phone rang.

It was too loud to ignore, so I got it out, intending to shut it off, but I hesitated when I saw the caller ID. "Shit. It's Bridget."

I shouldn't have picked up. But like when you're about to do something stupid, such as touch a hot oven, I watched my finger swipe the screen and answer the call even as I willed it not to.

Date, interrupted. Since I'd gone ahead and done it, I put the phone to my ear. "Hi, Bridget."

"I hope I'm not interrupting you. I thought I'd leave a message if you were busy."

I mentally kicked myself. "It's fine. I've got a minute."

Across the table Lucen's expression silently contradicted my words. I mouthed *Sorry* for all the good it did.

"Good," Bridget said. "I wanted to give you a heads-up and let you know I need you in by ten tomorrow morning for a meeting. This case got bigger. There's lots to discuss."

"Bigger? What happened?"

Lucen looked up sharply.

"I don't have all the information yet, but Marshall does not appear to be our only victim. Not any longer. I just got back from meeting with another family who experienced the same thing you did on Sunday. We've got a goblin, or possibly goblins, going on the attack out there."

I swore and reached for my wine. "So this might not have anything to do with Eric trying to break his contract after all?"

"Too early to say, but it's definitely something we need to investigate. Hold on." In the background, I could hear someone talking to Bridget, but not their words. Then she was back. "We've got another call. Be here at ten tomorrow."

I didn't want to ask, yet I knew I should. "Do you need me now?"

Lucen dropped his fork with a clatter. Even if Bridget said yes, his face said no way in hell was he letting me go.

Luckily, Bridget declined. "No, we should handle this part. I'll fill you in tomorrow. I've got to go." Then she hung up.

So did I, and I stuck my phone away, feeling guiltier than before for leaving early, and helpless too. On one hand, another victim might provide another lead. On the other, it might distract the Gryphons from finding the goblin who'd ruined Eric. Especially if, as Bridget suggested, they were two different goblins.

I stabbed a scallop, also feeling guilty for not enjoying my expensive dinner as well as it deserved.

"What was that about?" Lucen asked.

"That case I've been helping out with." I chewed slowly, trying to remember how much I'd told Lucen about it. "It blew up."

"Blew up how?"

The scallop landed in my stomach like lead. "How much did I tell you?"

"That Steph's cousin was magically attacked. You were rather vague on the details."

"Right." Shoving my plate away, I gave Lucen a rundown of the specifics. "Bridget was calling because someone else got drained the same way. Maybe more than one someone. Something came up that caused her to hang up on me quickly."

I expected Lucen to shrug it off or tell me to leave it alone and let the goblins police themselves, but instead he stared thoughtfully at his empty wineglass. "Two people? That's odd, and yet I'd bet it's two different goblins. It's unlikely whoever did that to Steph's cousin could have used up his soul so quickly. Then again, it seems odd that Gunthra would have two goblins acting so strangely. And so nastily."

Lucen's voice was laced with disapproval, and it surprised me. "What do you mean by nastily?"

"Just that. I know you think all of us are cruel, horrible people—"

"I do not."

"Fine, most of us." I started to protest, but it was true enough, and I wanted him to get out his information so I let it go. "But this is not good. It's not the sort of behavior any decent person would approve of."

"Any decent pred, you mean?"

He frowned. Lucen hated being called a pred as much as any pred did, but it was an easy way to distinguish them from humans. Nonhuman was too broad a term because it could include the magi, as well. "Yes, any decent pred does not approve of creating ghouls for obvious reasons. And for sucking someone dry like that—the magic that would have to go in to storing that soul, it wouldn't be pretty."

"You're speaking in riddles to those of us uneducated in the ways of magic. From everything I've seen, magic is never pretty. What's so much worse about this?"

"Degrees of badness. I can't give you the specifics because I don't know myself exactly how you'd make a container to store that much power. I'm only basing this on what I've heard."

"And what you've heard is?"

Lucen ran his hands through his hair. "You know that to create a spell requires using ingredients that relate to the spell's purpose."

"Like how a love charm requires pieces of satyr?"

"Exactly. A charmed container, like the sort you'd need to store a human soul, would therefore require some human magic. And like how the soul would have to be taken by force, the spell ingredients would have to be too."

And spell ingredients were rarely pretty. They weren't things that would be easy to take by force or otherwise. "But something taken by force could be anything, maybe nothing more than snipping off a strand of a Gryphon's hair?" I doubted it, but I made the suggestion anyway for my own sake.

"Could be. Or it could require Gryphon blood. I don't know. I can just tell you, based on how magic works, that something like that must be involved. Chances are, this isn't the sort of spell that most people are going to be able to work on their own. It would be extremely tricky."

The scent of my remaining dinner was making me sick. I had to get out of this restaurant soon before the seafood aromas made me hurl. But Lucen had just given me an idea too. "If it's tricky and something most people couldn't do on their own, they'd have to buy it. Right?"

"I'd think, although this isn't the sort of thing your average charm maker is going to sell. Like I said, it's a nasty business in many ways. We're not all evil. A decent charm maker wouldn't sell such a thing because it has no good purpose."

Maybe, maybe not. One reason humans risked bargaining with preds for magic was because they wanted items that were illegal or simply too immoral for the magi to create. Usually that meant curses, but evil objects made from evilly obtained ingredients didn't sound all that different to me.

Lucen's eyes bore into me though, so I refrained from asking if he could think of any likely suspects. Odds were, he couldn't unless they were a satyr, and I'd get nowhere with him if that were the case. And if it were the case, Lucen would bring up the matter with Dezzi, and they'd talk to the satyr in question themselves. The only way I'd find out about it is if I were a member of Dezzi's council.

Which you could be. I pushed the thought away.

"I think I'm ready to go," I told Lucen.

"I hope this hasn't ruined your appetite for dessert, little siren."

"Honestly, I'm feeling a bit queasy at the moment, but maybe some fresh air and a car ride home will help."

"They'd better, or I'm going to have even more reasons to hate the Gryphons. They ruin dates too."

He was smiling, so I neglected to mention that it wasn't the Gryphons going around sucking people's souls dry. Then again, it wasn't a satyr either.

Probably.

Lucen was right—not all preds were the same, and it wasn't fair to hate him for what he was. I just wished he'd had been more forthcoming about what he was before he was a satyr.

FOURTEEN

"Three more," Bridget said the next day.

We were gathered in the meeting room. Besides Brian and Wes, seven other Gryphons spread out around the table. Two had been part of the group that went to Gunthra's with us. The other five were unfamiliar, and no one introduced me to them.

That was fine. The people here weren't important. The three Bridget had just mentioned however—that was a different story. Three more people turned into ghouls? In one night? Shit.

Bridget directed a laser pointer at the photos hanging on the wall. Eric's photo was there, along with more unfamiliar faces. "They all were drained within hours of each other." She named off the victims as well as their locations.

"And those might not be the only ones," Brian interjected. "We know about their attacks because other people were with them when it happened and called us. The police could have an epidemic of missing person reports coming in soon as addicts who were alone at the time of the attack never arrive home, or never show up to work, or what have you. We won't know for a while. We might never know."

One of the unfamiliar Gryphons cleared her throat. "Of the three we do know about, what about their masters? Any way to find out if it was the same goblin?"

Bridget took a sip from her tea before responding. "We're not that lucky. Their masters weren't even all goblins. We haven't figured out who Chen's master was yet, but O'Connor and Klees were vanity addicts." She circled the two photographs in the center with her laser.

Great. Vanity addicts—sylphs. I felt the collective groan of unhappiness that went around the table.

"The good news," Bridget continued, ignoring the muttering and swearing, "is that the sylphs involved were less devious than the goblins. They left us a paper trail. We have the contracts and we know who they are."

Brian pushed back his chair and stood. "Which means you're all going to pay them visits today. Agent Nelson will lead one group, Agent Riley will lead the second. Gear up and head out ASAP."

Someone flicked on the lights. Amid the squeaking chairs and jumble of voices, I snagged Bridget's attention. "You want me to go too?"

"Only if you want to be a part of it. It could be dangerous."

"I'm in."

"Good. Let's get you a weapon."

I rubbed my hands together with fake glee. "Oh, I knew there was a reason I wanted to go."

Not ten minutes later we were suited up and ready to leave. For me, that meant putting on my Gryphon jacket and taking the knife Bridget offered. For the others, it meant adding charms to their uniforms, as well as swords.

We left in four cars. Two for us and two for Riley's team. Dumped in the backseat of one of them, I sat on my hands to keep from fidgeting. All the nervous energy my companions were attempting to hide from each other was impossible to hide from me. The citrusy, minty flavor of fear and anxiety was irritating.

It was also seeping into me. I hadn't had any qualms about coming along when Bridget asked, but as we pulled out of the Gryphons' private lot, my mood shifted. I was fairly certain the sylphs hated me on general principle, yet they'd been keeping their distance because of what I'd done to the furies last month. But after this, they'd start hating me with good reasons and possibly stop with that distance-keeping business.

I knew it was a bad idea to choose an apartment above a sylph's barbershop.

With my luck, one of the sylphs we were after was the barber. I'd checked the two names on Bridget's list, but neither was familiar. My involvement in their arrests, though, would be recognized, and no doubt it would be spread throughout Shadowtown. I wondered what Dezzi would think of that.

We arrived at our destination as I mused. Bridget parked behind the other SUV, along a mostly residential side street. I took a good look around as I got out. Narrow row houses fronted by tiny yet tidy yards slept in the pre-noon sun. Not a tacky piece of lawn furniture could be found, nor an untended flowerbed or any untrimmed foliage. I'd say it was the result of the very appearance-conscious sylphs, but all of Shadowtown was like this. The only aspect that could possibly be attributed to the sylphs in particular was the bright paint on the shutters and trim. That alone wasn't enough to throw off the aura of darkness that pervaded Shadowtown and gave it its name, but it was more colorful than anything I was used to seeing.

Bridget pointed out the house in question, and silently as the street, we split into groups. Two Gryphons crept over the grass, blades drawn, heading for a back door. I tailed behind Bridget and the fourth Gryphon to the front one. Standing several feet down the path so I wouldn't get in the way, I searched the windows for any sign of movement. Not a drape fluttered nor a shadow moved.

Bridget knocked twice, two hard thwaps in the stillness. I circled in place, checking for hints of life in the vicinity. Dreadfully early though it was for a pred, someone had to be up and watching us. Even now, a sylph was likely to be on the phone, calling their Dom.

I'd spun all the way around as Bridget knocked again. When nothing happened, she gave a signal to the other Gryphon to force the door open. Swallowing, I removed my hands from my pockets in case I needed them.

He managed to get the door open quicker than I was anticipating, and the noise rattled me to my bones. Bridget and the Gryphon rushed inside the house. She had her sword drawn. He had a gun. I left my hand on the knife's hilt and followed a few seconds later, not expecting I'd need it.

Sure enough, I was right. Nobody was home. I heard the "all clear" signal being given as I entered. Lucen and the satyrs derided the sylphs as being the least intelligent pred race, but this one had the good sense to get the hell out of town after ripping off some poor addict's soul.

Of course, if the sylph had been more clever, he might have destroyed his addict's copy of their contract first so we couldn't have found him.

I meandered through a living room so tastefully decorated and bland it could have served for a catalog shoot. Back through a stainless-steel kitchen, Bridget had thrown open a set of sliding doors to a tiny patio. As she checked in with the other team, I climbed the stairs to a balcony-style bedroom and listened in to the conversations below me.

Up here there was evidence of hurried packing. Several drawers were partially open, and the bathroom had been cleaned out of the usual supplies like a toothbrush or shampoo.

"Nothing, damn." Bridget paced below me in the living room, talking to Riley on the phone. "Make a thorough search of the place. If there's any hint of where they got to, we need to find it."

She assigned us the same task, but a couple hours later, we emerged from the house with empty hands, no new leads and still four souls in need of recovery.

Even Bridget was cursing as we left. "Let's question Assym," she said as we got in the SUV. "I want to hear his excuses. Jess, you in?"

Assym was the sylph's Dom. He had white hair, a pointed nose, and a wicked stiletto that he'd once almost slit my throat with. Although he couldn't touch my soul anymore, I'd just as soon not be in the same room as him.

"Actually, I think I want to follow up on a conversation I had with a goblin the other day."

Bridget was pleased to hear I was working my Shadowtown "contacts," so I opted not to enlighten her any further about my plan. She offered to drop me off, and I gave her the address of my apartment building.

I leaned forward in the car so I could talk to her. "I didn't get a chance to mention it earlier, but I also had a conversation with a satyr last night that could be worth checking out. He was telling me about the containers that would be required for storing all that stolen power."

Bridget wasn't driving, so she twisted around in her seat. "What about them?"

"He thought the magic involved in creating them would be difficult, and the preds who are using them would probably need to buy them from a master charm maker."

"Good to know. We'll follow up on that. He didn't say who made them, did he?"

"No. He claimed not to know." I unfastened my seat belt as my building approached. "You can drop me off here."

I waited until the SUV disappeared down the street before heading up to my apartment. While I hadn't been lying to Bridget about my intentions, it was too early for the conversation I planned. Pounding on Gunthra's door while she was in bed wasn't likely to win me any favors.

After I dumped my Gryphon windbreaker, I took out the cheap thumb drive I'd bought yesterday and copied Tom's files onto it. Then I passed the time by hanging more decorations and planning my goblin attack.

By three, my apartment was starting to look like a home, but I was no closer to figuring out how to handle Gunthra. Since I'd gotten by with her before on my wits, that would have to be good enough. I pocketed the thumb drive, strapped Misery to my hip, and left.

Gunthra's servant seemed tempted to slam his mistress's door in my face when I showed up, but he let me in with his customary disdain when I explained the purpose for my visit.

"Are you like this with all visitors or just anyone who's not a goblin?"

I almost said "with anyone human," and I barely caught my error in time. I didn't like that. It suggested that I was starting to get comfortable thinking of myself as a nonhuman. Lucen might be happy, but I wasn't.

The goblin sniffed. "Rumor is you raided the houses of a couple sylphs this morning."

"Damn. Rumor travels fast, but those weren't raids. We were there to arrest those sylphs."

"The sylphs are our allies."

In my pocket, I wrapped my fingers around the thumb drive. "Your people and your allies are breaking legal contracts, making ghouls, and probably violating a hundred other laws I don't know about."

And when I thought about it like that, why was I turning this information over to Gunthra again? Ugh. Deals with preds were deals with the devil. In fact, if there was a devil, he was most likely a pred himself.

This time the goblin butler didn't bother to respond. He opened the doors into Gunthra's parlor and admitted me. "My lady will be with you shortly. You should have made an appointment."

"Give me her secretary's phone number and I will next time."

Given the displeasure on the goblin's face, I thought for sure he was reaching for a weapon to hit me with, but instead he pulled a business card out of his jacket pocket and thrust it at me. Well, then. Guess I'd been told.

Once he left, I slipped the card away because it really might be useful to call ahead.

Hoping Gunthra wouldn't keep me waiting forever, I wandered around the room, inspecting her impressive collection of porcelain vases, jade and glass boxes, and gaudy wall hangings of every style.

The doors opened as I came to the framed dead butterflies over her mantel, which meant Gunthra must have registered the shivers they gave me. "Still wishing you were a mere caterpillar, Miss Moore? Or have you come to terms with what you truly are?"

I swallowed down my memories of our conversation about the butterflies. "You mean an abomination?"

"Are you?"

"It's what you called me."

Gunthra sat in her favorite spot and gestured for me to follow suit. "It's what you are to me. It doesn't mean that's how you should view yourself. Should I see myself as a monster because that's what humans think I am?"

"It depends. Are you doing monstrous things like allowing your people to drain away more lives?"

Gunthra's self-satisfied smile faltered. "I told you. I'm looking into the matter."

"At a caterpillar's pace." I sat, removing the thumb drive from my pocket, and smiled back at her.

"I appreciate that you expect I alone am capable of fixing this unfortunate situation faster than you and that massive Gryphon organization can, but you give me too much credit. I am but one person."

"Oh, I don't think so. I think I'm crediting you just enough. You're not alone. You have a council at your disposal for help."

Gunthra had a couple books open on the table between us, and a drawing on one of the pages caught my eye. It was nothing special, just a pen-and-ink sketch of a bowl, but the books themselves reminded me of the book Tom had given me. Old and decaying. Although Gunthra's books appeared to be textbooks instead of a journal.

Still, everyone, it seemed, was doing research, and I wondered why.

Gunthra caught wind of my curiosity and shut the books. "You have the information you promised."

I set the thumb drive on the table slowly and deliberately, trying to catch either of the books' titles on their spines. All I managed to note were the words "history of." "This is everything I was able to get on the furies' behavior around the time of the Aubrey case. I read through it myself, and I have to admit, I have no idea why you're interested in this."

"Why I'm interested isn't your concern."

I seriously wondered about that, so I plundered on. "I'm sure, but there's nothing much there that you can't possibly already know."

That was a bit of a bluff. What Gunthra might know or not was nothing I could know. But if I kept babbling, I hoped to push her into talking and get her to explain what she wanted from these files. I didn't like handing them over in the first place, but I especially hated it when I didn't have a clue what her game was.

Gunthra set the thumb drive on top of her books and stacked the two volumes so that their spines faced away from me. "Perhaps you're not reading carefully enough, Miss Moore. Or perhaps you're not reading to discover the correct information."

"Or perhaps whatever you want isn't there. If that's the case, I'm not going back for more. I couldn't without you being more specific about what you want to find."

"Understood."

I took a deep breath. "Then our deal has been fulfilled."

Gunthra held out her hand. "Assuming what is on this drive is what I asked for, it is fulfilled."

"It is." As she should damn well be able to tell since she could sense if I were lying.

I gritted my teeth and shook her hand. Cold power brushed my skin and slithered up my wrist. Since I wasn't immune to the sheer blast of magic caused by a pred's touch, that brief contact was enough to stir up my need to learn more. My greed for knowledge.

What could possibly be in those files that she wanted so badly as to waste her debt with me on them? What damning secrets had I turned over?

Gunthra made a move to dismiss me, but I kept my butt planted on the sofa. "Is there more?" she asked.

"Actually, yeah. Are you aware that three more addicts had their souls sucked away? And those are only the ones we're aware of."

The Dom's eyes fluttered wide for a half second, then she regained her composure. "I was not, although I was aware of the commotion that you and your Gryphon allies created this morning. I assume the two events are connected, and since you went breaking into the homes of two sylphs, I also assume the addicts in question had nothing to do with me or my people."

Good deflection, I thought grudgingly. "Two of the addicts were connected to two sylphs. As of this morning, the third addict's master hasn't been identified. It could be another goblin, possibly the same one who drained Eric Marshall. If you—"

"If you had proof of that, Miss Moore, you'd either be telling me about it or the Gryphons would be dragging me downtown for one of their entertaining chats. So how does this concern me? I already told you I'm investigating what happened to Mr. Marshall."

"I'm starting to think we have an epidemic of magical attacks going on, all stemming from Shadowtown, and the first-known victim was a goblin's addict. That's how it concerns you, and frankly, that concerns me, as well."

To my surprise, Gunthra didn't counter immediately. Her long, slender fingers grazed the hems of her sleeves. She appeared to be considering things, but what? At last she stood, and there was no question that she wished me gone.

"People are on edge, Miss Moore. And when people are on edge, they do questionable things. It's as true of humans as it is of goblins or sylphs. Or satyrs," she added after a heavy pause.

I stood too, because I disliked the Dom staring down at me. "And because they're on edge they're attacking their own addicts?"

As I said it, I realized that didn't make sense. Preds needed their addicts. So why would they attack them? Answer: they wouldn't. They *weren't*. Our theory that Eric's master had drained him in revenge had been shot to hell last night.

My jaw fell open as I put it together. "They're on a bender, aren't they? They're nervous, so they want to feed."

Referring to humans as food bugged me, but from a pred's perspective, that was exactly what they were—an emotional banquet. That left me with another question. Were the preds stealing and gorging on their stolen emotions like a type of anxiety eating, or were they stealing them and hoarding the power because the cause of their anxiety was something big. Like apocalyptically so. Were the preds acting like humans who stocked their survival shelters for the end of the world?

Gunthra didn't deny it, and her large brown eyes flickered to the books on the table. Or maybe not to the books at all. To the thumb drive.

I wet my lips. "This has something to do with why you want that information on the furies, doesn't it?"

She must have realized she'd given something away because her back straightened and she walked stiffly toward the door. "Our deal has been fulfilled, Miss Moore. If you want to make another deal for additional information, we can discuss terms at a later date. I have a busy day ahead of me."

Yeah, I bet. Going through that thumb drive. "Fine, but I want those souls back and those people's lives restored before it's too late. If you know anything, I will be back and with reinforcements. This isn't over."

"No, I very much fear it's not." Then she shut the door on me.

Bitch.

FIFTEEN

THE ADDICT SUPPORT GROUP MET IN A DRAB, WHITE FUNCTION room near Mass General's sprawling complex. A patient liaison pointed me in the right direction with a pitying expression. I wanted to explain that it wasn't nice to openly pity pred addicts—or any addicts—but I held my tongue.

About twenty people were mingling in the room when I arrived. Most hung out in groups of four or five, drinking coffee in paper cups and talking about last night's TV shows or their families. They were a diverse bunch—men and women, old and young. I counted addicts of every affliction, but only one rage addict. That itself could be interesting given that something might be up with the furies, or it could simply be that rage addicts needed more intensive interventions than a support group. Having met a couple, that was easy to believe.

But the most interesting part at all was that when I closed my eyes, they disappeared. I could hear them, but emotionally they were dead to me. Addicts could only feed their masters, so this wasn't a surprise, nor something I hadn't encountered before. Yet I'd never been around so many addicts at once. It was like losing one of my senses.

As I clung to the doorway, acclimating to their lack of presence, one of the men approached me. He held out a hand. "Hey, first time here? I'm Justin. Welcome to the group."

I took the hand warily. "Jess, and yes."

Was this the time to explain that I wasn't an addict, or would that make people uncomfortable? Would it be better to lie? Unlike me, these people couldn't tell if I was or wasn't. I'd asked Bridget for advice, but she'd had none. In retrospect, I should have asked someone like Andre. My ex-partner was a people person. Bridget was no more of that than I was.

Justin had been talking, but I'd been paying more attention to my thoughts, so I smiled politely and tried to catch up. He was in his early fifties if I had to guess, dressed in dusty jeans and a dustier jean jacket. A lust addict, smelling faintly of cigarette smoke. I wondered if I knew his master.

"So what's your sin?"

"Sorry?"

"Your sin. You know, which demon's got your soul by the balls?"

Soul by the balls? I gave up trying to form a mental image to make that figure of speech work. "You could say I've had my troubles with a lot of preds."

"Ah, I'm sorry to hear it." He clasped my hands in his, and the clunky ring on his left hand hit my knuckle painfully. "Well, we come together here to support each other. Sometimes that means sharing information on magic or what's happening in Shadowtown. Sometimes it means helping each other deal with family issues that arise because of our conditions. Other times it's helping each other cope in general, or hell, sometimes we just sit back and shoot the shit. I'm sort of the informal leader around here. Why don't you grab a cup of coffee and I'll introduce you to people? First names only. We want everything confidential, or barring that, anonymous. Get me?"

"Got you," I said, taking my hands back.

If this guy was in charge, then he was the one I should talk to, and I got the sense from him that honesty would be my best policy. Just as well. Laying everything out upfront was more my style than sneakiness. "I'd better explain. I'm not an addict, but I have a friend who is. Or was, I should say. I don't want to be here under false pretenses or make anyone uncomfortable, but I am looking for help for that friend. I'm not a Gryphon, but I work with them as a consultant. If it's okay, I'd like a few minutes to speak to the group about what's happening. I think this would fall under news about Shadowtown."

Justin scratched his chin. "I see. Well, I don't know how well we can help with anything—"

"The friend I'm talking about used to attend these meetings. His name is Eric."

Recognition brightened Justin's green eyes. "I know who you mean, yeah. Something happened to him?"

"To him and to others. Addicts are being attacked." I didn't like that I might need to repeat myself before the whole group, but if Justin was in charge, I had to impress on him why I was here.

"Jesus." He refilled his coffee cup from the carafe. "You talking like those murders the other month?"

I grimaced. *You mean the ones I was framed for?* Dragon shit on toast. I hoped he didn't recognize me. My face had been plastered on TV a couple times in the aftermath, and I did not feel like answering questions.

"Not quite like that. Worse in some ways because everyone is at risk this time."

"All right, Jesus. You don't mind speaking first and then leaving?" Justin glanced over his shoulder. "So we can talk about other stuff with just the group?"

"That's fine. I don't need to take up your whole meeting."

Justin spoke to me a bit longer, pressing for information on the attacks, until I explained it made more sense for me to talk to everyone at once. After that, he called the group together.

Metal folding chairs had been laid out in a rough circle in the middle of the room, and everyone grabbed one. I took a seat next to Justin and scanned people's hands. I had no guarantee that the mysterious Shawna was an addict or that she attended these meetings, but it struck me as a good possibility. And if Eric left these meetings with her to go to Vine, they must be cozy. She was my best bet for finding the goblin's name, assuming no one else here knew it.

"Tall and thin," the waitress at Vine had said of Shawna. With rings on every finger. That one detail was precious and narrowed down my search to a single candidate who sat directly across from me. Her height was difficult to judge while seated, but she was—as promised—model thin with long brown hair, and each of her fingers were covered in silver rings.

Perfect. I only had to hope she had useful information.

As people got settled, Justin welcomed everyone then introduced me. "Jess is friends with Eric, who I see isn't here tonight, and she might know something about that. She also has some news from the Gryphons that we should hear."

I couldn't sense a trace of surprise from the group, and it was weirding me out to be so lost among so many humans. To hide my awkward fidgeting, I folded my hands together. Twenty-plus pairs of alarmed eyes focused on me.

I thanked Justin and explained yet again what had happened to Eric, reminding everyone that they might have heard parts of the story in the news. "What the news hasn't gotten around to reporting is that there were three more similar attacks. Any information you can provide on the pred who addicted Eric would be extremely useful. As of now, we believe everyone could be in danger. The sooner we find the culprits, the better for all."

That was probably exactly the sort of thing Bridget hadn't wanted me to say. After all, she'd sent me because she thought sending a Gryphon would freak these people out. But screw that. If I were an addict, I'd want the truth. And as someone trying to bring down the goblin, I wanted to provide incentive for people to give me information.

"Do you know which kind of preds are doing this?" a woman with graying hair asked.

The man two seats down from her crushed his coffee cup. "What kind of problem did Eric have? That would tell."

Several others grumbled or jumped in with guesses. I kept an eye on Shawna before answering, waiting to see if she would volunteer information. Her head was bent and hair shrouded her face, but her fingers played with her rings.

She knew something, or maybe she was just upset. Without being able to read her, I was helpless. Body language was one of those things I'd stopped paying as much attention to over the last ten years. What was the point when I could sense how most people felt?

"There have been multiple types of addicts attacked so far," I said, cutting off the various debates. "Goblins and sylphs have been implicated, but there might be others involved."

A couple people groaned.

I answered a few more questions. No, there wasn't any known pattern with regard to the victims. This wasn't like Victor Aubrey's murders in which he'd targeted a certain type of woman vanity addict. And no, so far the Gryphons had no theories about motive.

Before I left, I wrote my name and phone number on one of the tablets I found by the coffeepot. "If anyone has information they'd rather share anonymously, here's where you can find me. I'm especially interested in talking to Shawna if she's here."

The woman I thought was Shawna hadn't said a damn thing. Maybe she'd do it over the phone.

I thanked Justin again and left, frustrated. Between the travel to get here and back, and talking to people without learning anything, this had been a colossal waste of almost two hours. It wasn't just two of my hours gone either. It was two hours slipping out of Eric's hourglass of unknown duration. Bridget had set a minimum of five days. Tonight marked day four. I did not want to be there in person when I told Steph our leads were turning into dead ends.

Halfway to the exit, a door down the hall opened and heels clacked on the linoleum. I thought nothing of it, then a woman's voice called out to me.

Keeping my hope in check, I turned around. "Shawna?"

"Yeah. Hi." She pulled her long hair off her neck, twisting it into a facsimile of a ponytail. She had a good several inches on me, willowy and delicate, and she dressed to show off her lithe frame. Her shirt merely grazed the waist of her low-cut jeans, and the jeans themselves could have been painted on. No wonder Jenny described her as looking like a model. "You said you wanted to talk to me?"

"You're friends with Eric, right?" I asked.

Shawna continued wrapping her hair around her hand. "Sort of. We've spent some time together, but I wouldn't say I knew him well. Did he mention me? Is that how you knew my name?"

Vanity addict. She'd like to hear that Eric had been talking about her. Yet even if I lied and said yes, it wouldn't make her feel all that great. The sylph Shawna answered to had seen to that. Just as I couldn't sense her emotions because of her addict bond, Shawna's ego couldn't be appeased by anyone except her master.

So I hedged. She might be more likely to say something useful if she thought herself important. "Sort of. I wanted to talk to you because it seemed like, of all the people at these meetings, Eric was closest to you. I was hoping he might have mentioned the name of the goblin who addicted him."

Shawna's face fell. "I wish I could help, but I can't. We talked about other things, you know? Our careers and art and, you know, fun stuff. We tried to leave the heavy topics at the meeting."

"Did he ever mention anything about the goblin at all?"

"No. We weren't really supposed to talk about them. It's part of the group rules to help people chill. I knew he was a goblin's addict, but that's it. This is so upsetting, you know. He was such a great guy and so talented."

Shit. I studied Shawna carefully. The way she played with her hair was like the way she'd played with her rings. It could simply be a quirk, or it could be a nervous tic. My gut told me she knew more than she was sharing, but there could be a hundred reasons for that. Without being able to read her emotions, I was out of luck.

"Okay, well, thanks for that. But it's really important, so I'd appreciate if you would continue to think on it. If Eric ever said anything that could point us in the right direction, it would be a help. Not just for him, but for you. Two sylphs' addicts were attacked. You could be in more danger than most people."

That did seem to register with her because she let go of her hair and wrapped her arms around herself. "I will. Do you want to give me your information again?"

Shawna handed me a piece of scrap paper from her purse, and I rewrote my name and number. "Thanks, and be careful."

Maybe that wasn't a total waste of time, I told myself as I left. But I didn't easily believe it.

Deflated, I stopped by The Lair on the way home to see Lucen, but the place was more crowded than usual for a Thursday. He gave me a heart-stoppingly hot kiss behind the bar, and that improved my mood significantly until he let go of me and I saw one of his addicts staring at us.

Mood. Killed. I left and told him I'd see him tomorrow.

Since it had been a long day, I made dinner, had a glass of wine, and typed up my notes from my conversations with Gunthra and Shawna so I could share them tomorrow with Bridget. Then I treated myself to more of Eric's latest book and went to bed late because I couldn't stop reading.

When my phone rang at six thirty the next morning, I was prepared to curse Bridget for calling, but it wasn't her voice I heard. It was Lucen's.

"Check the news," he told me before I could finish with hello. "Buenos Aires is the new Boston. This is bad."

I threw off my blanket. "Why are you awake? What are you talking about?"

"I'm talking about war. Check the news, little siren, and you'll figure it out. Then can you be here at eleven? Dezzi's calling a council meeting."

SIXTEEN

I STARTED THE COFFEEPOT, AND WHILE THE WATER BOILED, I dragged my laptop to my bed. Rubbing my sleepy eyes, I brought up the news.

By the time the page finished loading, I was awake and alert. It was impossible not to be. The coffee water boiled, but I made no move to get it, too engrossed and horrified by the photos and the story I was reading.

The city was a war zone. Like Boston and most major metropolitan areas, Buenos Aires was home to a sizable pred population. And last night, relations between the various pred groups had turned violent. Very violent. None of the stories suggested what had spawned the fighting, but it was clear that race had turned on race. Addicts had been dragged in, naturally, and the fighting had spread from the pred-dominated areas to the city itself. Curse grenades had taken out buildings, and salamander fires had destroyed entire blocks.

The number of missing or dead humans caught in the middle was not pretty, and it was likely to keep on rising. Although the worst of the fighting seemed to have died down by morning, salamanders remained on the loose, as well as other magical nasties, and violence continued to flare up. Fury addicts ran wild, attacking anyone and everyone they encountered, "like they were dosed up on some sort of magic steroid," in the words of one Buenos Aires-based Gryphon.

Unfortunately, that was all too possible.

Buenos Aires had its own Gryphon office that was working to control the damage, but it wasn't enough. Nearby offices were flying in reinforcements to deal with the salamanders and more. Vaguely, I wondered how this would affect our office, and I checked my email but found nothing. I was sure the local Gryphons were as freaked out about this as Lucen, but unlike the satyrs, they were leaving me out of it.

Surely that was a sign of who trusted me more?

To hell with it though. What happened in Buenos Aires was all too much like what could have happened in Boston last month. But that was all the more reason why I should focus on the situation at hand, and not on who was more interested in buying my loyalty.

APPARENTLY, I WAS THE ONLY PERSON THINKING THAT WAY. When I got to The Lair, Dezzi was already there, clutching a gigantic, steaming mug of tea and looking surprisingly alert for someone who should have been dead asleep at this time of day. Lucen had the coffee maker going, and a cup was put in front of me without me asking. It was just the three of us, although I was ten minutes late.

"I thought there was a council meeting." Sensing a trap, I held the coffee cup like a shield.

"They are coming." Dezzi checked the clock. "Soon. We have a lot to discuss. I want you to be a part of those discussions, but for me to bring you to a council meeting, you must be part of the council. I asked you to come early so I might get your decision and fill you in on your responsibilities."

My decision and my responsibilities. Because naturally I'd say yes. If I were a normal satyr, I supposed I would.

Never had I been normal. "I haven't made a decision."

Lucen hid his disappointment by turning his back on me while he moved tables around, but Dezzi closed her eyes in a long-suffering sort of way.

She inhaled deeply of the steam from her tea. I hoped it soothed her. "What I'm offering you is an honor."

"I'm conscious of that, and I do appreciate it." And I needed to tread carefully here so I stayed on her good side. "But under the circumstances, I don't think I can make the best decision. There's a lot I don't understand about how or why the Gryphons—"

"Really, Jess?" Lucen slammed a chair into the table. "About why they fucked you up when you were a kid? Why they took your choice from you? How they lied to you? Why do you care?"

Because Olef told me cities were going to burn in salamander fire and I'd be in the middle of them.

Dragon shit on toast, I did not want to think about Olef's visions coming to pass. Not now. And yet, how could I ignore those visions when another city had burned?

"I need to know," I told Lucen. "I need closure. I thought knowing what was done to me would give me that, but this is nothing like what I thought had been done. The people who did this had reasons. Seriously fucked-up ones, but reasons."

Lucen grabbed the chair he'd pushed around and sat. His eyes glowed that fierce blue-green they got when he was angry, a sure sign he was throwing off a lot of power, and it made me long for him more than I usually did.

Heat crept over me as my gaze traveled down the curve of his biceps from where they left his sleeves, to his strong forearms wrapped around the chairback. A slim patch of skin showed through the rip in the knee of his jeans, and I wanted to wiggle my finger through it. I wanted to...

Okay, suddenly I was having a hard time concentrating on my screwed-up origins or Buenos Aires or anything else important for that matter, and I took a long drink of coffee.

Lucen locked eyes with me over the mug, and now I could feel him touching me. His hands squeezing my hips. His tongue parting my lips.

Stop it! My command reasserted my willpower, and the sensation vanished.

Across the room, Lucen flinched but continued to glare heatedly at me. "Fucked-up reasons are not good reasons for hanging around with the people who, by your own admission, ruined your life. Let go of your past."

"Like you did?"

"Exactly. You're angry they didn't give you a choice. So now you can make the choice to tell them to fuck off. What's the problem?"

"The problem is..." I snapped my mouth shut as I put it together—not my problem, but his. "This isn't a choice between you and the Gryphons. Whether I say no now or later to being on Dezzi's council has nothing to do with you. I'm not choosing Team Human over Team Lucen. For now, I'm choosing Team Jess, and Jess has questions she wants answers to before she decides anything. But I'm not leaving you for a Gryphon."

"You're impossible. You get something in your head and you can't let go."

Dezzi set down her tea with a laugh, and I remembered Lucen and I weren't alone. "You mean she is like you then."

"I am nowhere near as stubborn as she is." His smoldering intensity was gone. He sounded like a chastised teenager.

Dezzi clucked her tongue. "No, you only followed her around for ten years until you got her. You deserve each other."

When Dezzi acted like that, it was hard to tell her no about the council. She might be the only one here with her head on straight. I nursed my coffee to hide my amusement, and my phone chose that moment to ring.

It was Bridget, so I let it go to voicemail. I should go into the office though. I didn't need her to tell me that. Buenos Aires aside, we had business to discuss.

Afraid of meeting Lucen's eyes, I turned to Dezzi. "When you were protecting me from the sylphs, I sat in on council meetings. I could do that again, couldn't I?"

She shook her head. "That was an exception because you were the reason for those meetings. We needed your information. Buenos Aires doesn't concern you."

Hopefully not, but Olef wouldn't be so sure.

I shivered as though untouched by my mug's warmth. "I need to go to work then. I'm still trying to retrieve Eric Marshall's soul, and the sooner that's done, the sooner I can tell the Gryphons to fuck off, as someone suggested to me."

Dezzi waved her hand. "Leave then. It's all right, Jessica. I need you to be fully committed to us and the council should you choose to join. If you can't be that, then it is no good. Take more time, but not too much more."

Lucen said nothing, but he followed me outside and grabbed my arm on the patio. I started to ask what he wanted, but he pulled me close before I could form the words and kissed me.

The last traces of my annoyance faded as I sank into him, wrapping my arms around his waist. His hands slipped under my hair, and his palm warmed the back of my neck. Gentle but possessive, he pressed me closer.

I'm not losing you, his body seemed to say.

I'm not leaving, I tried to respond back.

I couldn't tell if his brain understood me, but his body did. His breaths quickened with mine, and I could feel his arousal growing. My hands slid under his waistband, searching for bare skin, until I remembered we were outside on one of the main roads running through Shadowtown.

Breathing hard, I pulled away, but instead of letting me go, Lucen pushed me back into one of the patio tables, spreading my legs apart with his own. His lips found mine again, insistent. "You can't leave yet. We haven't finished the best part of a fight."

"Not here."

"It's okay," came a familiar voice. "We don't mind."

Swearing, I pushed Lucen away and snapped my head to the right. Coming down the steps to the patio was Devon with two other satyrs from Dezzi's council. He smirked at me.

I felt my cheeks turn bright red. "I'm off to work."

Lucen must have known better than to protest. The other satyrs moved aside so I could climb up to street level, but Devon stayed where he was so I had to push by his laughing face as I left.

Jerk, I thought as I hurried to the T station, although I didn't really mean it.

Lucen used to do that sort of thing with me. He'd stand in my way to try to make me touch him. From any other guy, it might have been a dick move, but Lucen had known I wanted to touch him and wasn't about to give in to the urge. Also, Lucen had known me well enough to realize that if I hadn't been willing to put up with his nonsense, I'd have kneed him in the balls and kept right on walking.

By now, Devon must know me well enough to understand that too. So what did it suggest that he was imitating Lucen's tricks? And maybe more to the point, what did it suggest that I hadn't made Devon pay for his presumption?

Ugh. I didn't have time to dwell on this crap. I had to concentrate on Buenos Aires.

GRYPHON HEADQUARTERS BUZZED WITH SERIOUS ANXIETY, and it didn't take a genius to guess why. Outwardly, all seemed the same, but the strong spearmint of everyone's unrest had hit me before I entered the building. Inside, it was worse.

It didn't do good things for my nerves. Jittery from all that unfocused energy I couldn't block, I stomped to my desk, my hands rubbing my arms like I could brush off the tension.

What I found in my inbox didn't make me feel any better. Olivia Lee had sent me an email. *Come see me when you get in.*

That didn't sound promising.

At last I checked Bridget's message and returned it with one to let her know I'd arrived. Then I took a deep breath and went to see what the good director wanted of me.

Olivia Lee's secretary buzzed me right in this time, and I entered her enormous office prepared for the worst. I discovered her standing over a cardboard box on her desk. "I don't suppose I'm lucky enough that you're giving me the box so I can clear out my things and be escorted from the building?"

"Funny." She didn't look amused. "Even if I wanted to hand you a proverbial pink slip, Jessica, it seems it's out of my hands. Other people in the organization want to keep you around. Why is that?"

Wasn't this interesting. While everyone else in the building was one giant stomachache of nerves over what was happening in Buenos Aires, Olivia barely registered anxiety. She was more like a blowtorch of suppressed wrath, and I was clearly in her line of fire.

"I don't mind pissing people off. It can be fun. But I don't like being the target of people's rage unless I did something to deserve it. You want to know why? I'm not the one you should be asking. Take it up with Tom Kassin, and if you want to punch him for it, I've got your back."

My answer surprised her, which frankly surprised me. After all, she knew he was the reason I'd stormed out of the building not that long ago. "I was under the impression you and Kassin were getting along these days."

"I don't know what could have given you that idea."

Olivia pulled a piece of paper from the box and handed it to me. "This is a good start."

Confused, I took it and read.

JESSICA,

The events in BA necessitated my immediate return to France, but I still expect to meet with you when I return from World. In the meantime, please read these books and keep this information to yourself. I trust you'll follow these instructions and know what to make of the information. I'll be in touch as soon as I return. I'm depending on you.

-Tom

TRUST I'D DO WHAT HE'D TELL ME, DID HE? DEPENDING ON ME, was he? This note reeked of manipulation. He wanted me to feel important, to return his trust in me with trust in him, and buy into more of whatever messed-up bullshit his fraternity was spewing for justifying why they had screwed me over.

And yet you're there, Jess. I could hear Lucen's voice in my head. *You're at Gryphon headquarters, and you haven't told Tom to fuck off.*

My hand clenched, crumpling the note. When I looked up, Olivia's dark eyes were demanding answers.

Too bad I only had questions. "If he left this crap for me, how did you get it?" And just what sort of crap was it?

I peered into the box. Tom had given me three more books. Peachy.

Although I wasn't watching Olivia's face, I could sense her frustration and discomfort. "I'm the director of this office. I deserve to know what's going on around here. I'm not a landlord leasing office space to you and Kassin."

I tossed the note on top of the books. "Look, I'm not the one cutting you out of the loop. I don't know half of what's going on myself, or why, and I'd tell you everything, but I don't trust that Tom wouldn't cut out my tongue if I did. His group has done far worse to me already."

"What do you mean far worse?"

I sighed. Although I'd threatened to go public with everything I'd learned about *Le Confrérie*, I didn't feel like sharing all with Olivia when she was venting her anger on me. "Let's just say I didn't get my freaky powers by some accident of birth."

Olivia pressed her lips thin. "No, I wouldn't think so." She fell silent a moment, pacing in front of the plaque hanging behind her desk.

For the Gifted Have a Duty to Protect Mankind.

I wanted to spray-paint a corollary beneath the motto: *Except When the Gifted Decide to Screw Them Over Instead.*

Olivia's anger was mellowing into more of the same generalized anxiety that plagued the rest of the building. "He's been meeting with the magi a lot."

"Tom?"

"Tom." She quit her pacing and rested her hands on the back of her desk chair. "Did you know about that?"

I shook my head. "Which magi?"

"Xander, and whoever Xander has brought to the meetings."

Olef, I wondered? Olef and his visions concerning me? Shit. If Tom knew about that...

Oh, who was I kidding? I'd already made the connection between the so-called prophecies in Tom's book and the visions Olef had described. Why should I think Tom wouldn't know about it too? Better to assume that I'd be the last to know anything. It was more likely the case.

I sucked on my lip, irritated by Tom's note, irritated by the way Olivia watched me, and irritated that I'd ever met Olef. If he hadn't frequented the diner where I used to work, he'd never have been able to identify me in his visions.

I was done here. "Tom wanted to meet with me this past week, but we never found the time. I came back here to help with the Eric Marshall case. Not because Tom Kassin and his secret society have some hang-up about me. I'd just like to be able to do something for Eric's family."

"Fine. Go. I have real work to do." Olivia sat down, sounding cross.

I picked up the box. "Great, and don't worry. I won't mention to Tom that you went through the box of top-secret books he left for me."

She scowled at me as I left. I didn't turn around to see it, but I could feel the burn on my back and taste her annoyance.

SEVENTEEN

"Jess?" Bridget had to say my name twice before it dawned on me that she was speaking.

I snapped upright and blinked. "Um, yeah. Sorry."

We were supposed to be discussing our next moves on Eric's case, but despite what I'd told Olivia a couple hours ago, my head wasn't into it. I wanted to help, truly. But all I could think about was Tom's books and what Olivia had told me about his meetings with the magi. Couple my own anxiety with the anxiety that coursed through the building, all feeding into my nerves, and I was wired and irritable.

And utterly, hopelessly distracted.

I put my pen to my notepaper, but I had no clue what Bridget had said. My brain had given up on the conversation after I'd shared my adventures with Gunthra and Shawna yesterday.

"Go home," Bridget said.

"What? No. I'm here to help."

"Jess, your body is here, but your thoughts are with that box Agent Kassin gave you. It's obvious, and since he's the highest-ranking Gryphon around, you should attend to what he needs. You've been a big help on this case, but we can handle the next steps without you."

I dug the pen tip into the paper in frustration, but Bridget had a point.

I wasn't helping anyone at the moment. "You're sure? It's just I can pick up on all the anxiety around here, and it makes it hard to concentrate."

"I'm positive." Bridget took my pen away before I hurt anything. "Go home. I'll call you when we need you. If you want to help, and get the chance, keep asking questions around Shadowtown."

"Right, okay." I felt crappy about cutting out, but I wasn't doing any good here. That was for certain.

Taking Tom's box with me, I left. If I couldn't dedicate my day to finding Eric's goblin, I'd dedicate it to reading Tom's books. I didn't like that he'd probably think his BS flattery had nudged me to it, but against my will, I'd grown curious. And what happened in Buenos Aires wasn't BS. Cities were burning like Olef had said they would. I still wasn't willing to forgive and forget what the Brotherhood had done to me, but if there was the slightest connection between Tom's crap and Olef's legit visions, I needed to know.

Without all the anxiety at HQ screwing with my head, I was focused. Ready. So it just figured that as I entered my building, my plans were upended.

Because my attention had been on Tom's books, I hadn't noticed the shadows lurking behind the apartment building door until one of them clasped a hand over my mouth.

In surprise and fear, I dropped the box. Even as I did, my brain identified the cold insecurity caused by the creature's touch. A sylph. Fuck. I should have seen this coming after the attempted arrests yesterday.

I struggled, slamming a heel down on the asshole's foot and about to wedge an elbow into his gut when a second sylph emerged from the dim alcove beneath the steps. He was on me in a flash of silver hair. His knife shone dully in the low lighting.

"I wouldn't," he said, holding the blade to my throat.

I might have risked it if I had Misery on me, but alas, my knife was in my apartment.

Mental note: If I survived this, use Tom to get me special permission to carry my own weapon into the Gryphon building.

While I thought of useless ideas for the future, the sylph behind me wrapped his free arm around my torso, pinning my arms down, and now a second knife was poised to stab me in the gut if I moved badly.

The first sylph with the knife kicked my box aside. "Upstairs. Assym wants a chat with you."

Who else? Slowly, I was recognizing the sylph's face. He was one of Assym's thugs.

Awkwardly, the three of us made it up the stairs. The sylph who was holding me grunted with each step, and I felt the cool knife blade through my thin shirt with every movement. Guns would have worked better, I wanted to tell them, but I also didn't want to give them ideas.

Assym waited for us, pacing on the landing outside my door. Impatience and cold fury were written all over his flawless face. "It's about time."

"You said not to damage her unless necessary," the sylph holding me said. "She fights."

Unless necessary, huh? Did that mean Assym still thought he could addict me one day? How much could I get away with before he declared that hurting me was necessary?

Assym must have read my thoughts or gotten the gist through my emotions. "I can cause you quite a bit of damage without ruining you permanently, satyr's pet. I just want your soul intact. I don't care if your body has scars."

Oh hey, satyr's pet. There was a blast from the past. I hadn't missed being called that.

I ignored Assym's bodily threat because I was intrigued by the one to my soul. So Assym didn't know what I was or what I could do. I'd really thought the news would have traveled by now, but maybe Dezzi had commanded Lucen and Devon to keep their mouths shut. It was easy enough to believe that anyone who'd overheard their joking about my council initiation at The Lair wouldn't have taken them seriously. But the question, then, was why? Why didn't Dezzi want this to spread?

Because you're a freak, Jess. An abomination. Dezzi only wants you on her council so she can control you, but even that won't save you. One day, Assym will have you just like he's promised.

That was the sylph's magic talking, reminding me that I wasn't immune to pred power when they touched me.

I squirmed, and the knife blade at my gut sent me its own gentle reminder—that this was the wrong time to be contemplating Dezzi and the satyrs.

Unfortunately, I couldn't speak because the sylph still had a hand over my mouth.

Assym turned his icy glare on me. "I can't decide whether you were very brave or very stupid to move into our neighborhood. Did you think your friends in the satyrs would continue to protect you?"

Actually, Assym, you have no idea what my friends in the satyrs might do for me. But since I couldn't speak, any witty one-liners that came to mind had to be silent. That pissed me off. Trading barbs with Assym was the only fun he provided.

Assym resumed pacing the length of the tiny landing. At his sides, his hands opened and closed, and his fingers twitched. Nervous. The silver-haired asshole was nervous. "You'll leave off this investigation with the Gryphons if you know what's good for you."

He motioned to the sylph who was holding me, and the thug removed his hand from my face. Finally, I could breathe again. The sylph kept the knife on me, but I didn't even care about that as I gulped down the musty air.

"Do you understand?" Assym asked. "Quit the investigation if you want to live here unscathed."

"Then your people need to quit attacking their own addicts."

To my amazement, he laughed once, sharply. "You have your priorities all wrong, satyr's pet."

"What does that mean? My priorities are protecting humans from your pathetic goons."

"I will deal with my people. The Gryphons need to stay out of it, and if I find out you haven't, next time we meet we'll see how much you can bleed without dying." Assym flicked his wrist a second time, and the thug released me completely. With a shove, I went flying into my door.

As I got up, the sylphs disappeared down the stairs. I cursed and pounded my fist into the wall.

After I caught my breath, I pulled myself together and retrieved Tom's box. Assym and his thugs were gone, but that was little consolation. There was no way I could sit here and calmly read about the end of the world. I was shaken and needed company. Steph would be at work for another two hours, so I headed to one of the few places in Shadowtown where I felt relatively safe.

THE LAIR WOULD BE BUSY TONIGHT, BUT IT WAS TOO EARLY YET for Friday's crowd to form. I slumped on my favorite stool with my head on my arms while I waited for Lucen to finish his conversation. He came up behind me and rubbed my shoulders, and I let out a contented sigh. Sometimes sex had nothing on a good massage.

Luckily, Lucen excelled at both.

His breath tickled my ear when he spoke. "Little siren, if something wasn't bothering you so much, I'd remind you that you owe me some make-up sex."

"I think *you* owe *me*. You were the one being unreasonable."

"Whichever. So long as this ends with your naked body curled around mine, I'm happy."

I closed my eyes. "Yup, just keep rubbing my shoulders a bit longer first? I've had a weird day, and that doesn't count waking up to your phone call."

"I can guess. You're tense, and as I said, something's bothering you."

"Assym ambushed me in my building. I spent some quality time with one of his sylphs holding a knife at my gut."

The rubbing stopped abruptly. Damn it. "What? Are you okay?"

Groaning, I straightened and pressed a hand to Lucen's clenched jaw. "Yeah, but he's gone, so calm down. I'll tell you all about it."

"Damn right, you will. Then I'm gathering some friends and dealing with him. I'm sick of the sylphs and their shit."

"You know what?" I grabbed his hands before he could get away. "You're not. Because we don't need to start a pred-on-pred war here too. Let Buenos Aires hog the newsfeeds for a little while. Okay?"

That actually seemed to cool Lucen's temper. He still looked ready to punch someone, but his shoulders slumped. "Yeah, true enough. Let's talk."

I took a quiet corner table, and he brought over a coffee with a shot of Baileys in it for me and a beer for himself. "How do you do it? Is it your magic? You drink and eat whatever you want, and you're still sporting those abs."

"You mean these?" He grinned, lifting his shirt so I could admire them. "We've been over this. I'm amazing."

I poked him in the amazing with my nail. "Show off."

"It would be a sin to hide them." He slipped into the booth across from me, and his expression turned serious. "Nice distraction, by the way, but what about Assym?"

There wasn't much story to tell, but I shared everything. "I think he was nervous. So what is it—Buenos Aires? The Gryphons are freaked out over that. Dezzi called a council meeting about it. Is *everyone* losing their shit?"

Lucen contemplated his beer. Three drops of condensation snaked down the glass before he responded. "I'm not sure it's Buenos Aires that's tying up Assym's knickers. It probably hasn't helped any more than it's helped ease our concerns, but..."

I let two more drops of condensation fall before I pressed. "But what?"

"I shouldn't be sharing Shadowtown gossip with you since you haven't agreed to be on the council." His smile was thin but mischievous.

"Uh-huh. But you know you're going to so get it over with. The longer it takes, the longer until that sex happens."

Lucen kissed my hand. "Very persuasive. Fine. Something spawned that fighting in Buenos Aires. The question is who arranged the something."

I raised an eyebrow. "You know things I don't? Why are you more interested in the *who* than in the *what*?"

"Because the who might be more important. Remember when we discussed whether the furies were trying to start fights here?"

I drank heavily of my coffee, wishing I'd asked for something stronger in it. "That was a theory, yes. So the idea is that the furies tried to start trouble here, and when that failed, they tried in Buenos Aires?"

"It's possible. Framing you for those murders, implicating the magi—it could have boiled over into something nasty real fast. It's kind of a miracle that it didn't. Conditions in Buenos Aires could have been riper for success."

"But why?"

Lucen yawned. "That's what no one knows, and until we know that, this is all idle speculation. But something seems to be up. Raj left town two weeks ago."

"Raj is the fury's Dom, right?" I'd met him once, and that was enough. His appearance—never mind his personality—could alone explain why people had once called preds "demons." He was a walking nightmare among the nightmares. "What does him leaving town suggest?"

Lucen laughed, this time without humor. "That's the thing—no one knows. But it's very strange for a Dom to leave their domus. Unheard of, more accurately. If Dezzi had important business that had to be taken care of elsewhere, she'd send Devon. That's a lieutenant's job. For Raj to go off on his own and leave his lieutenant in charge? Damned if I know what would require that."

"I'm guessing something that couldn't be handled with a phone call or video chat?" I was trying to be flip to lighten my own tension, but it didn't work, and the expression Lucen shot me was less than amused.

Right. What sort of business had to be handled in person? Anything politically fraught was one possibility. The other involved magic.

"Are we talking high council kinds of business?" I didn't have much of a clue about pred hierarchy, but Lucen had explained that each race had a council they answered to and that made the decisions that were then passed down to each domus. It was part of how they policed and governed themselves.

"Possible. Even so, it would be unusual for Raj to leave. Anyway." He yawned a second time. Last night's lack of sleep must have been catching up to him. "Everyone's been on edge since what happened with the furies last month, and Raj's vanishing act only upped the tension. It's going to make people act more and more unhinged. Lucrezia was a prime example."

I bit my lip, remembering Dezzi's former number two. She had never spoken of the specifics around me, but Lucen was right that she'd been jumpy about something. It was purportedly why she'd tried to overthrow Dezzi. She'd claimed Dezzi wasn't doing enough to protect people.

"Everyone's twitchy, and that's why the goblins and sylphs are draining their addicts," I muttered.

"That might explain it. Have you gotten any closer to finding the ones responsible?"

I frowned into my coffee. "No, and time is running out. It's been five days. Not to mention that I now have Assym's death threat hanging over me if I don't quit."

"One day I will strangle Assym with his own flowing tresses. But I can't object to his notion. You should quit."

"Don't start."

"And moreover, you should join the council." He grinned at me. "It's the ultimate protection from Assym. He'll lose his half-baked mind when he hears about it."

I smiled. "That's true. It might be the biggest inducement yet."

A shadow fell over our table as someone approached, and then Devon dropped into the booth next to me. Uncomfortably aware of his body, I shifted over until I hit the wall, leaving myself trapped.

Devon's cool blue eyes seemed to laugh at the distance I'd tried to put between us. "Do I smell bad?"

Nope. You smell like cloves, and I don't like that I can smell it and what it does to me.

Being backed into a corner by him and Lucen made me feel way too much like I used to feel in the presence of any satyr. Dangerously aroused, like I might say or do something I'd regret later.

"I enjoy having my space," I said.

"Since when?" He raised an eyebrow, and I could tell from his smirk that he was thinking of that time at Purgatory when I attempted to tear off his clothes. Which, of course, now I couldn't stop thinking about either. "I'm trying not to be offended, but it hurts."

I pulled my knees in so my legs were between us. The position caused Misery's sheath to dig into my thigh, but I'd live. "Then you're not trying hard enough."

"If you moved closer, you could help me get hard enough."

Flipping him off was easier than thinking of a good retort, so that's what I did.

As expected, Lucen was stifling a laugh. "Go easy on her. She was assaulted by Assym. She might be a bit, uh, touchy."

"Seriously? I had a knife at my throat recently, and you're both making bad puns?" I banged my head against the wall. "That thing I said about sex? Forget it."

Lucen pouted, but Devon's face turned serious. "Assym put a knife to you? Why?"

"Does it matter? I've noticed you haven't asked if I was okay. Your lack of concern is sweet."

"Really, Jess. I can tell that you're fine. There was no need to ask." He glanced at Lucen. "Why was she attacked?"

"Assym wants her to quit working for the Gryphons." Lucen gave me a pointed look. "It's the only intelligent idea he's ever had."

My phone buzzed with a text, so I ignored him to check it.

"Intelligent for him," Devon was saying. "Not for us. Dezzi's right that Jess should continue working for them."

"Can we not talk about me like I'm not here? I mean, I was here first." I pointed to Devon. "You interrupted our conversation."

Devon's expression was an annoying blend of pity and laughter. "Normally I'd apologize for that, but since you're being so rude, I don't feel the need. Lucen and I have council business to discuss."

Lucen made a sour face.

I turned my attention to my phone, deciding it was less likely to give me a smart-ass response and therefore more deserving of my brain.

Miss Moore, this is Gunthra. Please come by ASAP.

What in the world? And how the hell did she get my cell number?

Both were good questions, but the best part of the Dom's request was that it got me out of here with my dignity intact. "Move," I told Devon.

"Leaving already?" he asked.

Putting my phone back in my pocket was too difficult while trapped in the booth, so I poked Devon in the arm with it. "Move. I have to leave, and you can discuss your council business without me."

"Jess?" Lucen asked. "What's up?"

Devon finally moved his ass so I could climb out. "Gunthra wants to see me immediately. It must be about the case. I'll be back later."

"We're going to be really busy here later."

Alas, that was true, but there was nothing I could do about it. "Looks like you're plenty busy now with your council business. We'll figure something out. I need to see what she wants. Sorry."

"I wasn't going to make her leave," I heard Devon say as I left. "I think she's avoiding me."

I picked up my pace, not wanting to know what Lucen would say to that.

EIGHTEEN

THE DOOR OPENED BEFORE I COULD KNOCK. CLEARLY, I WAS
expected. Gunthra's butler ushered me inside, but his large eyes took a
long look at my knife.

There was no way I was removing it. After my run-in with Assym, it
wasn't leaving my side.

Perhaps my mood conveyed this, or perhaps Gunthra's business with
me was too urgent to debate it. The goblin simply opened the parlor door.

In I went. I was starting to become way too well acquainted with
Gunthra's digs. "You beckoned?"

"Sit, please." She had the tea set out again. Scones today, not muffins. I
supposed it was about that time of the afternoon, but I was tired of being
polite and eating her food and drinking her tea when I didn't want it.

Gunthra had nothing to lord over me anymore. No secrets, no deals. I
sat but refused her offer to drink. "What information do you have about
the attacks?"

"About the attacks?" Gunthra raised an eyebrow and calmly sipped her
tea. "I have been making inquiries, yes. But that's not why I invited you
over here. Please, Miss Moore. Try a scone at the least. I realize you don't
enjoy tea."

My fingers curled into fists, so I sat on my hands. "I'm not hungry, but thanks. What is this visit about then? Does it have to with what Assym said to me?" Dragon shit on toast. I should have guessed that first. Why would Gunthra change her mind and help me find the culprit of the attacks? That would be stupid.

But for the second time, it appeared I was wrong. "Assym? What did he do this time?"

The way she said "this time" reminded me of a parent despairing over a no-good child. I almost laughed, but instead I tucked that information away. The goblins and the sylphs tended to stick together, but apparently relations weren't all that cozy at the moment.

"He threatened me, at knife point, to back off the case. Funnily enough, it struck me as a demand you might be wanting to second."

Gunthra spread her hands open on her lap. Was she pointing out that she held no weapons, or saying she was helpless to control Assym. Technically, both were true. "I don't follow Assym's lead. Quit, don't quit. It doesn't make much difference to me. But if you do quit the Gryphons, I would appreciate if you'd wait a touch longer. I have use of you there."

"You and everyone else, but sorry. Our deal is done. You said so yourself, and don't try claiming that I didn't give you exactly what you asked for yesterday. I did."

Gunthra bristled and waved her hands in front of her face in a very goblin-like gesture. "A goblin doesn't lie, Miss Moore. I have no intention of making any such claim. That deal is done, as you say. I asked you here because I'd like to make a new one."

Gunthra ought to be happy I wasn't drinking her tea. I'd likely have dropped the cup. "That's going to depend on what you want from me."

"It's not what you're thinking."

"I wasn't aware that you read minds as well as emotions."

Gunthra set her tea down, her smile forced. "You're adamant that you won't turn over any new case files or anything that might be considered sensitive. I don't need to be a mind reader to understand that."

I shrugged in acknowledgment. "Fair enough. So what do you want?"

"The Gryphons have an extensive library and access to information that's not generally available to the public. They are also meticulous record-keepers, one has to assume. I'm working on a bit of a history project. You saw the books I was reading yesterday. But there are other documents that might contain the information I need, and I can't find them at any public or university library."

For someone who usually liked to come straight to the point, Gunthra was taking her sweet time. In the past, she'd done that in order to hook me, to feed my need to know whatever she was holding back. In this case, however, I got the sense that she was trying to do the opposite. She wanted to convince me there was no nefarious purpose to her curiosity.

Just a history project, my ass.

"So you think the Gryphons have a book that you want. Forget it. I'm not stealing books out of their library even if I could."

Gunthra sighed. "It's not a book, Miss Moore. It's information that I want. It might be contained in a book or in many books. It might not be found in book-form at all, but rather in records or other archived materials."

"Information on what?"

She clasped her hands together. "Objects referred to as the Vessels of Making."

I thought on the words for a moment, but I'd never heard of them. Gunthra had piqued my curiosity, after all, but not in a good way. This was probably some seriously evil magic. Otherwise why couldn't she find what she wanted at a normal library? "What are—?"

"They're historical artifacts, nothing else. More legend than history, but there are fascinating tales surrounding them. As I explained, it's a history project of mine."

I sat back, crossing my legs. "A history project is never just a history project. As you're so fond of saying, knowledge is power. So excuse me if I don't believe your interest is benign."

"Believe what you want, but you'll make the deal with me."

"I will? You're going to hand over to me the goblin who stole Eric Marshall's soul?" That was the only way I could see myself doing this, but so far Gunthra hadn't even admitted that she knew who it was.

I waited her out.

Gunthra's ears flattened, and she paled ever so slightly. "Yes. I'm prepared to do that once you've told me what you could learn."

I locked my lips shut, but my heart beat faster. Damn it, damn it, damn it. Any second, Gunthra was going to wise up to what she'd said. Tipped off by my racing emotions.

She was desperate. It was the only explanation. Desperate enough to make this deal. Desperate enough not to even make it well. "What you could learn." So vague, such poor wording. If she'd done this right, she'd have said "what I need to know" or words to that effect. Then she could have strung me on forever.

Gunthra was losing her shit. Like Assym. Like Lucrezia. Like the nameless goblin who'd attacked Eric. And whatever these Vessels were had to be part of it. That was why Gunthra was interested. Possibly, this even had something to do with what she'd hoped to find in the files about the furies.

So to hell with what Gunthra wanted to know. I should probably be researching these Vessels for my own sake.

"Agreed. Deal. But." I held out my hand and raised one finger. "Time is running out for Eric's soul. I can't wait a week or longer. I have access to the Gryphon library on the weekend. I will do whatever research I can between now and Sunday evening, and I'll start immediately. However, I will likely have to wait for books or records to be sent from other locations. You'll need to take my word that I will pass on whatever I find out when I get them. But anything I learn by Sunday evening, I'll share. Consider it a deposit. I want Eric's goblin then."

Gunthra's folded hands clenched, tendons popping to the surface in her frustration. "Fine. You've demonstrated you will keep your word."

Damn. Well, that was also unexpected. I shook quickly before she changed her mind.

"One more thing." I snatched my hand back and tried to discreetly rub off the unsettling sensation Gunthra left on my palm. "Assym is giving me shit about working for the Gryphons. It would make my life and fulfilling my end of this deal easier if you could talk to him and tell him to back off."

Gunthra closed her eyes. "Assym and I are not friends."

"No, but you're the closest thing each other has to an ally in

Shadowtown. If he fillets me, I can't get you the information you're requesting."

The Dom chuckled. "Assym won't kill you, and you know it. He wants your soul and thinks he can have it eventually. If he makes a play for it, you've shown yourself quite capable of making him regret it."

"True, but he's pointed out that he can try for my soul if pieces of me are missing. I don't want pieces of me to go missing."

"Not my problem, but understandable. This time, I will talk to him and encourage him to focus his energy elsewhere. Just don't expect me to have much success. I can no more control him than he can control his own people, it would seem."

I paused at her door. "It was a goblin who began the string of addict attacks. One could say the lack of control started here."

Gunthra's ears were so flat against her head that she appeared to have none. With my parting shot, I exited before she could retaliate.

This time, I hoped she was the one calling me a bitch as I did.

I CHECKED THE TIME WHEN I GOT HOME, TRYING TO FIGURE out how to proceed. I'd given myself a tight deadline to get this research done, but what choice did I have? Sure, Bridget and I might be able to crack Eric's case another way, but it might also be too late by the time we did. Gunthra's desperation could be Eric's lucky break.

As for me, though, it meant a long weekend poring over dusty books. I couldn't do a half-assed job and expect Gunthra would turn over her information. She could sniff out a lie from me as easily as I could from your average human. If she asked the right questions, which I would if I were her, I'd be busted if I hadn't made a legit attempt.

My stomach rumbled as I kicked off my sneakers. Hauling my ass to the library might need to wait a bit longer. Although Gunthra's scones hadn't done it for me, it was getting close to dinnertime. Reluctantly, I wandered into the kitchen to cook something.

Times like this, I missed living with Lucen. I could cook, I didn't even mind cooking, but he was so much better at it. Besides, cooking was a lot more enjoyable with and for two people. When it was just me? I hated bothering. It seemed like a waste of effort.

I didn't have much food in the apartment either. Shopping had not been high on my priorities list. I dug out the bread, some tuna and cheese, and congratulated myself on going through the effort to actually make a melt instead of a regular sandwich. Look out, Julia Child.

As I ate, it dawned on me that I'd be better off if I went to headquarters late tonight. Since I had no good reason to be searching for information on these Vessels, the fewer people who saw me and asked questions, the better. On a Friday evening, it shouldn't be too crowded unless something big went down. And as far as I knew, the biggest thing going down locally was the case I'd been working on.

I made good use of the next few hours. I updated Steph, made a grocery list so I didn't have to keep eating tuna, and frowned a lot at the new books Tom had left me. I randomly opened a couple on the off chance that they, by some miraculous coincidence, contained information on these Vessels Gunthra was interested in, but I didn't find anything. Without a clue where to start looking, they were fairly useless. Gunthra had given me shit to go on, but at least experience had taught me that the Gryphons kept a well-organized library system that was connected across all offices and linked to their central archives in France.

I was going to need it.

When eight o'clock rolled around, I figured it was late enough to head downtown. Naturally, that was when someone knocked on my door.

I froze with a hand on my sneaker, and my heart skipped a beat. I couldn't sense anyone outside, nor did I have a reason to. This was Shadowtown. Whoever was there wouldn't be human. So who was it?

Lucen would be busy at The Lair, and he'd have texted me before randomly stopping over. Dezzi never dropped in anywhere unannounced, and she had no reason to visit anyway. Devon then? But that didn't make sense. He also had to work Fridays. Purgatory would be every bit as busy as The Lair. And as for Gunthra, I'd seen her a few hours ago. Besides, she always expected me to go to her.

That left only one person I could think of—Assym again, or someone he'd sent. Shit.

I backed away from the door and grabbed my knife from the bedroom where I'd left it when I got home. The old floor creaked under my feet, and I cringed with each breath.

The person at the door knocked again. "Jess, are you there?"

I stopped stupidly several feet away. That female voice was familiar, but I couldn't place it. The best I could say was that nothing about it set off any alarms in my head.

Nonetheless, I opened the door with my knife poised to strike.

On the landing stood a beautiful satyr with long dark waves and pouty lips. She was dressed head to toe in black leather, and the black satin scarf tied above her nose was as seductive as it was practical for concealing her empty eye sockets.

Beneath the scarf, her blood-red lips parted, and she beamed at me. "Don't be scared, silly. I'm here to make you happy."

NINETEEN

LETTING OUT A BREATH, I LOWERED MY KNIFE. "ANGELIA, HI."

"Hi yourself. I hope you weren't planning on staying home all night. I want to take you out." Oblivious to the knife I held, she offered me her hand.

Behind Angelia stood two beefy satyrs, also dressed in black, who weren't so oblivious. They kept a sharp eye on the blade. I tucked it behind my back, contemplating how weird this was.

The seductress before me was basically the satyrs' very own drug kingpin. Or make that queenpin. Angelia made and dealt—through her network of addicts—a drug called F. If you imagined an aphrodisiac on crack, you got the idea. F wasn't exactly harmful unless you considered losing your pants and possibly your dignity dangerous, but like any drug, it had the potential to be greatly misused and abused. Some called it the ultimate date-rape drug because one dose in an unsuspecting person's drink could turn a demure nun into a sex fiend.

I didn't precisely have a problem with F. So long as it was taken by consenting adults, it wasn't much different than being blasted by a satyr's power. Plus, it offered zero risk of turning someone into an addict—magical or mundane. But the one time I'd met Angelia had been when I'd suspected her of making a tainted batch that was killing people. She'd convinced me of her innocence—I still wasn't sure how—but I wouldn't have called us friends. I barely knew her.

So yeah, this was weird.

"Um." I took Angelia's hand and led her into my apartment. "I appreciate the offer, but I'm kind of busy."

"On a Friday night? That's not good. Lucen said you might be shaken up after what happened with the sylphs, and since he's busy working, I thought I'd drag you away from home and take you to Purgatory with me."

Purgatory. That explained her attire. That one time we'd met, Angelia had looked like an angel, but the angel could apparently go vamp quite easily. Her scarf was the only part of her outfit that was unchanged.

Silky and suggestive, the scarf hid the fact that Angelia had lost her eyes in a vicious attack. To add insult to violence, she'd been branded as imperfect because of that and kicked out of her old domus. Dezzi had taken her in. It was one of the reasons I liked Dezzi, and I guess I held a bit of a grudging admiration for Angelia too. In spite of what had been done to her, she seemed to have a gentle spirit.

"Surely you can spare a few hours to do something fun?" She drew a soft finger over my hand.

The hyacinth scent of her pheromones temporarily overpowered me, and I caught myself contemplating her full lips and the swell of her breasts that were so close to popping out of her leather bustier.

Like I didn't have enough problems with male satyrs and their damn magic. I did not need one more working her mojo on me, no matter how attractive she was.

Angelia giggled, obviously sensing the desire she aroused. "Come on, Jess. I want to take you up to the VIP room with me and kiss you in front of all the humans. They'll go wild. Just think about what a head rush that would give you."

I pulled my hand away, and the wave of lust receded. Thank dragons she wasn't another Devon. "I don't think it's a good idea."

"No, it's a great idea." She grinned wickedly.

Lucen would think so too. He'd probably ask to watch.

"I really do have work."

Angelia's perfectly red lips fell. "You can't put it off for a few hours?

When's the last time you went dancing? Oh, and I want to tell you about what I've been doing with the F."

"Okay, that's definitely something you shouldn't tell me. I'm working with the Gryphons."

Angelia dismissed the Gryphons by blowing hair out of her face. "This is good. You'll like this. I told you how I was fiddling with the spell to make it so it can't be used to assault anyone? I'm making progress."

"That is good."

"Very good. Come on, your drinks will be on me. Literally, if you like."

I rolled my eyes, a gesture that was lost on her, but her mood was contagious. I could take off for a couple hours to do something fun, couldn't I? I wouldn't stay out late, and I'd hit the library first thing tomorrow morning. I was tired anyway since Lucen had woken me up so early. I wouldn't be as productive tonight.

I was full of excuses.

"You are a master pusher, aren't you? Definite drug queenpin."

Angelia tossed her head back and laughed, but her stoic bodyguards didn't so much as flinch. The contrast between them made *me* laugh.

"Put on something hot," she called after me as I went into my bedroom to change.

"Anything I wear will look frumpy next to you."

"Nonsense. That's my appeal. I bring out the best in everyone."

THE TRUTH OF ANGELIA'S WORDS MIGHT HAVE BEEN debatable, but I sure felt frumpy next to her. All satyrs gave off a kind of glow, for lack of a better explanation, that could draw heads. Even the less attractive ones. Like their magical healing abilities, however, or their need to feed from addicts, that kind of magnetism was not included with my particular brand of satyr subspecies. I gave off more of the stay-away vibe than the come-hither sort.

To cover up their more obvious satyr traits, Angelia and her bodyguards wore charms to disguise their horns. I simply wore my leather pants and a lacy, red, midriff-baring tank top that didn't see enough use these days since I no longer went clubbing.

At Purgatory, my outfit was tame. The line stretching around the building was a shifting mass of black, including large quantities of vinyl, fishnet, and spandex. Most of the color people sported was in their hair or tattoos, the latter of which could be viewed easily. Fridays went by the moniker of "Fetish Fridays," and in addition to the spectacle I was certain to find inside, many people chose to see just how little cloth they could get away with wearing.

With Angelia, getting in was simple. We passed the rope and entered the club in record time. Before I could fully take in the chaos or let my ears adjust to the music, I was ushered to the second floor and tucked into the VIP room.

This was one of the few areas of the club that I'd never seen before. Some sort of red and silver lights covered the walls in sensual patterns, and the chair I sat on felt more like real leather than the vinyl downstairs. The music was quieter too, thankfully.

A waitress came over to take our drink orders, and I settled against the soft cushions. "So this is how the other half parties, huh?"

Angelia laughed. "How is it that you've never been back here when you're friends with Devon?"

"Calling Devon and I friends might be more than is deserved."

She pooh-poohed that thought, and our drinks arrived. On the waitress's heels came two lust addicts. Both were young women, which meant both were probably Angelia's dealers for the evening. I pulled out my phone so I could pretend to ignore their conversation and the F changing hands.

Yet Angelia wouldn't let me ignore her business completely. When the women disappeared, she filled me in on what she'd been doing with the F, and although I should have been thinking about turning her in for all of this, I couldn't do it. That was what made Angelia so alluring—she cared. Or so she made me believe.

Angelia claimed that she didn't want her drugs to be used to force people to do things against their will. If she ever was busted, there was a good chance the satyr who took her place wouldn't bother with these safeguards. So Angelia got a pass from me.

One way or another, Dezzi was pulling me to her side. Arresting Angelia would be a huge score for the Gryphons, but I wouldn't be the one to turn her in. And Angelia knew it, or she wouldn't have invited me along.

"This was Dezzi's idea." I set down my Jack and Coke, realization dawning. "Dezzi suggested you hang out with me so I'd start feeling more like one of the gang."

Angelia rested her head against the chairback. Her brown hair fanned out around her, and she looked sweet in spite of her outfit. "No, Dezzi didn't tell me anything. I wanted to get to know you better. You have a reputation—the girl who traded souls, the woman who beat the furies, the human who's stolen satyr hearts. You think that's normal? You're fascinating. A legend."

"A legend? What's this about hearts, plural?"

Angelia sucked on a fingernail. "I said nothing."

"That's the problem. This *is* Dezzi's doing, isn't it? Admit it."

"No." She slapped my arm. For someone who couldn't see, she had excellent aim.

I swished my drink around to stir up the whiskey that settled to the bottom. "Lucen then." When Angelia didn't deny it immediately, I slammed back the remains of my cocktail. "Damn his manipulative, scheming ass."

"Don't be too hard on him. It's a nice ass." She grinned into her wineglass, sensing my confusion. "I can't see it, but I've grabbed it."

I choked on my ice.

That made her laugh some more, and she pulled me closer. "I'm not getting into your relationship issues, but I do—as a friend—have some advice."

Warily, I spit out the remains of the ice cube. Angelia had offered me advice before, namely that I should trust Lucen. "Uh-huh. Advice, and that is?"

Her head swiveled, taking in the room. I wondered if she was listening to voices or otherwise sensing the other occupants by their emotions.

Although disguised satyrs worked the bar, most of the occupants were human.

"Your left," she said at last. "The bartender with the golden skin and black hair. The one with tattoos on her arms. See her?"

"Yeah?"

"Her name is Nora. She's a sweetheart and very talented with her tongue piercing, or so I hear. Take her for a spin. You'll have fun."

I needed another drink and motioned for the waitress. "Right. Fun."

Fuck Lucen. This was his real plan, wasn't it? It wasn't about me hanging out with Angelia, becoming friends with her so I'd join the damn council. It was about me hanging out with Angelia so she could help cure me of my monogamy.

"Not your type?" Angelia asked.

I rested my head on my knees. "Sorry, but my type is not the kind of person who's into screwing random people."

Our waitress brought us over another round, and Angelia smiled prettily at her. The waitress was human and definitely Angelia's type, from what I'd observed of her addicts.

"Nora's not random. I'm vouching for her. She's a good person. You'll like her, and she'll treat you right."

I raised my head long enough to drink deeply. "I appreciate that your job is supposed to be to help me select partners, and I do want to make my relationship with Lucen work, but I'm not sure this is the way. Nora's hot, I'll give you that, and I'm glad to hear she's nice, but I need more. I can't just fuck people like that. It's not me. I don't work that way."

Angelia made a thoughtful noise as she sipped her wine. "Have you tried?"

"No!"

"Then how do you know you won't like it? I'm only asking because we are satyrs. We have that effect on people."

I laughed ruefully to hear her fling my own words back at me. "That's beside the point. Maybe I'm being a brat, but I don't want to try. I told Lucen I would, but I don't want to do it."

I expected a scolding or something like it, but Angelia fell silent. "A lot of humans are like that," she said at last. "They need that emotional connection. Lucen said you're one of us, but you're also very different in a lot of ways. You're much more human."

"Yeah, I am. As far as my relationship with Lucen is concerned, I might as well be completely human."

Angelia reached over and squeezed my wrist. "Even among humans, there are a lot of types of relationships. If you can't separate sex from love, then maybe you need to find the right sort of balance is all."

Her words swelled with hope. She wanted us to be happy. Angelia wanted everyone to be happy. It made me wonder how she treated her addicts.

"What I need to find is a way to..." I chased down that thought with a drink.

What I needed was a magical cure that would stop Lucen from needing addicts. He could stay a satyr, but he could feed off me only. Or better yet, off no one.

And that made me wonder... If he hoarded a lot of energy the way Eric's soul-sucking goblin had, could he last a long time without feeding? And if he didn't need to feed himself, would that mean he didn't need to feed his addicts with sex as well?

But that was an awful thought. That would require turning an addict into a ghoul, and from what Lucen had suggested, the containers to store such magic were also nasty. Bad Jess for contemplating any of this.

"What you need is what?" Angelia asked.

I shook my head, watching the carbonation in my drink, trying to shake away the evil, selfish idea like I could shake the bubbles right out of my soda.

"What she needs," Devon said, "is to come with me."

Startled, I shook my glass too hard, and a spray of carbonation landed on my chin. Peachy. Given my conversation with Angelia, Devon was so not the person I wanted to see right now.

TWENTY

DEVON STARED DOWN AT ME WITH A DEVIOUS SMILE ON HIS face. He also had a charm hiding his horns, and he was far better dressed than anyone else in the vicinity—black pants and shirt, black tie, black jacket. Expensive-looking. It was what I'd come to identify as his typical work clothes.

"What did I do this time? I've been sitting with Angelia, not breaking and entering." Every time I'd come to Purgatory in the last month, I'd gotten in trouble with Devon for doing something I wasn't supposed to. Just this once I was innocent. I did not need a lecture.

Devon rubbed his chin. "Guilty conscience? Who said you did anything wrong? I'm sure we can come up with something to punish you, though, if that's what you're into."

"Funny."

"Yet you're not laughing. Tough audience." He held out a hand. "Come."

I made no move to get up, hating that he could sense the way my stomach twisted. "Why?"

He sighed. "Because you've been avoiding me, and I want to talk."

"I haven't been avoiding you." That was a lie, which he could tell. I should have weasel-worded my response more cleverly.

Devon's smirk broadened, confirming it. "Then you should have no problem talking with me."

"I don't mind," Angelia said, so helpfully.

Of course not. She, Devon, and Lucen were probably all in this together.

"Fine." I hurriedly finished my drink, expecting Devon would insist on going to his office, but instead of moving toward the elevator, he led me around a corner.

We landed in an alcove off the very back of the VIP area, one almost impossible to see from the lounge proper. A gap in the wall provided a window onto the main dance floor, and cushions surrounded it. I took a seat next to the gap so I could stare out of it when I needed an excuse for not looking at Devon.

He sat on the other side of the gap and stretched out his legs. "So what's wrong?"

His feet were too close. I pulled my legs in, then decided that made me appear defensive. Damn it. I had to shift positions entirely. "Nothing's wrong."

He threw his head back and laughed. "You've been avoiding me since that night when Lucrezia tried to kill you, and now you've either got the world's worst wedgie, or you're squirming for some other reason. If it's your unders, I recommend ditching them, but I suspect it's not."

I began to say it wasn't him, but that would be a lie and he could tell. Best to deflect. "I'm having relationship issues with Lucen, and since you're his best friend, I'd rather not talk about them. Okay?"

Devon scratched his chin again. Was he growing in a goatee, and why hadn't I noticed that before? Oh wait, probably because I'd been avoiding him. I had to admit it was a good look. Devon had a bit of a baby face, but the scruff gave him an edge to match his personality.

A different waitress entered the alcove and set down a fresh drink for me, and one for Devon. That would make this my third in an hour. Tempted though I was to reach for it, doing so was a bad idea. My tolerance was pretty high, but some situations called for stone-cold sobriety. It was too late for that, but at the very least I could refrain from making my head fuzzier.

"I think since you can't avoid me at the moment, you're avoiding the question," Devon said, "but I'll play."

"I'm not asking you to play."

He leaned toward me. "I like to play."

I leaned away, and my head rocked as though the alcohol was hitting me all at once. Funny—I'd swear it was clove-scented alcohol. In other words, I couldn't tell how much was booze-induced intoxication and how much had to do with Devon's power. I considered moving farther away from him, and to hell with rudeness, but what good would that do? He'd simply laugh about how uncomfortable he made me.

"I don't need to discuss my relationship issues with you. If you want to gossip, do it with Lucen."

"Is this about your sex hang-up? I've told you before. I want to help."

"Yeah, I bet." I threw all the sarcasm I could muster into the words, but it didn't change the fact that when I met Devon's bright eyes, my body became very ready to take him up on that offer. My heart beat harder, and I wrapped my arms around myself, suddenly self-conscious of all my exposed skin.

Devon said nothing. He didn't have to in order to make his point, and he continued to watch me with great amusement.

Fuck it. I drank more. "It's not just the monogamy thing. He doesn't talk to me, and that pisses me off."

My brow furrowed at my own admission. Well done, alcohol. Not only had I *not* planned on talking about this crap with Devon, I hadn't fully acknowledged the truth to myself before now.

Yet it was definitely true. Lucen's silence did piss me off. It *did* make me wonder if he was hiding things from me.

Surprised as I was to hear it myself, Devon seemed to be just as taken aback. He poked at the ice in his drink. "Interesting. When you say he doesn't talk to you—can you be more specific? I find he never shuts up."

"Well, no, not if you get him started about certain subjects, but he won't talk about himself. Why am I telling you this?"

"Probably because you're drinking, and you're desperate to avoid that other topic."

I groaned and pushed my glass away. Both of those answers were correct. "Can we pretend we never had this conversation? I should go home. I have work to do tomorrow."

"That you admitted anything tells me you had too much to drink for me to allow you to leave by yourself. That means you'll need a ride. I'll be the one who provides it, which means you'll end up talking to me longer anyway. So really, you should stay here where it's comfortable and talk instead."

"I can leave just fine."

"You can lie to yourself but not to me."

"I hate you."

"Another lie, but back to Lucen. What do you want to know about him that he won't talk about?"

I draped my arm over my eyes, wishing I'd kept my mouth shut. When I peeked out from under it, Devon was still there. No surprise.

Resigned, I let my arm flop back to my side. "Anything. Everything. I want to know if he chose to become a satyr. I want to know what he was like, what he did before he opened The Lair. I want to know where he's from. But all he'll tell me is that the past isn't important. I guess that worries me, like there's something about his past he doesn't want me to know."

"There isn't." Devon sounded so certain.

I narrowed my eyes. "And you know this how?"

"Because I know why Lucen isn't telling you about his past."

"And?"

Devon set down his drink, but he didn't answer right away. I had to motion for him to get on with it. "I'm trying to decide if this is something I should tell you."

"If you're going to betray Lucen's secrets..." Well, he shouldn't and that would make him a very crappy friend, but I really wanted him to do just that, so I couldn't finish my sentence.

Damn, first wishing for ghoulish magic and now this. I was truly a horrible person for having all these thoughts about Lucen tonight.

"It has nothing to do with Lucen's secrets," Devon said, "whatever they are. I was wondering if there was a reason Lucen didn't tell you these things himself. Since I can't figure out his reasons, I don't see the harm. You might as well know since you are one of us."

"So they're satyr secrets?"

"You're obsessed with secrets."

"Well, yeah. Because no one tells me anything. So go on. Why isn't Lucen telling me about his past?"

Devon took his time, putting his feet up on the table first. "Because, like most satyrs, he doesn't remember."

"Doesn't remember?" I repeated. And then, through my alcohol- or pheromone-induced fog, I got it.

I didn't remember either.

The last time I'd been home I'd found an old photo of myself. It was from a camping trip, and in the picture I wore glasses. Glasses I had no memory of ever needing. That was when I'd discovered my childhood memories had become the equivalent of Swiss cheese.

Together, my mother and I had gone through more photos under the pretense that I was feeling nostalgic, and I'd discovered more and more missing pieces. Yet there was a pattern to the missing information. I remembered people and places just fine. It was my personal history that was screwed up.

I'd suspected the magic worked on me had something to do with it, and Devon was confirming my suspicion.

I picked up my glass but didn't drink. "I have a lot of missing memories from before this happened." I waved my hand over my body to indicate what I meant. "I assumed that it must have been something abnormal about me. Since I wasn't supposed to be able to turn, the spells had somehow screwed me up."

"No, that actually makes you normal. It's mostly personal details that you lost. Right?" When I confirmed it, he continued. "You lose something of yourself in the process, but memories of other people remain. That's what's hard to deal with."

There was a wistful undertone to his voice that surprised and confused me. I'd never heard Devon sound…sad? Feeling both alarmed and awkward, I tilted my glass back and sucked on the ice melt.

Devon snapped out of whatever reverie had brought him down and straightened his shoulders. "Coupled with the agony of having gone through the change, it's enough for most people to want to forget their pasts entirely. So they ask, and most Doms are only too happy to make sure they receive. I'd say a complete memory wipe is standard. No one, except certain freaks, would want to remember everything, so they don't."

"You mean like me? I don't think I had a choice."

"I mean like us actually, and I'm sure you didn't have a choice about it given the circumstances surrounding your change. Normal people—stable people—like Lucen, would not have wanted to remember their pasts."

I swallowed the feeble remains of an ice cube, hoping I could hold on to each enticing piece of information I'd been given long enough to ask about them all. "But why wouldn't he tell me that then? Why not say, 'Hey, Jess, I took some memory-cleansing potion, sorry'?"

"That much you'll have to ask him. I'm only telling you stuff that would be common knowledge for all satyrs who came about the usual way. You should know these things if you take up Dezzi's offer. I guess we expect you know more than you do, but that's not your fault."

"I should know more." I entwined my fingers and stretched my arms, careful to keep them away from Devon. This space was too cramped. Alas, my shirt slid up as I did, and I could feel his heavy gaze on my torso.

If you didn't want guys staring at your stomach and cleavage, you should have worn a different shirt, I reminded myself. But this was different. This was a guy I was attracted to.

A guy I didn't want to be attracted to.

And the reason for that?

Your sex hang-up. I heard the words spoken in my head with Devon's faintly British accent.

Cringing, I closed my eyes. That shadow of a goatee worked very well for him, indeed. He still had nothing on Lucen, but I had to admit it was sexy. And hey, we were finally having a serious conversation that didn't involve him being angry at me. Amazing.

And um…shit. I squirmed in my seat, this time because I could feel my body getting hot. If just Devon's gaze could do this to me, his touch might make me ignite.

I shivered with the thought of it. Before Lucen, my sex life had been as nonexistent as my love life, and I rarely spent much time thinking about its lack. Thanks to Lucen, however, I wasted a lot more time with sex on my brain, and oh hell, was it on my brain now. I wondered what Devon's lips would taste like. I wondered what his body would feel like. I wondered how similar the experience would be to Lucen since I had so few other experiences to compare it to.

Lucen would like this.

It was a sobering—cooling—thought. Lucen would like this because it was a very satyr thing to do, and I was a satyr. So I should be okay with it.

Human Jess would not have been. At least I didn't think she would have been. She'd been taken from me so long ago it was pointless thinking about it, and anyway it didn't matter. Satyr, human, or whatever I was—I wasn't the sort of person who could separate sex from emotion. Great if it worked for others, but I couldn't deal with it. I wanted them to stick together.

Devon hadn't taken his eyes off me. How long had my thoughts rambled for? Worse—did he know I'd been thinking about him? He wasn't smirking for a change. Instead his face was hungry. Predator-like.

Had he been thinking the same things?

I had to get this conversation back on track ASAP. I cleared my throat. "You said you remember your past. Why didn't you get your memories wiped since they bother you?"

Devon's eyebrows shot up.

Oops. Maybe I should have left that bit out, but I'd been thinking of the sadness in his voice. And well, my mouth was functioning somewhat independently of my brain, which was still fixated on more deviant and tangible things than memories.

Gradually, the surprise faded from Devon's expression, and he responded before I could form a less-than-coherent explanation for my poor word choice. "The change wasn't as traumatic for me as it is for most people. Because of that, I didn't have the same motivation to forget. I wanted to remember."

I chewed on this a moment. Curiosity was a great antidote for unwanted lust. "Why don't I remember it being traumatic, and why wasn't it traumatic for you? For that matter, what's so damn traumatic?"

"You're full of questions tonight."

"Like I said, nobody tells me anything. Which begs another question of why you're suddenly being chatty, but moving on. Don't stop now."

"Words I've been wanting to hear from you."

I flipped him off. "You're going to tell me, right?"

He chuckled. "These are things you should know, so why not. I can't answer the question about you. I can only guess it's because you're different. You don't need addicts like we do. That's got to be part of it. As for me, I knew what I was getting into, so I was prepared. Dezzi told me everything."

Lucen had explained to me that Dezzi had turned Devon, and that was why he was so loyal to her. Why he was willing to remain as her lieutenant instead of moving on to become a Dom himself. "So you're saying most people don't know what they're getting into? Does that mean they don't have a choice? It's just done to them?"

This was the answer I wanted most. To know that Lucen hadn't chosen this life.

But Devon's expression shot down my brief moment of hope. "I'm sure some don't choose it. Some Doms are cruel like some people are cruel. But no Dom that I've ever met tells people what to expect after the change. What Dezzi did with me was an exception because she was trying to talk me out of it. If people knew, I doubt most would go through with it."

I should have been sober for this conversation because with every word Devon said, I had a hundred new questions. Trying to keep myself focused on the main point was difficult. "Why not?"

Devon rested his head in his hands and glanced up at me with an oddly —and endearingly—wistful expression. "You don't need addicts, Jess. Do you know how lucky you are? Has Lucen ever explained why we need addicts?"

I rubbed my eyes, confused. "I'm not that buzzed, which means you're not making sense. You need addicts to feed on. Everyone knows that."

"No, not just to feed." He stood abruptly and stuffed his hands in his pockets. "Why do lust addicts crave sex all the time? Why do greed addicts covet everything they can't have? Why do vanity addicts feel so worthless? Why are rage addicts perpetually angry?"

"Because your addict bond makes them that way so you can feed off their misery."

"Partially." He knelt in front of me. "But we can feed off all kinds of negativity. So why does the bond do that?"

Devon had gotten way too close to me again, but I did my best not to fidget, and concentrated on his words. "You've lost me. I assumed it was just how the bond worked."

"You were in that fury's head, Jess. You know from experience that the bond goes two ways. It's a circuit."

"And your point?"

He stood once more and moved away. "We don't just feed on an addict's emotions. We dump *our* emotions on *them*."

Devon paused a moment to let this sink into my thick head.

When I didn't respond, he continued. "We dump our emotions on them, they chew them up internally—so to speak—and suffer for them, and then we can feed on their misery, as you so eloquently put it."

I floundered for a response to that. "So it's not the bond magic itself that creates the misery. It's you?"

He paced against the far wall, seemingly too agitated to sit or stand still, despite the lack of space. "Remember how you felt under Lucrezia's curse when it combined with the F? You said it was like you were going to tear off your own skin with uncontrollable lust. That's us, every day, unless we can get rid of it. And we get rid of it by giving it to our addicts. The misery we feed on is, essentially, our own. The magic that created us makes it. We're the miserable ones, and we need to get rid of that pain to survive. It's just convenient how we can offload it on others and feed on their suffering."

I swallowed and stared at the floor. Needing to tear off my skin with an insatiable lust—that was exactly what it had been like. Not a pleasurable pain, but one so overwhelming and all-encompassing that I could barely think straight. One I'd have done anything to get rid of. Only I couldn't.

I was having a hard time comprehending what Devon was telling me because nothing I'd ever learned about preds had so much as hinted at this. It changed everything. Lucen didn't just need his addicts to feed on. He needed them to take away his pain. To live.

I wasn't sure what I felt about that. Pity? Anger? Shock at this revelation, for sure.

"The Gryphons never taught you any of this, did they?" Devon sounded amused, but his smile wasn't as bright as usual.

"Nope. Maybe I'd have learned it if I hadn't gotten kicked out."

Devon sat, rubbing his neck. "Now do you see why it's so traumatic when you're first changed?"

"You don't have any addicts to take away the pain."

"No, you don't. So you're so filled with this intense, insatiable lust, and you remember what you gave up to become this way. For what? Power? You have none yet. A longer life? Who wants to live like that? It hurts to remember the past, so people choose to forget."

I picked at the seam on my pants. My heart ached for Lucen. No wonder he hadn't wanted to talk about his past. I just wished he'd have been the one to explain.

"Except you," I pointed out. "You didn't choose that."

"Because I knew what to expect, unlike everyone else. Because I wanted it in spite of that. I wanted to remember because for me, remembering what I left made it easier to suffer through the pain, not harder."

"So you're saying you had a shitty life as a human, huh?"

Devon's face finally broke into a real grin. "You could say that. So have I satisfied your desperate curiosity well enough for the evening?"

"I suppose so." I had other questions, but he'd given me plenty to think about. Possibly too much, considering I had to research entirely unrelated questions tomorrow, and my head felt stuffed.

"Good. Then how about satisfying my curiosity now."

I quit picking at my seam, a cold dread creeping over me. *Please don't go there.* I'd just gotten my body back under control. "About what?"

"At the meeting when you told us what you were and what you could do, you mentioned that you were largely immune to our power these days. That explained a lot, and it certainly seems to be true. You were sitting so close to Angelia and her bodyguards, and yet I didn't notice an effect on you." He crossed the space between us in less than a heartbeat and stood inches away. The heat from his body radiated onto mine.

My breath caught in my throat. I could close that last amount of distance just as fast. I could feel how hot his skin truly was. My lips were dry, and I struggled not to wet them. He could do that for me.

But I didn't move. I was determined to keep a nonchalant expression even though my body betrayed me.

"So why is it—" Devon didn't move either, yet I could have sworn he was touching me, "—that I can sense so much lust in you when we're together these days?"

Don't twitch. Don't flinch. Don't give in.

"Wishful thinking?"

In the second it took Devon to think of a witty reply to that, I darted around him, banging my shin on the table, and re-entered the main VIP area. There, I took a deep breath of Devon-free air. I could hear him laugh behind me.

On the sofa, Angelia was talking with one of her dealers, so I waved good night and got the hell out of Purgatory before anyone tried to stop me.

TWENTY-ONE

I WAS HELLACIOUSLY TIRED THE NEXT DAY. ON THE WAY HOME from Purgatory, I'd stopped by The Lair, filled with the delusional hope that I might grab a moment with Lucen to discuss my conversation with Devon, but the place was jammed and he was busy. Apologies and a quick kiss were all I got. I went to bed frustrated, mentally and physically.

Armed with coffee, I'd arrived at Gryphon headquarters this morning and checked my inbox. But although I'd been cc'd on a bunch of emails so I knew Bridget and company were busy shaking down their pred informants, there was nothing for me to do.

From my computer, I went straight to the library, which was where I'd been hanging out for the last several hours. When I wasn't thinking about everything I'd learned from Devon last night, or how close I'd come to kissing him, my eyes were glazing over as I searched the Gryphons' database for anything to do with Gunthra's Vessels.

Tom had told me once that World had storage rooms full of books, manuscripts, and equipment that was too rare to keep in the regular collection. Not all of it was even catalogued. If he were here, I might have asked him if he'd heard of the Vessels, but he was still gone.

Mostly, I was grateful for that, but I was becoming less so as the day wore on and my search proved fruitless. Logically, it shouldn't matter if I learned nothing. Gunthra had worded her end of the deal so poorly that if I found nothing and told her that truthfully, it ought to count as upholding my end. But deep down, I wasn't satisfied with nothing, and maybe Gunthra had me figured out well enough to know that I wouldn't be. She'd put me on the hunt, and it had become a mission. I had to know why she wanted to know.

The single history book I found that actually contained a reference to the Vessels in its index treated them more like a legend than a fact. They were, apparently, the Holy Grail of the magical world.

According to the book, the Vessels of Making were five objects of such significant power that their very existence had been deemed a threat thousands of years ago. A group of magicians had once created them to do "great works," whatever that meant, and had then destroyed them.

Or that was one theory for the reason of their disappearance.

Other theories were that they'd merely been lost. And still others were that they'd never existed in the first place, and this had become the dominant theory. They were a legend, something to drive fortune hunters and conspiracy freaks mad with over the millennia.

And just who were these magicians alleged to have created the Vessels anyway? The book didn't say, although the way it was written suggested they were either gifted humans or magi. Maybe both.

I slammed the book shut in annoyance and checked my coffee cup, but I'd drunk the dregs a while ago. It was time for more, but first a phone call. Thinking about magi had given me an idea. The last time I'd gone looking for information that didn't exist in the Gryphon library, I'd checked in with Olef. Granted, he hadn't been able to help then, but that was Gryphon-specific information I'd been searching for. These Vessels sounded more like general folklore, and general folklore sounded right up Olef's alley.

I got out my phone and jumped when it rang in my hand. As my heart returned to normal, I frowned at the caller ID. Unknown number. It was probably a telemarketer, but I picked up anyway. "Hello?"

"Hi, is this Jessica Moore?"

The voice was vaguely familiar. "Yes. Is this Shawna?"

"Yes. Yes, it is." Her voice sounded higher than I remembered. Taut. Like she was scared shitless.

"Are you okay?"

"Yeah, fine, yeah. You said to call if I could think of anything, and I did. It's just...wow, this is kind of scary, you know? I've been thinking about what you said about those other vanity addicts, and I'm freaked out."

I closed my eyes, steadying my breathing. I needed to project calm so she held it together, but damn. I needed her information. "Okay, just relax. What do you know? Anything you tell me is going to help keep you out of danger. I'm at Gryphon headquarters. If you know the names of the people involved, we can head out immediately."

That wasn't exactly truthful, but we could do something. I'd call Bridget the moment I got off the phone with Shawna.

"I'd rather not talk on the phone, you know? Could you come here, to me? I have questions too, and I'd feel safer doing this in person."

I grimaced, not liking how long the travel would take. But then, I'd made a good start on my research task. I could afford to follow leads on Eric's case. "Okay, sure."

"Alone?"

"If that's what you want." I had no one with me anyway.

"It is. It's just, you know, I feel like a fool about this whole addiction thing, and talking in front of Gryphons..." Her voice trailed off in a nervous laugh.

Hence why Bridget hadn't wanted to send Gryphons to the support group meeting. "Yeah, sure. Give me the address. I can leave now."

Shawna gave me an address in one of the outlying towns, and I hung up. After looking up the directions, I sent Bridget a text to let her know I was following up on a lead, and headed out.

Gunthra and her Vessels were going to have to wait a little longer.

***

SHAWNA LIVED ON A QUIET STREET ABOUT HALF AN HOUR outside the Greater Boston urban sprawl. I found her house easily and parked my Dragon'sWing next to a sign by her driveway that advertised her yoga studio. Without the rumble of the motorcycle's engine, the air was eerily peaceful.

The street dead-ended at an elementary school, which throughout the summer had a playground doubling as a park. Kids shouted as they raced across a baseball diamond. I tore my attention away from them and traipsed past the white farmhouse to the carriage house in the back. Shawna had said she'd be in her studio stretching because it kept her calm.

I knocked once on the large door, and no one answered. Noticing it was slightly ajar, I pushed it open. The hinges creaked, and the scent of sandalwood incense wafted outside.

"Shawna?" I stepped in and discovered an enormous and airy space. Part of one wall had been hung with mirrors, but the ceiling was high and open. Another temporary wall divided the room, and a desk stood in front of it, as did a stereo that was playing relaxing music.

Shawna herself sat on one of the mats by the mirror doing some pose that required her to touch her toes. Her chest rose and fell with peaceful breathing, but she made no move to acknowledge me.

"Shawna?" Annoyance colored my voice, and I spoke louder. She might be meditating or whatever, but she wasn't deaf, and she'd asked me to drive all the way out here.

When she didn't answer a second time, suspicion cooled my blood. Shawna had sounded one breath from a heart attack on the phone, but this did not seem like the reaction of a scared woman.

Now it was my turn to get worried, and I swore silently at my stupidity as suspicion hardened into certainty. She'd lured me out here, and I'd walked into a trap.

With one hand, I reached for my knife. With my other, I took out my phone.

Still, nothing happened. Maybe I was being paranoid, but so what? I'd call for Gryphon reinforcements. Just in case. Every sense on alert, I adjusted my grip on my knife so I could bring up the Gryphons' phone number.

That was when they struck.

Sylphs, at least three of them. They were white-and-silver blurs in my vision, decked out in some serious charms to make them move so fast. Before I could finish dialing, the phone flew from my hand. I swore again, not so silently this time.

One of the sylphs went for my knife, but I managed to maintain my grip. Ducking as a pale object streaked by me, I swung out my arms and slashed at anything within my vicinity. Someone cursed. All at once the blurs formed into people.

There were three as I'd first guessed, a woman and two men, although with sylphs it could often be hard to tell the difference. They circled around me at a safe distance. None appeared willing to get too close, although they were armed as well.

Blood rushed by my ears. Three on one—not good odds, especially when they had speed charms. The only point in my favor was that the sylphs had seen Misery's black blade and were wary of it. But dragon shit on toast—I'd been tricked by a sylph. My opinion of my intelligence took a hard blow.

I swallowed, regathering my wits before they had a chance to regroup. "What did you do to Shawna? Is she a ghoul?"

The taller of the two men gave me a deranged smile. He stood closer than the others, but the knife he held was longer than Misery, as was his reach. "She served her purpose and is being punished for her insolence."

"Which was what? Why try to get me here?"

He raised a perfectly formed eyebrow. "To see if you'd come. Assym told you to leave this Gryphon business alone. When he found out Shawna had spoken to you, he decided to test you. See if you would take his advice."

Great. Just what the world needed. Sylphs that were growing brains. "So I'm here. What does Assym expect, a trophy for you to take back and prove it? None of you seem eager to get any closer."

I spun slowly in place as I spoke, trying to get a better bearing on my surroundings. Eventually the sylphs were going to remember they had the upper hand and attack again. One knife versus three, and all that. I needed something else to defend myself with, but the carriage house held no promises. The walls were bare and the floor empty.

"You're going to drop the knife and come with us," the sylph said. "We're taking you back to Shadowtown."

"Um, no. You want the knife, you're going to have to pry it from my hand." I backed my way into the wall opposite of the mirrors and adjusted my stance. Now they would all have to attack from the same side, and unless they moved together, there was a good chance I'd get in a couple hits first, even with their charms. We were far from Shadowtown, and they'd be in deep shit if they hadn't brought anything with them to stop the bleeding. Those wounds wouldn't clot on their own.

The sylphs, on the other hand, wouldn't want to kill me because Assym wanted me alive. They'd have to be careful not to do too much damage.

This realization didn't even the odds, but it made me feel a bit more confident. Judging by the sylphs' faces and their reluctance to attack, they'd had the same thoughts. I hoped like hell that my less-than-cowed reaction was pissing them off. Angry people made dumb mistakes.

The sylphs glanced at each other. How soon until the tall one ordered the others to disarm me? It didn't look like anyone was willing to volunteer.

"I can make you drop it," the tall sylph said.

I bent my knees, keeping loose. "I'm trembling. So have at it, or are you afraid you'll damage me too much for Assym?"

Drop the knife.

The words slipped through me, cool and sharp, like taking an icicle to the brain. Chilly hands seemed to wrap themselves around my chest, constricting me. Since they were too wary to attack me physically, the tall sylph was attempting a magical assault instead.

Do it. Listen to me. Make this easy on yourself. You can't fight three of us, and you can't fight Assym. You know it, Jessica. Cooperate and you won't get hurt. You need us.

My muscles clenched. Every instinct screamed at me to fight, to throw off this sylph's hold on my soul. I could do it too. In spite of the insecurities the sylph fed into my head, I was stronger. I had more resistance than they'd be expecting because I wasn't human.

Get... But I cut myself off even as I prepared to throw all my willpower at the sylph.

I didn't need to release his stranglehold on me. I could use him. Use his power. Maybe he knew where to find the sylphs who'd fled the other day, or which goblin had attacked Eric. But to find out, I needed to let him in completely so I could take control.

Breathing heavily, I sank to my knees, cold with terror. I could do this. I'd done it before, but I so did not like the idea of doing it again.

Above me, the sylph grinned, sensing my will collapsing, and his icy, magical fingers probed what was left of my resistance. I closed my eyes, struggling with my own revulsion at letting him forge a bond with me.

"Assym wants her," the female sylph hissed. "You can't have her."

"I'll release her to him when we get back. She'll be easier to deal with this way." The sylph lowered his blade, returning his attention to me. "Won't you? Be good, and put down the knife."

My grip tightened on the handle, but only for a moment. *Listen. Obey. Let him in.*

This wasn't like when the red-eyed fury had made a play for me. His power had been strong and hot. The power washing over me now was cool and steady. Then, I'd been hurt badly. I'd also been filled with rage. Giving in had been easy because my body had wanted nothing more than relief from the pain and an outlet for my vengeance.

This time, my body rebelled. There was no pain relief in this sylph's touch, only humiliation. But if I could do what the sylph asked, that would be enough. I would open myself to his power completely, and that was what I needed, loathsome as it was.

My hand trembled, but I set the knife on the mat.

Good, weak little human.

The act of obedience blew open our connection. The bond between us formed and solidified. As I had the first time, I could see it in my mind's eye, a circuit of glowing power between us.

I reached out with my will and grabbed at the connection.

As I raised my head, the sylph shuddered, but whether from the force of my pull or the shock, I didn't know.

More—that was all I understood. I needed more.

I yanked harder on his power, and the circuit changed direction. Cool and forceful, the magic poured into me and over me like the wind. Hair lifted off my neck, and my pores tingled. I let it fill me, propelling me to my feet, and that was all I could do to keep from raising my arms and throwing my head back in delight. I was caught in a windstorm, carried above everything by a glorious gust of sheer power.

I was a goddess, and the three sylphs in front of me gawked, immobile with panic. Unbidden, laughter bubbled up from my lips. I barely felt my body move as I reached down and picked up my knife. It was as though my head—my soul—was disconnected from the rest of me. It was almost too much.

Yet the sylph didn't break our bond like Red-eye had. With Red-eye, my burst of power had been put to immediate use and then cut. For whatever reason, the sylph was too stupid or too in shock to release me. I was going to burst as a result unless I did something to expel this energy.

So I struck. Physical activity had worked last time. I hoped it would again.

The female sylph scrambled away as I snatched at her arm, and she dropped her knife. By the time I kicked it away, her male counterpart had recovered his wits. Bewildered, he lunged for me with his weapon, and I dodged easily. His speed charm was nothing compared to the magic that I controlled. He seemed to move so slowly, so clumsily. One swipe of my arm and he flew back several feet. He landed with a cry, and the woman shrieked.

"What the hell happened? What did she do?"

I ignored them. They weren't a threat any longer, and I pushed the sylph who'd addicted me in the chest. "Where are the sylphs who attacked their addicts? Who has Shawna's soul? Which goblins are you working with?"

The sylph's jaw worked, but no words left him.

"Answer me."

"Cut her loose," the woman yelled at him.

"Answer me!" My voice echoed off the ceiling like a burst of thunder, but he still didn't respond.

Shit. Had I taken too much power from him, or was he in some kind of magical shock? I didn't know how to control this.

The woman yelled his name and ran over to shake him.

I grabbed her arm. "Answer my questions."

She clawed at me, so I sheathed Misery and snagged her other arm too. It was ridiculous how weak and insignificant she felt in my hands. I could snap her in two on a whim. "I don't know," she whispered.

Annoyed, I tossed her toward the other male. She landed on her side with a thud. Retrieving Misery from my sheath, I advanced on her, but a flash of white flew by in my peripheral vision. She screamed.

I gasped as my connection to the first sylph shattered. Power drained away in an instant, leaving me lightheaded and swaying on my feet. I felt its remains crackling over my skin, but I was empty inside—a sad and hollow letdown that made me think of a junkie coming off a high.

Then Misery slipped in my grasp, and I snapped back into myself. Danger. Without the connection, I was only Jess again. But as I spun around to face the sylphs, two of them dashed out of the barn in another blur. The door slammed in their breeze.

I let them go and focused on the sylph who'd addicted me. He remained on his knees, unmoving with his back to me. As I took a cautious step forward, he fell over. His head landed at an unnatural angle, and the mat began to pool with blood. So much blood.

That's why the connection had broken. The other male sylph must have had a salamander-fire-forged blade and slit his friend's throat.

Clasping a hand to my mouth, I stumbled backward until I found my phone. Luckily, it had landed on a mat so it wasn't damaged, and I finished dialing the Gryphons before I got sick.

TWENTY-TWO

MY SIMPLE QUEST TO ASK SHAWNA QUESTIONS TURNED INTO hours of post-sylph murder cleanup. The Gryphons, including Bridget, had arrived with alacrity, but I had a lot of explaining to do.

The easy but unfortunate parts related to Shawna. The dead sylph, on the other hand—that was complicated. No one truly doubted me when I said I hadn't killed him. Why would I deny it? The Gryphons wouldn't care, not much. As long as I claimed he'd attacked me, they'd call it justified self-defense.

I should have done that, but I hadn't been thinking clearly. Upset over Shawna and disturbed over what Assym's next move would be, I'd failed to think through my explanation. The Gryphons knew I had freaky magic, so I'd forgotten they weren't aware of the extent of its freakiness. They didn't know I could reverse a pred-addict bond, and I wasn't ready to tell them.

I rested my head on my knees, sitting on the warm grass by the carriage house. No longer could I hear children playing on the school grounds. Only Gryphon voices filled the air. They'd cordoned off the area.

Bridget squatted next to me. "Jess, you really need to be clearer about why that sylph is dead."

"I told you. One of the other sylphs killed him because he was doing something stupid and they were scared." I brushed dirt off my jeans and stood. "I'm not sure I should say anything else until I talk this over with Agent Kassin."

"I thought you didn't like him."

"I don't."

And yet, here I was using him as an excuse. It was the least he could do for me. Hell, he might even thank me for not spilling my guts about what had actually happened. My entire existence had been concocted in secrecy, after all. Surely, the extent of my power was part of that. Not that I would be pleased for Tom to find out about it, but realistically, that had been bound to happen. I couldn't avoid him forever, and I owed him a conversation.

Bridget smoothed the wrinkles from her shirt. "Fine. He's due back soon, and we've got enough issues with the case at hand for me to worry about. But once this report is filed, you know the director is going to have questions about your nonanswers."

Ugh. No doubt. "Won't be the first time I piss off Olivia."

The sound of a car pulling into the driveway ended our conversation.

"That must be Shawna's family," Bridget said.

Peachy. It sucked being a bearer of bad news, but since I'd known Shawna—however barely and briefly—I felt responsible for telling her family what had transpired.

It was late afternoon by the time I was ready to leave, and as happy as I was to get out of the way, returning to Shadowtown was not an appealing thought. Why, oh why, had I chosen to live around so many people who hated me? My only consolation was that the two sylphs who'd gotten away had seen what I'd done to their friend. Maybe Assym would also be scared and keep his distance.

Yeah. And salamanders might spit water.

To top it off, I'd lost hours upon hours of research time, and my head was in no place to return to dusty books.

I rode straight home, parked my bike, and went to The Lair. It would be busy by now and only getting busier, but I wasn't ready to return to my research, and I sure didn't feel comfortable being home alone. Besides, I'd texted Lucen to let him know what had happened, and I wanted to talk it over. More than that, I wanted to stay at his place tonight.

Paulius was behind the bar, as was usual on a Saturday, but I didn't see Lucen. Sauntering over, I waved to catch the bartender's attention.

He came over a minute later. "Lucen's not back yet if you're looking for him."

"Not back yet? Where is he?"

"He left you a message. He told Dezzi what happened to you with the sylphs, and she called him and a few other people together to discuss the situation. I don't know what they're up to, but he left about thirty minutes ago, and I don't expect he's going to be back for a while because he called in help to cover his shift."

I swore, checking my phone. Sure enough, Lucen had called. I must not have heard the phone among all the commotion at Shawna's.

"Can I get you anything?" Paulius asked.

Whiskey, a double sounded good, but I shook my head. My nerves were frayed, but drinking in Shadowtown did not feel wise. Not tonight when I half-expected retaliation at any moment.

I took to a quiet corner and listened to Lucen's message. He didn't say much of anything that Paulius hadn't related, although he'd expressed far more concern and outrage on my behalf. Whatever he was up to with Dezzi, I got the feeling Lucen was out to kick some sylph ass.

Sighing, I hung up. Dezzi would talk him down from his righteous anger and probably attempt to speak with Assym. Assym would want to know why she cared. It could be an interesting conversation. I wished Lucen had waited for me so I could take part.

But you're not a member of the council and wouldn't be allowed to participate. Dezzi is making that clear.

Scowling, I sent Lucen a new text, telling him to let me know when he was back. Then I called Steph. If I couldn't be surrounded by satyrs who had my back, I wanted to be in another neighborhood.

An hour later I met up with Steph at Kilpatrick's pub for dinner. Guinness and greasy fish-and-chips made excellent comfort food, and I deserved some comfort.

"I hope I didn't make you leave Jim behind," I said. "I wouldn't have minded if he came."

Steph coated her fries in ketchup with an annoyed face. "He was thrilled that you called. One of his friends is hosting a poker night, so now he can go without feeling like he's ditching me."

"Good."

She stuck her finger in my face. "Not good. If he loses money, I'm blaming you."

"You realize that's terribly unfair. It's not like you were going to stop him from going in the first place."

"I might have tried, but you sounded upset, so I couldn't say no."

"Yeah, there's a reason for that." I peeled excess batter off my fish and chewed slowly, wondering how much to divulge. "I was attacked by a few sylphs today while following a lead on Eric's case."

Steph smacked her beer bottle against her mouth in surprise. "Are you okay? Why didn't you say something on the phone?"

"Because I'm fine, relax. I just needed to get out of Shadowtown for a while until my head cleared."

"No kidding. I told you not to live there."

"Yeah, you did. But I'll be fine."

She rolled her eyes. "Of course you will. That's why you're not there tonight. Because you feel totally safe surrounded by preds."

I am a pred. But I swallowed down that thought with my beer. "I'm no less safe around preds who have it in for me than I am around humans who have it in for me. The really bad news is that I lost my lead, although in retrospect, I'm not sure she was much of a lead. The sylphs used her as a lure to get to me."

"What do they want with you?"

"Everyone wants me. I'm that cool."

Steph snorted. "Please. If you're not going to be serious about being attacked, then give me an update on Eric's case."

That much I could do without reliving my afternoon, so I shared everything that had happened since the last time we'd talked. It wasn't much, and Steph figured that out pretty fast.

"So you're telling me they have nothing. It's been almost a week, and the Gryphons have nothing." Steph shoved her half-eaten burger away.

I played with my fork, drawing swirls in my ketchup and searching for an explanation. "It's not nothing, but it's moving slowly. For whatever reason, Eric didn't seem to have a written contract with his goblin. It happens. Either that, or the goblin destroyed Eric's copy to keep us from finding it. But we will find out who it was, and we will make them pay for it."

"But it might be too late by then. Your Gryphon friend said there was a limited window to get his soul back."

So Bridget had, and I had nothing to say to make Steph feel better about that. I also suspected mentioning to Steph that I was working an angle with the goblin Dom would only infuriate her more. "We're trying."

"I know you're trying. I don't doubt you." She let out a frustrated cry and finished her beer. "I just hate it, Jess. I hate them. Every single damn pred. Why can't we kill them all like the Gryphons used to do way back when? They're all in Shadowtown. Just raze the entire fucking neighborhood, you excluded. They're all evil parasites, and it's not fair that we're supposed to play nice with them when they don't treat us the same way."

I winced. "Some are bad, yeah, I won't argue that. But..."

"Nuh-uh. No buts. Jesus, Jess. Three of them tried to kill you today. Why are you defending them?"

"I'm not defending those three. I'm just saying evil is a strong word. Evil suggests they like being cruel."

"They turn people into fucking addicts. They feed off of suffering. That is the very definition of evil."

Steph's anger burned hotter with each word, and I couldn't blame her. She was upset about what happened to Eric, worried for me and...wrong. Just wrong too.

I couldn't help but think of Lucen, and not only how he was good to me, but how I'd seen him take care of the homeless ghouls wandering

Shadowtown, and how he told me he thought it was wrong to let that happen to addicts.

I thought of my conversation with Devon too. How he claimed that most people had no idea what they were getting into when they changed, the longing in his voice when he'd commented on how lucky I was that I didn't need addicts to survive.

And Angelia, brutally attacked by humans but still determined to make sure people didn't get hurt with her magic.

Yes, their power hurt people, but I could not accept that they were all evil. Once I'd have agreed with Steph, but not anymore.

I wrapped my hands around my beer. "Evil suggests they enjoy being cruel. That's not true of all of them, just like it's not true of all humans. Some are evil, and some aren't."

"Bullshit. You've been spending too much time with that satyr so-called friend of yours, drinking their pred-flavored Kool-Aid. I'd have thought working for the Gryphons would counteract it, but it's like you forget that you're human just because you're not as vulnerable to their magic."

"I'm not human." The words tumbled out of me by accident, a simple, automatic correction to her false statement.

Fuck.

My eyes opened wide. This was not how I'd planned to confess. I must have been too lost in my thoughts to hold my tongue.

Across from me, Steph blinked. "What?"

Blood rushed to my face, and I pressed my sweaty hands tighter around my beer glass to cool off. I had a choice. I could go on and tell her the truth, or I could keep lying. It would no longer be a lie of omission at this point. It would be a calculated, deliberate deception to my best friend of ten years. It would—no way around it—be a shitty thing to do.

Whatever I chose, this wasn't going to end well. I might be able to smooth things over temporarily with a lie, but when I did admit the truth one day, she'd have every reason to be furious, and I would deserve her wrath. Shit, I deserved it now.

So screw it. It had already been an awful day. I might as well continue down that path and be a better friend even if I regretted it later.

I took a deep breath. "I'm not human."

Steph's anger was receding and fast, overwhelmed by confusion. "I heard you. What does that mean?"

I choked down a laugh. What could it mean except for exactly what it sounded like? She was in denial and no wonder. I'd been too, when Gunthra had told me the truth.

"It means I'm not human. I'm..." Deep breath. "I'm a satyr."

Steph's face went as blank as her emotions went numb. Then she was the one who laughed. "Is this a joke to make me repent and rethink my opinion on satyrs? Because it's not funny. I know about your gift, but you don't have horns, Jess. You don't have addicts. I've known you since the day the Gryphons kicked you out of their stupid Academy. You were wearing their uniform that night. You can't possibly be a satyr."

I swallowed. "And you know why the Gryphons kicked me out—my gift went rogue. They didn't understand it, they thought it was vanishing. But it didn't vanish. You know that too. It became a satyr's power."

"Yeah, but—"

"No buts, remember?"

Steph pushed her hair behind her shoulders. "Stop it. You're not a satyr. Preds are a threat to you. They can work their magic on you. They can't do that to other preds, and besides—you don't have fucking horns. You don't have addicts. You can't arouse lusty feelings in people by standing next to them. Just because you were cursed—"

"I wasn't cursed. I was wrong about that. I'm an anomaly, like a satyr subspecies that you've never seen before. And there's so much more I could tell you about what I can do and how I got this way, but I don't know if I'm allowed to because it's really complicated." I paused to gulp for air and reached for her arm. "But you deserve to know the truth."

Steph snatched her arm away, and my stomach fell to the sticky floor beneath me. "No, don't do that. I don't understand what you're telling me or why, and I don't like it. You are not one of them because they are evil, and you've always been a good person."

"I am one of them, and we are not all evil."

"Do not say we."

So conscious of every one of my breaths, I tried to gauge her emotions, but Steph was unfathomable. Her emotions were too wild, too screwed up for me to dissect them. But they were unhappy, that much I could tell, and it drove home how much of a pred I was. Breathing her in, I could get high enough to run circles around the city. It wasn't like when I'd fed on the sylph's power earlier, but it was close enough.

And it made me ill. The hurt and confusion and denial in her eyes sat in my gut like poison.

"Steph…" My voice trembled, and I searched for the right words that would help her deal. But what were they? I had a hard enough time dealing myself.

Eventually, she exhaled a slow, loud breath. "You're telling me the truth."

"Yes."

"You're a satyr."

"I am."

"Shit." Steph reached into her wallet and threw a twenty down on the table while I watched, frozen. "Sorry, Jess, but I need time to process this."

Then she got up and left, and I slumped in my seat, feeling more alone in the world than ever.

TWENTY-THREE

After Steph left, I stared into space. How many minutes ticked by, I couldn't say, but I watched people come and go at the bar, listened to different voices laughing and swearing at the pool table, and smelled my dinner as it congealed on my plate. My stomach was too twisted to eat any more.

Well, I couldn't say that had gone any worse than I'd feared. I could only hope that once Steph had a few days to think things through she'd get over it.

Like I'd done. Who was I kidding?

Cursing under my breath, I pulled out my phone. It would be nice if I had a message from Lucen, telling me he was back at The Lair, but naturally that didn't happen. Why should anything good happen? That would be someone else's life.

So where did I go? I didn't want to head home and pace about my lonesome apartment, jumping at every noise and wondering if sylphs with straight razors were going to invade. I could go to Gryphon headquarters, I supposed, and resume my research for Gunthra. That made the most sense, except my head was spinning. The ability to concentrate was not something I had in abundance. And that left me where?

When I was younger and in this sort of mood, I sometimes went to

Purgatory to dance off my stress. Maybe that was what I needed then. Not Purgatory, per se. I wasn't dressed to get in, and I wasn't sure I wanted to run into Devon two nights in a row, but physical activity might do me good. Boston was a great city for walking.

I finished settling the tab and left. The night was warm and humid, and I kept a brisk pace. It wasn't long before my mood improved, and my heart beat a steady rhythm. Fear and angst were like a toxin that could be cleansed through a good sweating.

I wandered aimlessly and until my feet hurt, only stopping to check my phone at various crosswalks in case Lucen had gotten back to me and I hadn't heard it over the traffic. But he didn't, and after a few crosswalks, I quit checking, content to be left alone.

The night was alive and vibrant, filled with the rush of cars and a thousand lights lining the streets. I reveled in the anonymity. Here I was one face among many, not a freak but another twenty-something, so easily overlooked and forgotten.

At the next turn, I followed a group of men and women about my age as they crossed the street, and I realized I'd ended up along the row of clubs and bars where Purgatory resided. Outside the buildings, lines of impatient people snaked down the pavement, and Purgatory was no exception. Only the clothes people wore and the unnatural colors of their dyed hair distinguished them. Thudding bass emanated from the various establishments, and the air was thick with the tang of alcohol and smoke.

Exhilarating as it was, however, my feet were getting sore. I'd easily walked a few miles, and though the city seethed with negativity and excitement to keep me fueled, turning around and going home might be wise. Or it would be if it weren't for the sylphs that could be waiting.

But maybe Lucen... I checked my phone for the first time in a while, but I had zero messages. Damn.

Sticking my phone away, I was suddenly irked by the laughter and good moods surrounding me. A woman in line at Purgatory screeched with delight about something, shattering the last defense I had against the darkness of my day. So much for my exercise-induced euphoria. I was crashing and burning, doomed to feel every last blister forming on my feet during the long walk home. Plus my stomach was realizing that I never gave it much for dinner.

"Jess?" Lost in my sour thoughts, I jumped as a clove-scented arm landed around my shoulders. "Just who I was hoping to find."

I stiffened, then extricated myself from Devon's hold. "Were you? And what are you doing out here? Club's that way." I jerked my thumb behind us.

"I'm aware of that." He adjusted the sleeves on his sports coat. "Dezzi's got Lucen and a few others busy with the sylph issue, and we wanted to make sure you weren't..." he examined me up and down, "... going to do anything reckless. You have a history, if you recall."

Mostly that history involved sneaking into Purgatory and doing things Devon disapproved of. Fortunately, that wasn't on my to-do list tonight. "Your faith in my good behavior is sweet. What could I possibly do?"

"I don't know—stick that knife of yours into Assym?"

I ran my hand over Misery. "Tempting, but that would assume I knew where to find him. I was hoping Assym would be cowering from me in some dark hole, actually."

"That's conceivable. He's a coward. As for me, since you asked, I just got here. When I sensed you nearby, I went looking. And here you are."

This wasn't the first time Devon had indicated he could pick my emotions out of a crowd. Lucen could do it too. According to Paulius, there were a few possible explanations. Either the two of them were simply that damn powerful, or they noticed me in a way they didn't notice other people. Like how you could pick a friend's voice out of background noise.

"I was out for a walk," I said, wiping the sweat off the back of my neck. How bad did I smell? "A crappy day required exercise. But I'm leaving now."

"Why don't you come in?"

I pulled at my T-shirt. "I'm not exactly dressed for it."

"It doesn't matter. You're with me. You're tired. Have you eaten?"

"Yes." My traitorous stomach rumbled. It didn't consider a few bites of my fish to count. "Sort of, but I'm fine."

Devon held out a hand. "Come along, little siren. Isn't that what Lucen calls you? Why is that?"

"It's a long story." Actually, it wasn't, but I didn't like Devon calling me by Lucen's pet name.

"You can tell me about it while you eat, and also tell me why you're in such a bad mood."

I crossed my arms. "Do you have to pry into my head like that?"

"No, but I do enjoy it." He waved his hand in front of me, urging me to take it. "Lucen should be free in about an hour. I don't think you want to hang out by yourself, do you?"

I silently cursed preds and their emotion-reading abilities. *There, that make you happy, Steph?*

It didn't make me happy, and I relented with a sigh. No, I did not want to be alone. "Yeah, okay."

Devon took me around back, and we entered through the kitchen. "What is it?" he asked again after requesting food and wine be sent up to his office.

The commotion and normality of the scene weirded me out. "I'm remembering that the last time I was in this part of the club, it was deserted and one of Lucrezia's addicts was holding me at gunpoint."

"Oh, dearest Crezi. Fun, wasn't she? I wonder how she's holding up in prison."

"Badly, I hope."

Devon unlocked a door that opened into a dimly lit stairwell. "Someone's feeling vindictive."

"She tried to kill me. Plus someone's in a bad mood."

"Noted. Maybe I should have requested multiple bottles of wine."

We climbed several flights and exited the stairwell into the end of Devon's office opposite the elevator. I scratched my head. I should have known there would have to be a way to enter and exit other than the elevator in case the electricity went out, but when Devon closed the door, it blended so seamlessly into the striped pattern on the wall that it was near impossible to see.

"So why are you in a bad mood? Is it the sylphs or something else?"

I glanced over my shoulder as I paced in front of the wall of one-way windows that provided a view of the main dance floor. Devon's office was soundproof, which made the spectacle two floors below amusing. People looked silly when they danced if you couldn't hear the music.

Devon stood over his computer while it booted. No tie for him tonight, and he'd abandoned the all-black look, substituting a deep blue shirt that he'd left artfully untucked. It brought out his eye color, and once again, I had disturbing thoughts about how good he looked.

Not my type, I told myself. I liked guys like Lucen with his jeans and leather jacket, and his broad shoulders and chest. A guy who portrayed a rough-around-the-edges appearance, but who was anything but. A guy who could kick bad-guy ass, then go home and prepare a four-course meal and pair it with the perfect wine.

Which, of course, didn't explain why standing next to Devon got me all hot and bothered these days. Devon did not do jeans and T-shirts, and although he might be hiding the compact body of a martial artist under his expensive clothes, he struck me as the sort to shun physical violence except when left with no alternative. Devon would whip out a gun or a knife sooner than throw a punch. Or, more likely, he'd call someone else to do it for him. That was the benefit of being Dezzi's lieutenant. He was —almost—the boss.

Even with my immunity to pred magic, I could have blamed my attraction to him on his power, except my blood quickened at only the thought of standing near him. That, no matter how desperately I rationalized it, could not be blamed on satyr pheromones.

I should not have come up here.

"Distracted?" Devon's smile was all too knowing. "I asked why you were in a bad mood."

I cleared my throat and sat on an arm of one of the several couches by the window. "No, it's not the sylphs. I finally told my best friend that I'm not human, and she reacted pretty much how I was afraid she'd react. She stormed off in the middle of dinner."

Devon tapped a few keys, then sat on the front of his desk. "So you were hoping your friend—who, if she's anything like a normal human, loathes us—would miraculously be okay with your revelation?"

"Yes. I mean, it would have been nice."

He made a thoughtful noise. "I never pegged you for an optimist. Reckless, yes. But this sounds delusional, even for you."

"Gee, thanks. You're really doing a good job of making me feel better. I should go home."

"Jess, *you* can't accept what you are. How can you expect anyone else to accept it?"

I'd gotten off the couch, but Devon's accusation stilled my feet. I plopped back down. If he wanted an argument, I could do that. Bad moods provided me with plenty of energy, and I felt ready to channel it. "I do accept it. I am accepting it. That I could tell Steph the truth is proof that I'm okay with it. That I chose to live in Shadowtown is also proof."

"Yes, you're finally willing to call yourself a satyr. It's a first step, but it's not acceptance. Deep down inside, you don't believe that's what you are. You're afraid."

"Afraid?" I laughed, but it was a fearful laugh. Yet I wasn't afraid. At least I hadn't been until Devon's words had sparked some fear in me. What the hell? "Your emotion-sucking sensibilities are on the fritz. What can I be afraid of? Losing my humanity? It was taken from me before I knew it was gone."

"Exactly." Devon slid off the desk and stalked toward me, hands in his pockets. His eyes shone with that same intensity Lucen's got when he was riled up. It was both unnerving and mesmerizing. "You say that, but you don't feel it. I think it's a fear of losing the image you have of yourself as human. You have this ideal version of who you are in your head. You're Jess the Martyr who was denied entry into the Gryphons because some evil people ruined your gift. So you became Jess the Vigilante, fighting the good fight for humanity against the terrible preds. And now you're Jess who is a pred, and you can't be the rejected martyr or humanity's savior anymore, but you want to be. That's who you believe you should be because that Jess is a good person. And this other Jess—you're afraid she's not good because she's not all those other things. So you hate her, and you fear letting her to the surface."

I moved away, trying to keep distance between myself and Devon. My hands shook, so I balled them into fists. He was not right, and I didn't need to hang around here and listen to him psychoanalyze me.

But if he wasn't right, then why had his speech cut me to the bone? Why was I shaking? Why was my mouth dry?

"You're wrong." Brilliant rebuttal, but it was all I could get out. Wrong. Devon had to be wrong. I didn't carry around some idealized version of myself in my head. I knew I wasn't perfect. I was so very far from it that the idea was absurd.

Case in point—I wasn't watching where I was going and I backed up into his desk and almost fell over.

Devon shrugged. "I could be. So prove it."

"And how am I supposed to do that?"

"Idealized Jess is the perfect should-have-been Gryphon, but an edgy one. She's even tamed a powerful satyr and is determined, despite all logic, that she can make her relationship with him work exactly the way she believes it should."

"I'm well aware that my relationship with Lucen has to be fucked up by all human standards."

"You are. You're also aware that Lucen takes a satyr's view of relationships and is encouraging you to do the same, and you're resisting. Why? Because you're afraid. Because even though not all human relationships are monogamous, you associate that sort of behavior more strongly with satyrs and don't want anything to do with it. So you bury your fear and lie to yourself."

I gripped the edge of the desk, wishing I could crush it. "I'm just not the sort of person who can dissociate sex from emotions. It has no interest to me."

He laughed, pushing his hair out of his face. "You don't have to dissociate anything to prove me wrong. That's another lie you tell yourself."

"I am not—"

But I didn't get to finish my denial because suddenly Devon's mouth was on mine, stealing my denial along with my breath. Stealing my resistance.

His lips were fierce, demanding I yield. The sweep of his tongue, his teeth lightly pulling on mine—the sort of insistence that drove pangs of longing straight through me, pooling between my legs.

I didn't put up much of a fight. One heady whiff of his clove scent, one hint of aftershave the next time I breathed in, and I lost myself. I opened my mouth and welcomed him. His arms pressed against my own, the heat from his body making every muscle in mine tense. A soft moan rose in my throat as his hands cupped my cheeks, less forceful now that I'd surrendered, and I melted into his kiss.

Stop this, Jess. You don't want this. But that was the fear talking, like Devon had said. The rest of me knew the truth. I wanted this. I didn't want to, but I had for too long.

What if Devon was right about why?

Tentatively, I released my grip on the desk and slid my hands over Devon's shirt. Beneath the smooth fabric, I could feel the firm outlines of his stomach muscles. And pressed against me, I could feel his arousal. Growing harder, growing stronger, the more I explored his body.

Need strengthened inside me, aching to be released. I had to have more of him. So much more.

Oh, shit.

Devon pulled his face away before I could decide what to do, and I wasn't sure whether to be grateful and relieved or sad and frustrated.

He breathed as heavily as I did, and the scent of cloves hung in the air between our faces, leaving me dizzy and disoriented. "Prove me wrong, Jess. No more lies. Admit that you want me, that you like me. Admit that no one has a problem with that except you because you hate the thought that you're capable of wanting Lucen and me."

His breath was so hot on my skin. His body so deliciously hard through his clothes. I closed my eyes so I didn't have to look at him too. The longing on his face was enough to seduce my better judgment.

No one else had a problem with it. It was true. Neither Lucen nor Devon seemed to care, so why did I?

Because I didn't want this to be me. I wanted normal, and by normal, I meant normal human. Even when I'd told Lucen I was ready to embrace my satyr side, I'd never let go of wanting that normal human relationship.

But this? This was doubling the non-normality of my life.

I couldn't have normal human. How many times did I have to be faced with that before I let the idea go? Before I let the fear of not having it go?

Devon was right about that too. I was afraid of letting go of the life I'd pictured for myself. I didn't know if I'd call it my idealized self, but it was my idealized life.

"Jess?" Devon ran his thumb over my mouth, and I couldn't stop myself from reaching out for it, taking it between my lips slowly and sucking. I wanted to taste him, to take every part of him inside me. His eyes widened, and I could sense him growing more aroused. One hand rested on my hip, and he squeezed. "Admit that you want me because I have wanted you for weeks now."

I was trembling, and I forced my hands to unclench his shirt. "Of course I want you. You're a satyr. You do that to people."

"True. So why can you sense my power and not other satyrs'? It's because you like me. Just admit it, and admit that it's okay."

When it came to relationships, one of the hardest things I'd ever had to do was admit to myself that I trusted and cared about Lucen. He was so different from me. Entrusting your heart to someone was scary enough normally, but with him, all my fear was amplified.

In some ways this was worse. I wasn't just making myself vulnerable to Devon. I was allowing my entire life to be flipped around.

My heart pounded so hard I should have passed out, but I managed to fling the words off my tongue. "Fine. I like you. Are you happy?"

Devon rested his forehead on mine. "You don't have to sound so miserable about it."

"If I'm miserable right now, it's because you're an awful tease."

"Oh, I can be. But I always deliver in the end, and you've been at the top of my list for too long."

I slipped my hands under his shirt, and still my brain screamed that I shouldn't be doing this. But I couldn't stop. He felt so good, smooth skin over tight muscle, and I needed to be touched. "Then deliver. I said it, so finish this. I want to be rewarded for my honesty."

Devon stiffened as I glided my palms around his ribs, higher up his shirt, feeling his body rising and falling with his breaths. He waited for me, unmoving except for the rhythm of his breathing. Waited to see what I did. What I would do, maybe.

I waited for the same, willing the last of my fear to release me.

His hands rested like weights against my hips, so heavy they pinned me in place with no force at all. And still he didn't move them. A few inches in either direction, that was all I needed.

So I slid mine down him instead, letting my nails lightly brush his skin, entranced by the way he held his breath as they caressed his abs. Lower still, as though they were drawn to the bulge in his pants, and my gaze drawn with them.

Then my hands faltered, hindered by the waistband. It was like the air had turned to honey, thick and sweet, making it hard to move. I knew what I wanted to do, glide my hands lower, unfasten his belt, wrap my fingers around the erection pressed against me. I wanted to breathe him in, taste every delicious inch of his body. Wanted him to burrow himself inside me. Wanted him to make me forget my fear, my hang-ups, myself. Just like Lucen had done our first time together.

I wanted to be changed by his hands.

But I also wanted to pause. Or was that the last traces of my fear slowing me down?

"Jess." Devon's fingers finally trailed up my hips. My clothes shielded me, but it didn't matter. I tensed, my skin coming alive beneath those faintest of touches. My ache growing stronger with each inch of me he covered—hips to stomach to breasts. My nipples hardening as his thumbs grazed them. My eyes closing in my best effort to remain in control.

His lips found mine again, still insistent but gentler this time, teasing as I tried to kiss him more deeply. When I reached for them, he left me groping at air. My tongue longing for a taste denied.

Instead, he nibbled down my throat until he reached my collar. My shirt landed on the floor. I wasn't sure how, and I moaned as he slipped from my grasp, his mouth working down my chest, lingering over the skin between my breasts, licking and biting, making it hard to breathe. Then I was back to squeezing the life from his desk, succumbing to the throbbing between my legs, while he took his time unbuttoning my jeans.

He toyed with me, as promised, slowly and deliberately sliding my jeans down my hips. His face was a study in focus, his eyes lit with a beautiful hunger. And I had to look away. Had to close my eyes again in order to hold still.

I released the desk to grab his shoulders, urging him on.

"Oh, Jess, I've been waiting for this." Desire had thickened his accent. "You're not going to make me go faster."

"I don't want you to go faster." I did, but I didn't. The ache between my legs was growing more intense by the moment, harder and harder to fight.

Devon slipped his hands up my thighs, and I held my breath as his fingers wrapped around the lace band of my underwear. "No, you don't."

I whimpered as he drew his face over the satin fabric and draped the waistband in more delicate kisses. My hips gave in to him, wanting and needing to move.

"I think you've wet these things through. Best to remove them." He tugged my underwear off, and it fell to the floor with my jeans. I swallowed, stepping out of them and feeling his breaths on my most sensitive skin, the way he barely touched it with his lips. Closer and closer, until we met.

With just one delicate kiss, my knees threatened to give out.

He looked up at me, smiling. "I think I'm going to have to tread very carefully here, aren't I? Why have you been fighting so long against something you want too much?"

I couldn't answer him in words.

He didn't seem to expect any. He grasped my backside with one hand and slipped a finger through my folds with another, and I lost track of everything but his touch. His tongue.

My breaths came in ragged bursts, and I whispered his name over and over to keep from letting him tear me in two. Each syllable felt heavy in my mouth, each letter like a note to myself, a reminder of who I was with, the life I was embracing.

And that it was okay. More than okay. It was fucking amazing.

"Get up here, please." I tangled my fingers in his hair, trying to pull him onto me.

He took his time obliging, but when I moaned again, he clasped my ass tightly and straightened. I gasped for air, fighting to bring him closer, deeper. My hands fumbled with his pants button, and his sharp breath when I wrapped my hand around his cock made me shiver.

"Now." I burrowed my face against his neck, hungry for the salt of his skin, but he cupped my cheeks and lifted my head away.

"What are you, Jess?"

There were too many choice answers to that, but for once, my smart-ass mouth couldn't be bothered. I had to give him the one he wanted, or he was going to leave me desperate like this. The sweet agony of him pressed against me, but not in me, was too much.

"I'm a satyr," I whispered.

He leaned into me, nipped at my lip, then pulled harder at it with his teeth until I cried out. "Yes, you are."

Then he lifted me onto the edge of the desk. My legs curled around his hips and my arms around his back, and he plunged inside me. I grabbed him harder, tighter, working toward his mouth again, then wrestling with his tongue and tangling my hands through his hair. Trying to take everything he was able to give until I finally did with a scream torn from my throat and my hands locked around fistfuls of his shirt.

Devon shuddered with me, his moan increasing the residual spasms still flowing through me. Then his breathing settled into pace with mine. His arms held me upright, and I clung to his back, feeling sweat drip down my neck. When I rested my head against the hollow of his throat, it was the scent of cloves I breathed in.

It wasn't the same as cinnamon, but it was damned good too.

TWENTY-FOUR

I ROLLED OVER, AND CRACKED MY EYELIDS OPEN. A SLIVER OF light peeked around the edge of a heavy, gray curtain.

I frowned. This was not right. The window was way too close to the bed.

Wakefulness intruded on my sense of peace, and more wrongness occurred to me. The sheets felt strange, and they smelled stranger. This was not my bed. Nor was it Lucen's.

I sat up with a start, and memories of last night rushed to the front of my thoughts. Letting out a breath, I checked the clock and sank back onto the mattress. I needed to go home.

Next to me, Devon stirred. For once, he didn't look so perfectly put together. His hair was a mess and he needed to shave, but under the sheet, his naked body called to me. Those memories threatened to stick around for a while.

"What are you doing?" The way he forced his eyes open looked painful.

I bid the memories and the feelings they aroused to go away. "I need to leave."

"Already? It's only..." he rolled onto his side to see the clock, "...early. Too early."

"I have work to do. Stuff I should have been working on yesterday when I got sidetracked by the sylphs, and then you. I'm behind." I tossed off the covers so I could climb over him more easily.

Devon reached out and yanked me back. He looked alert now, and his hands slid around me, grabbing my backside and waking up more memories. I shuddered with them. "You weren't really planning on sneaking out on me, were you?"

"It's not like I'd never see you again." And if he didn't release me soon, I wouldn't leave. The promise of what he was hiding beneath the sheet tormented me.

"True." He let go and proceeded to watch me as I got dressed. "Remember when we first met. I told you never say never."

I ran my fingers through my unruly hair, wondering how ridiculous I looked. Spending the night at Devon's had not been in the plan.

Okay, so none of what happened had been in the plan, but sex was one thing. Spending the night in his bed felt way more intimate. What if I snored? Or drooled? It had taken some coaxing before I'd been willing to sleep in Lucen's bed. So what did this suggest? That since I'd finally agreed to sleep with Lucen I was willing to sleep with anyone?

To be fair to myself, I'd had a strong motivation not to go home. But once Lucen had returned from whatever business Dezzi had sent him on, I hadn't left. He'd known where I was, and as expected, had encouraged me to stay with Devon. By then, I'd had a couple glasses of wine and was much more open to the suggestion. Not to mention I'd gone a couple rounds with Devon and my body had ached for more.

And speaking of aches, I wondered how long this soreness would last. And whether normal female satyrs had to deal with it.

Willing my thoughts back to the task at hand, I rummaged in my pocket and found a hair tie. Victory. "Yeah, yeah. I remember, and let's forget it. Don't make me regret this more than I'm already going to."

"Please, Jess. The only thing you should regret is not doing this sooner."

"I'm warning you."

He grinned up at me, smug but charming. "You won't regret it, and you shouldn't. It's not the end of the world, though it may be the end of your worldview. Embrace it. You might find you can be happy for a change."

I put my hands over my ears. "I can't hear you. You're not my therapist."

"Thank all that's unholy, no. This would have been a serious breach of ethics."

I left him there, hoping for his sake that he went back to sleep. It was early, by pred standards, but I was working on a human schedule. By that standard, I was running late.

I found my shoes in the living room and took a second glance around Devon's apartment while I put them on. I didn't remember much of it from last night, having been preoccupied with its owner.

The place fit him. Everything was modern with white walls and black furniture. Very much the opposite of Lucen's apartment, which was filled with heavy wood furniture and earth tones.

Both of them stood in stark contrast to mine, what with my no furniture and few decorations. I felt very much like a little girl fresh out of college, although I was twenty-eight and had never gone. Adulthood? What was that?

One of these days, I promised myself. One of these days I'd pull myself together and get a real life. Who knew—maybe sleeping with Devon was one more step down that path. It was certainly a change.

I kept my eyes open for sylphs as I walked home, but like Devon, most of Shadowtown was in bed. No nasty surprises awaited me at my apartment either. I showered, ate breakfast, and headed downtown.

Before returning to the Gryphon library, I stopped at The Feathers's branch of the public library to see if Olef was around, but he didn't work on Sundays. I left a message with my phone number for him to get back to me.

Alas, although I resumed my research at the Gryphon library, it proved just as hopeless. A couple of the books I found in their online system seemed promising, but they weren't in Boston. I figured out how to put in a request for a loan, and that was that. For all my worrying about how I should have been researching more yesterday, I'd hit a dead end awfully fast. The only thing I might have missed out on was catching Olef at work.

I tapped my fingers on the table in annoyance. It was three o'clock. It was too early to go bug Lucen about what he'd been up to last night, and I had a few hours before my meeting with Gunthra. I should do something productive, but what? I supposed if Bridget were in, I could ask if she needed my help with Eric's case.

Before I could leave the library, however, my phone buzzed with a text. Hoping it was Lucen, wide awake and ready to talk, I pulled it out.

Instead it was Tom. *I'm flying back to Boston tomorrow. Have you had a chance to read those books I left you?*

Ugh. I stared at the message, reluctantly realizing that here was the task I should probably work on the rest of the afternoon.

Reading them now, I wrote back.

At home, I spread out on my floor with the books. A light rain had started falling when I left Gryphon headquarters, and the sky had darkened early. I dragged my one lamp into the middle of the room to augment the fading sunlight.

Tom must have left in a hurry because he hadn't provided any directions or specific instructions along with the books, just the note that had pissed off Olivia and a list of page numbers unconnected to any individual book.

That was unfortunate. Even though I was determined to read everything, there was an awful lot, and much of it was snoozily dry. In school, history had never been my favorite subject, nor one I'd excelled at as a result. I'd liked languages and math, but alas, it was history I was supposed to be studying.

I soldiered on for about an hour when I got a new text. It was from Lucen and only one word. *So?*

Does this mean you want to talk about the sylphs? I wrote back, ignoring his more obvious meaning.

A phone went off right outside my door. "You've got to be kidding."

I threw the door open and found Lucen on my landing. Smiling like a fiend, he offered me a bakery bag.

"What is this?"

"Open it and let me in."

I stepped back and opened the waxy paper. Inside were two chocolate croissants. Couldn't say the man didn't know my weaknesses. "Ooh."

Lucen pulled me into a hug, and tension that I hadn't realized lingered in my shoulders and back drained away. I rested my head on his chest, reveling in the sense of security his arms provided.

And waiting for guilt to kick in.

He seemed to know what I was thinking, and he held me tighter. I dug my nails into the cotton of his T-shirt, remembering everything I'd gotten up to in Devon's office last night. But those memories didn't stir up guilt. They only made me more aware of Lucen's sweet cinnamon scent and the way his hard muscles rubbed against my breasts. They made me want to pull him into my bedroom and see what more fun I could get up to today.

"I'm so glad you're okay, little siren." He cupped my cheek and kissed me slow and deep before I could respond, awakening stronger desire. I chased after his lips as he pulled away, and settled for his chin. "I hate that I wasn't there, but I'm glad someone was."

"Me too," I said, sad when he removed his hands. "I mean, ugh. Never mind. That didn't come out right."

Lucen grinned wickedly, and I reddened as he grabbed my hand. "You sure? No guilt. No shame. I like this side of you."

"I guess it's hard to feel guilty when your boyfriend is encouraging you. Sex and emotions though—I still can't separate them. Devon isn't some random stranger. I guess I don't hate him as much as I want to."

I mumbled the last part, and Lucen laughed. "About time. He's someone I trust."

"But it's not like I'm emotionally empty around him. If that's what you want, I don't think it's possible."

"Jess, all I want is for us to work. If my idea about needing lots of emotionless sex wasn't the right one, so be it. I need you to be okay with the way things are, and I'd say this is a big step forward. If you don't feel guilt over Devon..."

Then how could I feel upset over him and his addicts? I got it. But thinking of addicts made me think of what Devon had told me about them. It was so different than everything I'd believed, and it opened up a whole new way for me to dream about fixing Lucen's need for them.

I'd just keep that dream to myself.

"So what's the reason for this?" I asked, holding up the bakery bag. I opened it and inhaled the sweet butter and chocolate. Oh, yum. Possibly the only thing I'd like more on my tongue than the satyr before me.

Lucen peeled off his rain-soaked jacket. "A celebration?"

"You are so weird. I was thinking it was more like an apology for not being available last night when I needed comfort, but no. You're happy that I slept with your best friend."

"I am happy that we're taking steps to make this work, and yes, I'm happy that you weren't with a stranger." He made an apologetic face. "And I'm sorry that Dezzi called me away last night, but hey—you did have pleasant company from the sound of it."

I set the croissants on my counter. "Tell me you weren't comparing notes."

"Only humans are that crass. If we're going to talk about you, it will be to share tips for your benefit."

I winced. "How thoughtful."

While I took another whiff of the goodies, trying to drive away the image of Lucen and Devon discussing how best to stimulate me, he perused the books. "What are you doing?"

"Oh, just a little light reading for work."

"Light reading, clearly." He thumbed through one of them while I started coffee. "I came over to make sure you were okay with what happened and to talk about the sylph situation, and you're deep in history books?"

I collapsed to the floor and offered him Tom's note. "I promised him I'd take a look."

Lucen's face darkened as he read it. "After everything, you're taking this seriously. Jess—"

"Look, it's not because I want to work with Tom. Okay? There's more to it than that. There's Olef's visions too, and I can't help but wonder if the two things are related. Olef's visions sound an awful lot like the prophecies described in some of these books."

If anything, that made Lucen unhappier. "This is what you told me about the cities burning?"

"Yes, and here." I thrust the book that had the similar passages at him. "Tell me that doesn't sound like this prophecy. I know it's absurd. I don't even know the difference between a prophecy and a vision, but they have too much in common for me to discount it all."

Lucen sucked on his lip and opened to the marked page. "The magi consider a vision that's shared by three or more of their people to be a prophecy. The logic being that the more people who have the vision, the more likely it is to come true."

"Oh." In the kitchen, the coffee water finished boiling, and I paused a moment, parsing Lucen's words before getting up. "You're a right fountain of knowledge at times. Why don't you tell me these things?"

"Why don't you ask?"

"No way. We're not going down that road again." I wanted to explain to him that Devon had told me all about the memory loss, but this didn't seem like the time. Besides, knowing Devon, he'd probably already told Lucen everything about our conversation. It wouldn't be the first time. "While we're at it, I don't suppose you know anything about the Vessels of Making?"

Lucen looked up sharply. "The Vessels of Making? Is this something to do with the case you're working on?"

I spilled coffee on the counter in surprise. "The Gryphon case? No. Why?"

He stretched out on the floor with one of the books, looking very pleased with himself. "There are a bunch of legends about the Vessels. Not so much today, but back in the Middle Ages they were a big deal. Point is, the only thing all the stories have in common is that the Vessels are considered repositories for massive amounts of stored power."

I brought two mugs of coffee into the living room, pondering this. "Repositories for power. Like the containers the goblins and sylphs must be using to hoard the power they stole from their addicts."

"Exactly, only we're talking on a massively larger scale. Power that could feed a domus, or power that a few individual people could channel into one hell of a spell. See?" He handed me the book.

The page it was open to showed a fairly plain cup, somewhere in shape between a bowl and a goblet. It was different than the drawing I'd glimpsed at Gunthra's, but it suggested the same idea. "You found all that in here? I was hoping there'd be information, but I didn't know where to look."

"No, I knew all that already." He tucked his hands behind his head and stared at the ceiling. "But there's a bit about them in the book. They're in the index under their Latin name."

I swore, and Lucen continued to bask in his superiority.

Sipping my coffee, I paged through the brief text related to the Vessels. Alas, it contained nothing that I hadn't found already, and only reiterated that the Vessels had been lost for centuries. "Why would a legend like this be in Tom's so-called history books?"

"Legends and history often go together, particularly where magical lore is concerned. What I want to know..." he sat up and cupped his coffee mug, "...is why you're interested in this if your curiosity wasn't sparked by the case you're on?"

Briefly, I told him about my new deal with Gunthra. He had a few choice words about that, but he found her interest in the Vessels as strange as I had. In return, he told me about his meeting with Dezzi and Assym last night.

He'd been there as backup for her, along with a couple other particularly threatening satyrs. Devon had been left out in case the meeting didn't go over well and he had to take on Dezzi's duties during the fallout. Although Dezzi hadn't shared any details about what I was, nor her offer about the council seat, she'd threatened Assym with something—here, Lucen refused to provide details—and it sounded like Assym was going to back off. Temporarily anyway. According to Lucen, he wanted desperately to know how I'd done what I'd done, and as long as that was a secret, the satyrs had power over him.

I wanted to make a snarky comment about pred politics, but I held my tongue. I was a pred, after all. The more I thought about it, the more I accepted that Devon was right. I had to own it. That led me down another path, and I told Lucen about my conversation with Steph.

"You blew her mind, little siren. That's all."

"What if, in the end, she hates me?"

He took my hands. "She's not going to hate you. She just needs to reconcile two very different opinions. Cognitive dissonance is a bitch, as you should know. Give her time."

I sighed, kicking one of Tom's books aside. "What if that's in short supply? What if this prophecy is on a collision course with us?"

"What if you get hit by a bus tomorrow? No sense worrying about what you can't change. But on the off-chance that the bus is coming, you shouldn't wait to thank me for my extensive brainpower."

"Brawn and brains all in one." I climbed onto his lap and draped my arms over his shoulders. "How did I get that lucky?"

He rested his hands on my hips, sliding his thumbs along the bare skin at my waistband. "I don't know, but I think you should show me some appreciation."

TWENTY-FIVE

I COULD THINK OF ONLY ONE REASON WHY GUNTHRA MIGHT BE interested in the Vessels of Making, and I suspected she wouldn't be pleased when I brought it up.

She already was not pleased because I arrived at her house with Misery strapped to my hip again. "It's unnecessary and unfriendly of you to arrive at my house carrying a lethal weapon."

I tapped my fingers against my legs. "I wasn't aware we were friends, therefore I don't see how unfriendly applies."

Gunthra could make a face every bit as disdainful as her butler. Impressive. "You are in no danger from Assym or the sylphs. I heard that Dezzi had a rather forceful chat with him last night concerning your safety. Seems she intends to bring you into her fold."

I held my face impassive, hoping it would quiet whatever errant emotions might give something away. "Dezzi was clear with me that the choice to join her domus was mine."

"And yet she's taken up on your behalf. That suggests a rather strong interest. I think she's recruiting you."

I tapped my fingers harder, studying my nails as a distraction. I should have known Gunthra would want to discuss recent events. No doubt she was hoping to get me to spill satyr secrets.

"It would be quite a coup for her to have a satyr in her domus who was also trusted by the Gryphons," Gunthra continued. "I've never heard of such a thing. Plus with your unique abilities, you'd make an important asset. Assym is seething with curiosity as to how you did it."

I flattened my hands to stop the damn tapping. "You haven't told him?"

"I don't give out information for free."

Of course not.

"Speaking of which, do you have any for me?" She crossed her legs and settled back against her cushions.

"I have some, but it might not be anything you don't already know. The Gryphon library here in Boston wasn't exactly teeming with details. I had to put in interlibrary loan requests."

A muscle in Gunthra's ear twitched. She had no reason not to believe, seeing as she could tell if I were lying, so maybe she was displeased by the ineptitude of the Gryphons' Boston librarian. "Tell me what you did find out."

I wanted the name she owed me first, but I also knew better than to think I'd get it. So I recounted everything I'd read, as well as the information Lucen had given me. When I finished, Gunthra fell still.

"It occurred to me," I said, watching her closely, "that the Vessels share a striking resemblance to the containers that your people and the sylphs must be using to store those addicts' souls."

I expected derision from her, or denial. Maybe that she'd want to deflect. But Gunthra merely nodded. "It is the same concept, although the Vessels were designed for a greater purpose. Much blood and sacrifice went into making them, far more than what would be required to make the containers you're searching for. The scale is nowhere near the same."

"You believe they're real, not a legend."

"I know they're real. That doesn't make them any less of a legend." She smiled.

I acknowledged the point with a grunt. "Fair enough. You said they were made for a purpose. What purpose? Why do you want to learn more about them?"

"Knowledge." She raised one hand. "Price." She raised the other, then clasped them together.

I flopped backward. "Fine, but if you know so much, what more were you expecting me to be able to tell you?"

"Where to find them, primarily. What they look like. How to use them. Also confirmation that what I believe is true actually is true. All of which, Miss Moore, you've failed to deliver."

That was quite the list.

My hands clenched at my sides. "I told you everything I could find out, and you know I'm not lying. Maybe now that you've given me more to go on, I'll have a better chance of discovering what you want when those books arrive from the library. But meanwhile, I did what was requested. If you want more information than we originally agreed on, then tell me this —does your interest in the Vessels have anything to do with the containers your people used to steal those souls?"

Surprise flashed over Gunthra's face, then she slammed her mask of indifference down on top of it. "I can't tell you for sure, but I would certainly hope not."

Then why do you want them? My best—and only—idea was wrong.

"Just curious," I said, trying to play it off as a random thought. "So what about your end of the deal. I'd like to get Eric Marshall's soul back."

Gunthra pressed her lips together. "You're not lying about what you found, Miss Moore, but you've hardly done much. You haven't given me anything that I wanted to know."

"Our deal was that I'd tell you what I could learn by Sunday evening. I warned you that it might take longer than that to get information."

"Yes, but Sunday evening was an artificial time limit stuck on this deal by you."

"Doesn't matter. I upheld my end."

"Yes, it does matter." Gunthra's words ran together as she clenched her jaw. "You said you would hand over more information, though it might take longer."

She wasn't the only one on the verge of losing it. My fingers itched to caress my knife. There was no way in hell I was letting her get away with reneging on our deal. "I did say that, and I will hand it over. But first I want to know the name of your goblin, *as we agreed on.*"

"When you tell me all you could learn."

I jumped up because I could not control my limbs any longer. "That wasn't the wording we agreed upon."

"That's my interpretation of it."

"Oh, this is a pile of salamander shit." I smacked a pillow. It was that or lunge for her, and I couldn't get away with that. "Forget it. You are not getting any more information out of me until I have Eric's soul back in my possession. That is my priority. Not you and your nefarious history concerns. I don't have time for this."

"Fine." Gunthra's word came out like a punch, startling me. I held my breath as she stormed over to her mantel and picked up one of her glass-encased butterflies. She held it to her chest like it brought her comfort. "You realize what it means for a Dom to sell out her own people to the Gryphons?"

I crossed my arms. "Not exactly, no."

"Our job as Dom is to protect those under us. If we can't do that, we fail at our only job. It's like selling out one of your children."

"My heart breaks. Your child turned someone into a ghoul. What's his name?"

"I tell you this, you'll tell me what else you continue to learn?"

I chewed this over. It sounded an awful lot like what we'd originally agreed upon, but apparently Gunthra hadn't expected me to walk if she'd tried to be sneaky. I couldn't trust her anymore. "Yeah, okay, assuming your information pans out, that is. You'll forgive me for being less than trusting at the moment."

Gunthra clucked her tongue in disapproval, and I wanted to smack her more than ever. She was the one reneging on our deal. "Silas. He runs the dry-cleaning shop by the bookstore."

That couldn't be right. Silas didn't sound like a goblin name. "This is the goblin who has Eric's soul?"

Stiffly, Gunthra set the butterfly back. "No. This is the sylph who makes the containers that my goblin and the others used to capture those souls."

"That was not—"

"At his place of business, you'll find the names of everyone to whom he sold those containers, along with evidence to support arresting him for doing it. Trust me, Miss Moore. Arresting Silas is a much greater victory than arresting a single goblin, and I won't have betrayed my own people by pointing you toward him. I think that's more than fair."

I gritted my teeth. Much as I longed to pull Misery from its sheath and threaten the goblin's name from Gunthra, I fought to keep my temper in check. "You know how long it will take the Gryphons to pull off a raid like that. How do I know you won't tip off Assym?"

She sighed. "Because I have to assume if you don't find what I'm telling you is there, you won't continue to cooperate with my research. I am certain the Gryphons have records that will give me what I need, and unfortunately for both of us, you are the only person I know with the remotest chance of accessing them. So." She raised her hands in defeat. "I won't be tipping off Assym anytime soon. His inability to control his people isn't my problem."

"Then let's hope you're right if you want anything else from me."

"How did you get this information?" Bridget asked.

I paced in circles around my living room, holding my phone to my ear. Books were strewn all over, turning it into an obstacle course. "You told me to work my contacts in Shadowtown. I worked my contacts in Shadowtown. Can we leave it at that?"

"Jess, between this and the lack of details you provided yesterday about the sylphs, people are going to ask questions."

I stepped over a history book. "Let them. Those are two completely unrelated events, and any questions about yesterday can be directed at Tom Kassin."

"Who's conveniently out of the country."

"But on his way back." Unfortunately. I adjusted the phone. "Look, it's a good lead. I have reason to be confident about it. Are we following up on it or not?"

If not, I might have to do it by myself, and I didn't see that going over well. Dezzi might have threatened Assym on my behalf, but the sylphs would not roll over and let me raid one of their businesses. And I was certain that, even if she was trying to court me, Dezzi would not back me up on such a hostile act.

"We are," Bridget said. "But it's a Sunday evening, so it's going to take me a couple hours to pull a team together for something this big. I'll get started as soon as we hang up."

"Whoa, wait." I reached for the wall as I tripped on the lamp cord. "Tonight? What about waiting for morning and catching everyone unawares?" That was how the Gryphons preferred to operate, and it made sense.

"This case is time sensitive. I don't want to do this during prime pred hours either, but the sooner we have leads for tracking down the preds involved, the better. I don't want to wait, and I don't know enough about your informant to trust him."

I grimaced. "I wouldn't recommend it."

"Then as soon as I get a team together and a warrant, we're going. Can you come in? I assume you want to be a part of this."

"You know me. Wouldn't miss it."

BEFORE I WENT IN, THOUGH, I STOPPED BY LUCEN'S. THE LAIR was closed since it was Sunday, but that was often the day he took care of backend business if he hadn't had time during the week. So when he didn't answer his apartment door, I knocked on the bar's.

He opened it so fast he must have known I was there already. "Need to talk about your meeting with Gunthra?"

"Sort of. I've got to be quick."

I didn't owe the satyrs a warning about what was going to happen. Theoretically, they shouldn't even be involved, and the gods knew how illegal tipping off Lucen must be. Yet my conscience wouldn't let me leave Shadowtown without letting him know what was coming his way. If nothing else, I wanted him to be forewarned about what I was up to so there could be no arguments about it later.

Lucen stepped aside so I could enter the bar. He had boxes sitting out on the tables, music playing, and he seemed to be in the middle of some reorganizing.

"Hey, Jess." One of the boxes slid to the side, and Devon's face came into view.

I managed to hold in the whimper that crawled up my throat. Seeing him and Lucen together was too weird, and clearly not a situation I'd been prepared for.

It was also irrelevant at the moment, but that didn't make the weird feeling any less intense, nor stop Devon from silently laughing at my reaction.

I pushed my hair behind my ears self-consciously. "I wanted to give you a heads-up. The Gryphons are coming this way. Not after you, but after a certain sylph. It shouldn't concern you at all, in fact, but I feel this sense of obligation to warn you."

I was pleased to see my news wiped the humor from Lucen's face, but Devon just popped the cap off a fresh beer and shrugged. "Dezzi will be very happy that you're so considerate. Care to offer more details?"

"Not really. I shouldn't be telling you this much."

Lucen pulled me close. "Why are we being invaded?"

"Illicit magic operation."

Devon let out a whistle. "Better the sylphs than us. Those are always exciting. I should grab a rooftop seat to watch. Want to point me in the right direction?"

"Not really."

"You found who's making the containers?" Lucen asked, and I nodded. "Nothing we need to worry about then, but thanks, little siren."

"No problem." I kept my eyes averted from Devon as I kissed Lucen's cheek. Would I have felt as much like a traitor if I hadn't told him? Gryphons or satyrs—I needed to straighten out my loyalties. "I need to go."

Lucen kissed me back, not content for anything so chaste, and I could feel Devon's gaze on me. My cheeks flushed.

When I pulled away, he was watching me intently. "You're going along?"

"My case. My lead. Hell, yes."

Devon set his beer down and walked over. "Then you'd better give me a kiss for good luck too. The sylphs already have it in for you. You need to be careful."

You need to be careful. Devon's words rang in my head as I joined Brian's team in the Gryphons' conference room.

Bridget had turned my information over to her supervisor, and over the past hour, the Gryphons he'd called had been trickling in. There were ten, not including me, many of whom I hadn't seen before. For the most part, they weren't investigators like Bridget. More like the equivalent of a SWAT unit.

In the past few minutes we'd apparently reached some critical mass because Brian dimmed the lights and the briefing started. After providing a summary of what we'd been up to, he turned the floor over to Bridget, who related what I'd told her. Then we moved on to the logistics and other practical matters—who the sylph was, where his business was located, what we were likely to find.

This amounted to a lot of speculation because this sylph didn't have a criminal record. That made the people around me nervous, which made me jittery. When I asked Bridget about it, she explained that a lack of history meant they were dealing with the unknown.

"Usually we have a good beat on preds, an idea of who it is we're dealing with. Without it, it's harder to anticipate what sort of resistance we'll be met with."

"For one sylph?"

She obsessively undid and redid her ponytail. "It's never just one. When we raid this guy's shop, the sylphs as a whole will be pissed." She tapped me on the back. "Your protection charm okay still?"

"No worries there."

I was the only one who could say that, though. Getting out the door was a slow process for a group of people who seemed capable of moving at light speed in an emergency. But aside from weapons to hand out, charms needed to be assigned, as well. Recalling yesterday's sylph encounter, I didn't say no to the speed and strength charms Bridget offered me. I slung them around my neck, grateful for the additional protection. My soul might be safe, but I didn't need another reminder that my body was not.

Three hours after I'd called Bridget, I returned to Shadowtown.

The sun had finished setting, and the sky glowed with light pollution. Sunday night meant the streets were less busy, but plenty of preds were around to gawk when the Gryphon SUVs pulled up outside an innocuous-looking dry-cleaner's shop.

A goblin and two harpies who'd been exiting the bookstore next door cursed and darted back inside. Nervously, I fidgeted with my knife and wished I'd snagged a disguise charm. My presence would not be winning me any friendly neighbors.

Three of the Gryphons took off around the back, but up and down the street, preds were whipping out their phones. Even if this Silas guy didn't know we were about to knock down his front door, Assym and his council would soon.

I swatted at a couple imps that were hanging around the streetlamp we'd parked by and trailed the Gryphon team across the street. Bridget was on her walkie-talkie, letting the Gryphons in the back know an OPEN sign hung in the store window.

Hands on their blade hilts, the first two Gryphons threw open the door. When the "all clear" rang out, all but two of the Gryphons headed in. I followed.

The lights were on, and the faint strains of classical music played from unseen speakers. I let the door close behind me while Bridget yelled Silas's name. A long counter separated us from the back of the shop, which was a maze of racks and plastic-sheeted clothes. In all, the place appeared to be exactly what it was purported to be. Gunthra had better not have lied.

"You smell that?" one of the Gryphons asked.

I inhaled deeply, but I wasn't sure what I was supposed to be sniffing. A faint chemical odor laced the air. Not owning the sorts of clothes that required dry cleaning, I had no idea whether that was abnormal.

A few of the Gryphons shrugged, and Bridget called for Silas again. This time her inquiry was met with a banging noise, and a "Fucking Gryphons" from somewhere in the back.

A moment later an old and extremely pissy-looking sylph hobbled to the counter, holding a phone in his hand. "Can I help you?"

Bridget slapped the warrant on the counter. "We got a tip about some unregulated and illicit charm making going on at the premises. We're taking a look."

"I see." The sylph drew out the word, his gray eyes filled with cold menace. He slid the phone into his pocket, and I'd have bet anything that he'd been in the back getting tipped off when we arrived. How else would he have known that the humans entering his shop were Gryphons?

The Gryphon closest to the counter gate opened it, and one by one, we filed through. There was little room to move and less room to see thanks to the hanging clothes. I pushed a plastic-wrapped shirt out of my face, disturbed but unable to say why.

That was when the rack started moving.

I jumped back, the sound of the machinery competing with the shouting Gryphons, several of whom were stuck in the middle. Dodging clothes, I made to grab for the sylph, but he flew out of my reach, no longer frail, but spry. Swearing, I ducked low, maneuvering my way to where he'd been standing, certain the switch for the rack had to be nearby but I couldn't see it.

"Down there!" I heard Bridget yell.

Breaking free of the moving clothes, I saw a flash of white disappear through a doorway. Abandoning the switch, I charged after him.

Bridget and two other Gryphons got to the doorway first and disappeared. I stumbled through on their heels only to discover a narrow landing and set of rickety wood stairs. Whatever smell had lingered in the main part of the store was stronger here, a mix of harsh chemicals and something pungent. Something that conjured memories of the compost pile in my mother's backyard. Rotting food.

"Holy shit," one of the Gryphons muttered.

Holding the baluster, I continued my descent, landing in a creepy, dark basement. Only a couple bare light bulbs illuminated the dark wood that seemed to be everywhere—the floor, the ceiling, and row upon row of shelves.

"Where the hell did he go?" Bridget asked. She'd pulled out her sword and a flashlight, peering into the narrow aisles between the shelves.

It was a good question. Judging by the upstairs, the basement could not be that large.

I temporarily forgot about the sylph, enthralled in a horrified way by the objects that sat on his elaborate worktable. Glyphs and diagrams had been carved into the top, and the tools of the magical trade were everywhere. Obsidian bowls, a bloody knife, and jars filled with a variety of items that once belonged to living creatures. I simply couldn't identify what those creatures had been at this point, or what pieces of them had the misfortune to end up here. It was from one of those containers that the stench emanated.

Footsteps pounded down the stairs behind me, and dust fell from the ceiling with the vibrations. Another Gryphon joined us in the basement. Tearing my eyes from the table, I rested my hand on Misery's hilt and moved out of his way.

A stained shop sink sat beneath a narrow window at street level, and next to it sat a shelf filled with books. While Bridget and the others continued the search for Silas, I grabbed one, trusting a hunch that these weren't spell books.

I was right. Preds, especially older ones who'd been around since long before the digital revolution, shied away from computers for magical work. I'd bet if Silas hadn't made such a dash to get away, these books would have been burned and the most damning evidence against him destroyed.

But he had, and they weren't. I flipped through one of the ledgers, which was filled with row after row of charm orders and invoices. Score. All I had to do was find the newest one, the one that detailed the orders for the containers used to store Eric's soul, and let the Gryphons bring in Silas.

I tossed the one I held on the table and grabbed the least dusty book.

And my world exploded. A flash of light blinded me a split second before the building shook, and I hit the floor.

TWENTY-SIX

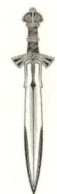

Books slammed into my back. Beneath my knees, the floor moved, and I could hear people screaming over the crashing of shelves and breaking of glass. But everything sounded wrong, and the air felt heavy. It was like the world—and me—moved in slow motion.

Curse grenades. The sylph had launched a fucking curse grenade at us.

I coughed, clawing my way free of the debris, fearing what sort of spell had been released in the explosion. One that distorted my perception of time, clearly. The explosion seemed like it had taken forever. How long since it had gone off?

"Bridget?"

My body ached, and I sneezed, but I clutched the ledger to my chest. One by one, Gryphons checked in, shoving off the shelves and whatever else had descended on them. More glass shattered.

"My charms aren't working," someone yelled.

"Anti-magic." Bridget coughed. "And some kind of disorientation curse."

From upstairs came a scream, and I remembered there was at least one other Gryphon who hadn't made it down the stairs yet, not counting the ones outside. Bounding over pieces of shelving, I lumbered up the steps.

My sense of time and place were returning to normal. The world resumed its natural pace, but I still felt sluggish.

Behind me, Bridget was getting on her walkie-talkie, calling in backup. Without their protective charms working, she and the other Gryphons were vulnerable to magical attacks.

I reached the top of the stairs and poked my head out carefully. The rack had been shut off, but I couldn't see where the screaming was coming from. Fighting my way to the front of the store, I pulled out my knife. My left shoulder whined in pain where a shelf had collapsed on it, and I adjusted my grip on the ledger.

I was at the counter when someone crashed into me from behind. I didn't hear footsteps and had no time to brace myself, so I flew forward, my knees once more colliding with the floor and my head smacking into the counter. The ledger fell from my hands, and my head swam. Or maybe the store did.

Dazed, I forced my eyes open and turned around just in time. Silas had somehow freed himself from the basement and was coming at me with a knife.

Shit. So much for Dezzi's talk with Assym.

I rolled out of the way, cursing my ineffective charms. Silas's momentum worked against him, and he had to hold out his arms to brace himself so he didn't get beamed on the counter too. Praying my vision was working better than it seemed to be, I shot out my legs and jammed him in the shins. He fell over, his knife arm colliding with the counter.

Seeing my opening, I reached for his wrist, using my own knife to scare him into not resisting. Silas did exactly what I wanted. He dropped his weapon to get out of my way. Then he reached around me, aiming for the ledger.

Twisting around, I flung it farther from him. Silas lost his balance, and his cold magic jolted me as his hand bumped against my arm. The touch of it was like a snake against my skin, and I shrank back before I kicked out at him a second time. He was ready and dodged, and on his feet so fast he had to be wearing a speed charm.

I reached for the ledger, determined to keep it from him, but he ignored it. With a curse, he suddenly bolted for the door.

I screamed in frustration, amazed by the guttural sound of my voice, and hauled myself upright. Temporarily leaving the book, I stumbled around the counter and out onto the street to see where Silas had gone.

And froze in the doorway.

The Gryphons who'd been waiting by the cars had vanished, and two of the SUVs were on fire. Up and down the street, sylphs were gathering. They lurked in doorways and huddled together in the intersection. The streetlamps' glow reflected off the metal they carried. Some had blades. Others possibly had guns. And still most were unarmed, but they kept coming. A panting Silas had joined his brethren at a grocer's across the street.

All the other preds who'd been gawking had disappeared.

My mouth went dry. Too scared to even swear, I backed into the shop.

"Bridget, do we have reinforcements coming? There's an army of sylphs gathering outside."

More crashing and muttering came from downstairs. Then Bridget's voice. "They're on the way. How many?"

"Ten that I could see."

I dove to the floor and peeked out from the window, wary of the guns. Preds so infrequently used them, mostly because they didn't work well on other preds.

Wetting my lips, I got out my phone and dialed Lucen. He didn't give me a chance to speak.

"Jess, are you okay? What's going on?"

I squeezed the phone. "That's why I'm calling. The sylphs are going on the offensive. They have guns. I'm trapped in a dry cleaner's until backup gets here."

Lucen swore. "I know. Assym seems to be panicking. A few minutes ago, Dezzi started getting reports that something was up. They're taking to the streets."

"Gunthra said they were panicky. I can't believe Assym is allowing this. They're really going to bring the Gryphons down on them."

"Not your problem, little siren."

"No?" I raised my head, and the storefront glass exploded with a bang that rattled my bones. I might have cried out, but my brain emptied of conscious thought. I flattened myself against the floor, listening to the sound of my heartbeat. It was so loud, even through the ringing in my ears.

Lucen was yelling. "Jess? What happened?"

I pulled the phone back toward my head, vaguely aware that the area was covered in glass. I probably was too. Was probably cut to hell and back and bleeding like crazy, but I couldn't feel it. Adrenaline had turned me numb.

My fingers shook so hard it took a moment to place the phone properly to my ear. "I'm here. I'm okay. I was just shot at."

"What? No, that is *not* okay." Lucen swore and yelled at someone, but I couldn't hear what was going on. The ringing in my ears was too much.

On my stomach, I wormed away from the window and back behind the counter. How many minutes had gone by since Bridget called for reinforcement? It couldn't have been enough.

"Jess, are you there?"

"Yeah, I'm here."

"Don't go anywhere or do anything stupid. Stay where you are until the Gryphons arrive. I have to go."

I rubbed blood from my hand on my jeans, debating whether to risk another glance out the window. "You're hanging up? Is it Dezzi calling?"

Lucen didn't respond. The sound of new shattering glass came through the phone before the line went dead.

"Lucen!" I stared at the phone. What the hell was going on?

I got to my knees, my muscles creaking in protest. Something hot and sticky ran down my neck. Sweat or blood? I didn't want to know.

My phone rang with Lucen's number as I peered around the counter. Quickly, I dove back down to answer. "Lucen?"

"No, he's busy at the moment."

The voice was familiar, yet I didn't place it right away. When I did, my blood chilled. "Assym?"

"Good ear."

No thanks to his people shooting at me. "What are you doing? Where's Lucen? Have you lost your shit? Dezzi's going to kill you, and so are the Gryphons."

"So many questions, so little time. The only one that matters is the one you need to answer—what are you, and what did you do to my associate yesterday? Come prepared to talk. You know where to find me."

"That was two questions, dumbass. And if you want to talk to me, you need to tell your people to stop shooting at me."

There was a pause, and I imagined Assym silently cursing me. At least I hoped he was because I was sure wishing him a very painful death. "They'll stop." Then he hung up.

"Shit." I repeated the word a few times for good measure, like a mantra to refocus myself. I had to get to The Lair, which was exactly what Lucen had told me not to do.

He didn't really think that would work, did he?

"Jess?"

I turned around, dropping my phone. Bridget had worked her way up the stairs. Blood ran down her forehead, and she was covered in dust. "What happened?"

"They're shooting. Keep your head down."

"Shooting, huh? This is new for them." Her eyes widened, and she shook her head slightly. For Bridget, that was one hell of a shocked response.

Another Gryphon appeared in the doorway, and I could hear others moving about on the creaking stairs. Keeping close to the floor, I worked my way through the rows of clothing, figuring there had to be a back exit. The acrid chemical stench strengthened as I passed by stainless-steel tables and machines unfamiliar to me. I scarcely noticed my surroundings, looking only for unfriendly movement and a door.

My gaze settled on an industrial exit sign at last, and I pushed it open cautiously, not trusting Assym's goons to refrain from shooting. But the alley was silent and dark. Slowly, I stepped outside, leaving Misery sheathed. If I had to duck for cover, I didn't want to cut myself in the process.

A shape moaned by a reeking dumpster, and as my eyes adjusted to the lack of light, I realized it was one of the Gryphons Bridget had directed this way. My feet sounded so loud on the pavement as I ran over and checked him for injuries. I saw none, which suggested he'd either been clonked on the head or hit with a disorientation curse. That whoever had done this hadn't killed him was a miracle, but maybe they'd been in a hurry. The Gryphon's partner was gone, and I hoped she was busy chasing down the asshole who'd attacked.

Swallowing down my concern and fear, I jogged to the end of the alley far from the street where I'd seen the sylphs gathering. I was near the back of the bookstore, and not too far from Gunthra's narrow and quiet street. I cursed the goblin Dom's name, not entirely trusting that she hadn't known what would happen when we went after Silas.

When no one jumped out at me, I dashed around the back of the bookstore and came out on the street that ran perpendicular to the dry cleaner's. Emptiness greeted me, and I shivered at the slight breeze. After escaping the violence and chaos nearby, this deadness was eerie. Had all the other pred groups retreated inside?

I could see silhouettes moving about in some of the windows, but there was no life on the street except for imps buzzing about the streetlamps. I prayed they stayed there. An imp sting would dull my magical senses, and while I couldn't sense preds in the first place, I wanted every advantage my gift gave me just in case.

Brushing my fingers over Misery's hilt, I wondered if I was walking into another sylph trap, then I pushed aside the idea. Of course I was walking into a trap. But it was a couple blocks over at The Lair. Assym wanted me. I simply didn't know whether he wanted me dead or alive anymore.

There was only one way to find out.

I was about to start forward again when the air filled with a rumble. I blinked into a bright light flashing across the sky. The Gryphons were out in a helicopter. I suspected that after Buenos Aires, and Boston's own misadventure with salamander fire not so long ago, they were taking this very seriously, very quickly.

Good.

New sounds—sirens—pierced the noise above. Holding back, I watched headlights from three Gryphon vehicles tear down the street. And here were the reinforcements. Also good.

I wiped sweat from my forehead, feeling better about leaving Bridget, but the feeling was short-lived. The first of the three cars had passed me when an explosion detonated right in front of it.

Instinctively, I crouched down, although I was out of the blast area. Brakes and metal shrieked, and the darkened street lit up in flames. Foul smoke and burning rubber thickened the air.

My first horrified thought was that the car was on fire, but it had only overturned with another curse grenade. Besides, the flames moved too abnormally to be true fire, which meant my second thought was even more horrifying—someone had let out salamanders.

I gave up on swearing. I'd run out of words. Helplessly, I watched Gryphons pour out of the overturned SUV, and the night erupted in shouting. Sylphs descended from around the corner, charging from the dry cleaner's block. More curse grenades exploded, and foul-smelling smoke burned my nose.

Catching my breath, I made my decision—let them go. The Gryphons were better trained for this sort of fight than me, and I had my own destination. While a battle brewed to my left, I raced to the right.

TWENTY-SEVEN

THE SYLPHS HAD SHOT IN THE WINDOW AT THE LAIR, JUST LIKE they'd done at the dry cleaner's. Thousands of glass shards reflected the light from the bar's overhead lamp, glittering like dangerous diamonds over the patio and its upturned furniture.

My hands sweat as I crossed the street, listening to the sounds of a struggle inside that I couldn't yet see. Annoyed, I rubbed them on my jeans. I needed them dry to hold Misery.

Needed to hold Misery so I could drive the knife's blade into Assym's scrawny chest.

He'd gone after Lucen because of me, and me only. I was certain of it. And that made this my responsibility. I didn't know whether he'd done it because of what I'd done to his thug yesterday, or because I was working for the Gryphons. Frankly, I didn't care that much, but it would be nice to know whether this would have gone down if I'd stayed away from the Gryphons like Lucen had asked.

Actually, no. It wouldn't be nice to know that. It would make me feel worse if that was the case.

Bracing myself for a fight, I withdrew Misery and started down the steps to The Lair. Glass crunched under my feet, and a stillness settled over me. I was so ready to kill.

"Jess, get away!"

Lucen's voice rattled my calm, but instead of taking his suggestion—he ought to know better—I jumped down the last steps and peeked through the broken window.

I winced.

Devon had disappeared, but Lucen and Gi, a satyr I barely knew, were locked in fights with three sylphs. Lucen's lovely face was bruised and bloody, but he seemed to be holding his own despite them being outnumbered. It was hard to tell much more though. They were all amped up on magic and moving so fast that without my own charms working, I mostly saw blurs.

A Lucen-colored blur slammed a sylph into the wall, then slammed the sylph's head against it one more time for good measure. When he let go, the sylph slumped to the floor, but he wouldn't be down for long. They healed too quickly.

I scanned the room for other blades like mine, but I didn't see any. I didn't see Lucen's gun either, but I was sure it was there in the rubble. If I could only find it before the sylphs did.

"Jess, I said go!" Lucen wasn't even looking my way. He'd abandoned the downed sylph and was trying to pull one of the other two off Gi. I could tell them apart only from the color streaks they left behind—Gi dark, Lucen light, and the sylphs creepily white.

To hell with going. It was time to even the odds in there. I might not have the preds' speed or strength, but I had magical steel.

I got as far as the door when I was yanked on from behind. Unlike the last time sylphs had grabbed me, I was expecting trouble and my reflexes were sharp. I turned the sylph's momentum on him, twisting and jabbing with my elbows before he got a firm grip. With my right arm mostly free, I slashed at him with my knife. All it would take was a nick, and I got him way better than that.

The sylph screamed, releasing me and clutching his arm. Blood oozed from the wound, seeping between his fingers. Anticipating backup, I spun around.

Assym cocked a gun at me.

Genuine panic bloomed inside my gut, and I fought to control it. My own fear I could feed on for strength, but panic would overwhelm me. Anyway, Assym might well have decided to kill me, but he wouldn't yet. If that was all he'd wanted, he could have shot me in the back as I entered The Lair.

My lips were dry and tasted like blood when I wet them. "Where's your favorite knife? Too scared to get closer when I'm armed?"

Oh yeah. I could spew bravado, but we both knew it was a load of crap.

I cringed as something inside the bar crashed.

"I'm done playing games." Assym cast a withering glance at his bleeding sylph. If I had to guess, he was annoyed the thug had ruined his entrance. "I want to know how you did what you did to my associate yesterday."

I backed into the door but didn't dare open it. So it was information Assym wanted. Alas, he could shoot me and still ask questions. "Why don't you ask your associate? Oh, wait. You can't. Your other fearless associates killed him. Seems like your anger is misdirected."

Assym's face hardened. "They said they had to kill him because…" His jaw quivered. It was as if he was in such disbelief that he couldn't get the words out.

"Because?"

"It's not possible, so tell me what you did." He raised the gun, which had formerly been pointed at my chest, to head level. Not being human himself, perhaps he failed to realize that a shot to either location could kill me.

Someone was shouting down the street. Tires squealed, followed by gunfire and an explosion. Was the fighting getting closer? Were more satyrs on the way? Where had Devon gone? And how about some Gryphons?

Fuck, I'd take Tom right about now if he could supply a solution.

I had to get a grip.

"What incentive, exactly, do I have to tell you anything if you're going to shoot me when I'm done?" It was a pointless question, and I could predict Assym's answer, but I had to buy time. Just in case someone at street level could help. Just in case Lucen could break free of the fighting in the bar.

Assym cocked his head from side to side. "It depends on your answer. You are so very interesting to me, satyr's pet. I need to know what you did. I want to know if I can prevent you from doing it again. Because if I can, well, we still have a future together."

"You don't believe what I did is possible, yet you think you can neutralize my ability? I can't decide if you're merely lacking brain cells or drowning in arrogance. Then again, you're a sylph. They go together."

Assym's gaze darted toward the bar window for a second at the sound of more banging, but he was too fast for me to make a move. He smiled, daring me to attempt it. "I will shoot you if I have to. I'll take you one shot at a time to motivate you to talk."

That had been the answer I was anticipating. "I've never found that sort of drill-sergeant-like pain-as-motivator crap effective. Yell at me, hurt me—it only pisses me off and makes me more stubborn."

"Should we see about that?"

I cast about for a retort that would lengthen this conversation, but none came to mind. Trust all my ideas to run out too soon.

Fuck you, my body seemed to say to my brain. *Now is definitely the time to panic.* The surge of fear shot through me so hard, so cold, that I had no choice but to move. The energy hit it provided me demanded it.

I dove for Assym, my ears buzzing with more gunfire. It sounded like he'd fired before I moved, but I felt nothing. Not until we hit the ground together, that was.

Broken glass and concrete slammed into my palms and dug into my skin. I fell on top of Assym, who was screaming in rage. My knees landed on top of his legs, and I rolled off him, hissing to control the shrieking pain in my hands.

Misery had slipped from my grip when the ground and I collided, and I lunged for the knife. My fingers screeched in protest and trembled with adrenaline. Then I was pushing myself to my feet. Remembering Assym's gun. Adjusting my hold on Misery.

I had to finish the sylph before he finished me.

But there was blood everywhere. Assym was already coated in it, all streaming from the single bullet hole near his shoulder.

I scrambled up, found the gun and kicked it away from him. Assym wasn't knocked out, but he thrashed and moaned, seemingly senseless. The sylph I'd cut earlier flew up the steps, clutching his arm without a backward glance for his Dom. So much for loyalty.

"Lucen?" I reached for the gun, realizing as I said his name that it couldn't have been Lucen who shot Assym. The angle was wrong.

"Want to take a second guess, girlie?"

I spun toward the speaker and tripped over an overturned chair. Mace-head was staring down at me, a deranged grin on his face.

The fury was scary enough without that expression. Dressed in his usual black leather and with his gun hanging lazily from his hand, he reminded me of a comic book villain—the absolute batshit kind who thrived on violence.

"You?" I struggled for something coherent to say. Mace-head continued to grin, most pleased with himself. It certainly didn't seem like he intended to attack me next. It made no sense. "Why?"

Sirens wailed on the street above, drowning out whatever the fury had started to say. Four Gryphons on bikes, plus a cop car and an ambulance whizzed by.

Mace-head scratched his neck with his free hand, watching them go. He seemed completely unconcerned about the war breaking out in his neighborhood.

But of course, he wasn't concerned. The furies had tried to cause fighting here before, and he'd been an integral part of it. But how? Why? I had a million questions all of a sudden. So many I couldn't even process them. They dangled before me like threads, and I needed to weave them together to get my answer. A very complex and exciting answer—I could feel it.

I tried, but with everything going on around me, I couldn't concentrate.

At the sound of metal scraping the concrete, I spun around. Assym was climbing to his feet. His eyes were glazed with pain, but his face declared murder as he gawked at the fury. "You son of a—"

"Nuh-uh, Mister Assym." Mace-head waved his gun at the sylph. "Let's keep this polite, right? Beat it before I shoot you again. Next time I aim for your pretty face. Got it?"

Assym's jaw worked, but nothing came out. "This... You'll pay for this." He limped up the steps and disappeared from view.

"Funny, isn't he?" Mace-head said. "Like there'll be anything left of him once the Gryphons clean up here."

"You're not worried about that yourself?"

"Nah. Gryphons aren't really my concern. You, on the other hand, you are my concern. So take this."

I flinched as he reached into his pocket and tossed something at me.

It was a charm container. "What is this?"

"A little thing to speed your healing along, is all. You look a might beat-up, and the night is young. This could get uglier before the dawn. Take care, girlie."

"Wait!" My world spun—literally and metaphorically—as I lunged for the steps. "What the hell are you doing? What kind of game is this?"

Mace-head holstered his gun, leaning back on his heels. "I'm saving you, or I did. And it's a good game, girlie. It's a very good game, indeed. 'Til we meet again, try not to get dead. And oh, you might want to hang by your satyr boyfriend there. Sounds like the fun's breaking up inside, and he might be useful."

Then he turned around and left. Mouth open, I let him go. He'd given me as much of a weird nonanswer as I should have expected, so I couldn't complain. As much as I wanted to shake him until it rattled loose the truth, or at least something sensible, I knew it would be pointless. Besides, I had Lucen in the bar and had to make sure he was okay.

I clopped down the steps toward him, but my brain couldn't let go of Mace-head's words. Nor his actions. When I considered it a second time, his response, bizarre as it sounded, wasn't actually nonsensical. I didn't believe that for a second. Something big was going on, and him shooting Assym for me was part of it.

He wanted me alive. The furies had *always* wanted me alive.

But why? After what I'd done to them with regards to Victor, I should have been at the top of their hit list. Instead, when three of them had harassed and threatened me a couple weeks ago, Mace-head had chased them off. I hadn't thought much of it at the time. It had been weird, but I'd had plenty of other issues to keep me from dwelling on it.

I couldn't not dwell on it any longer. None of these incidents were random.

"Jess!"

The Lair's door crashed open, and Lucen emerged, bloodied and in a ripped shirt, but alive. I threw my arms around him and silently cried in pain when he did the same to me. My adrenaline was wearing off, and with it came awareness of how damaged I was.

With some trepidation, I stuck the pain-relief charm around my neck, trusting that if Mace-head had wanted to hurt me, he could have done it some better way. Hell, he could have shot me. For some reason, he wasn't a threat.

"What happened with Assym?" Lucen had retrieved his own gun, and he stuck it awkwardly in his waistband. "I could sense you out here, little siren, but I couldn't get to you."

I wiped the trickle of blood off his lip. "I'm fine. Weird story. I'll tell you about it later. What's going on?"

"I don't know."

I followed him inside, mourning the damage to The Lair, which was extensive. The place looked more like it had hosted a train wreck than a bar fight, but a large part of that was probably due to the broken window.

Among the overturned tables and chairs, and general disaster of broken glasses and bottles, the important thing here was clear—Lucen and Gi had subdued the sylphs. Two of them slumped unconscious against a booth, while the third glowered at us. Gi or Lucen had stuffed a dishrag in his mouth while Gi finishing tying the three of them together.

Thanks to the broken bottles, the smell of alcohol hovered in the air, so strong a lightweight might get drunk off it. Stepping around a pool of Absolut Vodka, I turned on the tap at the sink and began rinsing the blood off my hands and removing the glass and pebbles from my skin. Even with the charm on, the water stung.

Lucen had gotten on the phone, but I wasn't sure who he was talking to. Shutting off the tap, I closed my eyes. I needed time to think everything through. The threads knotted and unknotted, but I couldn't see the final pattern they would produce.

I just knew there was one.

IT WAS ALMOST DAWN BEFORE THE THREADS FORMED A picture for me, but even then, it was incomplete. I needed other threads. Fortunately, I knew where to find them, but I would have to wait a few more hours.

Overnight, the fighting in Shadowtown had spread. The sylphs had collectively lost their minds. That was my opinion.

Officially, the story emerged that they were acting on Assym's orders and a good bit of their own paranoia. As soon as we had descended on the dry cleaner's, Silas had alerted his Dom. We already knew he wasn't the only sylph who would be in trouble before the night was over, but the number of sylphs he'd sold his illegal containers to was higher than anyone could have guessed. This racket was big—the number of addict victims was over a dozen and growing. So was the number of guilty sylphs, many of whom were on Assym's council. They'd decided they weren't going down without a fight.

That Assym thought to take his revenge on me in the middle of it was just the fucked-up cherry on top of this evil Sunday night.

It was also Assym's biggest mistake. Once he set his sights on me and targeted Lucen to get to me, he'd picked a fight with the satyrs. Thank dragons Dezzi wasn't so shortsighted as to forgo assisting the Gryphons. In my adrenaline-fueled, sleep-deprived stupor, I started calling the battle the Boston Pred Party.

Too bad none of the sylphs got dumped in the ocean, but I'd settle for arrested or dead.

Dezzi had gathered her council a couple hours ago, which was when I'd finally parted from Lucen. He'd wanted me to stay close and hole up in his apartment, but I had my own problems to deal with. There was still the matter of finding Eric's soul, as well as those of the other addicts. My threads continued to wait.

In the end, we collected almost all the containers, and the Gryphons arrested almost all the sylphs—and the one goblin—responsible. Amazingly, in spite of the destruction and fighting, Silas's ledger books had remained intact.

What to do about the containers was the next question, but not one for us. The Gryphon healers took over from there.

Around five in the morning, Bridget sent me home. She'd survived with only a few scratches, in better shape than most. "We're done. Nothing left for us to do tonight."

Dazed, I rubbed my eyes. I was exhausted, but all the negative emotions around me kept me unpleasantly alert. I felt like a rubber band stretched to its breaking point. I'd snap soon if I couldn't relax.

I didn't have to feign concern when I offered to stick around, but when my offer was refused, I also didn't need to be told to go home yet again. I left, gladly.

Getting home, however, was not so easy. Shadowtown was in shambles. The damage wasn't nearly as horrific as it had been when the furies had instigated fighting last month, but it was a hell of a mess. Cars lay on their sides, a couple buildings had burned, and the windows of many satyr- and sylph-owned businesses had been smashed. Given how preds hated messes, I suspected the cleanup would begin shortly.

That worked for me. I didn't like living in a neighborhood that looked like it had seen the apocalypse.

The apocalypse.

That was when the few threads I'd been weaving began to form a coherent picture.

TWENTY-EIGHT

TOM WOKE ME UP WITH A PHONE CALL WAY TOO EARLY THE next day, considering I hadn't gotten home until the sun was rising. With my mind racing and my body coming down from an emotional feast, it had been even longer before I could sleep.

I swore at the phone and checked the time. Noon. I wasn't sure whether I hated my phone or Tom more.

My hand whined in pain from a million cuts and abrasions as I answered. "Do you know what time it is? Do you know how late I was up?"

"Five after twelve, and my apologies. I'm aware everyone had a busy night. But in light of that, I think it's more important than ever that we have our talk. When are you coming in?"

I fell back against my pillow. "You have no idea how right you are about the talk, but it's not happening today. When I finally drag my sorry ass into work, I need to fill out paperwork and generally deal with the fallout from the Boston Pred Party."

"The what?"

"Never mind." I yawned, wondering how long I could delay him. "How's tomorrow evening?"

"Tomorrow?" He sighed. "No, I'll be here late today. Your obligations to closing out the case can't take the whole time."

A thin band of sunlight sneaked through my drapes and landed on my futon. I pulled my blanket higher. "No, but I have other obligations tonight."

"What can be more important than this?" He sounded annoyed.

"A lot of things. And who said it didn't relate to this? I'll send you more information about when and where later."

I hung up to the sound of him grumbling in protest. Then, since there was no going back to bed, I forced myself into the shower. I'd have to make a strong pot of coffee because I had work to do. Tom might not believe me, but I hadn't been lying about my plans.

My life was at a turning point, and I could sense it right down to my bones. To my soul maybe, if there was something to this whole soul business other than emotional energy.

After my meeting tomorrow, nothing was going to be the same. I had to know who I could count on, and who would be better off keeping their distance. The sylphs had used Lucen to get to me, and if anything I suspected was true, yesterday was unlikely to be the last time someone made that mistake. It was only fair to warn those who might become bait and make sure they were willing to be risked.

***

STEPH AND JIM SHARED AN APARTMENT IN A PLAIN BRICK building just outside Boston proper. Jim frequently worked double shifts on Mondays, and I counted on him not being home. Although I liked Steph's boyfriend, he had no place in the conversation I'd planned.

A couple guys pulled into the parking lot around the same time as I did, and they let me into the building. I took the stairs slowly, playing through my planned speech as I traipsed to the fourth floor. It was sweltering inside, but I couldn't pretend I wasn't also sweaty from nerves. I didn't know how Steph was going to react to me showing up at her door.

In retrospect, maybe I should have called ahead. At the time, though, that hadn't seemed like a good idea. I had words to get out, and it was far easier for her to hang up on me and claim she wasn't ready to talk than it would be for her to ignore me while I kept knocking on her door.

Funny how I'd been less nervous about barging into Silas's dry-cleaning shop last night.

And look how well that went down, a particularly loathsome voice whispered to me.

I told it to fuck off, then knocked.

A TV was on in Steph's apartment, and through the door I could hear her swear.

"Logan, I told you I'm not—" She threw open the door and gaped at me. "You're not my neighbor."

"Not the last I checked."

Steph remained still for a moment, but I could taste her conflict. She was battling something out in her head, and I could guess what it was. Finally, one side lost and she did a very un-Steph-like thing. She pulled me into a hug.

Shocked, I patted her on the back. "I missed you too?"

She released me and brushed her hair away behind her shoulders. "Get in here."

I stepped inside and followed her into the kitchen. "Did you hear about Eric?"

"Yes, I heard about Eric." She handed me a beer. "Why do you think I hugged you? Some Agent Silverman, I think it was, called me earlier. She's the person monitoring Eric's progress, and she said he was recovering fine." Steph collapsed onto the sofa and turned off the TV. "Thank you."

I sat next to her but not too close. "You're welcome, but it's hardly all my doing."

Steph shrugged and pushed her empty dinner plate aside with her foot. "Well, no, but I heard it was your tip that led to the bust last night."

"Ah, yeah. And what a bust that was, in every sense. How did you hear that?"

"Your friend Bridget called to tell me they'd found Eric's soul. That was before the healer called about his recovery."

"Oh." I sipped my beer, temporarily washing away the taste of Steph's anxiety. "I'm glad they recovered it. With everything that happened, I was afraid the information we'd been after would be destroyed."

Steph just nodded, fixated on her bottle. "Are you okay? Your hands look bad."

Dozens of red scabs crisscrossed my palms. I flexed my fingers for her. "I've had worse injuries. Actually, given how badly I've been beaten up in the past couple months, a few scrapes and bruises is nothing."

"True. But I'm glad it's not worse."

We descended into an awkward silence. I picked at the label on my bottle with my thumbnail. The pretty speech I'd been rehearsing just didn't flow naturally now that I was here. And did I really want to make speeches anyway? That was silly. Speeches were what you gave to faceless, nameless people. They shouldn't be what you gave to the people who knew you.

Steph had been my best friend for ten years. Through the worst times of my life and her own. So to hell with speeches. All that I should need was a question.

I set down the bottle. "So now what?"

"Now what?" Far from putting her own beer down, Steph clutched the bottle tighter.

"Look, I know you said you needed time. I get that. I kind of dropped a bomb on you without any warning. On the other hand, you've known me for a decade, and you know more about me than almost anyone else on this planet. The entire time you've known me, you've known about my abilities. You were there when they developed. So even this 'without warning' thing almost feels like a cop-out. We knew I was a freak. You simply didn't know exactly what flavor of freak I am."

I took a deep breath. I shouldn't have put that bottle down. My hands twitched with the need to do something to release my tension, but curling them into fists was painful. "Things are changing, Steph. Not me, but the world around me. There's a lot I haven't told you, and it's partly because I was scared of your reaction, but it's also because I didn't want to dump a whole lot of weirdness on you. You have your own life, and it's a decent one. You have a good job. And for once, you have a decent boyfriend. You didn't need me to fill your head with magical crap that I only ever half believed or understood. But I can't ignore that crap anymore because whatever I believe or understand—I don't think that matters."

"You're scaring me, Jess." Steph finally relinquished the beer. "What are these things you're talking about?"

I held up a hand. "There are lots of them, but before we go there, I need to know where you stand. I could use your support, but if you give it to me, I need to know you mean it. People I care about were attacked yesterday because they're friends with me. I don't want to put you, or anyone else, at risk. So think about that before you give me an answer. I'm not just asking whether you can forgive me for hiding what I am from you, or whether you can overlook what I am. I'm asking whether it's worth it to you to do that. Really worth it."

So much for not giving speeches, but at least I hadn't planned that one.

I reached for my beer. My mouth was dry, and I needed to do something while I waited for Steph's response.

Besides feel my intestines tie themselves into a fun assortment of knots, that was.

I told myself I would walk if Steph couldn't handle this. Even if Steph lied and claimed she could, I would walk. For her sake. But the truth was I'd rather face down an army of sylphs.

Death was less scary than losing my best friend.

Steph picked at loose threads on her throw pillow. Her anxiety had been strong since I arrived, and her fear had grown stronger as I spoke. But there were other emotions buried in her too. Ones I didn't sense too often and therefore had a harder time discerning.

Abruptly, she punched the pillow and tossed it away. "This is stupid."

Well, that was unexpected. "Stupid?"

"You remember the night we met?"

"Not likely to forget it."

"Exactly." Steph drank heavily of her beer. "I'd gotten the shit kicked out of me by a few bigoted assholes, and you concocted what I thought was this absolutely fucked-up revenge plan to nick their souls and trade them away for some other girl's soul. For the record, when I say I thought it was fucked-up, I mean it was brilliant."

"For the record, you thought it was fucked-up bullshit and wouldn't work. I remember; I was there."

Steph waved away my disagreement. "Point is, you've had my back since we met. And when I decided I was done pretending to be something I'm not and started living openly as a woman, you were one of the only people I knew who didn't give me the side eye, if they didn't outright cut me from their lives. You've never had trouble accepting me for who and what I am. What kind of shitty person would I be if I couldn't do the same?"

Carefully, I set the beer back down, afraid I would drop it. "Being trans isn't quite the same thing as finding out you're a pred, even an abnormal pred."

"No, but it's not like you're a serial killer either."

"No, but I have used my ability to influence people's desires to my advantage."

"For good causes." She wrinkled her nose. "Mostly. Are you trying to talk me out of my decision? It's not like I came to this realization tonight. I've been thinking a lot and generally pissing myself off the past couple days."

I bit my lip, willing myself to relax so my voice would be steady. "I'm not trying to talk you out of anything. I just want to make sure you heard what I said and know what you're getting into."

"Bitch. I know my own mind, and you cannot toss me aside like an empty beer bottle. I'm not going anywhere, Jess. You're stuck with me. We're like family. More than family because my family mostly sucks, as you now understand firsthand. But I couldn't choose them. I can choose you."

I didn't move. All my attention was focused on Steph. I was prying into her head, which I tried never to do with her, but I had to be sure. Had to be so damned positive that she meant what she said.

The pessimist in me—which was basically ninety percent of my personality—could not believe she meant it. Yet I could detect no trace that she didn't.

Steph wasn't abandoning me.

I couldn't hold in my relief any longer and I doubled over, burying my face in my hands as it gushed out of me in a massive breath. Tears burned my eyes, and I forced them to retreat. Where the hell had they come from? I didn't cry. I never cried, not since I'd been kicked out of the Gryphon pre-training program.

Besides, nothing would freak out Steph more than me getting all teary.

Except maybe me getting all teary and telling her I thought the apocalypse was upon us. But really, the apocalypse was more than enough for one evening.

So I breathed. And continued breathing. Just a few more breaths until I regained my wits.

"Jess?" Steph whacked me with a pillow. "Don't get all emotional on me."

"I'm not," I said, keeping my face buried in my hands.

"Damn you." She shifted over and pulled me into an uncomfortably positioned hug. "I'm hugging a satyr. Do you know how strange that is?"

I managed a laugh. "Not so strange, considering what I've done with one. Er, one or more."

Steph pretended to shudder. "Yes, but you are one."

"So I'm starting to accept." I grabbed her hands. "Thank you for accepting it too."

"Don't thank me yet. After all that buildup, I'm not letting you leave until you fill me in on all that magical bullshit you were teasing me with. Plus anything else about being a satyr that you've been neglecting to mention."

"Everything?"

"Everything."

"Including how they have better stamina than your average romance-novel hero?"

Steph took the bottles into the kitchen. "Especially that. I'll make popcorn."

My smile faded as she turned away. All joking aside, I had a feeling Steph was going to want something a lot stronger than popcorn by the time I finished talking.

I could have spent the whole evening regaling Steph with all the sordid details I'd been keeping from her, but by eleven o'clock I was getting a buzz off the way her head spun. I'd started her off gently, sharing the fun bits before transitioning to the serious events on the horizon. But ultimately, what I had to tell her was not a happy story, and no amount of joking about satyr equipment could overcome the anxiety I'd seeded in her blood.

I left before Jim got home, sensing that she was overwhelmed. "You need to get up in six hours for work tomorrow," I reminded her.

"You think I'm going to get any sleep tonight?" Yet despite her potently tangerine fear, Steph yawned.

Yeah, she'd sleep, and I could use some of that myself. Fortunately, I had the hit of her emotions to keep me going for a bit longer. There was someone else I needed to talk to before falling into bed.

The Lair was closed and the front window boarded up, but I could see a light shining through the glass in the door. Before I could test whether it was unlocked, it swung open.

"Don't ever say again that I can't be bothered to get up for you," Lucen said.

"I thought we established it would be a tragedy if that were the case."

"Given I'm satyr, I think it would be more like a farce."

I stood on my tiptoes and planted a delicate kiss on his lips. His injuries had already healed, but I couldn't say the same for the damage to the bar.

Lucen pulled me into the room, then shut and locked the door behind me. "Everything settled with your case?"

"Mostly. There are still a few souls at large, but the Gryphons are continuing to track them down."

I watched him head behind the bar, admiring the way the warm lighting caught the palest streaks in his golden hair, how his dusty T-shirt clung to his broad chest, and the way his jeans hugged his ass.

Angelia had been right about that. It was a very nice ass.

Lucen glanced over his shoulder and raised an eyebrow, giving me the impression that he knew exactly what I'd been staring at. "Something to drink, little siren? I'm not going to be reopening for a couple days, I expect."

"Water would be good."

"Water?" He snorted in disbelief. "We're not doing that again, are we? I remember a time when you wouldn't accept alcohol from me."

I wandered over to the table where he'd obviously been working before I arrived. "I had a beer earlier."

Lucen's insurance policy was spread out across the table, and he appeared to have been making damage estimates. Although he'd already done a lot to clean the place up, it still was in disarray. Besides the boarded-up window, a stack of broken chairs sat in the far corner, and one table was covered with the random artwork that used to hang on the walls. Nearly all the glassware was gone too. Smashed along with the liquor bottles.

Lucen set a glass of water down by me. "It's truly exciting stuff you're looking at."

"Enough to make you wish you were fighting sylphs again?"

He pulled a chair over. "I'd love another fight with the sylphs. I dream of being the one to beat the ever-loving shit out of Assym." He swung his leg around the chair and sat backward on it. "Have you come to save me from my paperwork? Tell me you have."

"Maybe." I slipped my fingers through his hair, but the chairback dug into me as I tried to get closer. Damn his habit of sitting backwards.

On the other hand, his face was about breast height, and he nuzzled me through my shirt.

I sucked in a breath as Lucen kissed me through the fabric, his teeth lightly biting at my nipple. "I think you have."

I bent closer, gliding my nails over the back of his neck, burrowing my nose in his hair. I could detect rosemary among his natural cinnamon, the scent of his shampoo.

"More nails," he murmured into me, and when I pressed them deeper into the lightly sweaty skin on his upper back, I could hear his breath catch. He suckled me harder, and I gasped, every muscle clenching with my building desire.

"You're going to get my shirt all wet."

"Fuck your shirt. I want to get *you* wet. Take it off. In fact, can we just agree that whenever we're alone together, you should be naked? That would make me very happy." He glanced up at me with his most endearingly puppylike expression. "You want to make me happy, don't you?"

I couldn't help but laugh. "Always. But we do live in a cold climate."

"Yes, but it's summer." He reached around the chair and grazed the skin just below my shirt hem with his fingertips.

I shivered. I swore I could feel that touch everywhere, shooting up my nerves into my breasts and down to my stomach and my sensitive skin below. My nipples ached as they hardened, and I tossed my shirt on top of his papers. When he touched me that way, I wanted to do everything he asked. "Better?"

He licked his lips. "It's a start."

I could feel his gaze roaming over me as I drank some of the water. Heavy and hungry. I longed to give in to it, but not yet. I'd come over for a reason, and I couldn't let myself be distracted. No matter how hot my blood burned for him.

"Strip for me, Jess. I've been cleaning up this disaster area all day. I want to see something beautiful."

I closed my eyes. I loved the way he watched me when I did that for him. The way his eyes devoured me. The way he made me feel like I was the single most amazing thing on this planet.

I sucked in a breath through clenched teeth, my jeans suddenly chafing as heat gathered between my legs. "Not yet." I set the water down and returned to him, tousling his hair once more but keeping enough distance so that he couldn't touch his lips to my bare skin. I might lose the will to continue if he did. "Did Devon tell you what we talked about when I was at Purgatory the other night?"

Lucen sighed. "I take it you're not referring to the conversation in which he rhapsodized about your ass?"

"Um, no."

Lucen shook with silent laughter. "Yes, little siren, he told me your feminine wiles seduced him into spilling all our darkest satyr secrets."

"Oh, yeah. I seduced *him*. You're both hilarious." I slid my hand down his cheek, trying to turn this conversation serious. "I wish you'd been the one to tell me these things."

He grabbed my hand and pressed it deeper against him. Stubble bristled against my sore palm, but I made no move to withdraw it. Touching him would always be better than not touching him. No pain could change that. "I should have. You're right. And it's not that I didn't think you deserved to know, it's just..."

I waited while he closed his eyes. "Just what?"

Lucen swallowed. "I didn't know how to tell you that I chose to forget."

"Do you wish you could still remember your old life?" His expression was killing me inside. So sad. I wanted to drape his face with kisses until he smiled again, but he held my hand tightly.

"No, it's not that. How can you care about things you don't remember?" At last he loosened his grip on me, bringing my hand to his lips and gently kissing my knuckles. But he wouldn't look at me. He cast his gaze on the spot of floor between us. "I didn't want to tell you because I made the weak choice. I chose to lose part of myself rather than deal with the regret, the pain of knowing what I'd lost on top of the physical pain of the transformation. I didn't have the strength to see the whole thing through. I don't doubt that I chose this life for myself, little siren. But I was too weak to deal with the consequences of my choice. That's why I didn't want to talk about it."

There was no mischief, not even hunger, in his eyes when he raised his head to me now. Only regret and embarrassment.

But that was wrong. So utterly wrong for him to feel that way.

I removed my hand from his and cupped his cheeks. "You're not weak." I kissed his forehead, leaving my lips pressed to his skin. "I've felt that physical pain, or something close to it when Lucrezia cursed me. It was horrible. Torture. Wanting to forget what you had before makes perfect sense. There's nothing weak about that."

The memory of it, the thought of Lucen suffering with that same insatiable agony, made my heart wail, and I burned with this fierce desire to shield him from any more pain.

In that moment, it no longer mattered to me if he chose this life. I didn't care. He was right that the past was in the past, and the person he was before was not the person he was now. And it was the person he was now whom I needed in my life.

I kissed him again and again, drawing my lips over his eyelids, his nose, the blond hairs on his cheeks and chin. I took his bottom lip in mine and caressed it with my tongue. I kissed him to chase away any notion that he should regret what he'd done or be ashamed of it.

And although I intended the kisses to be sweet and chaste, desire stirred in me again, sparked by this hint of vulnerability I'd discovered. I'd always felt like I was laying myself bare before him, the one who needed him to assure me that everything was going to be okay.

Learning he had his own insecurities, that there were parts of his life he was nervous baring to me, just made my heart cry out for him more. And made me want him more. To show him how strong and sexy and perfect I thought he was.

"You're not weak, and you will never convince me otherwise after all you've done."

"I don't think you'd have done it. You're strong, Jess."

"We don't know what I'd have done. And you're plenty strong. However you started off, you rose to become Dezzi's number two, and then you risked that position to help me. You could have blasted me with your magic any time over these last ten years, and instead you waited patiently until I saw how amazing you are. Those aren't the things weak people do. They don't risk everything for others. They don't refuse to take advantage of others when they have the means." I crouched down to eye level with him. "And you put up with my shit. Not many people seem capable of that."

Lucen allowed himself to smirk. "It's only fair given what you have to put up with for me."

"That's true. Fucking your best friend was hard."

"It wouldn't have been a good fuck if it wasn't." He bounded off the chair and swept me up in his arms before I knew what he was doing. I put my head on his chest, feeling it rise and fall beneath me. "Thank you, Jess. Thank you for trying."

I clutched him tighter. "I'd try anything for you. I just don't know if I'll always be so successful."

"All that's important is that we keep trying. If we never give up, we never fail."

His hands slipped up my back, and he tangled his fingers through my hair. Warm lips found mine, a slow, lingering kiss that grew until I parted my mouth, taking him in, and he greedily stole my breath. A moan escaped my lips, and I dug my nails into his back. His erection pressed against me, hot through our clothing.

I backed away from his mouth, gasping, my hands wrapped around fistfuls of his shirt. "I need you. Now."

Lucen took my face in his hands and kissed me harder still. I clawed at his back, tearing his shirt out of his waistband, desperate for his skin, desperate to grasp that bulge I felt in his pants and make it mine.

He pulled my arms away and spun me around, pushing my back up against the bar. "I need you too, little siren. You have no idea how much."

Then his mouth was on my throat, his hot tongue sliding over my skin. He unfastened my jeans and yanked them down.

I tore into his pants, vaguely aware of my vision blurring. My eyes were getting watery? For the love of dragons, why were my eyes tearing up for a second time in one night? My breath hitched in my throat as my fingers danced over his hard length, and Lucen let out a most delicious moan.

His lips nibbled lower and lower down my chest. Firm hands cupped my breasts until his tongue found them, and he shoved aside the lace of my bra, his hungry mouth sucking and tugging relentlessly.

I collapsed on him, and we tumbled to the floor. Landing on top of him, I kicked my pants and shoes off so I could straddle him. Lucen reached for me, his mouth open for more, but I had to keep my distance. My ache was too strong, and I wasn't ready to be pushed over the edge yet. I wanted him inside me for that.

Breathing hard, I drew my nails down his abs, lightening my touch as I reached the more sensitive skin around his hips. His whole body twitched, and his sex rubbed against mine in a maddeningly enticing way. Teasing me, reminding me that I wasn't whole until he filled me.

"Damn it, Jess. Come closer." Lucen lunged for me, fingers digging into my thighs and just brushing the edge of my folds. I writhed under his touch but slid farther away, and he fell back to the floor. "I can feel your wetness on my legs. I need more of you. Please."

Slipping my fingers around his length, I gave it to him. I ran my tongue up his hard shaft, swirled it around his head, and licked the bead of wetness from the tip. Each moan, each time he growled out my name, stoked my desire hotter.

"You always say how you like to make me scream," I whispered, rubbing my face against him. "I want to do the same for you. I think I'm starting to get it now, this thing that we have. I want you to know that, but I want you to need my touch like I need yours."

"You think I don't?"

No, I thought he did, but I hadn't until tonight. Not until I realized he wasn't invulnerable, after all.

I kissed him deeper, harder, reveling in every gorgeous noise that he couldn't restrain. Only when he begged again did I pause, my tongue flicking the tip of his cock. "I'm learning."

"You've learned too well. Now take me inside you." His eyes blazed with raw power.

No, he wasn't invulnerable, but he was still capable of making my body obey his will. My thighs clenched, and I could feel my pulse throbbing between my legs. I couldn't hold out any longer. I climbed over him and glided him inside, and the last of my rational thoughts slipped out of me with a whimper as I enveloped his thickness. Lucen sighed my name, and I was complete. The ache I felt without him filled.

He grabbed my hips, hands sliding lower as he thrust deeper again and again, and his thumbs pushed aside my folds so he could stroke my clit. My heavy breaths became cries, and I closed my eyes as the room blurred around me. My hands pinched and hugged at his body, craving more.

Usually I let Lucen guide our rhythm because I liked him taking control. He was so good at it since he could feel my needs. But tonight I insisted, listening to his breaths and his moans for direction, pounding myself against him until he yelled my name and I exploded with him, helpless to resist that command.

When I laid my whole body on top of him afterward, he refused to pull out, and I realized how uncomfortable the floor must have been beneath him. But Lucen said nothing of it, he just kissed me and ran his hands down my back. Surrounded by the clutter and dust—and most importantly his body—I reveled in the contentment and safety of his arms, and hoped I roused the same emotions in him.

Because it wasn't going to last.

TWENTY-NINE

I'D CHOSEN VINE AS MY MEETING SPOT. IT WAS FAR FROM Shadowtown and far from Gryphon headquarters, making it about as close to neutral territory within the city as I could get. And besides, why not? The place was pricey, but we were all going to need a drink to get through this meeting. Myself included.

I made sure I got there early and explained to Cat, the manager I'd met last time, that I needed a quiet corner for a group. Vine didn't normally rearrange seating for guests, but my gift allowed me to be persuasive. I hit her with a touch of my satyr magic, and she acquiesced as easily as butter to a warm knife.

Like Steph had said, I *mostly* used my gift for good purposes. If the direct purpose here was a touch shifty, I still thought it should count because my goal with the meeting was nothing but good.

I sat with my back against the wall, watching the door and making the most of my overpriced glass of merlot. It was yummy, but no doubt I could have bought the entire bottle in any liquor store for the cost of this one glass.

Tom arrived first. He paused by the door, and judging by his confusion, he was counting the number of chairs surrounding me.

"Welcome back to Boston."

Tom pulled out the chair across from me. "You're saying that now?"

"I was too tired when you called yesterday." I passed him the extensive wine menu.

"Might I ask who the other chairs are for?"

"You might. They're for friends of mine. Well, friends and one business associate."

"When I said I wanted a meeting to discuss the material I gave you—"

"Trust me, we're discussing it and more. But this isn't just about you giving me stuff to read to make me buy into your end-of-the-world nonsense. This is me sharing what I've found out as well."

Tom pressed his hands together, his face strained. "With other people."

"Did you or did you not tell me *Le Confrérie de l'Aile* created me to be some kind of secret weapon to fight the good fight when everything goes to hell?"

"I don't recall saying it quite like that, but yes, that was the idea."

I sipped my wine with great satisfaction. "Good. Then this is me being all badass and warriorly. The first rule of battle is know your enemies. That's why we're here. To get acquainted."

"I see." He opened the wine menu snappishly.

Yup, this was why I'd chosen a bar.

The door opened again, and this time Olef appeared. Thank dragons. I hoped the magi's presence would calm down Tom.

I waved to Olef, and the owl shifter headed over. Belatedly, I wondered if magi drank wine. I knew they ate some human food, but their drinking habits were not something I'd ever had any reason to pay attention to. It was too late to worry about such a minor thing though. Of all the people I'd invited to this meeting, I trusted Olef would have the least demanding temperament.

He chose a seat by Tom, the brown and white feathers on top of his head narrowing in surprise. "Ms. Moore, it's good to see you looking well after what happened in Shadowtown the other day."

"Thanks." I shook his four-fingered hand.

"I brought my notes on the information you asked me to look up," he added before turning to Tom. "You're Agent Kassin?"

Tom closed the menu. "Yes. How did you know that?"

Because Olef knows everything, I thought. But I let the magi answer for himself.

"I understand you've been in contact with Xander regarding certain information," Olef said. "He's mentioned it to me, although he may not have mentioned me by name to you."

Tom's eyes widened. "You're the prophet Xander's been telling me about."

I sipped smugly while they did their introductions.

After they finished, Olef turned to me. "Will Xander be coming?"

"No. This is about your visions. Frankly, I don't want Xander within a five-mile radius of me after what he once did."

Olef shrugged helplessly, but Tom frowned. "What did Xander do to you?"

"Insulted me, assaulted me, and held me captive."

"He thought Ms. Moore was guilty of Victor Aubrey's murders," Olef explained.

"He also told me I was evil because I had a pred's gift."

Tom coughed into his hand. "That's unfortunate."

"No kidding. Oh, look." I smiled, anticipating—evilly—how all hell was going to break loose in a moment. "Our next three guests have arrived."

Olef and Tom twisted around in their seats. The magi were cut off to me emotionally, but I could taste the exact moment when Tom's curiosity turned to bewilderment and horror.

He spun around to face me. "Those are satyrs. What are you doing?" He kept his voice so low I could barely hear him.

I couldn't help but be impressed. Tom controlled his fear well. Mostly, now that his initial shock had passed, I sensed anger from him.

"Yeah, they're like me, remember? And they've been part of what's been going on since the beginning."

Lucen, Dezzi, and Devon were all wearing charms to disguise their horns, but their magical auras nevertheless managed to ensnare the attention of everyone they passed. We'd have an enthralled server over here any second, offering themself up with the drinks.

Lucen and Devon both insisted on making a show of hugging me in greeting, but Dezzi narrowed her dark eyes at Tom and Olef. The human and magi didn't appear any more pleased. Magi and preds notoriously didn't like each other, and, well, preds and Gryphons. Enough said.

Although Tom wasn't in uniform, Dezzi picked up on what he was just as easily as he had seen through their disguise charms. "Jessica, what is the meaning of this? He's a Gryphon."

"Yes, I am." Tom frowned. "And that's a very good question."

I shot him a nasty look. "It's called a temporary alliance. Kind of like what you had on Sunday. We can all sit and drink and have a conversation."

"We'll see about that, won't we?" Devon said cheerfully. "You do know how to keep everyone on their toes."

I smiled at Lucen and he returned it with a *why me* expression before taking the seat on my right.

Devon sat on my left, and Dezzi sat next to him. That left one chair belonging to the person who I was most worried wouldn't show.

As predicted, our server showed up the instant everyone got settled. I tapped my fingers together impatiently, my gaze glued to the door and my hopes rising and falling each time it opened. We descended into an uncomfortable recitation of what I'd already gone over with Tom and Olef until the server returned with everyone's drinks.

As the server left, the door opened one more time. In walked a short, elderly woman with iron-gray hair. Her clothes were extremely formal and old-fashioned, but her eyes were alert. Behind her were two short men of the same vintage.

Not a single one of them gave off any sort of emotions that I could sense.

I smiled.

Gunthra made a weird face. If she weren't disguised, I imagined her ears would have perked up or something. But although she could disguise her face as a human's with the assistance of some powerful magic, she had less success with her mannerisms.

She spoke to her companions, who headed over to the bar, then she joined us. Six heads turned her way as she stiffly took the last chair. "Miss Moore, you have piqued my curiosity with your choice of company."

"Not just yours," Lucen muttered.

I squeezed his arm to quiet him. "Thank you for coming."

"How long I stay," Gunthra replied, "will depend on where this conversation goes."

I squeezed Lucen again, sensing that another comment was dancing on his tongue. "Then let's get started."

I did a round of introductions after our server returned to take Gunthra's order. Most everyone here ought to have known everyone else, if not by name then by face. Gunthra's borrowed face excepted. The tension around the table was as thick as dragon hide and as dangerous as an uncontained salamander. Not even the wine could help that. The only thing that might would be reminding everyone that they all had one thing in common.

Me.

And Devon had accused me of self-hatred. Please. I must have an ego the size of Massachusetts to think I could pull this off, and yet I was strangely calm. Convinced I knew what I was doing.

Of course, it could also have been the result of having finished my wine so quickly.

I folded my hands. "I asked everyone together because I believe we're all investigating or chasing after or worrying about the same thing. It's taken me a while to figure that out for several reasons." Like I was in denial or too filled with rage to consider what I was being told. But hey, that was life.

No one questioned me, which was a touch unnerving. So I plundered on. "Here's what I know. I'll start with the magi. For hundreds of years, they've been having visions of an apocalypse. Enough of them, including Olef, have had these visions that over time they've been called a prophecy."

Olef nodded. "This is correct. And the role you—"

I held up a finger. "Sorry. I don't want to cut you off, but I think it would help if I go chronologically."

The magi threaded his fingers together. "As you wish."

I gazed longingly into my glass. My wish was that our server could read my mind and bring me a refill.

"In response to that prophecy, and believing preds were going to cause this apocalypse, the Gryphons began experimenting, trying to create super-Gryphons." Tom winced at my word choice but didn't interrupt. "They finally figured out how to turn gifted humans into preds, like I am. We look like humans, and preds can feed off us like humans, but we're not normal humans. The thing was, the Gryphons who were working on this —Agent Kassin's group—didn't realize their experiment had worked, and so they released a bunch of us into the wild. Me, Victor Aubrey, and possibly several other people."

"Several other people who we're now aware of," Tom said. "But this was not information meant to be shared, especially not with the present company."

"This is nothing that they didn't already know or figure out."

Tom's knuckles whitened around his glass. I hoped he wouldn't break it.

"Anyway." I drained my wine dregs. "One of us—Victor—was enamored with his misery-sucking power, and that's probably what brought him to the furies' attention. He became an addict, and as we all know, he murdered several vanity addicts at their behest and then framed me for it. Once we figured out the furies were behind those murders, we wanted to know why. I first heard the theory from Lucen that the sort of chaos and suffering caused by a magical war would be ideal for them to feed on, and I know the satyrs took that theory seriously, at least at the time."

I glanced at Dezzi, who nodded. Her face was calm, but the way she held herself suggested she wasn't pleased with something.

"You said the furies' behavior was unusual too," I told Tom, "when you first came here, although that was a cover story for investigating me."

"Not just a cover story."

I gave him a chance to explain, but he didn't. Big surprise.

Moving on then. "Gunthra also suspected the furies were up to something, and now I know for certain that they're up to something because one of them practically told me as much on Sunday."

"Who?" Dezzi asked sharply. "Why didn't I know this?"

"You were busy."

All three satyrs and Gunthra leaned closer to me. Lucen put his hand on my arm. "What did they say?"

"It was Mace-head." I answered Dezzi's question first. "You know the one with the spiky hair, dresses like he wants to be Sid Vicious?"

"His real name is Nyles," Devon said. "He was recently promoted to be Raj's lieutenant."

"I liked calling him Mace-head better."

"What did he say?" Lucen asked again.

I tucked my hair behind my ears, sensing I was about to make at least one person here unhappy. "He said he didn't want me getting hurt. Right after he shot Assym in order to protect me."

Lucen groaned.

"Your enjoyment of keeping us on our toes is starting to get irksome," Devon told me.

"A fury was protecting you?" Tom repeated. "Why?"

"Well, that's what I'm trying to figure out. This wasn't the first time it happened either." I searched the bar. "I need more wine. I've been talking too much."

Lucen pushed his half-filled glass my way. "Keep talking."

"Fine." I took a sip and continued. "So let's jump back to the magi's apocalyptic prophecy for a moment. Olef had let me know a couple weeks ago that he'd had visions—similar ones to all the others—but in his, he'd seen me."

Everyone but Lucen cast surprised glances at the magi. Olef modestly cleaned his glasses and said nothing.

"So," I continued, "to rehash—the Gryphons created me because of this prophecy, we have confirmation from Olef that I'm part of it, and the furies are acting weird, and as part of that weirdness, they want to keep me alive. Somewhere in the middle of all this, a pred war breaks out in Buenos Aires, very similar to what the furies tried to do here. Now we get to the part that explains why I invited Gunthra to join us. Still want to leave?" I asked her.

Gunthra spun the strand of pearls she wore around her wrist. "No. Proceed."

I blinked away my surprise. Gunthra did not strike me as the sort to cede the floor. Often enough she talked over people. I really did have everyone's attention.

"Gunthra's also been interested in finding out what the furies are up to, and she's interested in finding out more about the Vessels of Making. I'm going to assume everyone here is familiar with them." When no one objected, I went on. "I didn't realize the two might be connected until I saw a mention of the Vessels in one of the books Tom lent me. Since they all dealt, one way or another, with the prophecy, I'm going ahead and making a leap that somehow everything I've talked about here is related. I just don't know how. And now anyone can jump in and fill in the gaps for me because I need more wine."

Honestly, I needed something stronger at this point. The six faces staring at me around the table suggested their owners felt the same.

"Don't everyone start talking at once," I said when the silence grew too heavy.

"Very well." Gunthra tapped her spindly fingers against her glass. "You have intrigued me, Miss Moore, and I agree that a pooling of knowledge might serve us well at this point. So I'll explain why I became interested in the Vessels."

"Let me guess—it's not a history project?" I rolled my eyes.

Gunthra flattered me with a faint smile. "It's not exactly a secret that all the Doms in Shadowtown keep an eye on their neighbors. In the aftermath of Mr. Aubrey's arrest and the unsettlement that followed, one of my council members informed me that the furies had an object of extreme power in their possession. Right here in our own neighborhood."

"How did they know that?" Devon asked.

Gunthra regarded him disdainfully. "She saw it, and she felt it. She said the magic surrounding it was so strong, so powerful, that it made her skin tingle from yards away. She didn't get a good look at it, but she described it as a bowl. Ancient-looking, she called it. The furies were treating it as though it was made from the most fragile of china. Very odd for a race whose favorite pastime is destruction."

"What happened to it?" I asked.

"It would appear that Raj took it with him when he disappeared."

"Wait." Tom's blue eyes no longer fixed me with a death glare. He'd been hooked too. At last. "This Raj person is the local fury Dom. He left?"

Dezzi cleared her throat. "Yes, a couple weeks ago. Along with everything else odd about the furies, that's also been a concern. Gunthra, you do not know for sure that this object your spy saw was a Vessel?"

Gunthra's spine straightened. Either she didn't like her judgment questioned, her goblin being called a spy, or both. "My informer is not the type to exaggerate. If she said it gave off extreme power, it did. There are not many objects that would fit such a description. I began my research, which Miss Moore has been helping with."

Lucen's grip on my arm tightened. "Jess, why?"

"Long story?" I gave him an innocent grin.

"Irksome," Devon whispered to me while Dezzi and Gunthra debated what the goblin had seen. "You're like the unruly child of this domus."

I narrowed my eyes at him. "I'm neither a child, nor a part of your domus."

"Can I spank you anyway?"

I elbowed him. Hard.

Meanwhile, the two Doms had stopped talking, and Olef coughed politely. "If I may contribute something? I might know why the furies would be interested in the Vessels, historically speaking, that is. Legends have recorded that the Vessels were created to be objects of great power, but the legends rarely say what they were created for."

"You know?" I asked. Of course he knew. He was Olef. It was why I'd asked for his help.

Apparently I wasn't the only one in the dark though. Tom was back to looking smug, so he must have known something too, but the preds appeared clueless.

Olef donned his teacher voice. "The Vessels were a dirty business, born of desperation and formed by a collaboration between gifted humans, magi, and even some pred races. You see, there is precedent for this meeting Ms. Moore has called. But back on topic, the Vessels were used to create The Pit. Is that name familiar?"

"According to legend, it's a magical prison," said Gunthra.

"Correct. It's gone by many names, but essentially it's a magical void, a prison in which the original preds were sealed. It was only capable of being created by using the tremendous amounts of power that this collaborative was able to store in the Vessels. Hence, the Vessels of Making. Making The Pit."

Devon rubbed at his goatee. "But that's just a myth. I remember hearing that tale told to me as a child, only it was a religious story about how a band of angels locked the demons in prison to save humanity. The Vessels were the cups of God, et cetera."

"Oh, it's real," Olef said. "Many religious traditions laid claim to the glory, but the work done was absolutely real. I have no doubt."

Tom ran his finger around his wineglass. "There are many manuscripts at World Headquarters that deal with the subject. Some are over a thousand years old. What does this have to do with the prophecy though?"

"As for that, I'm not entirely sure," Olef admitted. "But I find it concerning that the furies might have an interest in the Vessels."

"Why?" I asked.

Olef turned his kind eyes on me. "Because the original preds—the people our ancestors called devils and demons—they are furies. All of them. And they are nothing like the furies we know today. They are far less human because they were never human to begin with."

Silence fell around the table. I didn't know what the others were thinking, but I was afraid if I moved, shifted even slightly, I might disturb Olef's words and they wouldn't penetrate my brain properly. It was taking them a while. Like my brain was rebelling, and I had a good idea why.

The conversation at Vine had picked up along with the clientele. People laughed, glasses clinked together, chairs squeaked on the floor. I felt as though I were in a different world.

Finally, Tom started saying something about records and manuscripts at World, but I didn't hear much. It sounded like he was confirming Olef's information, or close to it.

"But I'm not a scholar," he added. "My work has been focused elsewhere."

Lucen took my hand. "This is all a lot to take in, but none of it addresses the question of why the furies might have tried protecting Jess. That's a big gap here."

"That I don't know," Olef said. "It does seem counterintuitive to what Agent Kassin and myself know about Jess, or why she was given her abilities."

Once again, I was a freak. A missing piece.

It didn't matter so much. I had a bigger issue with what Olef had told us.

"If these Vessels were used to create this magical prison, then could they be used to uncreate it? Is that why the furies might have one? Is that why they could have been trying to start a war here, or why they did in Buenos Aires? Could they be gathering power to store in the Vessels?"

Lucen shook my hand. "There would be your apocalypse."

Tom rested his head on his hands. His face was pale. "It's certainly a possibility. We'll have to look into that."

I forced a smile although I felt sick to my stomach. Good thing I hadn't had a full second glass of wine, after all. "Aren't you glad I'm finally taking this seriously?"

Gunthra stood, the lines of her fake face stretched tightly. "We should all investigate this, and I propose we share what we discover. If Miss Moore is correct, we need to be smart about this."

"I agree," Dezzi said, and she stood as well. "We will be in touch." She offered a hand to Gunthra, and they shook. She did not offer a hand to Tom or Olef, and neither did the goblin, but she nodded respectfully in their direction. "Jessica, see me when you return to Shadowtown."

Dezzi left money on the table, then gave a signal, and Lucen and Devon followed her out. Gunthra followed suit after a few more words with the men.

Tom and Olef were lost in conversation.

I cleared my throat. "What about me?"

"I have to do some research," Tom said. "But I'll be in touch. This, though unorthodox, was well done."

Peachy. After what I'd put together for them, I was told I'd accomplished the equivalent of an overcooked steak.

"All right then." I clapped my hands together with sarcastic enthusiasm. "If that's it, I'm off to buy a lot of desserts and plan an orgy."

"Excuse me?" Tom gaped at me.

"If the end of the world is coming, and no one has anything for me to do in the meantime, I might as well enjoy myself. Eat, drink, and be merry. All that good stuff."

I said goodbye to Olef and left.

DEZZI WAS WAITING FOR ME IN LUCEN'S APARTMENT, ALONG with Devon. The Lair was closed until further notice, depriving the satyrs of their unofficial meeting space.

I wondered if Purgatory would become the replacement. It wasn't in Shadowtown, but it met what appeared to be the other prerequisites—a loaded bar and a healthy atmosphere of debauchery.

"Given what we learned today," Dezzi said, "I need to know your answer to my offer."

I'd been expecting the question and had thought long and hard about it on my way back to Shadowtown. Being offered the spot on Dezzi's council meant a lot to me, and it would offer me much in return. Some protection. A sense of belonging. Power. Since Devon had convinced me to accept what I was, I'd seriously considered it.

But everything had changed. Everything was shifting.

I needed to be able to shift with it. Declaring myself a member of Dezzi's domus wouldn't allow for that.

"I can't," I told her, walking toward the window. "I almost decided to, but with the way things stand, it doesn't make sense. You and Gunthra might have formed an alliance, but satyrs and goblins working with magi and the Gryphons... I just don't see that coming so easily." And really, Dezzi and Gunthra's alliance wasn't likely to be easy either. "But I believe that whatever happens, you're going to need to make this work. To do that, you're all going to need someone who can walk and talk both sides.

You'll need a middleperson or a mediator. That's me. I am a satyr, but I'm a very human one. The Gryphons created me. That means they'll listen to me. I hope, because I am one of you, that the satyrs—or other preds—will listen to me too."

Dezzi sighed, but she didn't look disappointed, and she rested her hand on my shoulder. "You are smart, Jessica. Although this wasn't the outcome I hoped for, I agree that it makes sense under the circumstances. We all have work to do in the coming days. Much work, I fear."

"You leaving?" Lucen asked as she headed into the kitchen.

"Did you miss the part where I said there was work to be done?" she asked.

"No, but you specifically said in the coming days." He grinned.

Dezzi shook her finger at him. "Be prepared to work tomorrow."

A moment later Lucen's door shut. A heavy silence settled over the apartment and over my mind. The sense of urgency that had kept me focused and moving forward was gone. Now all I had before me was the unknown—a big, scary unknown.

In his cage, Sweetpea snored in his sleep. Oh, how I envied the dragon right now. To be so blissfully unaware of what was coming.

"Well then." Devon bounded off the sofa with fake cheerfulness. "This all feels very gloom and doom. Lucen, did the sylphs destroy your stereo or just the bar? I'm in the mood for some R.E.M."

Lucen leaned against the doorway. "If you play 'It's the End of the World As We Know It,' the end of *your* world will be coming a lot sooner than you expect."

Devon shook his head sadly. "Sometimes you're no fun."

I tossed the bag of sweets I'd bought at Devon. "Sorry, I concur with the blond one. However, I do need a distraction before my anxiety gets the better of me. I brought the food, and we've got a bar full of booze downstairs. So which of you is bringing on the merry first?"

Thank you for reading! Did you enjoy? Please add your review because nothing helps an author more and encourages readers to take a chance on a book than a review.

And don't miss more in the Miss Misery series with book four, DARKEST MISERY, available now. Turn the page for a sneak peek!

Also be sure to sign up for the City Owl Press newsletter to receive notice of all book releases!

SNEAK PEEK OF DARKEST MISERY

Gryphon agent Tom Kassin might know more about what I was than most people on this planet, but he totally didn't get *who* I was. Which is how I ended up on a plane taxiing down the runway at Phoenix Sky Harbor International Airport.

Passengers shuffled in their seats, clearly antsy to get to the gate and impatient for the *Fasten seat belt* light to go off. I shared their impatience—literally. It tasted to me like bitter almonds. But that was as much as I shared with my fellow passengers. Though I wanted to stretch my legs too, I had little else to look forward to when I got off the plane.

"I still think this is a bad idea," I muttered, stuffing my water bottle into my duffel bag.

I could sense Tom was just as eager to get off this flying deathtrap as everyone else, but he hid his irritation better than most. Which was to say he was one of the few who hadn't actually made a move toward his phone yet. "You're too hard on yourself, Jessica. I truly think having you along will do a lot to reassure Mr. Johnson."

"See, this is why I keep saying you don't get me. You used my name and 'reassure' in the same sentence."

"I get you better that you think." His disconcerting accent, part Southern twang and part butchered British, always seeped out when his emotions were heightened. And they'd been heightened a lot lately.

Tom did not like me challenging his authority.

I could no longer keep from rolling my eyes. "Just because you have my magical profile and rap sheet memorized doesn't mean you understand my psyche."

In light of a looming apocalypse I could no longer ignore, I was willing to work with Tom and his secret Gryphon group of expert magic workers and highly trained fighters to prevent it, but it killed me a little inside to do so. The Brotherhood of the Wing, aka *Le Confrérie de l'Aile*, had created me to become a super pred-fighting warrior against my will and without my knowledge. Those actions had made my life hell for a multitude of reasons, and regardless of the Brotherhood's intentions, I had a hard time forgiving them for it.

If that made me petty or short-sighted or even vindictive, I could live with it.

After several torturous minutes, the plane reached the gate, and I stuffed my brand Kindle into my bag. Lucen had given it to me a couple days ago, just as Tom was starting to make noise about the value of having me along on his Arizona mission.

Over the years, Lucen had given me lots of things—a reason to live, a safe place to hide, all the free booze I could drink, and more recently, the best sex I could ever imagine. But this was the first present-like thing he'd given me.

Despite his bar recently being destroyed and his alliances turned upside down, Lucen had been in remarkably good spirits lately. Apparently me screwing around with his best friend Devon did that to him. For Lucen, it was a sign that I was becoming comfortable in my sorta-satyr skin and we could make our relationship work. While I was glad he was happy, and as much as I did like Devon, I couldn't kill my hope that one day Lucen and I could have a normal, human-style relationship that did not involve some form of ménage. I just wasn't about to tell either of the men that.

Missing Lucen already, I watched Tom worm his way into the aisle. After he grabbed his bag from the overhead compartment, I adjusted my grip on my duffel and followed his blond head into the terminal. There, I breathed deeply and stretched my cramping muscles, rejoicing in leaving behind the plane's odors of sweat and stale coffee. The airport was done up in shades of neutral, and through the wall of windows to my left, a line of majestic mountains jutted into a blue sky dotted with perfect fluffy clouds.

I gazed at them in delight. Although I still believed my presence on this trip was superfluous, maybe I wouldn't end up hating it so much. Dragging my longing gaze from the window, I turned to Tom. He was only my height, and with a disarmingly cherubic face, he inadvertently hid the extent of his magical and political power well.

"So." I yawned. "Do we have an actual plan, or are we simply going to knock on this guy's door? And do I have time to use the restroom before we do?"

Tom had his phone out, and he was staring at it. "We have time," he said, choosing to ignore what I thought was some obvious hyperbole in my question. "Mr. Johnson just got home."

"Good." I immediately took off toward the restroom signs, and Tom trailed behind me. I had a feeling he didn't intend to let me out of his sight. Lack of trust was one of the few things we had in common. "So you've been calling him?"

Tom shook his head. "Given the sensitivity of the situation, I've had someone at the local Gryphon office keeping an eye on him. This is a conversation we need to have with him face-to-face."

I merely nodded. Tom and the other members of our little apocalyptic prep group had all been in agreement about the need for discretion. For some reason, the furies were interested in me, and that meant they'd likely be interested in Mr. Johnson too if they found out we shared some traits. It was best, therefore, to keep our mission hush-hush.

"What does he do for a living?" I asked, thinking about Mitchell Johnson's strange talents and what sorts of occupations they might lend themselves to.

Tom stuck his phone away. "He's a psychiatric nurse."

I couldn't help myself. I snorted. "Oh well, then I think his job would have been the perfect place to tell him the truth. It's exactly the sort of story that makes people want to check themselves into a psych ward."

"Actually, I expect he'll want to commit *us*." Tom smiled grimly. "That's one of the reasons you're along."

Right. Because I was so mentally fucking stable.

I headed into the restroom, enjoying the image of Tom strapped into a straightjacket.

In theory, whether we accosted Johnson at his work or at his home or at the local McDonald's, it shouldn't matter. Our mission was simple: convince Johnson to come with us, both for his personal safety and because the Gryphons thought he would be instrumental in saving the world. But first, we would have to explain to Johnson what he was and find out what he could do.

The what-he-could-do part interested me greatly, but although I'd asked lots of questions, Tom only shared information with me when he felt like it. For all of his "we're in this together" BS, it was clear where he and his fraternity saw my place in the pecking order. I was their tool, a weapon they'd created to be used as they required, and no more. If I were feeling generous, I'd say they expected me to be a foot soldier to their commanding officers, but I rarely felt generous given what they'd done to me.

All I could do, therefore, was wait until Tom decided to spill his guts about the Brotherhood's experiments and those of us who'd survived them this long. We were three now. Two of *Le Confrérie's* test subjects were dead. Kyra McNaughton had committed suicide years ago, and Victor Aubrey was a twisted serial killer who'd been murdered in prison.

That left me, Mitchell Johnson, and another woman who lived in Chicago. After we convinced Johnson to come with us, we were supposed to swing by the Windy City and pick her up.

When I finished washing my hands, I pulled my mess of brown curls back in a ponytail. Whether it was the early flight or the horrible bathroom lighting, I couldn't tell, but my face seemed paler, and those circles under my eyes should not have been there. No way to deny it, I was stressed and tired. I felt like I'd been running on nothing but adrenaline for weeks.

But there was no backing out now. No getting off this roller coaster. I was the person who'd clued the Gryphons in to various parts of this prophecy, and I was the one who'd brought together the unhappy alliance of Gryphons, magi, and preds to deal with it. For the sake of everyone I loved—and maybe the world—I had to suck it up and act like something I didn't feel. A confident, competent warrior.

Too bad I couldn't shake the feeling that I was just a misery-sucking freak in way over her head.

Neither Tom nor I had any checked luggage since this was supposed to be a short trip, so after we picked up our rental car, we were on the road. Rubbing my tired eyes, I kept silent as Tom navigated us out of the airport morass. Once we hit the highway, however, I adjusted my sunglasses and seized the silence. "Tell me about Mitchell Johnson."

Tom was quiet a moment, frowning. "I can hardly tell you a lot about someone I've never met."

I glared at him, but the gesture went unnoticed because Tom kept his gaze focused on the road. "You said you'd tell me more about the experiments if I came to Phoenix. Well, I came to Phoenix. So tell me—how were we selected? Is Johnson also a satyr?"

"You're not a satyr." Tom's frown deepened.

I narrowed my eyes at him. "Really? Because the satyrs in Boston seem to think I am. They said I'm a rare subspecies." Thinking of myself that way still unsettled me. Mentally un-conditioning yourself to believe you're human was about as difficult as it sounded. Particularly when you grew up thinking the creature you truly were was evil.

Tom said nothing for a moment, but his grip on the steering wheel tightened. I waited him out. "You shouldn't listen to your satyr *friends*."

"Aw, and I thought we were all on the same side now. The enemy of my enemy is still my enemy then, as far as the Gryphons are concerned?"

They sure were as far as the satyrs were concerned. Lucen and others had made it quite clear to me that though we were all working together on this apocalyptic problem, the satyrs trusted the Gryphons not even half as far as they could throw one.

Tom sighed. "At best, the enemy of my enemy is my casual acquaintance. Nothing more. Something you'd do well to keep in mind."

It was my turn to stay silent. Neither Tom nor any other Gryphons knew just how close my current relationships with some of the satyrs were, or how far into my past those relationships extended. The animosity between all the pred races and humanity—especially the Gryphons—probably went back until the day the two groups had met thousands of years ago.

All pred races had to feed on human misery, after all. And they all had to "addict" some humans to survive. That is, the preds created a magical bond between themselves and a human whose emotional barriers—usually referred to as their soul—were worn down. Then the preds dumped their negativity on their addicts and fed on the suffering it caused.

As a result, the small pool of magically gifted humans who formed the Gryphons had always sought to defend humanity and fight preds. But centuries of laws and treaties codifying how the groups should behave around each other to avoid bloodshed couldn't overcome the natural fear and loathing between predator and prey.

"So back to my question—will Johnson share my lusty skill set? Or did you shake it up among the five of us?"

A muscle in Tom's cheek twitched. "Satyr magic was used on all of you."

"Well, that doesn't seem particularly experimental. Why?"

I was testing Tom's patience. I'd always suspected he wore some very strong charms to damper his emotions, which made sensing them difficult for me, but I was picking up on them now. "As far as pred races go, satyrs were deemed the best option. The Brotherhood felt the side effects of lust magic were less likely to cause issues."

I mused on this, twisting the water bottle cap around. "I don't know. The ability to wound a person's vanity doesn't seem so scary as far as things go. Although I'm just as glad to not be part sylph."

"The blow to the self-esteem faced by a sylph's addict is exceptionally detrimental to a person's mental health," Tom said. "Physically, too, satyrs appear more human. If there were any side effects with regards to appearance, we figured they would be easier to manage."

Okay, that made sense. Aside from the small horns on their heads, satyrs were indistinguishable from humans, something none of the other four races could say.

Tom preemptively hushed me so he could concentrate on the GPS, and I stared out the window, sucking up the view. Phoenix was so unlike Boston I might as well have been in a different country altogether. I was used to shining steel façades and lush green trees, to peeling houses whipped raw by the Atlantic, and tall buildings crowded together on narrow, winding roads that became other narrow, winding roads without warning until outsiders were hopelessly lost.

Here, it was as though someone had taken a city and squashed it flat. The buildings oozed away from the core and spread thin across the landscape. Everything was wide and open. Everywhere I looked was a palette of browns and oranges and subdued reds, except for the sky, which was a singularly amazing blue.

Lost in my thoughts, I only returned my attention to Tom as the car slowed. He parked along the street and waved at an unmarked SUV on the opposite side of the road. The driver, a Gryphon in uniform, returned the gesture then pulled away. Once she was gone, we headed up the stone path to a ranch-style house in what appeared to be a middle-class neighborhood. Even out of uniform, Tom looked every bit the professional in his button-down shirt, tie, and khaki pants. Me? I looked like exactly what I was—an unwilling recruit.

Tom knocked twice, then let the screen door creak loudly on its hinges as it banged shut. Someone must have been home because it sounded like a TV was on.

When no one answered after a moment, Tom knocked harder. I closed my eyes and stretched out with my gift, trying to sense the emotions of whoever was inside. They came to me faintly—irritation, confusion, sadness maybe. Or more likely weariness. All emotions had their unique taste, but within those tastes were variations. Sometimes the variations gave me useful information, but just as often my interpretation depended on my own mood. I could well be projecting my own weariness and making unwarranted assumptions.

"Someone's home," I said to Tom.

He gave me a funny look, then his eyes widened in understanding. "You're sensing him. Interesting."

I crossed my arms, wishing I could make Tom sense what it felt like to be a lab rat. "Yes, Doctor Frankenstein, I am."

Tom ignored the jab and knocked a third time. At last, I heard footsteps, and the door was thrown open. Startled, I straightened and wiped away my pissy expression.

On the other side of the screen door stood a guy about my age. Tall and thin, he wore a faded gray T-shirt that stood out in stark contrast to his dark skin. His black hair was shaved close to his scalp, and a heavy five o'clock shadow covered his chin. His dark eyes swept over us. Though they were small, they were expressive. You didn't need to be an empath to figure out what he was feeling.

"Can I help you?"

"Are you Mitchell Johnson?" Tom asked.

Johnson's irritation morphed into suspicion in my mouth. "Yeah, I'm Mitch. What's this about?"

Tom flashed his badge. "I'm Gryphon Agent Tom Kassin, and this is…"

I didn't hear the rest of Tom's speech because the strength of Johnson's panic almost knocked me over. The emotional rush left my head spinning.

Then the door slammed in our faces.

Don't stop now. Keep reading with your copy of DARKEST MISERY

And find more from Tracey Martin at www.tracey-martin.com

Don't miss book four, DARKEST MISERY, coming soon, and discover more from Tracey Martin at www.tracey-martin.com

---

Red sky at morning, satyr take warning.

Jessica Moore is about to lose her you-know-what. She did the impossible by convincing the Gryphons, the magi, the satyrs and the goblins to work together to stop an apocalyptic prophecy from coming true.

The one thing she can't do? Make them trust each other—which means their plans are already falling apart. With Gryphons and satyrs making plays for her loyalty, Jess is ready to cut through the crap and kill everyone herself.

The tentative alliance disintegrates even faster when a key member is murdered and Jess's supposed allies turn on her. Grieving will have to wait. Right now, she's forced to work closely with her least trusted coworker to flush out the culprit, even as she pushes Lucen away to keep him safe.

Dangers that will test her freakish powers await in the Alps, and this time Lucen isn't there to guard her back. Even if she finds what she's looking for, it'll come with a fury-ous heap of trouble.

Escape Your World. Get Lost in Ours! City Owl Press at www.cityowlpress.com.

ACKNOWLEDGMENTS

Thank you to wonderful editor, Danielle DeVor, my copy editor, Vanessa Wotjanowski, and all the team at City Owl Press for making this book happen, but also especially to Tina Moss for convincing me to put it back out there. Thank you, too, to MiblArt for the beautiful cover. And, as always, thank you to my family, friends, and writing groups for for supporting me on this journey!

ABOUT THE AUTHOR

TRACEY MARTIN lives in New England where she collects pen names, tattoos, and hoodies in shades of gray and black. Under the name Alanna Martin, she's the author of the *Hearts of Alaska* contemporary romance series. If you can't find her online, it's because she's lost in the woods. Send help.

www.tracey-martin.com

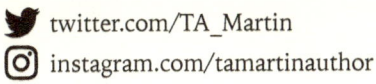 twitter.com/TA_Martin
instagram.com/tamartinauthor

ABOUT THE PUBLISHER

City Owl Press is a cutting edge indie publishing company, bringing the world of romance and speculative fiction to discerning readers.

Escape Your World. Get Lost in Ours!

www.cityowlpress.com

facebook.com/YourCityOwlPress
twitter.com/cityowlpress
instagram.com/cityowlbooks
pinterest.com/cityowlpress